Unaware

Unaware

If Only We'd Known

John Cox

RESOURCE *Publications* · Eugene, Oregon

UNAWARE
If Only We'd Known

Resource Publications
An Imprint of Wipf and Stock Publishers
199 W. 8th Ave., Suite 3
Eugene, OR 97401

www.wipfandstock.com

PAPERBACK ISBN: 978-1-6667-2893-4
HARDCOVER ISBN: 978-1-6667-2075-4
EBOOK ISBN: 978-1-6667-2076-1

08/27/21

For Vi

Imagine, journeying through life quite unaware of what might have been.

Do not forget to show hospitality to strangers, for by so doing some people have shown hospitality to angels without knowing it.

—*HEBREWS 13:2 NIV*

Chapter One

AGAINST A BACKDROP OF steep mountains cloaked in forest, the pale sky fading with the late evening sun, Jack floated aimlessly in the middle of a lake like a piece of driftwood. Along the shoreline, the maples and cedars parted where the railway carved a path high over a wooden trellis bridge. The setting should have lifted Jack's spirits, evoking a song of praise; instead, he barely noticed—or even cared. "It's a perfect day to get the hell out of here," he muttered.

Below him, dark water plunged to an undefined depth. He'd purchased his blue air mattress—a cheap Walmart special—that morning. Now, as the spindly fingers of the late summer sun reached out across the lake, he knew it was time.

A hundred yards away Bill Morris reclined in his boat. His feet rested on the dash; his cap tilted over his eyes to protect against the glare of the setting sun. He loved the play of evening light on the water, the changing moods, the stillness, the silence.

Beneath the shadow of the rim of his cap, he surveyed the crinkling water extending to the far shoreline. His gaze lingered upon a solitary figure lying on what appeared to be an air mattress. "He's got a long way to paddle if he wants to be home before dark," Bill thought before surrendering to heavy eyelids and the languid motion of the water.

Jack felt the evening chill brush his shoulders. He wished the boat idling in the distance would take off so that he'd have the lake to himself. *If I'd rolled into the water fifteen minutes ago, it would be over by now*, he thought. *I wouldn't be feeling the cold or thinking anymore. No more guilt, regret, and failure; no pressure or expectations. Done.*

He turned his head on the pillow as the water gurgled, hungry wavelets lapping across the surface. His eyes rested on the distant shore where a trail of cars wound their way around the lake's edge like ants. *Wonder if they can see me from there?* Jack pondered. He'd driven the road countless times to and from his home in Port Alberni.

The road was the only access to the West Coast of Vancouver Island, where the coastal towns of Tofino and Ucluelet had reinvented themselves as tourist destinations. One hundred years ago the first road West had skirted the other side of the lake where the railway now ran. Horses and coaches had carried passengers to and from the town, often overnighting in cabins still inhabited between the shoreline and the road. Years later a large landslide blocked the road. By then a highway had been constructed, blasting through rock on the opposite shoreline.

Jack's father had relocated to Port Alberni, a thriving hub of activity servicing the logging and fishing industries. Work was plentiful, wages good, and opportunities abounded for heavy duty mechanics—so much so that his father opened his own shop and never wanted for work. He was always quick to remind Jack that the secret to his business success lay in his tough, unyielding approach to life. "You won't get anywhere in life without hard work, Jack," was a familiar refrain of Jack's childhood. "Nothing came easy for me. You're certainly not getting it free, served up hot with gravy on a fancy china plate."

"I know that, Dad. I just don't find schoolwork easy," Jack would reply to deaf ears.

"Bulls**t, you're just lazy. Look at your sisters, how well they have done. There's nothing wrong with the brains in *this* family. You get your good looks from me but your mother's the genius." He laughed.

Jack's mother loved to read, which classified her as brilliant in her husband's eyes. She skimmed the newspaper only to find the crossword. The family were used to her asking out loud, expecting no answer, "What's the city in Russia beginning with 'V', eleven letters?"

Growing up, Jack had lived in the shadow of two older sisters, Helen, and Diane. Unlike him they excelled at school, they were outgoing, popular with their peers, and close friends. Of course, they adored their little brother, but their innocent teasing stung over time. Their response to his lackluster performance lodged in his heart. "Boys will be boys. Not the sharpest knife in the drawer. At least he's good with mechanical stuff."

His mother was a peacemaker, seldom challenging Jack's father, content to manage the household and remain in the background. And when Jack would vent his frustration to her, she'd invariably respond with, "He doesn't really mean it, honey."

Jack struggled academically—too much reading and writing. He found it hard to concentrate and follow along. He learned better by doing things, using his hands. But those skills were not tested in school. So, he did his best to adapt, like a chameleon—to blend in, to be accepted, to be popular. Though he labelled himself as stupid, dumbass Jack, to his peers he came across as nonchalant and cool. His dyslexia was only diagnosed years later; too late to erase his sense of intellectual inferiority.

Predictably, he fell in with the wrong crowd—drinking and doing drugs out at the gravel pit every weekend. It came as a welcome revelation to Jack that consuming these substances overcame his inadequacy, shyness, and awkwardness. They were having a good time, living in the moment, no worries.

The one place where Jack and his father connected was around engines. Jack loved the smell of grease, the thrill of speed, the challenge of fixing something mechanical and bringing it back to life. It wasn't so much that he felt close to his father in the workshop; it was more about winning his attention, at least for a while. But invariably it would end badly. "How many times do I have to show you?" knifed into him from his father's sharp tongue, usually wet with whisky, the stench hanging on his breath. No matter what Jack did, his father seemed forever impatient or disappointed. Jack seldom measured up as far as he could tell, and over the years his simmering frustration sparked into explosive anger.

Unsurprisingly, his father's constant disparagement took residence in Jack's head until, like a refrain on repeat, his inner voice accused him of incompetence whenever faced with a challenge. *Why bother? You won't be able to do it. You're not cut out for anything worthwhile.* And so, the wheel turned. He developed the habit of procrastinating over tasks, never really committing, and dragging his heels so as not to create false expectations. It drove those close to him crazy. "That's Jack for you, totally unreliable."

If he could have summed up the next twenty years with one word, it would be "failure." Despite his best efforts, his life had been nothing but a disappointment. He'd struggled to hold down a job; the marriage he thought was made in heaven turned out to be a hell of his own making.

It's not Brenda, it's me. His inner dialogue berated him. *I don't know how she juggles everything; I can hardly stay focused on one thing; I'm so easily distracted or discouraged if it doesn't work out the first time.*

Somehow, he had unwittingly become like his own father to his three children—whom he'd hardly seen since the separation nearly a year ago. The only things he did well, reliably, and with passion were procrastination and drink. Now, cold, and alone on a budget air mattress in the middle of a lake, his impending death seemed a predictable conclusion. *At least I can do this*, he thought. *It'll be better for everyone.*

The chill biting him as the sun sank further toward the horizon, Jack gulped the last mouthful of vodka and welcomed the burn as it slid down his throat. He wished he'd brought a new bottle rather than only a third, but it was enough. He held the bottle under the water and watched the bubbles rise as it filled. He gripped the neck between his fingers, then let it go. His limp hand dangled beneath the surface, catching the last bubble before it disappeared.

"F**k this," he sighed. He reached for the diving belt around his waist, ensuring it was secure. The weights pressed heavy against his back. He rolled over and sank like the bottle into the depths, leaving a trail of bubbles behind him, and the mattress bobbing in the dusky twilight.

Chapter Two

"WHAT DO YOU THINK it will be like?"

"Not sure . . . but should be fun!"

Five Junior Angels gathered at the entrance to what looked like a modest coffee shop. A dark red door with a steaming coffee cup sketched on it was ajar.

"I'm expecting it to be one of the best experiences I've ever had."

"Me too. I can't imagine wanting to be anywhere else."

They entered, single file, into a large, spacious interior. This was a common feature of buildings in heaven—small from the outside and much larger inside. The walls could even shrink or expand depending on how much space was required.

"I thought I'd be more nervous. Instead, I'm excited to get started."

Despite being strangers from distant heavenly villages, the five had eagerly anticipated this moment ever since learning of the meeting. Communication in heaven between people who were apart was exquisitely simple, thoughts dropping crystal clear as emails into the mind of the recipient. The message was activated by thinking of the recipient and speaking their name out loud. So, here they were.

What to expect? How to prepare? What to say? they all wondered excitedly.

The coffee shop and patisserie hummed, people sipping drinks and munching pastries at crowded tables, chatting happily, the air light with laughter. The aroma of baking and fresh coffee made their mouths water. Navo immediately disappeared across the room to where someone was singing, accompanied by a guitar and keyboard. He stood close to them, hands in his pockets, grinning and tapping his foot to the beat. The music wafted over at least three thousand patrons who spilled onto a terrace that overlooked a wide valley carved by a broad river.

Heavenly Ground was a favorite rendezvous; it was no surprise that the group huddled around their table had agreed to meet there. As five Junior Angels in training to become Guardian Angels (GAs), they'd received an invitation to get to know one another, before meeting with God later that day. First on the agenda were introductions. When Navo eventually rejoined them, they went around the table, asking each in turn, "Tell us something about your village and an interesting comment about yourself."

Jenny's long brown hair framed a delicate face with porcelain skin; her voice would have mingled easily in a crowd of friends gathered in a London pub. "My village is like a slice of Northern England—lots of sheep in the hills, pubs on the corner, and a fair amount of 'weather.' I love it. About me? I'm highly organized, I like to know what's happening, and I tend to ask lots of questions." She picked up a leather satchel by her side. "I'm never without this, always carrying a few books to read whenever I have the chance." She laughed. "Next, Navo, the music man?"

Navo was dark, his distinctive features hinting at a central African link. "Hey, that's me. I'm Navo and my village is straight from the heart of Africa. It's warm and we have lovely tropical fruit, which we supply to some of your villages. My passion is music and dancing, because when I sing, I have to move." He beat a rhythm on the tabletop. "And I play hand drums. I enjoy challenges and adventure and love to try new things, which is why I'm excited to be here with you today." Navo finished with another hand-drum roll. "That's me, for now."

None of the GAs were inhibited by the invitation to share. Nurtured in an atmosphere of trust and unconditional love, each considered vulnerable transparency as normal and genuine friendship, second nature.

Yesaidu was next. He had a stocky build, a golden coffee complexion, and the animated expressions and mannerisms of a South American native—Venezuela, to be precise. "I think we'll get on well," he said, turning to Navo. "I'm Yesaidu. My village has a South American theme expressed in our architecture and lots of dancing and singing in the streets." His legs jiggled constantly as he spoke, like a horse in the starting pen raring to go. "My village is surrounded by beautiful mountains; you must come and visit sometime. I love doing anything physical. My favorite sport is soccer, which I play in our inter-village league."

"That's sweet," said Navo. "I'd love to do that."

Seated next to Jenny was Asuka. Her black hair and narrow eyes sparkling above a gentle smile revealed her origin as somewhere in Asia. "Hi, I'm Asuka. It's so interesting hearing where we each live. The culture and buildings of my village represent South Asia. Many people love to visit us in the spring when the cherry blossoms are on full display. It's exceptionally beautiful. I would describe myself as somewhat introverted. I love to read and research. Like Jenny, I am curious and ask questions."

Asuka looked across at Nova and Yesaidu. "I'm afraid I'm not much good at sports at all. I hope you don't mind."

"Of course not," grinned Yesaidu. "I struggle to read much; it's never been really my thing. Is that ok with you?"

"I guess we can enjoy our differences, can't we?" Asuka nodded. "Sometimes I need to be prodded to speak, as I get lost in my own thoughts." Asuka smiled. "I'm also excited to be here and learn new things. Thank you."

Throughout the discussion Gregori had a wide grin on his face, framed by a mass of red hair exploding in every direction. When he spoke, his deep resonant European voice conjured up images of vast lands and deep forests. He had a great sense of humor and decided to introduce himself with a deadpan expression.

"My village is on the cooler side and is a slice of Northern Europe, with maybe the greatest ski hills in heaven. Of course, our onion-shaped domes are distinctive to our villages. I love people and enjoy making new friends and learning about them." He couldn't maintain his straight face so burst out in a loud laugh. "You know, just last week I was having coffee with Johan, a man who lived in second-century Earthtime. His stories and insights were fascinating to me. It's so interesting how people have lived their lives in Earthtime. I look forward to getting to know you all better. I think this is going to be unforgettable."

Not only did the Junior Angels' features display similarities with those who lived in Earthtime, but each spoke the language of their tribe and culture (French, English, Swahili, Spanish). Remarkably, fellow Junior Angels—as with all heaven's inhabitants—heard each other speaking in their "mother tongue," unaware of the difference. For instance, when Yesaidu spoke Spanish, Jenny heard English, and vice versa.

"It's great to hear a little from each of you," Nova said. "Thanks so much. What time is our meeting?"

"In about an hour," Jenny replied.

"Anyone for more coffee before we head out?" Gregori shoved back his chair and cleared empty mugs from the table.

"Let me help," said Asuka. With fresh steaming mugs, two creams for Gregori, they continued to swap stories, before stepping out beyond Heavenly Ground's doorway over another threshold that would change them forever.

Chapter Three

JACK DESCENDED SLOWLY INTO bone-numbing wet green.

He'd wanted to stick to the plan: to remain dispassionate, even as the weights of the diving belt pressed him ever deeper. But he couldn't sustain indifference. Despite his vodka-fueled resolve, his intuitive survival instinct began to kick and fight. Even dying was a challenge. Inexplicably, he felt the belt release. It relinquished its grip, like a monster letting go.

Reluctantly yet willingly, Jack fought his way to the surface, lungs bursting. *Don't open your mouth and swallow water!* his mind screamed. His body flailed wildly upward. *Open your f***g mouth and breathe!*

A cacophony of noise filled his head. In the chaos two voices clamored for attention. A familiar one mocked him: *How pitiful, you can't even kill yourself properly!* It was the other inner voice that surprised him. He hadn't heard it before, *Jackie, don't give up . . . I hear you.* He hadn't been called "Jackie" by anyone since he was a young boy hanging around his grandfather whom he'd adored.

Bill woke with a start; he must have dozed off in the rocking cradle of his boat. The sky had dimmed darker behind clouds tinged with silver. Glancing around the lake, as was his custom, he noticed the empty air mattress. Alarm bells rang and his stomach tightened. *Better go and check*, he thought. Firing up the engine, he raced across the lake, leaving a churning white trail in his wake.

As Bill approached, the blue mattress bobbed empty on the choppy surface. Suddenly, to his right, splashing boiled out of nowhere as a man's head broke through, gasping for air.

"Take hold of my hand," Bill shouted, reaching over the side of the boat after cutting the engine.

Coughing and spluttering, Jack grabbed his hand and the side of the boat. With a heave, Bill hauled him aboard. He lay shivering and gasping between the back seats.

"Dry yourself off with a towel and put this on before you freeze," said Bill, tossing him a sweatshirt before retrieving the mattress.

Jack had registered the hum of the boat in the background as he frantically clawed his way up to the light. He didn't know whether to be angry or relieved. He did know that he was frightened. How had the diving belt come loose? He'd been extra careful to ensure it was fastened correctly before he left the shoreline. Someone on the beach had asked what he was doing; he'd muttered something about a training program. Numb from the cold, he'd swallowed water as he broke the surface, his starving lungs prizing his lips apart sucking frantically for air. Before he knew it, a strong hand gripped his flailing, outstretched arm like a vise and he was being pulled over the side of a boat. He shivered uncontrollably and heaved to catch his breath. Waves of alternating frustration and relief broke over him as he lay, exhausted and ashamed, at the bottom of a stranger's boat.

"F**k, sorry man," he spluttered, as he mopped his face and struggled to sit upright. "Don't know what happened . . . Must've fallen asleep and lost track of the time."

"Bill Morris." Bill reached out his hand. "I wasn't sure whether I saw someone floating on an air mattress or not?"

"Jack Willard." He offered Bill a weak, wet handshake, then rubbed himself down with the towel. Still shivering, he slipped the sweatshirt over his head and sat in one of the front seats while Bill deflated the mattress, stowed it in a storage box, and strapped it closed.

"There we go," he said. "I often come out here at the end of the day for a few minutes. The solitude and stillness settle me down." Unscrewing a thermos, he poured steaming coffee into a mug and passed it to Jack. "Guess it's your lucky day—this'll do you some good."

"Thanks." Jack clasped the mug, both hands trembling, and drank with relish. His fingers tingled, sensation returning with every sip. Gradually, he felt blood pulse through his arms and legs, the cold yielding to the warmth of dry clothes and a hot drink. Taking a deep breath, he scanned the lake. In the distance, silhouetted against the fading light, a lone fisherman in waders cast for trout from a sandy spit. The lazy looping line flickered gold-flecks in the setting sun. He stared. *I wouldn't have seen this if that belt hadn't come undone—don't know whether to laugh or cry.*

Bill clambered back into the driver's seat and paused with his hands on the wheel. Jack could tell Bill was a tall man, at least a head taller than him. His face was tanned under a dark blue baseball cap. A question mark was stitched in white above the brim. Turning to Jack, he smiled.

"Hey Jack, how are you doing. Warming up, I hope?"

"Yep, coffee helps. Thanks man." He rubbed his arms as he bent over in the seat, hugging himself to cast out the chill.

"I'm sort of in shock myself." Bill looked across, clutching the wheel, concern in his eyes. "You weren't falling asleep, were you? I don't want to pry, but despair was pouring from your eyes when I pulled you from the water. I'm sorry"—he paused and shook his head apologetically—"it's really none of my business."

"No, it's ok. I'm kinda embarrassed. Where do I begin? I'm so tired, I . . ." Before he could utter another word, the pent-up emotion welled up in waves of sobs over which he had no control. He felt a strong arm on his shoulders.

Jack sniffed and wiped his nose with the towel and gazed at the floor—it was grey speckled vinyl. "I've cried out for help and nothing changes. It just gets heavier, and lonelier, and more and more desperate. I can't handle the hopelessness, I'm so f***ing angry."

"Any friends?" asked Bill. He never loosened his grip. Jack felt his strength and for once didn't bother resisting; he had no fight left.

"Not really . . . people tend to listen once and then don't want to know too much if you say the same thing next time they ask. To be honest, even I'm fed up with myself."

"Do you have children, a wife?"

"Yeah, three kids—two daughters and a son. My wife kept them with her ten months ago when I left."

"They'd care, if you took your life."

Jack shrugged, drying his hair with the towel. "I don't know, probably a shock at first. They'd get over it; I'm hardly part of their lives now anyway."

"I don't think children let go of their dad that easily," Bill said.

"Yeah, well, I'm always disappointing them—late for visits or don't turn up at all because I'm drunk or forget. Brenda called me a deadbeat when I left, and I can't argue."

"I don't see a deadbeat," Bill said. "Just a guy who's got himself lost."

"Easy for you to say," muttered Jack. For the first time he looked Bill in the eye. "Don't get me wrong, you dragging me out of the lake saved my life. But you get to go home, and I'm still stuck. Nothing's changed. The deadbeat can't even drown himself."

"More might have changed than you realize." Bill gave Jack a gentle nudge. "Where did you say you're living?"

"In a small mobile past Whiskey Creek, 15 Wagon Wheel Drive," Jack replied. "Turn first left beyond the store and it's about a mile down the road on the right, has a rusting red Chevy pickup outside."

"I know the area," Bill said. Firing up the engine, he thrust the gear lever forward. The nose of the boat rose, then flattened, as they picked up speed and headed for shore.

"Do you have a car?"

"Yeah, over there behind the trees," Jack replied, pointing.

"You sure you'll be all right? I'm not really comfortable leaving you on your own."

"Don't worry about me. I'll be fine, appreciate your time and kindness." He could sense the empathy in Bill as he held his gaze.

Bill guided the boat along the shoreline. "I'll drop you here and head over to the launch area." The boat's keel scraped the pebbled beach. "You take care, my friend, and don't despair; perhaps our meeting is no coincidence. If it's ok with you, I'll swing by tomorrow and pick up the sweater?"

Jack clambered out of the boat. "Sure, thanks. See you later." He gave half a wave and walked up the beach without looking back. He threaded a path through the trees to the road, retrieved his key behind the front fender, and unlocked the driver's door.

He'd forgotten about the envelope he'd left on the seat addressed to Brenda and the kids. For a long while he sat in the truck, staring ahead at the black garbage can bolted down next to a cedar. The engine idled a little rough, but it warmed the cabin and took the last of the chill out of his bones. He tore open the envelope at one end. His writing had always been an awkward scrawl; the letters seemed to jump around, making spelling almost impossible. Only a few hours earlier he'd written:

Sorry for the truble letting you bown and the kids. I Never get much rite. Am just a burden to you. Wen you read this note Ill be gone and you won't have to worry any more. Please forgive me be Happy you diserv it. Luv you, Jack

There were no tears to cry. He was dazed. Crumpling the note, he threw it on the floor.

He glanced through the trees toward the lake; there was no sign of Bill or the boat. He scratched his head. His hair was still damp. Leaning back in the seat, he closed his eyes and sighed. *I'm glad I'm not dead, but nothing's changed.* He thought of Brenda, Ricky, Kaitlin, and Jessica. Would it have been easier for them?

"I really don't know," he said to himself.

Jack revved the engine, released the handbrake, and waited for a gap in the passing traffic. Eventually he pulled out into a U-turn and drove slowly home, mentally adding "attempted drowning" to his running list of failures. God only knew what he would do next.

Chapter Four

"WELCOME, GOOD TO SEE you. Come in, come in, please."

The Junior Angels were ushered into a large, airy room, natural light flooding through a vaulted roof of glass. Couches and chairs framed a magnificent carpet, dyed wool, woven, blending every color on heaven and earth: the rainbow carpet.

Motioning them to be seated, God settled into an oversized, well-worn chair. Somewhere in the region of six feet in stature, he defied description, his face neither old nor young—timeless perhaps. His eyes were filled with gentle laughing smiles—and light; it was impossible to discern color. The most powerful quality was his presence—a presence that filled the room with kindness, peace, and a deep assurance of safety and acceptance. The Junior Angels already had a sense of that "presence"; they'd never known anything different. But to those in Earthtime it would have been overwhelming, in a wonderful way.

They sat silent, utterly transfixed; any initial nervousness faded as God leaned forward. "I want us to enjoy our time together, and you're going to help me with rescue missions. From now on you will be called Guardian Angels—or, more simply, GAs. That is what you're becoming. In Earthtime people work toward gaining a title. Here in heaven, we declare who you are and help you grow into that identity. Let me explain why we're gathered in the Rainbow Room. And by the way, call me Pappa G. I prefer that name to a title."

The newly named GAs smiled among themselves. "Ok, Pappa G," said Asuka and Jenny almost in unison.

"Thank you," Yesaidu added. "I was wondering what you'd look like. It already feels like I've known you forever."

"Indeed, you have," Pappa G replied with a broad smile. "I can also change my form at any time depending on the circumstance. Sometimes I'll appear younger, or older, as a potter perhaps, or a warrior when leading a battle charge, even a businessman, or a woman. It all depends. For now, with you, I'm Pappa G."

He unrolled a large document on the table. "Let's begin with the big picture. Here's a chart showing a small portion of the universe—where you'll be helping me. You can see a mighty expanse of stars, planets, galaxies, and other bits and pieces we won't bother with now. The area we're particularly interested in is over here." Pappa G pointed to a tiny dot in the top right-hand corner of the page.

"Can't see much, can we?" Pappa G waved his hand over the area; it began to enlarge. "That's better; there's a clearer view." An exquisite globe emerged of various shades of blues, whites, grays, greens, and browns suspended against a backdrop of satin black.

"This . . ." whispered Pappa G, "is my treasure, my pearl, my passion."

"It's gorgeous!" gasped Jenny. "Look at the colors."

"Wow!" was all the others could manage.

"This is where people in Earthtime live?" Yesaidu exclaimed, tracing the outline with his finger. "How lucky are they!"

Pappa G nodded. "Yes, they do. This is the center of my universe and what is closest to my heart. Unfortunately, the beauty is deceptive."

"I don't understand?" said Gregori.

"The earth from our vantage point is incomplete," Pappa G said while slowly rotating the brightly shining sphere with his finger. "This is the pinnacle of my creation, not so much in beauty, but rather in the complexity and fragility of the life it contains. It's the only place in the universe where I've shared responsibility and relationship with what I've created."

"You mean with people?" Asuka said.

"Yes Asuka, that's correct. However, the closer you travel to the surface the more you'll see scars, pollution, and damage done to the earth and its environment. Near to the ground you'll find all manner of divisions and countries where human beings have divided and conquered one another. They base their identity and security on power and, usually, wealth. Nations as well as individuals have become obsessed with independence and control. It breaks my heart."

For as long as the newly promoted Guardian Angels could recall, they had lived and matured in heaven. Theirs was a life of nurture, purity, love, affirmation, mutual trust, and beauty everywhere. They were unfamiliar with competitiveness and unkindness, envy, or fear. Their lives were completely devoid of malice, pain, and suffering. Everyone was a friend, and first meetings soon became relationships where it felt you had known each other for ever.

Just as children in Earthtime imagine and learn about life in other countries, the moon and Mars, the Guardian Angels were about to learn about life on earth. It was as much of a challenge for them to comprehend the turmoil and struggles endured by those living on earth as it was for those raised in Earthtime to believe heaven is real.

"Pappa G, I don't get it," said Jenny, leaning forward for a better view. "Imagine living in such a beautiful place. Isn't there enough for everyone?"

"Yes, there's more than enough for all. But, for a start, many people don't believe I'm real in a way that impacts their daily lives," said Pappa G. "There's a fierce battle raging for the hearts and minds of those who live in Earthtime, and—"

"Excuse me," Asuka interjected, "what do you mean by the word 'battle'?"

"Asuka, a battle is when some people don't like what others are doing and try to force them to give them what they want, even if it means killing them," Pappa G replied soberly.

"Killing? I thought all life is from you, so how can someone else come against what you've created and given?" Asuka asked with a puzzled look.

"I don't understand either," said Navo, shaking his head. "It looks so peaceful, and you're God Almighty?"

"That's why we're here," said Pappa G. He left the table and walked around the room. "You're about to learn what it feels like to live in Earthtime—Eden hijacked; my creation kidnapped. The people live incomplete lives in what has become a tired and fractured version of my original creation, quite oblivious to my existence. So, to help them you'll be entering into their world, becoming like them but not of them."

"I'm still confused," said Yesaidu, then added boldly, "What went wrong? How did you lose control and allow this beautiful creation to slip from your grasp?"

"Who said it slipped from my grasp?" Pappa G replied. "It's a long story; some of your questions will be answered, at least in part, during our sessions. My other two family members will help us. One of them should be here shortly."

For the next few minutes, they chatted excitedly about the vast expanse of the universe, each GA in turn puzzling over what God had told them about how humans had desecrated the very earth he had created for them. Their conversation was interrupted by a knock at the door, followed by a face peeking in. "You ready for me?"

"Always," Pappa G turned and smiled. "Come in, allow me to introduce you."

A woman entered the room with a broad smile and a spring in her step. Her long, shimmering, black hair tumbled in ringlets down her back. She wore a black top, loose black pants, and a multicolored long jacket crafted from pure silk. Her skin glistened translucent umber and her gold earrings and bangles sparkled in the light. She gave Pappa G a long, affectionate hug. Holding his hand, she said, "Hi, I'm Gale, I've been looking forward to meeting you."

Pappa G embraced Gale with one arm. He towered above her. "I couldn't do anything without Gale. She provides the power and the 'hands on' energy that makes everything happen, everywhere. I'm sure you'll enjoy your time together."

"This is a great project," Gale said. She rubbed her hands enthusiastically, bangles clinking, and approached one of the walls. "On each side of this room you'll have noted there are 'misty veils,' which from a distance resemble solid walls. They're our entry points into Earthtime. Given that we're not restricted by Earthtime's limitations, we can travel anywhere within Earthtime's history to observe people and events in their relative present. We'll walk around freely, fully engaged in their context and environment.

"However, because we're in a different realm, they won't be able to see or hear us. That means that we can communicate with each other and observe them without inhibition. My task is to transport us to the various historical destinations and enable you to interact in a real Earthtime environment. Each wall provides access to the same event."

The GAs looked at one another with a mixture of alarm and excitement. They'd never anticipated entering Earthtime like this, and so soon!

"Sweet," Jenny exclaimed. "You mean it when you say, 'taste and see.'"

"Can't wait," said Gregori. "It's going to be amazing."

Pappa G chuckled. "Gale's exceptionally good at this and has all kinds of tricks up her sleeve. Lots of fun. But before we begin, let me add this. The people we'll be observing and learning from are all well-known biblical figures. They've become heroes and celebrities in the minds of those in Earthtime—regarded more as saints, special, rather than ordinary people like them—which is a pity, because what you're going to witness is how we take regular men and women and make them extraordinary. In fact, all of them would have destroyed their lives if left to their own resources."

"One last thing." Gale held up a square object which she then distributed among the GAs. "I'm giving each of you one of these InSight tablets. They will enable you to observe a hurting and very dysfunctional family in Earthtime who are overwhelmed with their circumstances. The tablets will be updated every day. It's important that you watch, listen, and discuss among yourselves. Toward the end of our course, we'll have an open forum about what transpired."

"How does it work?" Asuka asked as she examined the flat screen, turning it around in her hands.

"Each InSight is customized for you and will be activated tomorrow morning. Just press this button," she pointed to a red button, "and look at the screen. It has been configured to recognize your eyes and will unlock. Then, follow the simple instructions. Now it's time to head out for our first assignment."

Mimicking a master of ceremonies, Gale bowed flamboyantly to the group and, smiling, waved her hand toward the wall behind her. "Action!"

Chapter Five

JACK SWUNG THE TRUCK into his driveway—nothing more than a cracked concrete slipway. No garage. Weeds and half-blown dandelions nodded balding heads around a ramshackle single-width mobile home. Three worn steps led up to a porch, blistered decking, and a tired front door with a diamond-shaped window at eye level. Jack unlocked the door. It protested with a shrill squeak. Closing it behind him, he noticed his phone blinking on the coffee table. He picked it up and listened to his voicemail.

"Jack are you there?" a familiar voice shouted accusingly. *"Please pick up. The kids need their father. There's been an accident—Ricky's at the hospital."* A pause, a deep sigh, then, *"What was I thinking? Had a fantasy you might answer the phone and help. You're probably hammered. God, sometimes I wish you were out of my life completely! Be easier than always making excuses and being disappointed. Thanks for nothing."*

Jack seethed. Brenda was always so negative and dramatic. She'd use anything these days to dig at him. Ricky probably had a scratch, and she was making a big deal to manipulate him into feeling guilty again. God knows, he felt the weight of his failure every day; he didn't need her to remind him.

This wasn't the first false alarm. There was the time Ricky hadn't come home and Brenda called in a panic. *"Ricky's always home in time for supper. Jack, I'm worried sick something's happened."*

"Calm down, Bren. Are you sure he's not with Paul or another friend?"

"Oh shoot, I totally forgot. He's spending the night at Paul's; they wanted to work on tuning up their skateboards. Sorry."

Or when she called him shortly after he'd popped in to visit the kids after work. He was at the top of the hump (the locals' name for the winding pass that cuts through the forests heading east of town).

"Jack, I think you've got my phone. You must have slipped it into your pocket after updating my iTunes."

"Then how are you calling me now?"

"I'm using Ricky's phone."

"Why don't you try calling your number; your phone's not with me."

"Oh my God, my bad. How stupid. Will do that. Thanks."

Brenda had the exasperating, yet endearing, ability to be absent-minded one moment, and brilliantly sharp the next. When she was like that, Jack used to feel needed. Strange how quickly the feeling had morphed into irritation.

He yanked open the fridge to grab the first of what would grow into a sizeable stack of beers. Collapsing onto the "pre-enjoyed" couch he'd picked up at the Salvation Army store, Jack vacantly watched the darkness outside descend. How long had he been living in this run-down mobile? Two, no, three months. Before that he'd crashed with his friend Bob after leaving Brenda, then couch surfed for a few months, and finally landed here.

For most of the year he'd been doing janitorial work at the hospital—until early summer, when he failed to pitch up for work again, for the third time. "Three strikes and you're out," his supervisor told him as he made a final, pathetic appeal for one more chance.

It was all Bonny's fault. He'd known her from his school days. They hooked up at a friend's barbecue out at the lake, water skiing, drinking beers, and flirting. A petite brunette a few years younger than Jack, she'd been married for three years, divorced, no children. Bonny worked at Shoppers Drug Mart as a cashier.

Jack was about to leave the lake that evening when she asked for a ride home. "I'll make it worth your while," she winked. One thing led to another. She invited him in. "Make yourself comfortable; I'll be back in a minute." Next thing he knew Bonny was sashaying into the room wearing a thong, the sheerest of gowns, and a broad smile. "Here, have another drink."

That was it, game over.

Next morning, he was meant to be at work at seven and woke up with Bonny by his side at nine. "S**t, I'm late for work, got to get going," he said half-heartedly. Bonny giggled. "Tell them you had a bad case of

Bonny-vitis. Came down with it last night and when you woke up this morning you just couldn't fight it off." She laughed and rolled on top of him. "I'm a very tough virus, Jackie boy."

Game over, again.

Later that day, when he drove away, he could have kicked himself for being so stupid. *When will you ever learn?* he chided. He couldn't shake the ugly picture his mind had conjured of the night before: the image of Brenda, Ricky, Kaitlin, and Jesse standing beside the bed watching. And Kaitlin asking, "Daddy what are you doing? Who is this lady? Why aren't you with mommy?" It had taken two more shots of vodka to erase the thought.

"Story of my friggin' life," Jack muttered, staring at the ceiling.

A lone corner lamp cast a dim light across the room. He retrieved cans from the fridge two at a time. Snapped them open, drained them mechanically—with little thought, let alone pleasure—then tossed them, crumpled, against the wall. Eventually he passed out, oblivious to the world, himself, and the urgency of Brenda's message.

Chapter Six

A VAST LAKE STRETCHED as far as the eye could see, wide then narrowing to where it spilled into the valley below, melting over the lip of a broad shelf of rock like wax cresting the rim of a burning candle. Its crystalline waters shimmered, before dissipating in a graceful freefall to a deep pool a hundred and fifty feet below. A misty haze rose through red-leafed orchards that clung to ancient crannies overgrown with tufts of thick, dripping moss. Further out from the waterfall, the daylight probed the pool depths, illuminating the pebbles and sand forty feet below the surface. Birds flitted among the branches of trees, some soaring high and others spreading wide. Lush green foliage stretched like a carpet into the distance. The sun shone warm and bright, suspending a brilliant rainbow in the spray. The tranquility and peace of the setting was tangible.

"Welcome to Eden, where it all began," Gale said, with an exaggerated sweep of her arm.

"Wow!" gasped Navo. "It's like the best of heaven all bundled together! Look at the size of these flowers, and the fruit—everything's so lush!"

A trumpeting sound caused the GAs to jump. Pappa G appeared, riding on the neck of a large elephant. "One of the first animals we created," he said. Smiling broadly, he stroked the wrinkled gray trunk that curled back to nuzzle him. He turned and whistled, and the most magnificent lion bounded up to join them. "This is my first lion, who accompanies me wherever I go when I visit this region."

"What's his name?" Jenny asked.

"Oh, that's our secret," Pappa G smiled. "Adam wanted to name him 'lion.'"

It wouldn't have occurred to the GAs to be afraid because nothing in heaven was dangerous, violent, or threatening. The lion did indeed lie down with the lamb.

Pappa G and his ancient elephant led them down a winding path lined with tall, bright, blooming flowers that appeared to bend in deference at the passing of their Creator. The air was humid but not uncomfortable, saturated with a bouquet of pungent perfumes.

The lion exuded majesty and muscle as he quietly padded along in their curious procession. "Whoa!" Yesaidu lifted his hand in surprise when he felt the rough wet tongue lick his fingers. Exquisite colors, shapes, and textures exploded in blossom everywhere. Rounding a bend in the path, they entered a clearing that offered a spectacular view of a shoreline. It must have been at least two miles away and a thousand feet below them. Lazy waves unfurled from an ocean of turquoise blue along a white sandy beach fringed with tall trees and dazzling red bougainvillea.

Behind them, the clearing where they gathered was the size of a magnificent amphitheater. In the center stood a large tree that towered above the surrounding vegetation, with massive branches protruding from an enormous speckled-gray trunk, gnarled, and weathered with age. Its broad canopy rose high above their straining necks. At the outer extremities, branches sagged heavy with fruit until they almost brushed the ground.

"This tree is ginormous," marveled Jenny, peering up into the thick green tapestry overhead.

"The tree of the knowledge of good and evil," Pappa G replied. "The fruit of this tree is reserved for Jesus, Gale, and me to eat. You might say it's our family tree," he added with a chuckle. "The instruction to my children was simple. One solitary rule: 'Do not eat the fruit of this tree. Everything else is for your pleasure and delight, to enjoy to your heart's content. But eat the fruit of this one tree and you will surely die.'"

"Who were you giving those instructions to?" Asuka asked.

"The couple over there." Pappa G pointed to the far side of the clearing where they could just make out two figures walking side by side engrossed in conversation and evidently enjoying one another's company.

"They're naked!" exclaimed Yesaidu. "What's with that?"

"So are the animals," said Pappa G. "They're innocent and have no sense of anything strange or unnatural about their bodies. Unfortunately, you'll be witnessing the last moments of that innocence. They're about to be enticed into decisions and choices they'll never be able to undo," he added, his voice heavy with sadness. Pappa G beckoned. "Move closer to the tree. Every time I watch I want to intervene."

The GAs gathered at the outer edge of the tree of the knowledge of good and evil, thick branches rippling above, the smell of ripening fruit mouthwatering.

A rustle in the leaves on the far side of the tree announced Adam and Eve's arrival. Just as Gale had explained, the couple appeared oblivious to the presence of the onlookers.

"Why do we always end up here? We know it's the one area of the garden Pappa G warned us to leave well alone," Eve said.

Smiling, Adam pretended to touch some of the fruit. "Looks good, doesn't it?"

∽∾∾

Adam knew the garden like the back of his hand. For quite some time he had been the lone human inhabitant. He had explored every inch of it, from mountain top to valley floor. He'd tasted the wide variety of food and enjoyed countless walks and conversations with Pappa G. He had even played a part in naming the animals, with a little coaxing when his creativity ran dry.

After they'd finished naming the creatures, Pappa G whispered to Adam that he had a surprise for him.

"When?"

"In a few days." Pappa G winked. "Don't worry, it's all good."

Sure enough, a few days later Adam awoke and felt a slight pain in his side. He didn't pay much attention as Pappa G joined him and declared, "Today's the day!"

"For what?" Adam asked, touching the tender spot on his torso.

"Your surprise."

"Give me a hint, please," Adam pleaded.

"Ok—it isn't good for you to be alone," Pappa G replied with a knowing look.

"But I have you!" Adam exclaimed.

"I'm flattered, but I'm not enough," was the response. "You need a companion with skin and bone."

Adam had no idea what lay in store. But he knew better than to argue. Pappa G called a name Adam had never heard before. "Eve, let me introduce you to Adam!"

A figure emerged from behind the foliage and Adam gasped.

"What . . . who . . . is this?"

The figure came closer and smiled. Adam was speechless. It was slightly shorter than him yet similar in many ways: it stood upright on two legs; it had two arms. He walked around the figure and touched it tentatively on the back. Its skin felt like his. Its hair was longer than his, but the face had no beard. He touched the chest; it was larger, rounder, and more formed. When he scanned down its body, he saw that it too was different. He looked into its face and two deep brown eyes stared back at him. Its features were softer, more delicate, and possessed a beauty he'd never seen before.

"Adam, meet Eve. Eve, meet Adam. I have made you both in my image and created you to be partners in love and friendship."

Adam and Eve smiled shyly.

Eve proceeded to inspect Adam. She walked slowly around him. She ran her hands along his back, patted his chest, looked down at his male appendage, touched it, and giggled.

"Eve is a woman, fashioned from your side, Adam. She is to be honored and cherished and will be with you always. Now I'll leave you two to get to know one another."

"Hello," Eve said softly.

"Um, hi," Adam replied. "Uh . . . let me show you around some of my favorite places."

"It's so beautiful." Eve looked around with eyes wide open, slowly turning around to take it all in.

"Wait until you see the beach, and the big tree!" Adam said excitedly.

Over the coming days they swam under the waterfall, walked on the beach, and on the way back often stopped in the opening where the big tree grew. They quickly became not only best friends, but lovers as well, delighting in each other's bodies in new and exciting discoveries. Adam grinned at Eve beside him, exclaiming, "Pappa G is full of surprises!" They ambled through the clearing and admired the tree. It was magnificent, effortlessly supporting the vast canopy overhead like a waiter holding a tray on the tips of his fingers.

The GAs watched intently, as Adam drew closer and closer to the fruit.

"Imagine taking a bite," said Eve, wrinkling her nose at Adam. "Mmmm, I can almost taste it. If we were allowed, I'd like that one right there," she said, pointing above Adam's head.

"I'll take that one," Adam replied, playing along, then realized they were treading into dangerous territory. "Ok, enough—let's get out of here."

They turned to leave as they'd done countless times before.

"Psssst!" a voice said.

"What's that?" said Adam, craning his neck to peer into the treetop.

"Up here."

Squinting into the foliage, Adam and Eve gasped. Emerging from the branches was the most exquisite creature they'd ever encountered. The markings and colors it displayed glistened with radiant splendor, like a long rainbow wrapped around the branches. What transfixed them even more were the eyes—gleaming yellows and browns surrounded with various shades of peacock blue, mauve, and flecks of ruby red and gold. It was breathtakingly beautiful. The creature slid toward them without hint of a threat, its voice soft and melodic.

"Adam and Eve, what a pleasure," the creature purred. "I've heard so much about you. Pappa G and I go back a long way—in fact, to heaven and back. Friends of his are friends of mine. Welcome."

"Strange he hasn't mentioned you before," said Eve, with only the slightest hint of hesitation in her voice. She reached out her hand without thinking. "Do you mind if I touch you? These colors are magnificent."

"Not at all; thank you for the compliment. My name is Prince; I live here. I've noticed you visiting my tree from time to time, and I didn't want to intrude."

"*Your* tree?" Adam looked at Eve, then back to Prince. "I thought everything was created by Pappa G and belongs to him?"

"Of course, quite right," Prince agreed. "We work together here on earth—that's all I meant. You know he's immensely proud of you. Always talking about how you're created in his image; his beloved son and daughter who will inherit and enjoy everything in Eden."

"He's our father whom we love very much," Eve said.

"You must be hungry . . . allow me to offer you the tastiest fruit in the entire garden from this tree that is my home," the serpent hissed, ever so sweetly.

"That's truly kind of you," said Adam. "Unfortunately, we cannot accept your offer."

"Why on earth not?" Prince looked puzzled. He lowered his head sadly.

"We would love to taste your fruit," said Eve, not wanting to offend the creature, "but Pappa G instructed us that the fruit of this tree is the only fruit in his garden that we're not permitted to eat."

"He said that if we eat this fruit, we will gain the knowledge of good and evil, and we'll die. I'm not too sure what that means," admitted Adam.

"My dear new friends," Prince drawled, "there's really nothing to fear; you're not going to die. After all, Pappa G's gone to all the trouble of giving you the gift of life—you're his beloved son and daughter . . . It wouldn't make sense to doom you to death, now, would it?"

Adam and Eve glanced uncertainly at one another and discussed Prince's proposition.

While conversing, they were unaware that they'd followed Prince as he slowly made his way to the outer edges of the tree, where his weight caused the branches to bend closer to the ground. The hanging fruit swung gently within an arm's length of the couple. Prince's beauty, his reassuring tone, and his hypnotic eyes were mesmerizing.

"Rest assured, my friends; I'd never do anything to upset Pappa G after all he's done for me—which is why I think you misunderstood his meaning. Why would he give you free run of this garden, create such a beautiful tree with the most delicious fruit, and withhold it from you? That's not the Pappa G I know . . ."

"I agree," said Adam definitively.

"Come to think of it," Prince continued, "perhaps, between you and me, Pappa G wanted to make you in his image but is now concerned that you'll become as powerful as he is." Then the serpent shook its head as if to dismiss the thought. "Sorry, I can't believe I'm saying such a thing. Please, forget I mentioned that."

By this time neither Adam nor Eve were looking at Prince, their gaze locked on the fruit.

"It's delicious to look at, isn't it?" said Prince. "I promise you there's nothing as refreshing and sweet as the fruit hanging before you." He plucked two off the branch before them with his tail and handed one to Adam and one to Eve. "Taste it. It's not going to bite you back." He laughed. "Go on. Then tell me if I'm right."

They stepped back and glanced at one another. "Why not?" they said, shrugging their shoulders. Trembling with excitement and anticipation, they grabbed the fruit in both hands, drew it toward their mouths, and bit into the soft, aromatic flesh.

"This is so good," said Eve. Juice flowed down her chin as she took another bite and smiled at Adam.

"Never tasted anything like this before," he agreed. "I could eat this whole tree. How does Pappa G come up with these masterpieces?"

"Thank you, Prince," Eve exclaimed, turning back toward him with delight.

But there was no one there.

Chapter Seven

BRENDA WAS BESIDE HERSELF.

Alone in the hospital emergency room, she bit her lip and cursed herself for allowing Ricky to skateboard in the road. But where else could he go to burn up his youthful energy? He was fanatical about his skateboarding. Fortunately, it was quiet in front of their apartment, one of four located on the corner of Seventh and Melrose in South Port. Ricky and his friends loved the road because of the incline, the light traffic, and their home-made ramp. It launched them airborne into a thousand different maneuvers that invariably ended in tumbles and scrapes. The one rule from all the parents: wear a helmet!

That Tuesday in early September had been no different—until it was. It would forever remain etched into Brenda's mind and memory.

Brenda had been preparing lunch for the children. Nothing flashy; they couldn't afford luxuries. The water was boiling on the stove and she was about to add the noodles when she heard the screech of brakes, then a scream. She'd recognize Ricky's voice anywhere. Dropping the packet, she ran onto the patio. Instinctively she looked to the left. There, at the intersection with Sixth Avenue, lay Ricky, still as a stone. A red Toyota Corolla was stopped in the street and a woman stood next to it, her hand over her mouth.

Brenda was rushing out when she heard a voice from the stairwell.

"Mrs. Willard! Come quickly, there's been a terrible accident—Ricky's hurt!"

It was Tyler, Ricky's best friend, pale as a ghost, tears running down his cheeks. "Oh God, please no," Brenda choked as she followed Tyler back into the street.

Ricky lay motionless, blood matting in his hair, his legs splayed awkwardly.

"Are you his mother?" the distraught driver asked Brenda, as she knelt at Ricky's side.

"I'm so sorry . . . he flew into the road out of nowhere . . . oh God, I hope he'll be all right!"

Brenda barely heard a word. Pushing emotion aside, she went into autopilot. She dialed 911 and was assured that help was on the way. Looking at Ricky lying there, she fought rising panic and grief. There was no movement, his eyes were firmly shut, and his breathing was shallow. She checked for a pulse in his neck. She'd learned First Aid at school and recalled the Glasgow Coma Scale; it didn't take her long to ascertain that he wasn't responding to her voice. He showed no sign of responding to pain. She begged for the ambulance to hurry up.

"Ricky, Ricky, wake up! Ricky, it's all right, I'm here, please wake up." She cradled his head on her lap and sobbed while she whispered to him.

Standing quietly, Ricky's friends watched, shocked and badly shaken.

"What happened?" Brenda asked, looking up at Tyler, who was wiping his nose with his sleeve. "I don't really know, Mrs. Willard," he began, the words tumbling out. "We were packing up to go home and Ricky said he was going to have one last try at a trick we'd been practicing. Then, at the bottom of the hill he lost control and skated into the road and was hit by the car. We saw him fall and roll and hit his head hard against the curb."

"Why wasn't he wearing his helmet, for God's sake?" Brenda cried.

"I don't know, Mrs. Willard. We were finished so had taken ours off. I guess Ricky wasn't thinking. You know how he always wants to have one more ride."

Sirens blared as the ambulance approached with flashing lights followed by a police car. It braked sharply beside them. Two first responders jumped out, flung open the back doors, and retrieved a stretcher. Having identified Brenda as the mother, they gently ushered her away from her son and assessed Ricky, asking the boys questions about what had happened. They checked for spinal injuries, carefully examining his neck. They decided to leave the legs for Emergency. There was no time to waste.

The responders placed Ricky on a backboard with a collar around his neck. They carefully placed him on the stretcher and fitted him with an ambubag to help with breathing. The bag resembled a small football and was attached to a face shield placed over his mouth and nose. An attendant would connect him to an oxygen supply on the way to the hospital.

As they loaded him into the ambulance, Ricky remained unresponsive. Sirens wailing, the ambulance left, headed for the hospital on the other side of town. Brenda impatiently answered questions for the police officer before rushing inside to collect her keys and her purse. By that time a few neighbors had gathered outside to see what was happening. One of them, her friend Sally, gave her a quick hug and reassured her, "Don't worry about the kids hon—I'll take care of them for as long as needed."

Brenda called Jack on her way to the hospital. No reply as usual. Emotionally raw, scared, and angry, she left a terse message.

She parked the car and half-walked, half-ran through the main entrance, across the bright courtyard with a glass roof, into the Emergency wing. Ricky was already being examined. The receptionist told her that the doctor would talk to her as soon as he'd completed his assessment. "We're doing everything we can for Ricky," she assured her.

Brenda waited alone. She wore a faded green tee shirt and blue track pants. She used to be petite, with short styled blonde hair, but in the past year she'd let herself go, the stress of coping with life as a single parent and an alcoholic, absent husband too much to bear. She didn't even try to kid herself anymore by making resolutions to lose weight that she knew she'd never keep.

Her stomach twisted in knots. Ricky was her firstborn—always so bright, outgoing, full of life, and adventurous. Afraid of nothing, he'd begged and pleaded for a skateboard when he was barely five. Initially Jack and Brenda had told him to wait until he was older. During the next year, Jack had googled for information on skateboards for young kids. He researched the shape of the board, whether w-concave, convex, asymmetrical, or radial, and got himself really confused. Eventually he ordered a Flybar board. Described as "ideal for a young kid," it boasted being "tons of fun, a smooth ride on chrome bearings and polyurethane wheels. Regular kick tale and nose." Whatever that meant.

The board arrived the day before Ricky's sixth birthday.

Four years later, the Flybar was history, replaced multiple times over the years with more customized boards by Baker. Ricky was a natural and was soon matching the older boys with his maneuvers. At supper he'd often describe the latest trick he'd learned.

"We're learning a heelflip. I've nearly got it!" he'd tell them excitedly, and launch into details, most of which Brenda tried to block out, wishing he would find a hobby less stressful—for her. But she didn't say this to him; she knew it was what he loved, and all she could do was try to encourage him to keep safe. He watched YouTube videos with his friends, which fueled their fantasies and aspirations. At any opportunity they took to the streets, pretending to be one of the legends in skateboarding, the likes of Tony Hawk, Ronald Mullen, and Luan Oliveira. Jack and Brenda did their best to cheer him on.

When Brenda privately voiced her worries to Jack, he would respond, "A lot better than sitting on the couch playing video games."

On one hand, she agreed. Skateboarding was Ricky's passion, it was a social activity, and it kept him active and engaged him. On the other hand—from the point of view of a mother—it unnerved her, and she found it frustrating that Jack didn't seem to share any of her worries. She often wondered if he cared at all.

And now this. The time dragged. People came and went from the waiting room in an endless stream. Brenda sat, rigid with fear, feeling as if her insides had been ripped out, dreading to imagine what was happening with Ricky. She closed her eyes. She'd carried the weight of responsibility for the household for so long, somehow managing to hold down her job as a hair stylist in a local salon, take care of the kids, and navigate her sense of despair and failure with Jack. She was exhausted. She fumbled for a Kleenex in her purse and dabbed her eyes.

"Are you ok? Haven't we met before? Brenda, isn't it?" a gentle voice said.

Brenda looked up into wide blue-gray eyes.

She'd been so absorbed in her thoughts she was oblivious to the woman who'd arrived five minutes earlier and was seated beside her.

"Yes, that's me," she spluttered. "Um, I'm not sure, perhaps at the school, Eighth Avenue?"

"That's it. I work with some of the kids there and we spoke in the parking lot last week. You were looking for jumper cables to start your car, and it so happened I could help."

"Oh yes, of course. You saved my life with the cables. And the car hasn't given me any trouble since. I don't know what you did, but it worked."

"That's good to hear. Just connected the cables for a charge and said a quick prayer." The stranger smiled. "I'm Rachel. I didn't mean to interrupt, but you seemed upset and . . ."

"It's all right, thanks," said Brenda. She couldn't stop the tears. "Well, not really. My son is in the operating room with a head injury and I'm going out of my mind waiting. I'm terrified."

"How awful. Do you have family?"

"No one here," Brenda answered. "I'm a single mom right now, and I'm so afraid that Ricky won't make it. I don't know what I'd do."

Rachel leaned in and touched Brenda's arm. "I'll wait with you if I'm not intruding. Sometimes things seem worse before they get better."

"Thank you," Brenda replied, looking up with a weak smile.

The two of them sat side by side on the hard, functional chairs. The cold, gray linoleum tile floor gleamed beneath the glare of the fluorescent lights. Together they waited.

Chapter Eight

WIDE-EYED WITH DISBELIEF, THE five GAs stood in the clearing only feet away from where Adam and Eve were embroiled in a catastrophe of their own making, with consequences far beyond anything they could have foreseen.

"Where's he gone?" Eve turned to Adam. "He was here a minute ago."

"Didn't notice him leave," said Adam, "Too busy enjoying the fruit. Here, you want another?" He plucked one from the branch and offered it to Eve. "He's disappeared before we can even thank him," said Adam, greedily taking a big bite.

"Thank him for what?" Eve asked.

"Thank him for giving us the courage to try the fruit. Strange that he should leave without a word or goodbye, isn't it? He seemed so pleasant and friendly."

Engrossed in savoring every morsel, they continued to eat without speaking. Slowly, reality dawned. No birds sang, and an eerie stillness pervaded the garden. Normally they would see animals around them—monkeys swinging in the trees, a zebra grazing on the lush grasses, or one of their favorite companions, the elegant tiger, basking in the sun's warmth. Now they'd all disappeared, even the sunlight through the tree-tops appeared to have dimmed.

"Adam," said Eve, with an edge to her voice he'd never heard before.

"Yes?" said Adam, putting his sticky fruit-stained arm around her shoulders.

"Something's strange." She leaned into him awkwardly. "I've never felt like this. I'm scared. Maybe Pappa G was serious and now we're going to die?"

"Nonsense," said Adam. "Here, join me in a few more mouthfuls." He plucked another juicy fruit from the branch above his head and bit hungrily into it.

"No, I don't think so," said Eve. "Adam, I'm not joking; I don't like this uneasiness inside me. What happens when Pappa G visits us? What are we going to tell him? I don't want to see him. I'm scared."

"We'll pretend nothing's happened," said Adam with a shrug of his shoulders. "We can tell him that this was a mistake, and we won't do it again."

"I think we should get far away from this tree," Eve said, clasping Adam's hand and pulling him away.

"Good idea. Let's go for a swim in the pool and wash away this juice; it's very sticky." He chuckled halfheartedly.

As they were making their way back up the path toward the waterfall, they heard Pappa G approaching from the opposite direction. Without saying a word, both ducked into the bushes.

Pappa G appeared around the corner. "Adam, Eve, where are you?" he called.

Silence.

Adam knew it was futile to remain hidden. Now he too was experiencing emotions he had never known before. He noticed his heart was beating faster and sweat beaded his brow, his throat was dry, and his whole body trembled. He spluttered the first thing that came into his head. "I . . . um . . . we . . . I heard you in the garden, and I was afraid because I was naked, so I hid."

"Who told you that you were naked?" Pappa G pressed him.

Silence.

"Have you eaten from the tree that I commanded you not to go near?"

"The woman you put here with me," Adam blurted accusingly, looking across at Eve; she began to cry. "It was her: she gave me some fruit from the tree, and I ate it. It was her idea—I tried to stop her."

"Eve is that true?" asked Pappa G, standing on the pathway speaking into the trees and bushes.

"It was the snake; he deceived me, and I ate," Eve replied, sobbing quietly, unable to hide the distress or control the tightening knot in her stomach. She wished Pappa G would go away and leave them alone for a while. How could Adam be so cruel as to blame her? she wondered.

"What will happen now?" Yesaidu turned to Gale, his face etched with sadness and shock at what was unfolding before them.

"Unfortunately, it's one of those situations where there is no going back. Pappa G is telling them they will have to live elsewhere. From now on, because of their disobedience, their lives will include hard work and won't be as pleasant as their lifestyle in Eden," Gale replied.

"But why did Pappa G place the tree in the garden if he knew this would happen? It's a cruel joke and they've been set up to fail. If there had to be a tree of the knowledge of good and evil, why not have no fruit on it? Or at least make the fruit too high for them to reach?" said Nova, visibly upset.

"Nova," said Gale, patting his shoulder gently, "If there wasn't a tree and no rule offering Adam and Eve the opportunity to make a real choice, there would be no freedom for human beings to choose. Then you'd complain that we created puppets, mere entertainment for a bored Creator." She cocked her head toward the action in front of them. "Watch this; you'll see there are many facets to who we are."

A loud roar rang out, or was it a shout? The earth around them trembled as a massive figure in battle armor approached the tree.

"Who's that?" whispered Gregori.

"That's Pappa G in battle mode; he's very angry."

The figure took hold of the massive tree and shook it like a sapling. "Come out from there!" he demanded. A dull brown snake fell from the branches. Pappa G picked it up in one hand. It writhed and wriggled like a worm.

"That's the same creature who told Adam and Eve to eat the fruit?" Gregori gasped at the nondescript snake with ugly black markings resembling a dead stick.

"Yes, it is," said Gale. "He always portrays himself as magnificent, powerful, and generous, but he's far from that now."

Pappa G's voice boomed as he shook the squirming snake by the throat.

"Will you never learn, you whom I created with love and elevated to the highest places to be with me? But it was never enough. You had to have it all, to be like me, so jealous for power and status. How you have fallen from the mighty expanse of the universe to the dust of the earth. I will not renounce the gifts I gave you, but I curse you above every living creature. You will crawl on your stomach and eat dust every day of your life. And there will be enmity between you and the woman, your offspring and hers forever. They will crush your head and you will strike their heels. You will be defeated, and my Kingdom will *never* be yours."

Pappa G tossed the snake to the ground and it slunk into the undergrowth without a sound.

There was a long silence.

"That was frightening," said Jenny. "I wouldn't want to have Pappa G angry with me."

"That's the anger of a father whose children have been attacked," said Gale. "A father whose heart is breaking because he has to exercise justice despite his passionate love. As do we." Gale turned away, her eyes brimming with tears.

"Let's walk by the ocean," suggested Gregori, attempting to lighten the mood. Everyone agreed.

The beach was a wide expanse of pure white sand stretching around a curved bay and disappearing into the distance. Wave after wave rolled up the shore and then receded with gently whooshing sighs. The rhythm and sounds provided a soothing accompaniment as they strolled above the water line.

"I thought beaches had shells on them?" said Jenny, bending down to scoop a handful of sand.

"Not in Eden," answered Gale. "Nothing dies here; all the shells have little creatures living inside them enjoying the rocks, the sea, and the sunshine. As I told you before, there are no predators, which means every animal is safe. Adam and Eve were unique in the garden. They were the only creatures in existence to whom we gave the ability to reflect, make choices, and have relationship, like how Pappa G, Jesus, and I relate."

"Someone's been here before," exclaimed Yesaidu. He pointed to three sets of footprints pressed into the sand.

"That's Adam and Eve," said Gale. "Pappa G used to walk with them here or through the garden every day. He'd show them new things and ask what they'd like to name them; they had lots of fun. Those prints will remain in the sand forever as a memory of what we shared and enjoyed. One day all our creation will once again walk with us along this beach, but before then we have much work to do."

Chapter Nine

"MRS. WILLARD?" A VOICE rang out over the waiting area.

"Yes, that's me." Brenda jumped to her feet. Letting go of Rachel's comforting hand, she approached the man wearing green scrubs and a green cap. She looked pale, eyes red from tears, hair disheveled, clothes crumpled. "How's Ricky?" she blurted.

"Hello, I'm Dr. O'Leary." He gestured for her to be seated beside him in a corner of the room. He was a man of medium height and build, with a ruddy complexion and kind eyes framed by black spectacles.

"Mrs. Willard, I'm so sorry about Ricky's accident. We're doing everything we can for him. May I ask you a few routine questions?"

"Yes, of course," Brenda muttered in a daze, her nerves shattered. Dr O'Leary checked with Brenda regarding allergies, medications, medical history, and whether there was any history of seizures. "We'll complete a family medical history later."

"Nothing," she replied. "Ricky is a normal, healthy, fourteen-year-old."

"He wasn't wearing a helmet?" Dr. O'Leary commented with a quizzical expression.

"Our cardinal rule was that Ricky always wear his helmet while skateboarding," Brenda replied weakly. "His friends told me he had made one more attempt at a difficult trick just before they were heading home. Ricky can get so focused that he forgets, and I guess that's what happened. Please, how is he?"

The doctor took a deep breath and began, "As you know, Ricky suffered a sharp blow to the head. He has also fractured his left leg which we've set in a splint. It will need plenty of rest and time to heal." He paused and met Brenda's eyes. "Of greater concern is the fact that Ricky's been unconscious and in a coma since the accident; that's troubling. We are monitoring the swelling and pressure on his brain. In these instances, it's difficult to say definitively whether there will be long-term effects. He has what we'd describe as a traumatic brain injury."

Brenda gasped and began to cry. "Oh my God—will he live?"

"We're doing everything we can," Dr. O'Leary reassured her. "The problem with these types of injuries is knowing the long-term outcome. The best scenario is that over time he regains his health with little, if any, lasting effects. But more likely, there will be some issues that may persist."

"What do you mean?" Brenda asked.

"The brain is an extremely fragile and sensitive organ," Dr. O'Leary explained. "We have Ricky on a ventilator to support his breathing. When you see him, he will be sedated and will have an intravenous saline drip and be attached to an ECG to monitor his heart. It can be a little over-whelming, but this is normal procedure. As we speak, Ricky is undergo-ing a CT scan which will provide us with a more accurate understanding of his injury. Of course, we'll keep him in Intensive Care under close observation."

"When can I see him?" Brenda asked, her mind swimming with worry.

"When we have him stable and comfortable; he has a tough battle ahead of him. You'll notice he's developed two black eyes, which is a sign of brain injury. I am trying to be as honest as possible, Brenda. We're doing everything we can, so let's take one step at a time."

"Thank you, Dr. O'Leary," Brenda said mechanically, still not quite comprehending his words.

"I'm sorry I can't bring you better news. We are a small hospital with limited resources. There's every likelihood we may need to air vac Ricky to Vancouver Children's Hospital where they're better equipped to deal with these types of injury. I'm afraid it's an hour-by-hour assessment situation."

Dr. O'Leary patted Brenda's shoulder as he got up and left. Brenda rose from her chair as if to follow him, then stood, stunned, as she grap-pled with the enormity of the doctor's words.

Watching it all unfold, Rachel rushed to Brenda's side, just in time to catch her as she fell into her arms and wept.

∽∘∽

The rhythmic slapping of hand drums pulsated across the rondavel, joined by a saxophone and guitars. It was a vast circular building with a thatched conical roof supported by massive wooden beams and posts. Colorful abstract designs covered the walls. A large log fire burned bright in the center where people danced to the beat of the drums. Lamps suspended from beams cast light over the table where the GAs planned to discuss the first downloads on their InSights.

"Jenny, come and dance before we get started." Nova reached out his hand. "How can you sit still when such beautiful music is playing?" He laughed, performing a little jig in front of her.

Jenny jumped up excitedly. "Sure, let's go," she said.

They headed toward the fire, soon to be followed by the rest of the group. All around them music filled the atmosphere as they twirled and moved to the slap of the drum and the soaring riff of the saxophone. Whoever said that heaven was dull evidently had no idea about the fullness of life celebrated.

They'd agreed to alternate the venue for their InSight discussions. On this first night they were meeting in Nova's village at a popular restaurant called Furaha. "It means 'joy'," Nova told them with smile, "and there is an abundance of it here. Enjoy!"

The GAs certainly enjoyed the dancing. Back at their table they found hot plates piled with Nova's recommendation: Jollof rice with goat meat, tomatoes, onions, and tomato sauce.

"Was that ever tasty!" Yesaidu exclaimed. "We'll definitely have to come here again, Nova." The others nodded in agreement. Eventually Jenny called them to order, and they retrieved their InSights. They had been following Jack's attempted drowning and Ricky's accident as part of their training, opening their eyes to an ugliness that they never could have fathomed existed.

"So, what do you think?" she said soberly. "I reviewed the material so far; I didn't realize how different we are to those in Earthtime."

"I was amazed how rundown and neglected everything looks there; I guess we're so used to our environment," Asuka commented.

"Yeah, me too," said Gregori, furrowing his brow. "I kept reviewing the scene of Jack wanting to drown himself. It was awful to think that someone could feel so defeated. I'm struggling to wrap my head around that."

"Did you notice that when Jack was about to drown, he was listening to the voice in his head accusing and belittling him? I recognized that voice from the tree in Eden—the snake. It gave me shivers." Jenny looked at her screen and shook her head.

"We're not used to hearing that sound in heaven," Yesaidu said. "It's so sad that the negativity of the snake infiltrates everyone; many aren't even aware and mistake the voice for their own self-talk. Gale explained that to me." The other GAs nodded solemnly in agreement. "So much of what we witnessed is filled with anxiety and conflict. How Brenda and Jack relate is hard to fathom. How can people who love each other become so angry?"

Asuka spoke so softly the rest had to lean in to hear. "I found Ricky's accident tough to watch. It raised emotions in me I find hard to describe. Unsettling, and yet it seems those in Earthtime live with such conflicting emotions all the time. I can't comprehend how they do it . . ."

"I guess that's why we're doing this exercise: We need to know how people function in Earthtime—what they do, what they feel, who they hurt—in order to do our job. Personally, I'd prefer not to know, but that would be selfish," Nova said.

"I'd probably get too impatient, particularly with Jack," Jenny confessed. "Their friends are exactly the opposite—so patient and gentle. I'm scared I'd say or do the wrong thing."

"Perhaps that will change as we go through the training," Gregori responded. "I feel the same as you do. I don't understand their mindset right now. I want to shake them." He laughed. "And tell them that it doesn't have to be this bad."

"Yes, but Ricky's accident would upset most people, don't you think?" said Yesaidu. "I've heard about them, but I've never seen an accident before, or someone, what do you call it—?"

"Unconscious," said Asuka. "We have a lot to learn hospitals, doctors, nurses, sickness, operations . . ."

"How about we run through the scenes together and highlight anything that is confusing or new?" Jenny suggested. Everyone agreed, powered up their InSights, and scrolled back to the beginning.

Chapter Ten

THE GAs WERE NOT expecting this.

They'd followed Jesus through the misty wall and immediately encountered heat—dry, dusty heat in a rock-strewn wasteland of mountains and valleys, brown pebbles, and rust-colored sand that stretched as far as the eye could see.

Jenny clutched her throat and stumbled. "I feel so tired and weak all of a sudden," she gasped. "What's happening?"

"Me too," said Yesaidu. "I have no strength at all." He sat down on a nearby rock and hung his head.

The rest of the group dropped like limp bundles in a semi-circle.

"What has this got to do with Adam and Eve?" Asuka asked, her voice dry and raspy.

Jesus stood on a rocky outcrop on a mountain ridge high above an ancient valley carved by a river that no longer flowed. They knew it was him even though they hadn't been formally introduced yet. The air shimmered above the baking earth, conjuring images of water where there was none.

The soft swish and crunch of hoofs on rock and sand caught their attention. A well-dressed herdsman led a camel laden with goods. He stopped and addressed them. "I greet you friends, in this barren land; you look exhausted. Allow me to offer some refreshments—water, fresh bread, ripe fruit? The tastiest you'll ever find."

"Yes please!" the GAs responded in grateful unison. They gathered around the camel as the man placed delicious-looking fruit and jugs of water in their hands. Smiles lit up their faces.

"Stop!"

They froze at the sound of Jesus' sharp declaration. The elegantly dressed man, the camel, the fruit, and the water vanished.

"What's going on?" Navo exclaimed. "That was a cruel joke."

"I'll explain," said Jesus. "This is the Judean wilderness—a stark contrast to Eden, isn't it? In some ways a spiritual metaphor. It used to be as lush as Eden, now look. Here is where I fasted for forty days when I lived in Earthtime."

"Why did you do that?" Jenny asked.

"You saw Pappa G cast down the snake in Eden. This is where the snake tried his tricks on me as well. The weakness you are experiencing is like mine after thirty-five days of fasting. The snake appeared to tempt and seduce me with false promises. He manifests like the kind man with his camel. When people in Earthtime are most vulnerable, he conveniently offers exactly what they yearn for. And they are so desperate they seldom suspect."

"How embarrassing," Yesaidu said, his face reddening. "We fell for it without a second thought."

"When he tried to tempt me, I was prepared for him," Jesus continued. "The point of the fasting was to affirm the strength of my spirit over my body. Life and resolve flow from the spirit, what we call 'living from the inside out.'"

"You mean a strong spirit is a weapon?" Jenny said.

"Precisely. The snake cannot destroy the spirit, but he will cause humans to unwittingly starve it by merely satisfying the body," Jesus explained. "Consequently, most people focus on the cravings of the flesh and psyche—they desire more money, a better job, the perfect body, drugs to make them feel good about themselves, which renders them extremely vulnerable to the charms of the snake. Once the spirit regains control, he is defeated—every time."

"But most people in Earthtime don't realize that their spirits are parched like this wilderness," Gregori said. "I get it. And our task as Guardian Angels is to be gardeners, restoring the desert to life."

"That's exactly right. Look over there." Jesus pointed across to the distant valley wall where green strips of vegetation dribbled down the mountainside. "That's an aqueduct. Wherever water leaks through cracks, green vegetation flourishes. There is life in this barren land. Add water and life returns."

"As it is with land, so it is with people," Asuka said.

"I merely wanted to demonstrate how easily you can succumb in Earthtime, if you're unaware." Jesus beckoned them to follow. "Now, we have an interview to attend to."

∽∾∽

"You know the routine," Pappa G said, addressing Adam and Eve. He and Gale had gathered the GAs into the Rainbow Room to allow them to question and learn from them. Facing the rest of the group, he continued, "It's one thing to try to comprehend what people are thinking and feeling by observing them. But hearing firsthand from them is the most effective and truthful way to really understand their experiences and perspectives. So, what questions would you like to ask?"

Nova started off the questioning with something he had been burning to ask ever since he'd watched the couple disobey God. "Adam, and Eve, how do you become disillusioned in a place like Eden? Did I miss something? It was beautiful, peaceful, tranquil, everything anyone could ever desire, and yet it wasn't enough?"

"You know what they say about hindsight and 20/20 vision?" Adam responded. "Believe me, we've had plenty of time to reflect on our actions. Eve usually gets a bad rap for tempting me, and admittedly I didn't help by pinning the blame on her. The truth is, we're both responsible for allowing the snake to beguile us."

"Of course," added Eve, "we'd never encountered lies before. The snake was gorgeous, and very friendly. It didn't occur to us that someone would want to deceive us or say anything bad about Pappa G, so we weren't suspicious at all."

"But you had been warned," Jenny interjected.

"You're right, Jenny," Adam said. "As soon as Pappa G told us that we couldn't touch the tree or eat its fruit, we were strangely fascinated. Eve and I would often hang out around there and tease one another about eating fruit, in a playful way. That was as far as it went."

"Wasn't that asking for trouble?" Jenny asked.

Eve nodded. "In retrospect I think we were naively playing with fire. We lulled ourselves into thinking that Pappa G might be irritated, but not respond drastically if we crossed his forbidden fruit line. The conversation with the snake nudged us in the wrong direction."

"Do you think that if the snake hadn't spoken to you, you'd have left the fruit alone?" Gregori scratched his tousled hair as he posed the question.

Eve smiled. "I'd like to think so. We let our guard down. When the snake spoke, we questioned why we were not allowed to touch the tree. For some reason, the thought of disobeying Pappa G at the time was intriguing, even exciting. All I could imagine was running around the garden telling Pappa G that I was smarter than him. It was a game in my mind. I never considered why obedience was imperative, or that I was actually being protected from something profoundly dangerous."

"It didn't enter my mind either," said Adam. "In conversation with the snake, I heard nothing other than the suggestion that we were being denied something more. How crazy is that when we had no right to anything in that garden in the first place?" He shrugged and shook his head, as if, millennia later, he still couldn't believe they'd been so short sighted.

"How do you deal with the guilt, knowing that because of your actions so many billions of people now suffer?" Jenny asked.

"Oh my," Adam sighed deeply, "we've had many conversations with Pappa G about those consequences. We've struggled to come to terms with what we set in motion. But his response to us was unexpected and comforting. Why don't you explain, Eve?"

"Sure, story is better than lecture, don't you agree? Here's what happened . . ."

"Adam and Eve, step out here into the open."

The two figures, once so happy to walk alongside Pappa G, reluctantly appeared from behind the bushes, almost cowering, awkwardly covering their nakedness.

"We're s-sorry Pappa G, we didn't realize."

"She made me do it," said Adam, pointing to Eve.

"What do you mean?" Eve retorted. "You weren't exactly watching passively. It was *you* who encouraged me in the first place. Pappa G, that's not true."

"Quiet, both of you." Pappa G raised a silencing hand. "As far as I'm concerned, you share the responsibility, no more pointing fingers. Follow me."

He led them back along the path until they arrived again at the large clearing around the big tree. They followed meekly, scarcely looking at the tree as they approached.

"Ever since I created you, I knew this situation was likely, indeed probable."

"You mean we were set up to fail?" Adam asked, mouth open, aghast.

"Not at all. You are created in my image with the capacity to think, reflect, create, have a conscience, and, most importantly, to make choices. Such is the essence of freedom, responsibility, and consequences."

"But why didn't you warn us about the snake?" Adam asked, anger rising in his voice.

"I warned you not to eat the fruit of this tree." Pappa G slapped the side of the trunk, plucked a fruit dangling from a nearby branch, and bit into it. "Jesus, Gale, and I are the only ones permitted to eat this fruit. That was the single restriction for you in the entire garden."

"You could have been a little more forceful, or built a fence around it," Adam said, pointedly. "Maybe?"

"No matter what I said, you'd have been tested." Pappa G took another bite of the juicy fruit. "You see, rebellion didn't start with you; it began with the snake. And because he is no match for me, he will tamper with all my creation, including you. It's a larger picture in play here."

"What happens now—are you going to kill us?" Eve whispered. Her eyes remained fixed to the ground as she spoke.

"I'd like to hug you and say everything will be fine, and that's what my love would prefer." Pappa G smiled. There was a compassionate sadness in his eyes. "Even I can't undo actions and magically dispel consequences. You'll have to leave the garden immediately. You can never touch me again."

Adam and Eve gasped. "What? Why? Where will we go?"

"Outside this garden is the snake's domain at present. My ultimate plan and purpose is to win it back, but that's a discussion for later. You will have to be careful of his cunning ways. And you will need to work the ground, collect your food, build a place to live, and raise a family."

"Won't you give us another chance and let us stay here? We've learned our lesson, I promise you that," Adam pleaded.

"Adam, my beloved son, I can't do that. If you remain in the garden, you will die. Through your actions a rebellion has entered your spirit and body, which means that the perfection of this creation can no longer sustain or nourish you. If you're going to live at all, it must be outside this place. I will help you and be with you, in a different way. If you've learned your lesson, we will return here again one day. I'm not abandoning you; I could never do that."

Eve looked at the GAs and smiled. "So that's our rather sad story. Adam?"

"We were so wrong to question Pappa G's motive," said Adam. "When we ate the fruit, we became wise—but not as we anticipated—knowing the difference between good and evil. Our problem was that having made a wrong choice, we had no clue how to handle the consequences. We learned by experience about a guilty conscience, except we were stuck with it. Stuck on the wrong side—left with our guilt, shame, and a fractured relationship. The desire to hide was overwhelming." He glanced at Gale and Pappa G.

"How would you suggest this helps us understand people living in Earthtime today?" Jenny asked, pen poised and ready. She'd already filled pages of her notebook with notes that she hoped would be helpful in her training. She'd promised the others that she'd give them copies.

"Great question," Gale affirmed.

"Probably realizing that they live in a battle zone," Adam replied. "Understanding that the snake continues to lie, is active, always accusing, wanting to destroy people's lives. Like us, many fail to see, or to be aware."

"Look, the world is a very different place today," said Eve. "Far worse than we ever experienced. However, the key issue remains the same for every generation following ours: the spiritual battle is real; the battle between good and evil rages."

"By the way," Pappa G interjected, "who do you think were the first inhabitants of heaven, apart from the angels, of course?" He smiled, gesturing to Adam and Eve. "These two. Defeat in Earthtime is of a temporary nature, as are the negative consequences of poor decisions. When my children admit their mistakes, we always find a way to restore."

"Excuse me," Nova raised his hand, "Pappa G, why didn't you just kill the snake and be done with it? End of story. And prevent ongoing suffering through all these generations?"

Pappa G leaned on the table his fingers intertwined, and smiled. "Thanks Nova; you're asking an important question that many have voiced over the centuries, usually out of pain, often concluding that I'm indifferent—which couldn't be further from the truth. For now, let's just say it's not a straightforward answer. There are many facets to be answered on our journey together. Next time, ok?"

Chapter Eleven

INSIDE INTENSIVE CARE, RICKY lay still and pale. A ventilator assisted his breathing, a tube down his throat. His head was bandaged, his face bruised. His left leg beneath the sheet was in a splint; an intravenous drip attached above the limp hand that Brenda would cradle and caress for hours in the days ahead.

Nothing could have prepared Brenda for the shock of seeing him lying there beaten up, looking so small, surrounded by tubes and monitors. She kissed him gently on the forehead.

"Hello Ricky, we're going to get you out of here as soon as we can, don't you worry," she said, struggling to keep her voice even.

No response.

A deluge of thoughts ticker taped through her mind, including the big "if only." *If only I'd called him in for lunch five minutes earlier. If only Jack had been here for his son, and for me . . .*

Rachel entered the room carrying two coffees. She passed Brenda a Starbucks cup with a lid. "Here you are."

"Thanks," said Brenda, pressing back the plastic cover.

They sipped in silence, staring at the prostrate, motionless shell of a boy in the bed.

"Any improvement, do you think?" Rachel asked.

"Difficult to say really," said Brenda. "He seems peaceful." She looked at Ricky and stroked his hand. "He still hasn't opened his eyes or said anything. Of course, he's quite heavily sedated to give time for healing, so I guess it's a waiting game."

Rachel stood beside Brenda at Ricky's bedside. One hand rested on Brenda's shoulder; in the other she held her coffee. "Well, at least he's in good care and is resting." She smiled and dragged over a chair to sit opposite Brenda.

"What's he like? How would you describe Ricky?"

Brenda smiled weakly. "Just like his mother and father—in better times."

Rachel didn't want to pry, being aware that she was still very much an outsider. She sipped her coffee thoughtfully, waiting for Brenda to continue.

"Loves his sport and having fun with friends, not so great at work— just like his father. Oddly enough, that's why I fell in love with Jack; he was such fun to be around. The lack of responsibility was only more obvious to me later," she explained, shaking her head despondently. "But Ricky's got my sense of humor," she continued, brightening. "He has a sensitivity to others who struggle, not a bone of a bully in him. I'd say that's like me. Really does light up the room, always looking out for his younger sisters. I really couldn't wish for a better son."

Brenda squeezed Ricky's hand and looked across at Rachel with a half-smile.

A tear rolled down Rachel's cheek. She pulled her gaze from Ricky and looked at Brenda. "Sorry." She dabbed her eyes. "I've had some longings and losses of my own. But that's a story for another day."

Brenda reached over and touched her arm. "It's kind of you to be here with me, a total stranger. You don't need to stay; you've already been so generous with your time."

"My privilege," Rachel replied. "I wouldn't want to go through something like this on my own."

"Why were you at the hospital?" Brenda asked, suddenly aware that she hadn't thought to ask earlier.

"I work part-time with young pregnant mothers and their families. Sometimes I pop into the hospital to see if there's anyone I know. It's amazing how often it's the right time and the right place."

"Are you married? Do you have children?" Brenda asked, then, realizing her boldness, added, "Sorry, it's none of my business."

"No, I don't mind." Rachel looked back at Ricky with his eyes closed, chest rising and falling in time with the ventilator. "Let's just say I haven't yet met the right guy. It's something I would love to have . . ." Her voice trailed into a whisper. "You know . . ."

"Strange how life goes," said Brenda. "Some of us get pregnant, have children, and a partner so young—like I did. We never really figure out who we are; it all just happens. Then one day the s**t hits the fan and there are more plates to juggle and pieces to pick up. I envy you your freedom, and perhaps you envy me having children and . . ." She paused. "Not sure about the marriage part."

Rachel smiled. "I'm content with who I am and my situation. I've learned that envying others isn't wise. We seldom see the whole picture. Everyone has challenges and circumstances that are less than ideal. I think that's why we need one another. As the song says, 'we all need somebody to lean on'—from time to time."

Brenda's eyes welled up. "I never saw this coming. Jack leaving was bad enough, but if Ricky—"

"Excuse me, Brenda," Dr. O'Leary knocked lightly on the door, "May I have a word?"

Brenda looked around, startled, fear in her eyes. "Hi, Dr O'Leary. Yes, sure."

He beckoned to her to follow him outside.

Rachel remained at Ricky's side, staring at him in the dim light. She placed a hand gently on his shoulder and softly squeezed. She could hardly fathom Brenda's pain, but hers gnawed from deep within her soul—the pain of knowing she could never have children, or be married, through no fault of her own. Those gifts had been snatched from her long ago. She wasn't angry or jealous, merely aware of the loss that lingered and surfaced from time to time in moments like this.

Brenda's return broke her thoughts. She was shaking.

"Dr. O'Leary says that the fact that Ricky's not coming out of his coma has them worried. He'll be airlifted to Children's Hospital in Vancouver in a few hours. He suggested I make arrangements and head over as soon as possible." For a moment Brenda stood there numbly, trying to absorb the news. She knew that breaking down would only make things worse.

Rachel stood up and held Brenda's arm. "I'm so sorry, Brenda. I can come with you for company if you like. I have the time."

Brenda hesitated.

"Look, I'm heading home. What's your number? I'll text you mine now. If you'd like me to join you just text or call in the next few hours, no pressure," Rachel said.

"Ok, thanks."

Brenda watched her leave. She lingered at Ricky's bedside before giving him a peck on his bandaged forehead. Walking out of Intensive

Care, she tried to block out thoughts of Ricky lying there alone, unconscious, being prepared to be flown to the Mainland. She wondered about her girls: maybe Sally would take care of them? She checked her phone, still nothing but radio silence from Jack. Outside the main entrance two patients in hospital gowns sat smoking, their IV drips suspended from portable IV poles. They nodded hello and Brenda nodded back. She skirted the turning circle and crossed the parking lot to her car in the last row. Dazed, she unlocked the door and slid behind the wheel. It was hot. She opened the windows and sat staring at nothing for a few minutes. As she gripped the steering wheel she began to shake. *Pull yourself together girl*, she scolded herself.

With a deep sigh Brenda picked up her cellphone and punched in the numbers Rachel had texted. It rang six times, which seemed like an eternity.

"Hello."

"Hi Rachel, Brenda here."

"Hi Brenda, I'm so glad you called."

"Thanks for your kind offer . . . I've been thinking, I really can't do this on my own. I hardly know you, but if you think you have the time—"

"Of course. Why don't I pick you up and we can go in my car? I have your address on my phone. I'll be there in about an hour. You ok with that?"

"Thank you, Rachel. I don't know what I'd do without you right now."

Chapter Twelve

"Push, girl, you can do it! That's the way."

An elderly man sat, legs splayed, behind the heaving goat. He gently pulled on two little legs protruding, soon followed by a wet nose and head. After a few more grunts and heaves from both goat and man, a bundle of soggy hair with four legs dropped to the ground. The exhausted mother turned slowly and began licking her new kid as he wobbled up-right to draw his first shallow breaths.

"Well done," the man said, patting the mother. "And welcome into this bright new world, young fellow." He scratched the kid's bobbing head before wiping his hands in the dust and rubbing them together in a crude attempt to clean them. "The rest is up to you, old goat. Take good care of him now."

Moses had done this hundreds of times over the years: overseeing his growing herd, bringing them into the world and usually sending them out when he butchered them for market. Every birth filled him with a sense of awe and wonder.

A response shared by the GAs who were watching from the Rainbow Room. "You've just witnessed your first creative miracle in Earthtime," Gale exclaimed with a broad grin. Earlier she had told them that they'd be meeting a famous man but first they would observe him from a distance.

"How amazing was that?" Asuka said. "All the struggle and mess and then there's the most adorable baby goat! Thank you for letting us see that Gale."

"Yes, one of the most astonishing things I've ever witnessed," Gregori agreed. "Does Moses have to be present for every birth?"

"No, it's not essential, but someone's presence and helping hand is always preferable in case complications arise," Gale replied. "I thought you'd find that interesting. Let's watch for a while longer and then we'll head down to visit in real time."

Moses sat on a nearby rock, wiping his brow and watching the proud mother cleaning her offspring, tenderly nudging the kid to stand precariously on its spindly legs. It wouldn't be long before he would be bounding across the arid landscape exploring his new home.

"Hope your life works out better than mine," Moses muttered under his breath.

He lifted his eyes and voice to the vast empty sky above with no hint of a cloud. "God, do you remember me? I wonder. My mother told me I was special when she floated me down the river in a basket to escape being killed. My parents in the palace in Egypt said I was special, a gift from the gods. Where's the evidence?"

Similar conversations with the Almighty had been repeated many times, his words evaporating in the hot desert air. Forty years ago, Moses fled Egypt in his middle years after killing a man—an Egyptian who had violently abused a Hebrew slave. Moses had struggled to restrain his dormant anger at the injustice that festered within him throughout his youth and early adult life. Now he lived in yet another foreign land, exiled, but with a wife he loved and two sons he adored. His life had been nothing but puzzling and mysterious—and here he was, light years away from his birth, his family, and his tribe.

He heard suckling and smiled as the young kid shoved a hungry mouth into its mother's side, instinctively locating the teat and gulping.

Moses often paced back and forth between his grazing herd talking to God as if he were right there by his side. A small part of him grimly held onto a faith he couldn't really explain. Nothing had turned out as he'd expected. The many years in this wilderness had blown like the desert sand by the wayside; until now he'd talked with no expectation of a response.

"Hey Dad, you whining to God again?"

Moses' thoughts were interrupted by a muscular man in his early thirties who loomed above him. He grinned and embraced Moses with one arm.

"Of course, I am, Gershom." Moses smiled. "We have this understanding: I talk, and he listens and never says a word. You know when—"

"I know . . . When you were my age, you were a prince in Egypt with the promise of greatness ahead of you, and now look," Gershom interrupted. Moses' eldest son teased him with deep affection. "You know Dad, I laugh, but I can't imagine having to leave this place and start again in a foreign land. I don't know how you managed. Do you still remember what it was like?"

"As if it were yesterday." Moses walked over to the doe with her new kid. "See, we had a healthy new arrival today."

Gershom picked up the newborn, now a shining black and white bundle of bleating fur. "I love the softness and smell of these young ones," he said, burying his nose into its side as it wriggled in his arms.

Moses looked on, leaning on his staff. "Sometimes I sit here and imagine Egypt in my younger days, as vividly as I can see you now, son. An enormous expanse of desert surrounding a fertile agricultural region, miles of vegetation flanking a broad meandering river. The air is hot and shimmers above the dusty road where I'm standing. People are everywhere working the land, conducting business along the river, transporting goods up and down the waterway. The silhouette of a city is etched against the distant skyline over there." Moses pointed to the horizon.

Gershom lowered the squirming kid to solid ground, and it bounded back to its bleating mother. *The story is always the same*, he thought as he indulged his father's reminiscences.

"I see the pyramids rising, the tombs of tyrannical pharaohs preparing for their journeys into the afterlife. Pyramids built with the blood and sweat of my people, the Hebrew slaves." Moses spat into the ground. "I still feel their pain and cry out to God for an end to the injustice and madness. Four hundred years it's been!"

"Do you think he'll ever answer?" Gershom asked. "What else do you remember?"

"I don't know what he'll do—nothing, probably, in my lifetime, maybe in yours. I see a field with a man behind two yoked cows. They're straining forward dragging a wooden plough. It's fastened by a rope to the horns. The churned-up furrow behind them is rich, damp, and reddish brown in color. So much fertile land along the banks of the Nile." Moses looked around the parched land where the goats foraged on grassy stubble. "It's very different to what you see here."

Moses drew a long, deep breath. He looked at his oldest son, who reminded him so much of the man he'd been forty years ago. "I can still smell those fields, the river, and the vegetation." He scraped the ground with the end of his staff. "But these years with your mother and you boys have also been good. Freedom is more precious than all the wealth and comfort of my life as an adopted son. Truthfully, it was never really my home."

"Well, I'm grateful for our years together, Dad. I love you, and the home you've provided for us. Talking of which, will you be heading back tonight?"

Moses and Gershom shared the task of minding the goats—a large herd that gave them a comfortable income and lifestyle. They relieved each other every seven days and spent two nights and a day together in the overlap. Home was half a day's ride on a mule.

Moses glanced at the waning sun. "It's getting late. I think I'll head out first thing in the morning."

"Sounds good." Gershom picked up a bucket and Moses walked with him to a flat slab of rock on a stony knoll nearby. He knelt and pushed the slab to the side, revealing a deep well with crystal clear water. Then, he tied a rope to the bucket and tossed it into the water, retrieving it effortlessly—filled, sloshing, and dripping. They took turns to drink, passing the bucket back and forth. When they had slaked their thirst, Gershom playfully poured the rest over his father's head. "You are anointed, Lord Moses."

"Anointed for what? To lead a bunch of goats?"

"You always told us to never give up," Gershom playfully chided his father. "Your life's not over yet . . . who knows what lies ahead."

Moses laughed and shook his long, shaggy wet hair, rubbing his face and flicking the water from his fingers.

"That feels better. Someone could die of thirst out here if they didn't know where to find water."

"Isn't that the truth," Gershom agreed. "Right beneath their feet and they'd never know it."

Chapter Thirteen

BRENDA AND RACHEL STOOD on the car deck as the ferry left Nanaimo bound for Horseshoe Bay, twenty minutes from downtown Vancouver. They'd managed to catch the late 10.10 pm sailing that Tuesday. It felt like days since Ricky's accident, so much had transpired. Brenda's entire world had twisted upside down since that morning.

It was good to breathe the fresh sea air blowing in their faces. The weather was mild, sky clear, and the fading light rendered trees and rocks as ink black silhouettes on the surrounding shorelines. They fast approached Entrance Island on their right with its cluster of houses and outbuildings, white walls, and red roofs.

"Do you know anything about that lighthouse?" Rachel asked Brenda, pointing to the structure that towered above the surrounding buildings.

"Not a thing," Brenda replied.

"It was built in the late 1800s when coal was exported from Nanaimo to the Pacific North West region. Two contractors absconded before it was complete. One of the first lighthouse keepers—Clarke I think his name was—ran it for twenty years. Except he was more interested in his ranch on Gabriola Island so was hardly ever there. He hired others to clean and tend the facility in extremely poor conditions and somehow got away with it. There's always a history behind a whitewashed wall."

Brenda shivered and folded her arms. Preoccupied with more pressing matters, she only half heard Rachel's explanation. "Let's go back to the car; I'm getting cold and can't face going upstairs with so many people."

"Good idea," Rachel agreed. "I'll nip up and grab us some fresh coffee and meet you there. Here are the keys."

Brenda sat in Rachel's black Toyota Rav with a lump in her throat. She thought of Ricky, so lively and excited this morning and now, twelve hours later, fighting for his life. At least Sally could take the two girls—one less thing to worry about. She still hadn't heard from Jack, which was no surprise. Increasingly, he seemed incapable of taking any responsibility and assumed she'd carry the load of raising three children. Whatever happened to the two of them? The question pecked at her mind like a persistent woodpecker hammering at a tree. What could she have done differently? His drinking and absence had left her wondering how long she could keep it all together. And now this. Fresh tears rolled down her cheeks.

The yellow lights of the car deck restrained the descending darkness beyond the outer railings, brooding over the sea. The vehicles around her stood silent and empty, no life inside—much like she felt, together with crushing fear and apprehension.

Rachel made her way back between the rows of cars. Climbing into the driver's seat, she handed Brenda a coffee. "Here you go, this will warm you up. And we can share some cake. I think we need something decadent to enjoy."

Brenda's lip quivered; it had been so long since she'd felt cared for. "Thanks Rachel, you've been unbelievably kind. I don't know how I could ever repay you . . . I'm just so scared . . ." She placed the coffee in a holder as waves of grief and pain washed through her with wracking sobs.

Rachel gently rubbed Brenda's hunched shoulders. "It's a lot to bear; so much unknown. Who wouldn't be afraid? I'm praying for God to give you strength and comfort, and to heal Ricky."

Brenda looked at her sidewise with shock and incomprehension. "God?" she scoffed. "What's he got to do with this? If he really does exist, why's everything so hard? Ricky didn't deserve this."

"Oh Brenda," Rachel soothed. "I'm not going to preach at you or exploit this terrible situation to guilt you in any way. Sometimes tragedy and hardship have a way of bringing us to the limits of ourselves. Not because it's our fault but merely because life is often tough and unfair, particularly when our 'why me?' seems to fall on deaf ears. All I know is that I wouldn't be alive and with you now if it wasn't for God. At least he's been faithful; I'm not so sure about the others. Here, have some cake."

Rachel broke the brownie in two, catching the crumbs in a napkin on her lap. She handed Brenda the larger piece.

"Thanks." Brenda nibbled at a corner. She hadn't registered hunger, but as the rich sweet chocolate melted in her mouth, she realized it had been hours since she'd eaten anything. "Tastes good." She rubbed her eyes and leaned back into the passenger seat. "What do you mean—about God?" She sighed, unsure of whether she wanted to continue this conversation. "I hope I haven't gotten myself into a situation with some religious nutcase. That's all I need right now."

Rachel appeared unperturbed by her question. "I've been called worse." She smiled. "I was orphaned at a young age and have no memory or knowledge of my mother or my father. Fortunately, I was raised in an adopted family who loved me dearly and loved God. That doesn't mean I don't feel my loss, but God has given me comfort."

"But aren't you angry at him for what happened? How can he love you and allow such a terrible thing? Losing both parents! I don't get it," Brenda responded incredulously. She gripped her coffee mug in both hands. Anger about Ricky rose in her. Her eyes scanned the rooftops of the cars. The gated bow of the ferry held its course through the darkness toward Vancouver.

"No, I'm not angry with God," Rachel said. "It would be like someone being angry with you for causing Ricky's accident. Your love and kindness allowed him to take risks and be exposed to possible danger, but an accident was never your desire for him. In fact, if you'd been selfish and over-protective, he would have been stunted and stifled."

"Yeah, but maybe I shouldn't have allowed him to play in the road."

"That's not what I was getting at. Please—don't beat yourself up. Freedom is an incredible gift, but it comes with unanticipated consequences—sometimes good, sometimes not so much. The God I know is like the father I never had: always present, never judging, faithful, and kind. He's incapable of being vindictive or 'causing' bad things to happen."

"Sounds wonderful," said Brenda, too weary to pretend, or to attempt to mask her sarcasm. She sipped her coffee in the ensuing silence.

"You remember the lighthouse we passed coming out of Nanaimo?"

"Yes, of course," Brenda replied.

"Not long after it opened, a boat was smashed on the rocks of that island in high winds. Seven people were drowned, including two women and some children. It must have been terrible. I'm sure they saw the lighthouse and the danger, but they had no power to overcome their situation. So many see God as a warning, like an overly strict teacher just waiting for us to fail so that he can punish us, but totally irrelevant to help in everyday life. I know him as a lifesaver who met me when I had no hope of rescue."

"What do you mean?" Brenda asked.

"I think I've said enough for now. It's a long story." Rachel smiled. "I wonder if Ricky's arrived at the hospital. Hopefully, we'll be there before too long."

The mobile trailer was quiet as a desert in darkness. Every now and then the silence was broken by Jack's snoring, a splutter, then stillness again. He was a restless sleeper. Brenda used to have a tug of war over the duvet as he tossed and turned through the night when they shared a bed.

They'd once been best friends—laughed together, swopped stories, and nurtured bottomless glasses of wine into the early morning hours. Brenda said their meeting was a dream come true, that Ricky was a gift from God. That first summer of marriage with a newborn Ricky was as close to domestic bliss as they could have imagined.

They muddled through the next ten years as couples do. For the most part Jack held steady jobs as a mechanic—a few years out at a logging camp, a stint with tow-trucks, and some decent years with his dad. Two more kids crawled and gurgled into their lives, Kaitlin and Jessica. They were welcomed, embraced, and adored. Jack played with them, made them toys, helped Ricky find new and better skateboards, and even built him and his friends a ramp.

They had a few great road trips on the Mainland, up through Hope and the Fraser River Canyon. Bundled the kids and tent into their Dodge van and headed off for "an adventure like I did with Grandpa when I was a kid." Those were the high points that kept them going, full of happy memories and laughter.

As the years wore on, they found it increasingly difficult to sustain that quality of life during the mundane months of everyday living. Jack still went fishing with his friends for days, leaving Brenda to cope. The drift apart was gradual, Brenda no longer asking for help, accepting with resignation her loneliness behind closed doors.

The cracks grew larger whenever Brenda finally spoke up and asked Jack for more support with the kids.

"JJ, I can't do it all," fell on deaf ears for the most part.

Her protestations invariably stoked the fires of his rage, and he reared up in defense: "F**k you Brenda, what's happened? You used to be fun to be around. Now all you do is bitch and complain. Who puts bread on the table?"

As their tenth summer faded and the leaves curled brown, Jack began missing work again, sometimes showing up hours late, other times not at all. He told Brenda not to worry and stayed out late. It was clear what he was doing; the smell of alcohol reeked on his breath at night. On those nights she turned her back and gazed at the window blinds, tracing the shadows of faint moonlight, wondering where to go from here.

"Just give him time; he's going through a bad patch," Sally had said.

But time was no friend or healer of theirs. Over the ensuing years they settled into a stalemate of mutual tolerance. Brenda said nothing and focused her attention and affection on Ricky and the girls. She stopped questioning what Jack was doing, where he was going, or expecting help at home. Sometimes, between Jack's months of no paychecks, she eked out the Employment Insurance support topped up with hairdressing, paid for under the table.

The kids adjusted, although they never stopped asking about their dad. Ricky was the most insistent. "Dad, you promised to take me fishing," he'd pleaded on multiple occasions. Being resilient, he settled for skateboarding with his friends.

It wasn't that Jack was oblivious. He knew that it was unfair to dump everything on Brenda, and that he should be spending more time with the kids. He would see the look in their eyes and feel terrible—at least for a while. He'd beat himself up for being so pathetic, making resolutions to change . . . But his resolve soon trickled away when Bob suggested meeting for a drink, or Gary organized a fishing trip out in the Broken Group, a stunningly beautiful collection of small islands scattered around the mouth of the inlet. He knew a friend with a cabin on floats moored there at the edge of the Pacific where they could camp. Those were the days, and nights when Jack felt most relaxed and himself. Fishing with his friends, beer in hand shooting the breeze, in the great outdoors of "Super Natural British Columbia."

Often, after returning from one of these outings, he'd try to get his act together, promising Brenda things would be different. He paid attention for a few weeks, assisted with the kids, stayed away from the beer, and laughter brightened the home. All was good. Brenda held her breath. *Maybe this time . . .*

It didn't help when Bob's marriage disintegrated, leaving him with more time on his hands to persuade Jack to join him. "Poor guy," Jack said solemnly to Brenda, "He's ripped apart since Jennifer kicked him out. That's what friends are for, to be supportive at times like this."

Brenda rolled her eyes. "You, supportive? Give me a break. It's just an excuse to get pissed with your little boy friends. They mean far more to you than we do."

"Come on Bren, that's not true. You know Bob and I go way back."

"Well, don't we go way back too?" She shrugged. "Whatever, I'm just letting you know I can't go on like this."

Ten months earlier Jack had returned home, mid-morning on a Saturday, after being out all night, disheveled and confused about where he'd been. When he brushed Brenda's questions aside with indignant irritation, she put her foot down. She'd suspected for some time that more than booze was being consumed.

"Pack your bags and leave. You go out and figure out who the hell you are and what you want from life. But I'm not taking this crap anymore!"

Jack seldom retaliated with much conviction; his inner voices were too self-deprecating. He knew that Brenda was right; what he didn't know was how to change himself. Asking for help was not in his nature. Anyway, where would he go for that? Instead, he focused on keeping guilt at arm's length, stuffing it down, denying and rationalizing, staying numb. He crammed essential items in a suitcase and headed over to Bob's, where they commiserated over cocktails of beer and dope.

A week later Jack was fired as a hospital janitor for poor attendance and was back on EI, most of which was garnished for Brenda and the children. He'd dug himself a hole that nearly buried him.

Chapter Fourteen

HAVING OBSERVED MOSES FROM afar, the GAs passed through the misty veil wall into a broad valley surrounded by rocks and mountains. A herd of goats grazed on the sparse scrubland interspersed with larger bushes and foliage, a stark contrast to the fertile green of Egypt. This land was for survivors and nomads, a tough desert breed who had learned how to adapt to, and even befriend, such an inhospitable environment. The air hung dry and parched beneath a clear blue sky. Goats foraged nearby—the larger herd scattered across the escarpment.

Gale's voice broke the silence. "Behold, Mount Horeb. Seated in the shade of that overhang is Moses." She pointed toward the slopes of the mountain, where there were signs of a camp and a lone figure reclining against the rock. "He's been herding goats for nearly forty years—you've probably gathered that it's been a rather mundane, and what he'd perhaps describe as an unexciting, existence."

"Because he would have been killed if he'd remained in Egypt?" Asuka declared.

"Quite possibly," Gale agreed. "Moses was born a Hebrew slave and raised a wealthy Egyptian, enjoying the finest education money could buy. Now he lives the life of a nomadic goat herder in the desert miles from anywhere, or anyone, of significance."

Jenny took in the landscape around her as she and the others walked up the slope, from the valley to the solid rock wall of mountain looming brown and weathered high above. Moses had set up camp against a large boulder leaning against the mountain, casting a distorted shadow across the stony ground. Black carbon from generations of herders' fires discolored the rock above a fireplace where smoldering coals released thin coils of smoke. Moses sat alongside, his hair and beard gray with streaks of black, his forehead glistening with beads of sweat. His eyes were closed. He leaned back into the cool of the rock, his lips moving as he conversed in a whisper to no one visibly present.

"He's older than I'd expected," said Yesaidu as they approached. The rest of them gathered around the gray-bearded figure.

"Probably in his late seventies," Nova muttered under his breath. Moses' skin was weathered from years of exposure to the wind and the sun, dark brown and wrinkled like ancient parchment. Angled in the crook of his arm was a wooden staff that he held like a king's scepter. Oblivious to the group gathered around him, he opened his eyes and surveyed the goatherd scattered across the foothills and valley.

"How does he survive here day after day, year after year, surrounded by goats?" Asuka said.

"It's not been easy," Pappa G replied. "Despite his circumstances, he has always held onto his faith." He walked over to Moses and placed a hand on his shoulder. "You'll come across many in Earthtime who identify."

Wiping his brow with a dirty sleeve, Moses slowly rose to his feet. He grunted with the effort, spat in the dirt, and walked about ten meters from the campsite. Thrusting his staff into the ground, he looked out over the valley.

Gale said quietly, "Moses' heart is exceedingly kind. We allowed him to remain here until conditions in Egypt were ready to set his people free from slavery under Pharaoh. Moses lived with his thoughts and unfulfilled dreams for at least a fistful of decades. He recalled a sense of destiny, a reason for him being rescued as a child. He thought he'd been strategically placed among Egyptian royalty and had high expectations for his life. Until he killed a man."

"I'll tell you the story briefly . . ." Pappa G stepped forward.

"The Hebrew slave was a mere fifteen years. He was assigned to making bricks, mixing mud and straw, pounding it into molds, laying the damp blocks out to bake in the sun. Exhausted by early afternoon, he was desperate for a drink. Thinking no one was watching, he raced to the river, submerged his head, and drank the cool water of the Nile. He felt instantly rejuvenated as he wiped the water from his eyes. Suddenly, the stinging lash of leather curled across his back, tearing his flesh. He cried out in shock and pain."

The GAs collectively winced, as if they, too were feeling the sting. Pappa G continued.

"Above him towered a notorious Egyptian slave master, renowned for his cruelty. The boy trembled in fear: he knew this was the end. He'd witnessed it many times before. Once a master started the lashings, he never stopped. A second blow crashed down hard, ripping apart his skin with the flick of the wrist. He cowered, anticipating the next, trying to shield himself with outstretched arms. But the lashing never came. Out of nowhere a man dressed in the fine clothing of a prince had grabbed the slave master from behind. One arm clutched his whipping wrist: the other locked tight around his throat. This was a man of immense strength. With a single wrench the boy heard a crunching sound as the slave master's neck snapped and he dropped to the ground with a thud, limp and lifeless."

At that Asuka gasped and covered her mouth with her hand. Pappa G raised a finger that signaled there was more to come.

"The stranger had Hebrew features but was dressed as an Egyptian. He bent down and heaved the dead slave master into the river. He spat with contempt on the corpse as it drifted away.

"Sweat poured from his face, his breath labored from the exertion. He turned to the terrified boy, anger flashing in his eyes. 'Go about your business, son. My tribe is your tribe. I couldn't stand by and watch that senseless brutality. Tell no one what happened here today, understand?'

"The boy nodded. With his back searing from the lashing, he scurried off to his bricks to ponder what had transpired."

The GAs listened, imagining the scene unfolding as Pappa G spoke, his voice gentle and strong, his inflection and delivery compelling.

Gale continued the narrative. "Now, many years later, Moses' expectations have evaporated like water in the hot desert sun. Nothing but a few puddles of hope lie buried deep within his heart. He hasn't sipped from them in a long while."

"We really are in a different dimension here, very close and yet he cannot hear, feel, or sense our presence," explained Pappa G. "If we revealed ourselves to him, or to any human being for that matter, they would be killed instantly by the exposure to our perfection and presence. Such is the reality of our distinctively different and incompatible 'states of being.' In Earthtime language, it would be like holding a match to gasoline. The fire would automatically consume the gasoline because that's the nature of those two entities when they come together. Gasoline cannot remain 'as normal' when in the presence of fire."

"If you appeared to him now, your presence would kill him?" Navo exclaimed, puzzled.

Gale nodded. "Therefore, let me ask you this. What are our options in this predicament? How would you communicate?"

For once the entire group was silent.

"Pappa G is going to attract Moses' attention. Watch this—"

Gale stopped mid-sentence. Moses was striding across the slope of the mountain, staff in hand. The GAs followed his gaze to a large bush ablaze with flames stretching high into the air.

"Follow him," said Gale.

They ran to catch up. Moses stood about ten feet from a tall bush engulfed in fire, an inferno of heat and hungry flames flicking skyward. The strangest thing was the absence of sound—no burning, crackling wood, no ashes. The bush remained untouched and undiminished as the fire raged through its leaves and branches. Moses gaped at the spectacle, his expression a mixture of fear and confusion.

"Moses, Moses!" a voice called from the midst of the rising flames, startling the old man, and causing him to step back in fright.

Moses hesitatingly stuttered, "Y-y-yes, th-that's me."

"Don't come any closer. Take off your sandals: you're standing on holy ground."

Moses hurriedly kicked off his dogeared leather sandals and leaned on his staff. He shielded his eyes from the flaming bush, his stomach tightened, and sweat poured from his brow. He had not experienced this intensity of fear since he'd fled Egypt. *What's going on? Am I dreaming? Is this desert heat finally making me mad?* he wondered.

"Moses, I am the God of your father, the God of Abraham, the God of Isaac, and the God of Jacob."

Moses trembled. He turned his face to hide from the flames and the voice, certain he was about to die. Memories blew like a desert sandstorm through his mind, whirling and lashing him about, sending him into a panic. He wanted to run but couldn't move; fear paralyzed him. His fumbling thoughts were interrupted again.

"Why is he so scared of God?" Asuka questioned, pulling her hair back into a ponytail and letting it fall loose again.

"At that time there was very little awareness of my love," Pappa G explained. "The people understood me to be mighty and powerful, a giver of commandments, and someone to fear. I spoke through various leaders, but ordinary people didn't believe I cared about them. Moses was a man of his time and acted accordingly. Nevertheless, I had to communicate with him and help him overcome his fear. Listen."

They watched the barefoot old man fall to his knees some distance from the flaming bush as God's voice echoed through the barren land. "I have seen the misery of my people in Egypt. I've heard them crying from their graves and noted their hopeless bondage in slavery. I am concerned about their suffering. I have come to rescue them from the hand of the Egyptians and to bring them out of their captivity into a good and spacious land, a land flowing with milk and honey."

Moses' heart pounded a thousand times a minute at the long-awaited words of hope and freedom for his enslaved tribe. Tears mingled with sweat on his cheeks. The prospect of being reunited with his people and family after the excruciatingly long exile cracked fault lines in his wall of despair and hopelessness. The heavens had been silent for so long. The bush burned hot and bright—no smoke rising into the clear sky above.

Moses wanted to ask, *How? When?* The voice in the fire spoke again.

"Moses, I'm sending you to Pharaoh to lead my people out of Egypt."

Stunned by the joy of the good news, Moses could only marvel at God's long-awaited words. Then, fear gripped him once again. "W-w-what? Me? Who, who am I, that I should go to Pharaoh and b-b-bring the Israelites out of Egypt?" He wanted to add, "He'll kill me," but the words faded on his tongue, vaporizing in the heat of the evening sun.

"I will be with you," the voice reassured the trembling figure who now stood, scratching his head, barefoot in the sand, sandals upside down in the dust beside the fire.

"Pappa G, why did you do that?" Jenny blurted out. "Sorry for interrupting."

"Do what?"

"Order Moses to confront Pharaoh when you knew that he was so afraid of him. Why not ask someone else who was unknown to Pharaoh and his family?"

"That's a fair question, Jenny," Pappa G replied. "As you get to know people in Earthtime you'll discover that many people are running away from something or someone. They live with a survival mentality, repressing, or denying their fears, many of which are wildly distorted in their minds and memories. I wanted Moses to face his fear with me and find freedom within his soul. After forty years out of Egypt, he remained trapped in a form of mental and emotional slavery himself."

Moses' anxiety was evident as he paced fitfully before the flames. Stabbing the ground with his staff, he punctuated each step in the dirt, stuttering, "Suppose I do g-g-go to the Israelites and say to them, 'The God of your f-f-fathers has s-s-s-sent me to you,' and they ask me, 'What is his name?' Then what shall I say to them?"

"Gale, why is Moses so reluctant and tentative?" Asuka's question broke the silence.

"He's scared of God, he's scared of Pharaoh, he's scared of the Israelites, and he's scared of himself," she replied.

"I feel sorry for Moses," said Yesaidu. "Poor man; he's been isolated for so long. Suddenly he's faced with a burning bush, God speaking, holy ground, orders to head for Egypt within the next twenty-four hours, and he's nearly eighty years old!"

"Let's see what happens," suggested Gale, drawing them back into the conversation that was still underway between Moses and the burning bush. "Pappa G is showing Moses that he will have supernatural power as he confronts Pharaoh."

Increasingly, Moses felt way beyond his comfort zone and out of control. He walked around the flaming bush muttering quietly, a goatherd of thoughts rushing through his mind. The flames rose like restless fingers to the sky grasping at unseen objects, or were they writhing hands pleading and straining from shackled wrists? Was he dreaming?

Eventually, he ceased his pacing, faced the heat once again, and pleaded, "Lord, I have n-n-never been eloquent, neither in the past nor s-s-s-since you have spoken to your servant. I am slow of speech and t-t-tongue."

Instead of empathic understanding, the voice in the flames responded with a frightening firmness. "Who gave man his mouth? Who makes him deaf or dumb? Who gives him sight or makes him blind? Is it not I, the Lord? Now go; I will help you speak and will teach you what to say." Moses was beginning to grasp that he was not being invited into a debate.

"Oh L-L-Lord, p-p-please send someone else to do it!"

The words were scarcely launched from Moses' lips when the fire increased in intensity, the flames shooting even higher above his head. He shuddered at what might follow: how was he to do all these things? He took a step backward and couldn't stop shaking.

"Your brother Aaron is already on his way to meet you. You shall put words in his mouth; I will help both of you speak and will teach you what to do. It will be as if he is your mouth and as if you are God to Pharaoh. Take your staff in hand; you will perform miraculous signs with it."

Moses said nothing. He bowed his head, silently clutching the staff as the fire in the bush subsided and within a minute was no more. The bush remained unscathed. He stood, mesmerized, for a long time. Finally, he put his fingers to his lips and gave a piercing whistle that echoed across the valley. The goats lifted their heads and slowly began moving toward him as he returned to the campsite to gather his meager belongings.

"That was intense," Gregori sighed.

"Sometimes it has to be," said Pappa G. "Often in Earthtime you'll come across people who see me as old fashioned or powerless. They think that my existence depends on them and whether they choose to believe or not." Pappa G smiled. "It's another lie of the snake."

"I'm beginning to catch a glimpse of the challenge in Earthtime to believe and trust in you, Pappa G," Jenny said. "I can't really imagine what that's like. In heaven it's easy to believe."

"That's because there is no snake, no lies, and no battle," said Gale.

"We often interview Moses, but we won't today. Just a quick hello."

Together they passed back through the misty veil, and Pappa G summoned Moses to join them in the Rainbow Room. The GAs had to look twice to identify the man before them as Moses: his demeanor and clothing had changed. Gone was the fear and frustration. Instead, he smiled and nodded a greeting to the startled group.

"Thank you, Moses my friend. After all this time you still carry your staff. Why?"

"It reminds me of you, Pappa G," Moses replied with a grin.

"An old, gnarled stick? How flattering!" said Pappa G, stepping back in mock offense.

"I remember the tree in the desert from which I cut a branch to carve this staff. I used to watch over my goats, whittling away, wondering what the rest of my life would be like. I so identified myself with the tree—growing where no one paid any attention to its existence. I broke off one of its branches to make a staff for myself. Later, as you know, Pappa G encountered me."

Moses rubbed the worn and shiny head of the staff that had become an extension of his body. "I guess it reminds me of myself too, hidden in the desert, feeling unloved and unattended. Pappa G saw something in me that I couldn't. He loved me enough to nearly scare me to death. He brought me out of that place and gradually whittled a stuttering, insecure, somewhat bitter and lonely old man into a great leader." He smiled.

"There's much in Moses' story you will discover is shared by those in Earthtime." Pappa G linked his hands behind his back. "Plenty of people think I don't care and feel sidelined. People hope life will be better and wonder why I let them down. Many are afraid of facing their past or use their weaknesses as excuses to not go out and do something great. You'll find multiple variations on those themes. And you, my Guardian Angels, will be there to remind them that I took Moses and used him despite all his excuses and inadequacies. They will learn that with me all things are possible, always, everywhere, with everyone."

Chapter Fifteen

THE FISH OGLED AT Brenda with brown button eyes before flicking its tail and disappearing behind a pile of black rocks. Sitting in the reception area of Vancouver Children's Hospital Emergency wing, she stared into the large, televised aquarium scene in a futile attempt at distraction. Her eyes followed a brightly colored fish and lingered on a languid small shark meandering across the sandy bottom. Nothing slowed her racing heart or relieved the tension.

In her mind's eye, a four-year-old Ricky jumped and grinned with delight as the fish swam by. Bubbling, tugging excitedly at her coat, he kept turning to her, exclaiming, "Mommy look!" They'd come to Emergency with Brenda's friend, Jill, whose daughter of eighteen months had contracted a virus that baffled the doctors. That visit didn't go well. A day later Jill returned home, empty handed and utterly inconsolable. *How does one recover from the death of a child?* Brenda had asked herself.

The digital aquarium stretched wide and tall across the wall, an underwater scene of constant movement and activity. She recalled a younger Ricky slapping the glass with excited delight. Tears welled up. Her chest tightened as panic gripped; she wanted to run outside and scream. Scream at the heavens, scream at the world, scream at God, whom she doubted anyway, and scream at Jack. Where was he? Why did she always have to battle alone? It wasn't fair.

"Please let Ricky be all right," she said to no one in particular. "Please help him; I couldn't bear to lose him." The lump in her throat exploded and her sobs erupted from a depth inside she couldn't fathom. Rachel's arm embraced her and pulled her closer as she whispered, "Let it out, Brenda, it's ok."

About twenty minutes later a man dressed in dark fuchsia scrubs with an unkempt mop of blonde hair and kind eyes seated himself alongside Brenda. "Hi, Brenda Willard? I believe you're Ricky's mom?"

Brenda looked up and nodded.

"I'm Doctor Pollard, a neurosurgeon. I've just spent the last hour with Ricky. I'm so sorry for what you're going through."

"Is Ricky going to be all right?" she sobbed. "How is he? What's happening? When can I see him?"

"It won't be long; you can see him shortly," Dr. Pollard assured her. "The accident happened nearly twelve hours ago, and Ricky remains unconscious in a coma. He's had a CAT scan and he's suffered a significant swelling of his brain from hitting his head. It's something we refer to as a diffuse axonal injury."

"Is that really bad?" Brenda could hardly get the words out.

"I'll be honest with you Brenda—it is serious. We may consider surgery to relieve the pressure. But first we'll try less invasive solutions as there are pros and cons to a craniectomy, as it's called. All we can do right now is keep Ricky as comfortable as possible and monitor how things unfold."

"Can I see him soon?"

"The nurses are taking Ricky up to the Intensive Care Unit on the fourth floor. You should be able to see him in about half an hour. You're welcome to be with him for as long as you want. If you need anything, the nurses are there for you, and I'll be checking in regularly."

Dr. Pollard reached out and squeezed Brenda's hand. "I'm so sorry, Brenda. Ricky has the best care and is in good hands, I assure you."

"Thank you, Doctor," Brenda replied. As soon as he left, she buried her head in Rachel's shoulder.

"Ricky will never be the same again—he might not even live," she spluttered. "What am I going to do. Oh God, what am I going to do? I can't bear it . . ."

Rachel held her tight. Silence was more eloquent than words right now.

Forty-five minutes later the two women were at Ricky's bedside in a dimly lit room. Brenda sat holding his left hand and stroked his shoulder. His head was still bandaged, his left leg in a splint. The ventilator sighed rhythmically in tandem with the quiet beep of the heart monitor. Rachel stood behind Brenda, her hands resting gently on her shoulders.

"He looks so peaceful, doesn't he?" said Brenda. "Hi Ricky, I'm here for you and won't be going anywhere. We need you to wake up now . . . Please wake up, my darling boy." More tears.

"Do you mind if I say a prayer for Ricky?" whispered Rachel.

"No, of course not. I'll take help from anywhere right now."

Rachel prayed quietly, laying her hand on Ricky's head. Brenda was numb, almost indifferent, with no expectation of anyone listening to Rachel or some miracle being forthcoming. *Whatever*, she thought to herself.

They sat in silence, pondering their private thoughts.

"Any word from Jack?" Rachel asked.

"Not a thing—no text, no call," Brenda replied. "Have zero expectation and am afraid I left him a rather nasty message. I'm so tired of having to initiate everything."

"Is it rude for me to ask what happened between you?"

Brenda sighed, shifting in her chair, clinging to her son's hand. "You really want to know? Well, it wasn't too bad in the first few years, just the three of us; we had some good times. When Kaitlin and Jessica arrived, I had my hands full." She paused. "But Jack carried on as if nothing had changed."

"Meaning?"

"Meaning he was in and out of jobs, drinking with his buddies, and leaving me to manage the kids, work part-time, and shoulder all the responsibility. I withdrew more and more in anger and frustration."

"That's a tough one," Rachel said quietly. "Did you try talking to him, or ask for help?"

"I tried a few times, but Jack would just get angry and leave. He gets so insecure and defensive when questioned. I didn't have many people to talk to except Sally next door. Her marriage wasn't great either. I just figured that's what happens."

"I hear you."

"Look, I'm no angel. I'm far from perfect and can be a bit of a nag at times. But I didn't have time to wallow in self-pity, not with three kids to look after, or four, if you count Jack."

"Was he ever unfaithful?"

"I can't be sure, but I certainly have my suspicions. When things were getting bad, I had a fling a few years ago. It only lasted a few weeks, but it was nice to have some attention—and to feel wanted." She leveled her gaze at Ricky's closed eyes. "Maybe I should watch what I say?

Probably shouldn't have said that. What if he can hear me? He's a smart kid; none of this would be a surprise to him," she reasoned aloud.

"Does Jack know about that—the affair?" Rachel asked, keeping her voice low.

Brenda shook her head. "I don't think so. He expects me to give him all the freedom he wants but goes ballistic and jealous if I hint at doing the same. The thing is, I don't want a great deal; I never asked for much. I just want my husband to be a friend, not an adversary. He was once . . . I don't want to find love in all the wrong places; it's way too stressful."

"What a difficult road it's been for you, Brenda. I wish I had some words of wisdom that would make everything better. I don't know what to say . . . Maybe this whole situation will be a wakeup call for him?"

"I don't know what to think about that right now." Brenda gave Rachel a weak smile and caressed Ricky's hand. "But I do know this young man would love to have his dad back."

Chapter Sixteen

THE GAs FOUND GALE alone in the Rainbow Room when they arrived for their next session. "Pappa G won't be with us, but Jesus will be here in a moment," she said, a glint in her eye.

The words were hardly out of her mouth when the doors swung open, and a wiry man appeared in a wheelchair. "Hello all," he said, as the GAs stared, open-mouthed. He waved and greeted each of them by name like long-lost friends. Of course, they'd recently seen Jesus in the Earthtime wilderness, but not like this.

"You're in a wheelchair!" Yesaidu exclaimed. "Why? I thought there's no pain or suffering in heaven?"

"That's true," Jesus replied matter-of-factly, rolling across the room toward him.

"Then why?" Yesaidu persisted with his question.

"It's linked to my identity when I entered Earthtime for thirty-three years. See these scars on my wrists and feet?"

"But wasn't that a sacrifice once and for all?" Jenny asked.

"Yes, it was." Jesus swiveled his chair to face her as she was seated behind him.

"It's not about what was accomplished on the Cross; it's about the lasting impact on me. Remember when Abraham wrestled with an angel at Bethel? He walked with a limp for the rest of his life. It's like that."

"But you're God," Nova said incredulously. "You don't have to go through this!"

"When I was born in Bethlehem, my mother was Mary, a human being from the line of David. I was conceived by the Holy Spirit, an act of

God. In other words, I was of mixed descent." Jesus smiled. "One parent from Earthtime and the other from heaven."

"Did people in Earthtime believe you?" Yesaidu asked.

"For the most part, no. The majority still find that fact impossible to accept, even though they claim to believe in a God who created the world." Jesus rubbed his palms on the top of the wheels of his chair. "Earthtime began as Eden but now it's become deeply corrupted, rampant with suspicion and doubt about our very existence."

"We are so naïve," said Jenny, shaking her head. "For years we've learned about Earthtime and the battleground it has become. But we've been so sheltered. It frightens me, to be honest."

"There's no need to be afraid; you're on the winning side," Jesus said. "But it's important for you to have a sense of what has been lost and the impact. When you walk alongside people, most will have extraordinarily little comprehension of me, or Pappa G, and certainly be oblivious to Gale. We need your help to open their blind eyes to the truth—there's so much to cover."

"Need *our* help?" Asuka looked incredulous. "You are God with power to do anything and everything. Why can't you do something so spectacular that people will have no doubt?"

"We get challenged with that line of reasoning often," Gale said. "The thing is, we've created people for relationship, thoughtfulness, and the ability to make their own choices in life. We did something spectacular with creation, and when Jesus walked the earth for thirty-three years— and when he died and was resurrected. Relationships rooted in our love will bring the revelation; and that's where you come in. In Earthtime the heart often leads where the mind cannot first comprehend, for our ways are not their ways."

"Meaning that sometimes people can sense things before they can explain them," Jesus explained.

"But Jesus, why the wheelchair?" Yesaidu persisted.

"When I took on human form, to reveal the love of God and to die on the Cross, my identity was changed, at least until heaven and earth are reunited. It's the resurrected human part of me that bears the scars of the Cross."

"Does that mean you're continuing to pay the price for the sins of the world?" Asuka asked softly.

"No Asuka; the work of the Cross is finished." Jesus paused and held one wrist in his fingers as if he were feeling for a pulse. "The wound scars are for me the equivalent of Abraham's limp. This wheelchair is a reminder in heaven that the battle is not yet over. Many, many people, whom we created and love, continue to be lost and orphaned. And we're not allowing that to happen without a fight."

"Can you walk at all?" Gregori wore a puzzled expression as he posed the question.

"On occasion," Jesus nodded. "For instance, during my resurrection appearances in Earthtime, because my mission there is fully accomplished. But in heaven, as I said, the bigger picture is incomplete. In the context of worship, I don't require a wheelchair."

The GAs were silent. Jenny had tears in her eyes—a rare occurrence in heaven. "After all you gave up, leaving heaven for earth, and suffering, the consequences never go away?" She sniffed and shook her head. "It doesn't seem right."

"There was no other way," Jesus said. "Don't be upset or pity me. That's one thing people in Earthtime do understand—the love of a parent for their children. It's in their DNA, from us. Most parents will do everything possible to protect and rescue their children. It's my honor and joy to lay down my life and have it raised up so that our children have the possibility of freedom. It's a small price to pay." He tilted his wheelchair backwards and spun it around a few times. "So, when we're on assignment in Earthtime, I'll be walking with you, and here in heaven I'll be rolling around in this."

"I don't know," Jenny shook her head, still unconvinced.

"I'm fine," said Jesus, rolling up to Jenny and patting her arm. "I'm in no pain, and as my friend Paul says—you'll be meeting him later—'When you suffer, count it all joy!' Now let's move on to the next assignment. We'll have plenty more to talk about before we're finished."

Chapter Seventeen

A PERSISTENT KNOCKING VIED for attention with the throbbing in Jack's head.

He'd fallen asleep on the couch, crumpled beer cans strewn across the floor, a half-empty vodka bottle tipped on its side under the coffee table. Jack had no idea how much he'd consumed. His attempt to bury his head under a cushion failed to block the noise. Groggily, he grabbed the cushion and tossed it aside, his eyes blinded by the sudden shock of morning light.

The knocking persisted and Jack realized it was at his front door. He stumbled, half asleep, into the hallway and opened the door after fumbling with the lock.

"Bill, what are doing here?"

Bill Morris smiled, taking in the sight of Jack, disheveled, still wearing yesterday's stained tee shirt and jeans, his hair tangled, face unwashed and unshaven. Little boy blinking at the front door.

"Good morning," Bill said. "Thought I'd drop by and see how you're doing and retrieve that sweater I lent you."

"Thanks man. Uh, sorry. I've just woken up. What time is it?"

"It's Wednesday morning, just after ten," Bill replied.

"Come in." He opened the door wider for Bill to enter. "Afraid the place is a bit of a mess, wasn't expecting anyone. I haven't had time to wash the sweater either."

"No problem," said Bill. He stepped through the hallway into a lounge that reeked of beer and surveyed the trash of the night before.

"Had a bit too much to drink," Jack muttered sheepishly.

"Have you had anything to eat? Want to join me for breakfast?" Bill asked. He patted Jack's shoulder and gave him a reassuring smile.

"Sounds great," Jack responded. "Mind if I have a quick shower and change? I won't be long."

"Go right ahead," said Bill, seating himself on the only chair in the room.

Bill heard water running as Jack cleaned up. It was clear that the mobile home had been well lived in. The walls of the open-plan lounge and kitchen were probably the original paint, now a faded, grimy cream. Sparse furniture consisted of a couch, the chair in which Bill sat, a coffee table, and a bookshelf against the wall, with few books. Magazines and papers were stuffed on the shelves, and on top stood two photographs propped up in cheap black frames.

One was a family portrait. A younger, clean-shaven, and clear-eyed Jack stood beside an attractive woman with short blonde hair cradling a baby in her arms. A young girl sat on his shoulders, gripping his head with both hands, and a boy of about ten by his side clutched a skateboard. Jack's arm was around the woman's shoulders as she snuggled into him. Everyone was smiling.

The other photo was of Jack and the boy. This time Jack stood behind him and rested his hands on his shoulders. The boy was wearing a helmet and holding the same skateboard proudly bearing the brand name for all to see.

Bill was pondering the picture in his hand when Jack returned. He wore clean jeans and tugged on a black tee shirt with "Metallica" emblazoned across the front. His Axel deodorant had been lavishly applied.

"Those were happier times a few years ago," he said.

"Looks like a cool family. What are their names?" Bill asked.

"That's Brenda, my wife, Kaitlin, our youngest, Jessica on my shoulders, and Ricky's the eldest." Jack pointed at each as he named them.

"Ricky's keen on skateboarding?" Bill said.

"A fanatic." Jack smiled. "Loves the challenge of tricks and riding with his friends. Was bitten with the bug from an early age and is better than guys much older."

"You're a lucky man. I've always wanted a family, but it's never happened," Bill said, then, quickly changing the subject, added, "Let's get that breakfast."

Fifteen minutes later they were seated at a table in a small café that boasted the best breakfast and burgers on the island. Tucked alongside a welding shop and the Co Op gas station, it was a pit stop for hungry locals and travelers to the West Coast. Formica-topped tables with stainless steel legs were arranged in three rows, alternating blue and red. Bill and Jack sat by the window facing the highway and were soon devouring eggs and crispy bacon, shredded potato, and multigrain toast. Bill said he'd have the same as Jack; and coffee for both.

"What happened, Jack?" Bill asked quietly, his voice gentle and nonthreatening. "The journey from the guy in those photographs to the man I hauled out of the lake yesterday?"

Jack poured ketchup on the side of his plate, plenty of it. "F***k, I don't know, Bill, I'm not really sure myself. I'm just a big screw-up." He fiddled with his food and kept looking down. "I can't keep a job, I neglect and betray Brenda, I don't have time for the kids, I drink too much, smoke joints, and am a total idiot. That's me in a nutshell."

"In the photos you seem happy and close to them, particularly Ricky. I can't help notice their names tattooed on your arm." He cocked his head toward Jack's exposed left arm, where "Brenda," "Ricky," "Kaitlin," and "Jessica" were inscribed like a double wristband. Above the names was a chain of armor design that Jack explained he'd found on the internet. "Made famous by the cool dude Jason Momoa, the actor. He said it was shark's teeth representing his ancestral guardian, the shark. It's about keeping out dark and letting in light. A benevolent spirit who protects, especially in the water. I liked it, so now I wear it." Jack rubbed his forearm and smiled at Bill. "Funny that, now I think of it—you rescuing me from drowning, the belt coming loose—maybe someone's looking out for me after all. But that sounds weird." He shook his head dismissively.

"Do you prefer being alone, away from your family?" Bill asked.

Jack took his time answering. He carefully positioned two slices of bacon on his toast and poured on more ketchup before devouring half the "toastwich" with a large bite. "The truth is, Bill, I love Brenda and the kids more than anything in the world. It's me I have trouble with. If everything's going too well, I sabotage and only realize later what I've done."

"Why do you think that is?"

"I guess I believe what others say—that I can't be trusted. So, instead of waiting to disappoint, I may as well pull the plug. I get nervous when too many expectations come my way. Brenda says I'm scared of responsibility and she's tired of being disappointed. Can't say I blame her."

Bill wiped his mouth with a napkin he plucked from the holder on the table. He leaned back with a quizzical expression. "So, you don't want to fight for yourself and your family? Jason Momoa says that the most important priority in his life is his family."

"How do you know that?" Jack asked, surprised Bill would even know the name.

Bill smiled.

"What if you'd died yesterday—would that have helped?"

Jack shrugged. "Well, I wouldn't have to feel like a loser and a failure anymore. Maybe I'm a coward, always want the easy way out."

"Drowning yourself doesn't sound like an easy way out to me. More like desperate. And sad." Bill pushed his empty plate aside. His forearms rested on the table as he looked across at Jack. "Nothing's wasted if you can learn from it, Jack. You can keep telling yourself you're no good, or you can change the narrative. How about stepping up and choosing to be a better man, like Jason, whom you admire?"

Jack mopped up the yellow puddle of egg yolk on his plate with his last torn piece of toast. "I don't know how to do that," he admitted.

"Why not start by thinking about something in the past that you wished had been different?" Bill suggested. "What might that be, do you think?"

Jack slid his empty plate to the middle of the table and stared at the space in front of him. "This is going to sound childish, I guess. But more than anything, I'd like my dad to have taken an interest in me. To have gone out for breakfast like this, listen to my crazy thoughts, and tell me that he believed in me. I never heard him say anything like that, let alone that he loved me." Looking out the window at the passing traffic, Jack added, "That's probably what I'd change—having a dad who could be my friend."

"Makes perfect sense; no harm in wanting that," Bill nodded. "Why do you think Ricky's standing so proudly beside you in the photo, and Jessica's giggling sitting on your shoulders? They clearly adore their dad. Maybe you can be that dad you never had?"

"Damn it, I forgot," Jack said suddenly. "Had a voicemail last night from Brenda saying Ricky had an accident and was taken to the hospital. It's probably nothing, but I'd better get over to the apartment in Port."

Bill settled the bill and offered to drive as they were already in his car.

As they wound their way around the lake where Bill had rescued Jack the day before, neither said a word about the incident. They slowed to a crawl through the towering old growth fir trees of Cathedral Grove.

Tourists, marveling at this last remaining vestige of what once was, crowded the narrow road as they did every day through the summer months.

Twenty minutes later Jack turned the handle of Brenda's apartment as he knocked. The door was locked; no one answered. Silence, heavy and ominous in a place where three children lived. He knocked again. "What's going on, why's no one answering?"

"Is that you, Jack?" Sally appeared at the door of an apartment down the hallway. She held Jessica in here arm. "Haven't you heard?"

Jack walked slowly toward her, scratching his head.

"No, what?"

It was the cherry blossoms that captivated them when they arrived in Asuka's village—deep, rich shades of pink lining every path and road. "They are in bloom all the time," Asuka explained, "changing color with the mild variation of seasons. The pink you see now will gradually become pale, then white, then a light blue, before returning to this rich pink."

"It's absolutely stunning," said Yesaidu.

"And the fragrance—I love it!" Jenny exclaimed, bending an overhanging branch and burying her nose in a cluster of petals.

They stood outside the Hao Shiwu restaurant where Asuka had arranged for them to meet. "It means 'Great Food,'" she told them, as they made themselves comfortable at a round table beside a fountain with bamboo growing lush and green. The room, curved like a crescent moon, contained about three hundred tables scattered among more fountains and bamboo. The gentle gurgling of running water filled the air. Large windows framed the cherry blossoms outside, almost close enough to touch.

"This is one of the most popular dishes in our community," Asuka explained when their meal arrived. "It's called Laksa and is made with spicy coconut, noodles, tofu, rice . . . I can't remember the other ingredients." She giggled. "And we eat with these chopsticks. I'll show you how." They practiced holding the lower chopstick still while moving the top one with their thumb and remaining fingers. "Hold it as if you were using it for writing and that will get you started . . ."

"Well, that was the slowest meal I've ever eaten," Gregori laughed once he'd finished his Laksa. "And one of the tastiest."

"I'm so poorly coordinated I ended up forming a shovel with the chopsticks, I'm afraid." Yesaidu pretended to look sorrowful before breaking into a wide grin. "Ok, time to dig into the InSight, without chopsticks. Where do we go?"

"I don't know how they do it . . ." Jenny tucked her hair behind her ears. "Ricky's accident, the unhappy marriage, the not knowing what will happen. It all seems too much. So many struggles."

Asuka nodded. "Am I the only one who finds it hard to open the InSight and watch? It's such a different world—so much conflict and pain. I'm afraid—a feeling I've never experienced before."

"Me too," Gregori said. "It feels like when I open InSight, I plunge into a dark hole. It becomes claustrophobic. I just want to come back here and pretend it doesn't exist."

"I think we all share those emotions," Nova agreed. "I look at Jack, so lost and estranged, and Brenda, alone and facing the unknown with little hope. Ricky, with his terrible injuries in hospital. What does one make of it? It's a totally foreign world to us and I'm not sure what we do." He shook his head, bewildered. "Where's Pappa G when we need him?"

"Maybe that's the point," said Jenny. "Maybe it's all part of understanding what it feels like to live in Earthtime."

"And then?" Yesaidu leaned forward. "What do we do with that?"

"Mind if I join you?"

The interruption took them by surprise. They looked up as a young man in casual dress pulled up a chair and sat down between Gregori and Asuka.

"Um, we're having a confidential meeting," Jenny said somewhat awkwardly.

The stranger smiled. "I thought Nova just said, 'Where is Pappa G when we need him?'"

They gasped in unison. They recognized the voice but not the person. "Pappa G?"

"I told you before that I can change my appearance at any time. This way I don't draw attention and can move freely among you. I'm in many, many places in heaven and earth at the same time, even now."

"I can't wrap my head around that but it's very cool." Gregori scratched his head, a faint smile playing on his lips.

"However you do it, thank you for hearing my plea," Yesaidu said. "I certainly never expected to be answered like this!"

"You're struggling with what you're witnessing through your In-Sights?" Pappa G leaned on the table, surveying their intrigued faces.

"I am," said Asuka. "It feels dark and makes me afraid, something I've never known before. I don't want to go there."

"Same for me," Nova affirmed.

Pappa G nodded. "I understand. If it helps, every Guardian Angel has a similar response at the beginning. It's unavoidable when you first encounter what darkness in Earthtime feels like."

"It's hard to watch," said Yesaidu. "There's almost no joy or hope that I could see, certainly not for Jack or Brenda. People are strangers to one another, like boats adrift that sometimes bump into each other."

"I find it sad to watch people feel so helpless and alone in their circumstances," Jenny added. "Fear permeates everything; I even notice it seeping into me. Fortunately, when we close the InSight fear disappears, but it's hard to swallow."

It took some time for the group to get used to engaging with such a young version of Pappa G, but they soon discovered that his voice and mannerisms remained the same.

"Yes, it is harsh," he said. "Which is why I need you to put flesh and blood on my love. People like Jack and Brenda have little comprehension of my being real and loving them. They have no foundation of faith to build upon. As far as they know, it's them against the world, and they're losing the battle. Evil and darkness take no prisoners; they will persist until death."

"So, what's the point?" Asuka looked sideways at Pappa G with a quizzical expression.

"I don't like what you're witnessing any more than you do." Pappa G looked stern and spoke with intensity. "It makes me angry. But you are bearers of light and hope. When you appear alongside, you carry with you my power and my presence. Evil and darkness know that, even if those like Jack and Brenda are unaware. Guardian Angels are creating space through their relationships with the Jacks and Brendas of the world for them to rediscover what has been hijacked and stolen."

"How is it possible to be so blind?" Yesaidu asked.

"I'm angry with evil—it's insidious, constantly maltreating all I have created," Pappa G continued. "I have enough grace for every person subjected to this toxic environment, but the fact is that it's easy to be unaware if you've never been introduced to what is good and true. Note how sur-prised you are of the conditions in Earthtime. The same is true for them, but from the other side."

"So how do we help?" Nova voiced the question forming on all their lips.

"They've been exposed to religious ritual but for the most part see no connection between God and their everyday lives. Ironically, the church, infiltrated by darkness, has helped inoculate many. And they become numb or indifferent to the institution. They need people who accept them unconditionally, people who will help them become aware that they're not alone and that my love is real, from a heart relationship. And you're the ones who can do that, following in the footsteps of other Guardian Angels and millions who have gone before you."

"What happened to the church?" Yesaidu asked.

"There are some good things happening in the church; it's not all bad." Pappa G leaned back in his chair and folded his arms. "But people in Earthtime struggle with me all the time. They tend to prefer rules, guidelines, and traditions. They even create their own faiths. It makes them feel secure, but it's a mindset that entraps and enslaves—a web of half-truths which the snake enthusiastically encourages."

"You mean it's like building churches in that wilderness Jesus showed us, except they're as hot and dusty as their surroundings?" Asuka said.

"Yes, something like that. A vibrant church in the wilderness should be an oasis—running water, verdant vegetation, a real contrast filled with hope."

"That sounds exciting," Nova said.

"My love, grace, and truth are rooted in relationship, which on oc-casion can appear to be contradictory, depending on the context. That's why GAs are so important. You meet people where they are and help them find me through relationship in a manner that rules can never accomplish."

"It sounds pretty simple, and obvious. Why is it so hard for them to grasp?" Asuka asked.

"Too many people try to think their way to believe and to follow my ways," said Pappa G. "Faith doesn't grow like that. Of course, the mind is important, but life-giving faith is walked out, step by step, not worked out premise by premise. The mind limited by Earthtime does not have the capacity to comprehend me rationally—much beyond the first baby steps. After that, faith requires the risky leaps, the bounds, trust, and, above all, friends."

"Ok, that helps." Jenny nodded thoughtfully. "Perhaps we should review Jack and Brenda's journey again with that in mind."

"I'll leave you to it. Remember, I'm always within earshot to lend a hand when needed." Pappa G winked at Yesaidu. He stood up and patted Asuka gently on the shoulder as he left.

"Thank you," they responded as they powered up their InSights once again, this time with a newfound confidence and sense of purpose.

Chapter Eighteen

IF A SCOOP PLOUGHED a furrow through a tub of ice cream, the result might resemble the valley of Elah—shallow and long, hills gently rising on either side, a small river roughly bisecting it—the place where a mere boy challenged a veritable giant of a man.

Some distance from that valley the Guardian Angels, accompanied by Jesus and Gale, assembled in the undulating hills. Given what they had witnessed so far, they were relatively certain they were about to face another challenge—probably upsetting them too. *All part of the training*, they told themselves. With a sweep of his arm Jesus directed their attention to the diminutive figure standing on the sheep-speckled hill, staff in hand.

At fourteen years old, David was increasingly restless with his isolated life in the hills, his only company a herd of bleating sheep. Yet, he accepted shepherding as a rite of passage that his brothers had endured before him. A few months earlier he'd been surprised when his brother Shammah arrived, breathless, in the hills outside Bethlehem.

"David!" he called. "Dad told me to bring you home. The prophet Samuel wants to talk to you."

"What does he want with me? Have I done something wrong?" he asked, panicked, as they ran back to the house.

"Have no idea," Shammah retorted. "We all had to meet with him, but he didn't seem satisfied. I can't understand why he'd want to meet with *you*," he scoffed.

They arrived about mid-afternoon when Samuel was resting. It was another hour before he appeared and asked for David to be brought before him. David had heard about the great prophet but had never met him in person. His pulse quickened as he entered the room where Samuel sat waiting. Wiping his clammy palms on his robe, he realized he was more nervous meeting him than confronting the wild animals threatening the flock in the hills.

Samuel was old, his long, wispy, white beard dangling from a gaunt face, weathered, and creased. As soon as he saw David, he smiled and beckoned him closer.

Slowly Samuel rose to his feet, raising himself gingerly with his arms and softly grunting with the effort. His watery eyes, milky opaque with cataracts, squinted over David's head as he declared the shocking news to Jesse and the rest of the family.

"This is the one the Lord has chosen."

Removing a horn from his belt, he uncapped it, dipped his thumb in the oil, and thickly smeared David's forehead until the oil dribbled down his face.

"David, I anoint you as the chosen one of the Lord Yahweh, to become king of Israel as successor to Saul in his appointed time."

David was speechless. What was happening? Was it a joke? There was no promise or warning he could cling to, no discussion, nothing. His older brothers shuffled together on the sideline, not knowing what to make of the proceedings. Then, Samuel turned David around to face them. Placing his hands on the boy's shoulders, he addressed the family.

"The Lord disregards outward appearances; rather, he focuses on the heart and spirit of a person. I have followed his leading and direction today. I urge you not to undermine what the Lord has determined to be the pathway for your brother and his nation."

"When will this be?" Jesse asked, aghast. "What must we do?"

"I have no way of knowing the will of the Lord concerning the time of fulfillment," Samuel said quietly as he sank back in his chair. "Continue your life as usual and he will lead you, have no doubt of that."

And that was the end of the matter. David returned to the hills; his brothers teased him and playfully call him names. Life did indeed carry on as normal—until today. Today David was delivering food to his brothers in the valley of Elah as his father had commanded. He'd found an army in disarray, muttering in fear. In response to David's questioning his brothers recounted the ongoing challenge between the Philistines and

Saul's army that had been underway for more than a month. The focus of attention was Goliath, who daily taunted Saul's men to step forward and fight him in a "winner-takes-all" contest.

"Why isn't anyone responding to the challenge?" David asked.

"Check him out for yourself," his brother Shammah replied, nudging David with his elbow. "He's huge; we wouldn't stand a chance."

David looked across the valley where smoke curled into a hazy cloud hanging over the Philistine camp. Every now and then light glinted off a helmet or spear as men waited for battle. About a hundred meters from where they stood, a giant of a man shouted obscenities, brandishing a sword above his head, and laughing derisively.

When David recounted the event later, he could never explain what came over him at that moment, other than a sense of great boldness, calmness, and clarity.

"I'll fight him," David announced matter-of-factly.

"Are you out of your mind?" his older brother Eliab exclaimed incredulously. "I could beat you in combat and you want to take him on? You're insane. Dad will never allow it. You came here with our lunch, not to fight. Who do you think you are?"

"Let's go and talk to someone who's in charge," suggested David, dismissing his brother's comments. "There's more than one way to slay a giant."

Saul was reclining beneath the awning of his tent, sipping freshly brewed tea with his commanders. When the two youngsters appeared, he looked up in surprise. The ensuing conversation fluctuated between a joking banter to earnest discussion. Eventually Saul realized that David was serious and would not be waylaid in his efforts to face Goliath. David explained his plan.

Having witnessed David's skill with a sling, Saul and his entourage agreed that such a tactic would probably come as a complete surprise to Goliath. As long as David did not intend to engage in hand-to-hand combat, then age and size were neutralized. Perhaps it was not such a foolhardy undertaking after all.

Saul insisted that David wear his armor, but the boy couldn't swing a sling beneath its weight. "This will slow me down; I can hardly move," David protested. Saul reluctantly conceded, and David was commissioned to fight the Philistine armed only with his sling and stones.

The shadows unfurled a dark carpet over the valley floor as David stepped out from the protection of Saul's camp. He strode resolutely across the empty terrain toward the Philistine line. The valley was wide and flat, bisected by a shallow stream, which is where he knelt, selected five stones, and placed them in his pouch.

As a shepherd, David had grown accustomed to self-sufficient isolation. But today fear and panic nibbled at his spirit. *What am I doing here? Who do I think I am? Maybe I should run back and admit this was a foolish idea.* He looked around.

He saw no one. All David heard was the cry of two eagles languorously circling overhead and the scrunch of his sandals on the pebbled ground. The deafening quiet was shattered as he strode toward the Philistine camp. A harsh guttural voice bellowed from the shadows across the plain. "Who the hell are you? Am I to be insulted with a challenge from a child?" More obscenities followed.

David's heart doubled its beat; sweat poured from his brow. Wiping his eyes, he beckoned with one hand for Goliath to come and fight. He shouted nothing in retaliation, whispering under his breath for God's presence and protection. He'd never felt so afraid; all his bravado evaporated. Suddenly a line from one of his songs popped into his head. He recited it like a mantra with every step he took. "Lord, you are my refuge and my strength, an ever-present help in trouble . . ." Mysteriously, courage and a deep assurance filled his being. He remembered the promise given when Samuel anointed him as the future king of Israel. He clutched to that promise as if it were a shield.

Goliath's frame appeared even taller with a brass helmet perched on his head that shone in the setting sun. His body was massive, encased in a coat of mail, breastplate, and bronze shin guards. His forearms were sheathed in leather. One hand clamped a bronze-tipped spear; the other brandished a sword high above his mocking mouth.

Greedily anticipating the ruthless slaughter of a brave but foolhardy boy, the gathered Philistines jeered, the sound reverberating through the valley. Behind David, his brothers and Saul's army rose to counter the Philistines' heckling. Their cheers melded into an ancient song of worship to Yahweh—a song of defiant declaration that David had first learned at his grandfather's knee. The familiar tune crescendoed from the camp, rolled across the valley like a wave, and broke over his shoulders with an affirmation that emboldened his young spirit.

As the distance between David and Goliath decreased, the giant became more uncouth and animated, furious that Saul would humiliate him and force him to even acknowledge the presence of a mere boy.

This wouldn't take long; by the time he was finished, they'd have to carry pieces of the child away and deal with their cowardice in offering up such a pathetic sacrifice.

When he was within slingshot range, David gestured at the raging giant. He deftly placed a stone in his sling and walked quickly, almost breaking into a run, until he was close enough to see the engravings on Goliath's helmet, the bulging biceps, veins popping in his neck, his face red with fury.

On top of David's diminutive size and youth, to his great bemusement Goliath also noted that his opponent carried no sword. They were a mere fifteen feet apart when the boy's right hand swiftly lifted. Surprised, the giant raised his shield as the sling twirled above the boy's head with increasing velocity. That was Goliath's last thought and action. The river pebble struck him with such accuracy and force that the giant crashed face down into the dust with a sickening thud. Silence fell over the valley as both armies witnessed the unexpected outcome.

David scampered over to the fallen figure, grabbed the heavy sword in both hands, and with a loud shout swung it as hard as he could down upon the base of Goliath's neck. He severed the giant's head from its body with his second blow. Removing the helmet, David lifted the bleeding head by the hair and shook it defiantly at the Philistines, who were already turning on their heels. Behind them, Saul's army charged forward with loud cheers and newfound boldness.

"Come back and fight!" David taunted them.

"I don't understand what we've witnessed," Asuka said, looking visibly upset. "Why such violence and anger between these people? There's enough land and food for everyone, isn't there?"

"I agree," said Yesaidu to Jesus. "Everywhere you take us, we watch people destroying each other without seeming to benefit much."

"You're capturing a glimpse into my heart. It's a tragedy to watch what is tantamount to blind savagery . . . look how far it's regressed since our talk with Adam and Eve," Jesus responded, shaking his head.

"Why don't you step in and do something?" Gregori asked.

"Freedom is complicated," Jesus replied evenly. "We can't flick switches and force people to bend to our will."

"But you had Samuel anoint David as king, and he had no idea," Asuka said.

"Ah, you're correct. However, we never call without equipping," Gale reassured her. "While it was understandably a shock for David and his family, we knew that he had the capacity and gifting to fulfil the mandate—with our help, of course. Some stumble into their destiny, and others, like David, have it declared over them."

"So, you're saying that sometimes you do initiate more than at other times?" Gregori asked.

"Sometimes. You will discover in due course just how blind and pig-headed people have become in Earthtime." Gale shook her head. "It's heartbreaking. We don't have favorites, nor do we take sides like they do. Goliath is loved as much as David, but generations of 'free choices' have multiplied into horrific consequences."

"Sounds as if the snake is winning?" Jenny exclaimed warily.

"No, there's no danger of that. But he has created enormous turmoil and suffering, and we have a tough battle to rescue millions who don't even realize that they're captives." Jesus stroked his short beard. "Their mindset is that they're free to do whatever they choose, which is the ultimate deception and lie."

They surveyed the jubilant brothers of David hoisting him high upon their shoulders while he clutched Goliath's dripping head.

Jesus continued. "This is what humanity is reduced to when infected with the rebellious venom of one who was once much loved, but who is now our enemy. He has no power over us. The best he can do is attack our creation and manipulate them into all manner of insanity. He manages to twist every exciting contrast and nuance in our creation into a reason to arouse fear, animosity, or suspicion." Jesus shook his head. "If there was another way, we'd know about it."

"Couldn't you have created people on earth without so much enmity and suffering?" Gregori asked. "It doesn't seem fair for generations to inherit stuff they had no control over, and then suffer for it."

"Believe me, they'd have it no other way." Gale wiped dark wisps of hair from her face. "As Jesus alluded to, their greatest deception is that they can rule themselves and that we're a cruel dictator, or don't even exist. They're trapped and prefer unstable leaders who are heroes one day and villains the next. Unfortunately, even David, a man after our own heart, is a prime example. Watch and see."

Chapter Nineteen

JACK EMERGED FROM THE apartment block in Port Alberni with a panicked look on his face. "They've taken Ricky to Vancouver Children's—in a helicopter. The neighbor's minding the kids. She said it's serious." He slumped into the seat and shut the door. "What a f****d-up father I am. This is all my fault. If I'd been around my children, and paid more attention, they wouldn't spend all their time playing in the street. I can't even answer the phone when my wife calls in an emergency."

"What do you want to do now?" Bill asked quietly. "It's never too late to change and make a difference. What would Ricky want, do you think?"

"For me to be with him," Jack blurted, wiping his nose with his sleeve. "Do you think we could go to Vancouver now? Please, man? You and me?"

"Absolutely," Bill turned the key in the ignition. "Let's go."

They talked almost all the way to the Departure Bay ferry. Fortunately, the 3:30 sailing that afternoon was not full. The ferry slowly inched and bumped toward the loading ramp as they were guided into their boarding lane in a large parking lot. The loudspeaker blared news of the pending arrival and advised drivers to return to their cars and prepare for boarding. Twenty minutes later they had crawled in a long line of cars like a mechanical centipede across heavy duty loading ramps onto the lower deck. Locking the car, they made their way up three flights of stairs to the passenger deck.

People trudged on board from the overhead passenger walkway pulling suitcases, carrying overnight bags, or with hands in pockets and backpacks. Others appeared from the car decks like rabbits popping out of warrens, many rushing to the cafeteria and joining the long lines that soon formed along the aisle.

"Want a coffee?" Bill asked Jack.

"Yes please, thanks."

They headed to the front of the boat, past the gift shop. Bill punched the buttons on the coffee machine for two Americanos. "Have a nice day," said the teller dressed in white shirt and dark blue pants. "You too," Bill smiled. Eager beavers had already claimed seats at the front providing panoramic views of the voyage ahead. They found two seats further back on the aisle and sank into them as the ferry shuddered and crept forward out of the dock.

Bill kept the conversation flowing to engage Jack rather than have him wallow into self-deprecating introspection.

"Canada's a land of immigrants," Bill noted. "How did you end up here?"

"Well, we've lots of time so may as well give you the rundown on my family." Jack told him about his grandfather, a heavy-duty mechanic, meeting his grandmother one summer in Kelowna, picking fruit. She was new to Canada and recently arrived from Scotland. When his grandad saw her, Jack said he knew right away that she was the one for him. They were married six months later.

His grandmother was born in Aberdeen and grew up in the war years. "She told me stories of German bombings in Scotland, the worst being the Aberdeen Blitz that killed over a hundred people. During one of the raids, to calm her nerves an aunt gave her a cigarette; she was only thirteen. That was the beginning of a lifelong habit."

"Your grandmother emigrated to Canada alone?" Bill asked.

"After the war she and her brother came over to see if they'd like it here. Nan stayed and he went back. I used to love the sound of her voice with her Scottish accent. She'd sing songs at bedtime. I can only remember part of one called 'Ally Bally Bee.' I used to sing it to my kids as they went to sleep."

Jack began to softly sing. He had a surprisingly good voice.

"*Ally, bally, ally bally bee,*
Sittin' on yer mammy's knee
Greeting for a wee baw-bee
To buy some Coulter's Candy.

Poor wee Jennie's lookin' awful thin
A rickle of bones covered over with skin
Now she's gettin' a wee double chin
From sucking Coulter's Candy."

Jack smiled. "Not sure if I got all the words right, but that song always makes me feel warm and safe," he said wistfully.

"Why do you think that is?" Bill asked.

"It's my nan and my mom. They were always there for us kids, you know. I dreamed I'd be like that when I had a family." He shook his head. "Mom always fussed and hated conflict. She lived for her family, making sure our clothes were clean and there was a hot meal on the table. Was quite naïve really, probably spoiled me in a way I guess and let me get away with stuff."

"Is she still alive?"

"No. She had an aneurism shortly after Brenda and I were married. Never even got to meet Ricky, although she knew he was on the way. I was shattered and drowned my sorrows in more drinking. For some reason I found it hard to accept."

"It's never easy processing the death of a parent," Bill responded with empathy. "I never knew mine . . . Back to your grandparents. What happened after they married?" Bill asked.

"They settled in Kelowna where my grandfather ran his mechanic shop for years. By the time I was born, he'd retired and sold it. We used to take family trips up there every year. My parents were great Legion supporters and would stop along the way for a beer at the local Legion halls in Hope, Penticton, and various other places. We loved those road trips."

"How did you end up in Port Alberni?" Bill asked, sipping his Starbucks. The ferry glided across the calm waters of the strait, churning up a wide wake trailing back to the island. Tourists leaned over the guard rails snapping selfies. Inside, around Bill and Jack, there was the constant bustle of people coming and going with animated chatter. Not far away young children squealed in the play area.

"My father apprenticed as a mechanic with his dad and then moved to Campbell River before eventually heading to Port. It was a busy logging and fishing town in those days—high wages, plenty of work in the mills. My dad was in heaven as a mechanic. He opened his own shop, just like his dad did, and never looked back. Shortly after arriving there, he met and married my mom and we never wanted for anything."

"Your mother's family already lived there?" Bill asked.

"Yep, she was a local island girl. Her father worked in the mill and they had a family home and acreage on the outskirts of town."

"And your wife, is she also local?"

"Sure is. I met Brenda at high school. She was good looking, lots of fun, and we hit it off from the beginning. I felt accepted by her and understood, which was new for me. She couldn't wait to finish school and train as a nurse. We graduated together and had a wild celebration out at the gravel pit and the lake. That's where Ricky was accidently conceived. We married a few months later, so Brenda's plans for nursing had to be parked. Ricky was our pride and joy. Best 'mistake' we ever made." Jack smiled. "Brenda took courses and worked as a hairstylist. Kaitlin appeared five years after Ricky, and Jessica two years later."

"How did you plan to support your new family? Were you scared?"

"No, actually I was excited. I was working for my dad again. When I have my act together, I'm a decent mechanic. Have been to trade school and got my red seal certification. Also learned a ton of stuff from dad. I remember my first motorbike was a small Yamaha 50cc that sounded like a sewing machine. I stripped it down, resprayed it, and Dad helped me rebuild the engine with new rings and gaskets. I loved that bike!"

"Sounds like fun; you're quite accomplished," Bill said.

"Grease flows like blood in the family genes and I guess I inherited them. I was expected to follow my father and work in his business with the possibility of eventually taking it over." Jack paused, taking a long sip of his coffee. "I let him down, of course."

"What happened?"

"Usual story: I fell in with the wrong crowd. Kept missing work because of parties, drugs, and just having a good time, particularly in the summer out at the lake. Then friends would go fishing down the inlet for a few days and I couldn't resist. I'd work for six months, swearing to Brenda that things would change. Then I'd drink or snort too much cocaine and not be home for days. I don't blame my wife for getting fed up. She held the family together and kept taking me back. When she did, we had great times . . . until the next 'bender.'"

"And your dad tolerated this behavior?" Bill asked incredulously.

"No way. After the second 'incident', he fired me. Said he wasn't going to put up with attitude and have me ruin a lifetime of work. I worked with a landscaper for a few months until being fired for not showing up for two days. Drove a truck up and down the island for a while, same result. Then did some grunt work at one of the smaller mills down the inlet. Was even hired as a janitor at the hospital Every time I ended up being fired for poor attendance. It was embarrassing, yet I kept repeating the pattern."

"Does that mean you're a victim and that no one understands you?" Bill scratched his forehead, a smile playing on his lips. "Now, at the grand old age of, what, thirty plus, you're giving up on what could be an amazing forty years ahead of you?"

Jack leaned back, clasping his hands behind his head, and looked at the ceiling. The thrum of the ferry engine vibrated beneath them.

"Despite a family with a wife and kids I adored, I guess I was restless, even though I hate to admit it. I couldn't handle responsibility and the thought of anyone relying on me. Never felt I could measure up and be the son my father wanted—or the husband either. If you know you will fail and are already a disappointment, you give up caring. I mean if I were my dad, or Brenda, I'd have done the same."

"And yet you can't help but care," Bill said. "Why were you trying to end your life in a lake if you didn't care?"

"Because the shame and guilt eat at me. I even get tired of myself but that does not seem to change anything. I just fall into the same f***d up cycle." Jack sighed.

"Remind me why we're heading to the hospital in Vancouver?"

"Obviously because Ricky is seriously injured, and I need to be there. I'm his father, good or bad, the only one he has."

"Any other reason?" Bill pressed in gently.

"I guess I feel guilty about abandoning Brenda and her carrying the weight of this situation alone."

"Those are good and normal responses, Jack. You have the capacity within you to do the right thing; you just need encouragement and some self-belief. You are not all bad. I would not be taking this trip with you if I thought there was no hope, or you weren't worth it. Don't allow the past to determine your future. In the end it's you who gets to decide."

"But I have done that so many times Bill: I make promises, start with a bang and lots of good intentions, and by next week my resolve's gone to hell. Even I've given up on myself. I have zero confidence in my ability to follow through on anything."

Bill leaned forward resting his elbows on his knees and looked sideways at Jack. "Well, we're here today heading for Vancouver. Your son is in a critical condition and your wife is beside herself with grief, worry, and probably a weight of guilt as well. Brenda's likely furious that you're not with her—again. And she's terrified about what may happen and how she'll cope. When we get to Vancouver, should we go to a pub and drink, or—?"

"Of course, we can't do that," Jack retorted. "We have to be with Ricky and Brenda. I want to be there, even though it scares me to death." Jack muttered a few obscenities under his breath, just audible enough for Bill to hear.

"I'm glad you feel that way, believe me," said Bill. "How do you think Brenda's going to react when you arrive?"

"That's what scares me," Jack said. "She doesn't trust me for a second. I'm not sure how to face her, or even how to be there with Ricky."

"Words are not as important as your actions, Jack. What do you want? I suspect your wife still wants her husband and family together. And if that's not what you're interested in, then it's probably best not to go there now."

"I do want things to change, and for us to be a family again," Jack replied, tears filling his eyes. "I don't usually get like this, but for some reason I'm feeling it in a different way. I'm just not sure what to do or how to be."

"Why don't we get some fresh air and walk on the upper deck?" Bill stood up and stretched.

"Good plan." Jack responded, bouncing to his feet, and wiped his eyes with his sleeve. "Let's go."

Chapter Twenty

THE SUN BAKED HOT in Jerusalem.

Evening shadows silently stretched across the city like an incoming tide. In the king's palace, a man languished in the cool shade cast by the wall protecting the stairs leading down to his private chambers. David, king of Israel, was normally away in the spring, leading a military maneuver to consolidate and protect his kingdom. He usually relished the life with his men—the physical exertion, the camps, the exhilaration, the adrenalin rush of another campaign. He'd never anticipated a time when he would grow weary of the adventure, or tire of the prospect of a new conquest. But this year he had felt disinclined to venture out. Besides, he told himself, there was enough for him to attend to right here at his headquarters. Now he was kicking his heels on the highest tower in the region. Before him, stunning views of Jerusalem and rolling hills folded into a blurred and hazy horizon.

Gale and the GAs stood in a corner of the king's rooftop patio, sharing his view. Gale gave them some necessary background information.

"Uriah left home three weeks ago to fulfill the annual military obligations. He and Bathsheba had only been married five months and were settling into their new life when the order was issued to march. She'd dreaded the moment and did her best to hide her tears as his day of departure approached.

"The men, of course, relished the prospect of adventure. King David's army was feared throughout the entire region and they were proud to be soldiers enlisted in such an elite group. It was never clear how long the campaigns would last; they could be away for one month, three, sometimes more."

"Every year?" Gregori shielded his eyes against the glare of the sun.

"Yes, they had to maintain a presence to discourage their enemies from getting any ideas. They had to be vigilant."

"More violence. Seems to be the norm around here." Nova shook his head. "It's not good."

"No, it's not," Gale sighed. "And you're about to see more." She continued with the story.

"Uriah and Bathsheba lived in soldiers' quarters close to David's palace down there." Gale pointed to a section of housing. "Two rooms with access to the flat roof overlooking the valley. Uriah was ecstatic when the opportunity to move there presented itself; otherwise, it would have meant staying in the extension they'd built onto his father's house—adequate, but now they enjoyed more independence and privacy, at least until the birth of their first child. Both were excited about the future and agreed that four children would be an ideal number of siblings. But, as you'll see, their lives would take a different turn."

"If you're not already expecting," Uriah whispered to Bathsheba with a smile as he left for the campaign, "We'll make sure one's on the way as soon as I return." The young couple lingered in an embrace and then he was gone. Bathsheba stood for a long time in the doorway staring at the empty space Uriah had left as he disappeared around the corner. She tried to imagine his homecoming, but it failed to temper the ache in her chest.

A few weeks later Bathsheba's heart dropped at the first sign of menstrual blood. She wouldn't be surprising her husband with their longed-for child after all. It took a while for the realization to sink in. All she could do was remind herself of Uriah's promise—that they would try again when he returned. Some days later, as she noticed the sun sinking, she hurried downstairs to fetch water for bathing; it was time for her ritual cleansing after the end of her period.

Lounging on his patio, David was bored, regretting his rash decision. He wasn't used to having time on his hands. He bit his finger—an old habit—stood up and strolled from one side of the tower to the other. His eyes scanned the rooftops below like an eagle hunting and hovering in the sky. The shadows brought welcome relief from the heat as the sun descended. A gentle breeze brushed the face of Israel's most beloved monarch.

He failed to notice her at first. In the encroaching dusk he surveyed the soldiers' quarters below, the flat-roofed buildings that housed the elite Royal Guard. The air was still and quiet, punctuated by the joyful shrieks of children and the occasional bark of a dog. His gaze wandered lazily over the valley, then closer to home, sweeping the rooftops, doorways, and windows, until his heart missed a beat and he paused.

King David's eyes were sharp, trained over years in battle to pick up the slightest movement. He was no longer in the prime of his youth, but at fifty he was still in better shape than most men half his age. Through a large window he spotted a woman. She was naked. She knelt, dipped a bucket into the water, and poured it over her head. Three times she repeated the ritual before she stood up and began to wash, quite unaware that every finger trace was being monitored from the rooftop above. She stretched like a lazy cat in the warmth of the sun's rays cascading over her body. Slowly she washed her neck, her shoulders, her breasts, her stomach, her legs, gently caressing her bronze gleaming skin with a dripping cloth she'd dabbed in olive oil.

In the warmth of the setting sun, after a long, hot day, she found the ritual sensuous and refreshing. It made her feel alive in her blossoming womanhood. It was pure and filled with thankfulness and anticipation of a long life with her husband.

David's heart raced. He drank, or rather gulped, in her beauty. He couldn't have fashioned her more exquisitely in his wildest fantasy—her wet hair tumbling down her shoulders, full breasts teasingly half-hidden by her back that tugged his eyes down to her rounded hips. *Those legs are like a gazelle by the springs of Ein Gedi*, he mused. What he wouldn't like to do with her. He beckoned to a guard standing by the stairs and pointed to her. "Bring her to me," he ordered. This was what he'd been missing: the thrill of the chase, the excitement of adventure, the break from the mundane.

Half an hour later the guard returned with the woman by his side. Dismissing him, David stood before her. She was just a girl, her skin glossy and smooth with youth. His throat was dry; he tasted the delectable copper flavor of lust on his tongue. She was even more striking than he'd imagined, damp tresses tangled, brown eyes large and afraid, the scent of oil and perfume driving him crazy with desire.

"What have I done, my lord?" she asked, her voice wavering.

"Absolutely nothing," he smiled. "But I hope that will change. Come over here."

David led her to the side of the tower and pointed downward. "I saw you bathing through your window earlier."

The girl stepped back and averted her eyes, embarrassed. "I thought I was alone," she whispered.

"You mean you didn't see me admiring you? You put on quite a show. You looked lonely, which is why I called you here."

He turned toward her, his hungry gaze exploring her. Gently he lifted her chin with his forefinger until their eyes met. This was not David the warrior. This was David the poet, the charmer, the singer of songs who plucked feelings and emotions like the strings of a harp to evoke much more than music. "What's your name?"

"Bathsheba, my lord."

"And your husband has gone to war with my armies? For how long?"

"It's been three weeks, my lord. He may be gone for three months."

"You must miss him," David said, taking hold of her shoulders. He could feel the warmth of her skin beneath her cotton robe. "I could order him home sooner," he crooned "If you don't resist me now."

He drew her closer and kissed her passionately on the lips. She gasped and pushed her hands against his chest in futile resistance. She was no match for this royal warrior lusting like a lion. His hands tore the cloth from her shoulders, exposing her breasts. Her arms folded to cover her nakedness, her clothing spilling onto the floor.

"Please stop, my lord!" Bathsheba cried as David pushed her down onto a mat, tore at his loose clothing, and raped her. With each thrust of his hips, she gasped and pleaded for him to stop, until, powerless, she went limp and let him have his way with her.

"What's your name again?" David asked, sweat pouring from him as he lay by her side, breathing heavily.

"Bathsheba, wife of Uriah," she gasped. Eyes red with tears, she turned away and curled up into a fetal position and whispered, "God help, why me?"

At last David stood up and pulled on his robe. He paced the outside terrace, enjoying the cooling evening air as his adrenalin subsided. Bathsheba captivated him. God, he loved women! But he was satisfied, for now. He looked down at the whimpering girl on the mat, without regret or remorse.

"You can go now." Sobbing quietly, Bathsheba hastily pulled on her cloth garment.

The king clicked his fingers and a guard appeared to accompany her out.

"I can't believe or process what we've just witnessed," Jenny said, tears streaming down her face. "It hurts my heart so much."

The others nodded. It was an awkward, bruised silence back in the Rainbow Room.

Everyone was quiet, in a state of shock, hearts and thoughts in turmoil. Their foundation was rocking and their compass spinning. They'd lost their bearings. This was far beyond what was comfortable or familiar. Neither Jesus nor Gale seemed in any hurry to intervene or break the tension.

Nova couldn't sit still. He paced along the wall. "I don't understand how David could do that to a helpless young woman? Take advantage of her. He'd everything from riches to power, affluence, and even the women in his palace. Is it never enough? Why the need to violate the wife of a man serving in his army?"

"And David's the most famous king of Israel, described as a man after your own heart? I don't follow how that can be," Gregori added, shaking his head. "I was ashamed to be a man when I saw that. We've never encountered this in heaven. What's the term in Earthtime?"

"Rape," said Yesaidu. "Gale and I were just talking about it earlier. When someone uses their power and physical strength to force another to do their will. It's horrible."

"You'll discover this theme frequently arising in your future missions," Gale said. "Men and women abusing power like the snake in the garden. They grab it with both hands, seldom possessing real strength, wisdom, or generosity of spirit."

Asuka hunched over her folded arms in tears. "I just can't get over how the king, of all people, rapes and defiles Bathsheba—and for what? Because he can? He's meant to protect her! I feel as if I've been violated with her."

"Many would share your response, Asuka." Gale shook her head.

"I'm afraid I can't protect you from the ugliness," Jesus said softly. "It can be much worse than what you witnessed. It's always hard for you GAs to comprehend how people in Earthtime can behave toward one another. It's a battleground down there raging in the heart of every man and woman."

"But evil's so clearly destructive," Yesaidu exclaimed. "Surely your goodness is more attractive? Can't they see?"

"You'd have thought so." Gale nodded in agreement. "But evil is not the mere absence of our goodness. It's energized by satan, the snake. He detests the fact that we cast him down because of his rebellious and jealous spirit. And remember, evil invariably masquerades under the guise of good, initially."

"But why do you allow him to continue to destroy the beauty you created?" Yesaidu pressed.

"Because the greatest gift I bestow on all created beings, natural and supernatural, is the freedom to choose. And then there are consequences to follow. Even when it hurts me, and those I love."

"Could you kill satan right now, if you wanted to?" Gregori interjected.

"Of course. He's no threat to us; after all, we created him in the beginning."

"Then why . . . ? I don't get it." The same question arose from their lips again. "Why so much suffering in all its forms?"

"I understand that it's hard," Jesus said. "Most people beg me to wave my hand and end all suffering. The trouble is that freedom is beautiful and terrifying. With each choice comes a consequence. Every consequence either draws closer to fulfilment and truth, or it leads further away into destruction and lies."

"Are you saying that you want to give all people whom you've created another chance to come closer to you rather than stay far away?" Asuka said.

"That's exactly what we're saying," Jesus replied. "Many chances are given. We love all and have no favorites. The last thing we desire is to see any lost for eternity in a place where our presence is absent—which is, in fact, hell. Many in Earthtime can't comprehend that the real essence and meaning to their physical life is supernatural."

"How would they, when they experience so much anger and pain?" Nova protested.

"Quite right, Nova," Gale said. "It is impossible from earth's perspective to conclude that there is a God of love amid the chaos and apparently meaningless and random affliction of the innocent, I agree."

Jesus nodded. "Which is where you come in. They need help to renew their hope and vision. We entered Earthtime history to break the logjam and to bring greater revelation. But not even my becoming human, dying, and rising could overcome generations of cynicism and suspicion. And that's still apparent, even among those who claim to believe and serve in the church today!"

"Isn't that disappointing?" Yesaidu asked.

"It's the nature of the battle in Earthtime," Jesus said. "The challenge to our presence and authority is everywhere."

"It's not just unbelief," said Gale. "There's a deep rebellion that is perpetuated through every generation. The snake's not smart but he is consistent. He attacks us by planting the same lies in the heads and hearts of men and women repeatedly: God doesn't mean what he says, nothing bad will happen, he doesn't have your best interests at heart, he doesn't exist. That's why Israel asked for their own king rather than have us lead them. They wanted to be like the other nations; little did they know."

"You'll see this time and again in Earthtime," Jesus added. "The same person who is capable of great good is also capable of great evil. My disciples are an example of that, as are Moses, David, Abraham, and everyone else. We love each one, but we hate the evil that is manifest. Our enemy is the source of evil, the snake, not the ones he influences and uses."

"As David fell to lust, so do many others, I'm afraid," said Gale. "They crave love and settle for a sexual encounter that gratifies for a moment and destroys infinitely more. The snake poisons everything, given half a chance. What begins as a dream ends in a nightmare. Lust for power, for money, for ambition, for what another has, for beauty and for a thousand other 'if onlys.' All offering a fulfilment that we alone provide."

"The snake lusted after 'being God,'" Jesus added. "We cut him loose with an army of his followers to pursue their impossible dream. Too late they discovered that power without us, without love, is a voracious monster. The Kingdom he once surveyed by my side has shriveled into something humiliatingly small, dark, and cold, in his demonic claws. His kingdom is hell."

"This is a tough mission. To walk alongside those in Earthtime, you must lose some of your innocence and be exposed to evil and its consequences. You can't help them unless you empathize and understand their dilemma," Gale said. "Be assured, I will always protect you and you will never be overcome, as they are. Your assignment is to help those we love to glimpse this world that we know—where the snake has no influence. The world as it was always meant to be."

Chapter Twenty-One

A PURPLE-GRAY FOG SHROUDED Vancouver, a cluster of high-rise buildings only faintly visible on the horizon. The city disappeared behind the hills of West Vancouver, bedecked with forest and residences that clung like barnacles to every nook and cranny. Jack and Bill were sailing up the Queen Charlotte channel, entering Howe Sound. Fishing boats bobbed in the ferry's wake beneath a clear blue September sky. They were about twenty minutes from Horseshoe Bay, the terminal tucked into a cove sheltered by mountains and providing access to communities on the West Coast shoreline.

The two men walked the gray circuit on the upper deck around the blunt bow and stern and past the smokestacks. People of all shapes and sizes lay sunbathing or sat at small round tables enjoying the passing scenery. It was the final week of the holidays, which meant every sailing was crowded with tourists intent on squeezing the last drop out of their summer reprieve.

Conversation flowed easily between Jack and Bill, which surprised Jack as he'd never talked like this with anyone before. The ferry engines vibrated the grey deck beneath their feet.

"Jack, you've done plenty of mechanical work over the years, haven't you?"

"Yes, I have, ever since I could hold a spanner and annoy my dad with questions and offers to help in the workshop." Jack smiled.

"Did you learn to fix these machines by trial and error or were you taught by your dad showing you how? Were manuals helpful as well?

"Of course—all of the above. With computerization things became simpler and more complicated at the same time. There's much more to working on engines now than merely knowing how to use a spanner. I seem to have an aptitude for troubleshooting."

"Do you think it's weak or degrading when someone brings you their vehicle and asks for help because they can't fix it themselves?"

Jack sensed he was being led somewhere but went along with Bill's line of questioning. "No, of course not. No one can know everything. Just as we go to doctors for medical issues, a mechanic's specialty is diagnosing and fixing problems with machines. In fact, I'd say someone was crazy if they didn't come to us; by ignoring the problem they could make matters much worse, even blow the engine."

"And where do you acquire the information about the particular vehicle and model you're working on?" Bill continued as they strolled into the headwind and rounded the bow.

"From the manufacturer, naturally. The people who made the engine. They provide support materials for every model they produce so that mechanics like me are not in the dark when we're asked to do maintenance. It's not rocket science. What are you getting at?"

"Well, I'm wanting to run something by you, but I'm afraid it's a touchy subject. For some reason I frequently get pushback and even anger when I raise it."

"No worries with me, Bill—fire away."

"Excuse me," Bill said as they nearly bumped into an elderly couple walking slowly around the deck, the man supported by a walker on wheels.

Turning back to Jack he continued.

"Ok—I found you in the middle of a lake yesterday wanting to end your life. Almost at the same time your son had an accident and is in danger of losing his. You've described to me the troubles you've had and admitted you have no faith in yourself to change things around. Correct?"

"About sums it up, although I hate to be reminded of Ricky's situation. That terrifies me right now." Jack's words trailed into a whisper lost in the wind.

"It's not easy for sure, I think I understand," said Bill. "It's just that if you were a machine like the ones you repair, you'd be regarded as, well, broken and requiring a mechanic to help with some changes."

"I wish it were that easy," said Jack. "Drop me off somewhere for a service and tune-up."

"Which leads into my question." Bill smiled. "Who created us? Where's the manual when we break down? Who's the mechanic, the go-to guy?"

"Haven't a clue," said Jack with a shrug of the shoulders.

"Ever thought about God?"

"Oh s**t, here we go. I'm not into church and religion, sorry Bill," Jack replied, raising a silencing hand.

"Told you I'd get pushback." Bill laughed. "Or a kneejerk reaction."

"Well . . ."

"I'm not into church or religion either, Jack. I'm talking about a God who is a friend, knows you and what makes you tick, and who could be more real than you realize."

"When you mention God, I go cold," Jack said. "All I hear are rules and judgment, anger, and my not being acceptable. I think of always doing wrong and certainly not being a good churchgoer like some I know. I've always steered clear of them anyway—my parents' best friends were a couple who never missed a service, and you should have seen how they behaved when they all got together—the language, the drinking, the judgmental attitudes. Not for me, thanks."

Bill nodded. "There's much in the world that doesn't give God a great reputation. It makes it hard to know who he really is—if he exists at all. Probably like struggling to find an honest mechanic who'll do a good job and not rip you off."

"Steady on, they're not all like that," Jack protested.

"Exactly, that's my point," said Bill. "Likewise, what if God is real? Like the good and reliable mechanic, you know. Those who exist among the frauds and the gangsters. What if he's the greatest father you could ever hope for? Maybe that would be a little more attractive? Someone who's always looking out for you, never makes you feel ashamed or a fool when you make poor choices. Someone who encourages you and believes in you. Someone who wants to help you become the best version of yourself possible. On a par with, or better than, the best mechanic in the world?"

"Sounds like a dream."

"Jack, you remember when you were out on the lake, drowning your sorrows in vodka before attempting to drown yourself? Do you remember crying out to God in your black despair? 'God help me!' you whispered as you rolled into the water and began to sink. Do you remember?"

"Not really, to be honest." Jack stopped and stared at Bill. "Hey, how do you know that's what I said?"

"That's a topic for another time." Bill smiled. He draped his arm over Jack's shoulders as they continued to walk. "Jack, what if my coming to your rescue and being here now is part of God's answer? Would that be a good thing?"

"Well, yes. If it weren't for you, I'd be dead."

"And Ricky would have no dad to visit, and Brenda would be isolated, left to deal alone with a suicide snatching her husband and a serious accident landing her son in Intensive Care."

The loudspeaker blared across the deck: "Attention all passengers. We will shortly be arriving at Horseshoe Bay; will all car passengers please make their way to the vehicle deck."

"Let's chat about what you can do to support Brenda when we get to the hospital," Bill suggested. He opened the heavy steel door from the upper deck and Jack led the way downstairs to the car.

Chapter Twenty-Two

"ALLOW ME TO INTRODUCE Bathsheba," Pappa G said.

"Hello," she bowed her head slightly, "it's good to be with you."

The GAs were reflecting on the traumatic encounter between David and Bathsheba when Pappa G joined them in the Rainbow Room. Holding his arm was a beautiful woman with braided hair and a demeanor radiating peace and serenity.

"They're still in shock at what we witnessed—King David violating and abusing you," Pappa G said as they took their seats. "It hurts all of us to face these realities."

Bathsheba looked around the group with an empathic expression. "I've had a long time to process that terrible event," she said softly. "But when it's new to you, it's a shock that no words adequately convey. I understand."

Addressing the GAs, Pappa G said, "You need to know that after this shameful incident, my priority was Bathsheba. King David did a terrible thing that can never be excused or condoned."

Bathsheba nodded. He continued.

"He used his position and his power to intimidate someone with no ability to resist him or to defend herself. Then he made matters worse by trying to cover up his actions by having Bathsheba's husband killed in a battle he should have been leading."

"Why did you allow him to continue as king?" Gregori's deep voice boomed with consternation.

"For the same reason, every human being receives second chances a thousand times in their lifetime—grace. David acknowledged his irresponsible behavior and his gross misuse of power, to me and to Bathsheba.

He didn't run away or make excuses. He owned the consequences. His son with Bathsheba died and he never disrespected her again. He had to deal with his children over the years who struggled with what he did, when they learned about it. And it has been a stain on his character down through the ages. Bathsheba, anything to add?"

"It's strange how after even a few thousand years, I still feel the pain and sorrow of those times. Perhaps, more for the women who continue to be in the same position I was many generations ago. That's why your training and mission is so important. To help bring about lasting change and a deep transformation of heart. Healing may be possible, but prevention is the best answer, surely?"

Jenny, always willing to pose tough questions, smiled at Bathsheba. "I don't want to be insensitive, but may I ask you a personal question?"

"By all means, go ahead."

"After David raped you, he had your husband killed as an attempted cover up. Gale told us you went to live with him—and stayed. How's that possible?"

Bathsheba gave a shy smile. "I was naïve and young. I'd been married a short while and was still getting to know Uriah, whom my parents had introduced me to. He was a good man. It was hard not to be attracted to his optimism and deep sense of loyalty and duty. Of course, I was distraught when I received news of his death. What would become of me? Our hopes and my dreams died as well.

"I had no idea that King David was the instigator. I wasn't even aware that Uriah had returned home, as I never saw him. I only learned those details months later. I was grieving and very vulnerable. When invited to the palace, I was grateful for what I understood to be King David's kindness and sensitivity. It seemed to me that I meant more to him than just a fleeting object of lust and pleasure. He genuinely appeared to care about our baby and my welfare."

"But he raped you!" Gregori raised his hands in exasperation. "It was brutal!"

"Indeed, it was," Bathsheba replied. "I was young and severely traumatized by that event. But you need to remember that women at that time and in that culture were regarded as little more than servants for men. I didn't have many options."

"And when you finally learned the truth? What then?" Gregori continued.

"It was after the prophet Nathan visited that King David told me and asked me to forgive him. I'll never forget. He was shaken to the core. It was as if a lamp were lit in his head, shining the light on the offensiveness of his actions both to me and to God. I was shocked, sad . . . betrayed, hurt, angry. It took me time to process. I didn't speak to him for a while. What probably saved us was that we'd begun to establish a solid relational foundation that grew into mutual and genuine love."

Asuka's eyes were wet with tears. "I'm amazed how gracious you are." The others murmured in agreement.

"Why don't we meet David?" Pappa G rose and walked toward the wall ahead of him. "Follow us. You first, Bathsheba." They disappeared through the misty veil.

The GAs followed onto the paved floor of the patio overlooking Jerusalem. The air was warm, the slightest breeze wafting and shifting distant palms and cypress trees. The evening sun melted into a dusty horizon.

Bathsheba stood beside a bearded man with long, reddish-brown hair. They recognized David and felt an immediate tension within. He was at least twelve inches taller than her diminutive four foot eleven. His left arm encircled her shoulders as she pressed into his embrace. He greeted the GAs with a warm smile. His eyes were piercing, sometimes intimidating. He had the confident authority of a soldier king, a man at ease with himself and those around him.

"Welcome," he said. "Enjoy the view over Jerusalem when I was king . . . a long time ago now."

Bathsheba moved toward the edge of the parapet and pointed to a collection of buildings below. "And that's where I used to live, before I came to the palace, but you know that," she said waving her hand.

Pappa G, turning to the GAs, said, "I presume you know where you are? You could call it 'the scene of the crime.'"

The GAs were silent, feeling awkward encroaching on the place of David and Bathsheba's intimate indiscretion. *Why do we have to do this?* they thought, but no one dared voice the question.

"I suspect I know what you're thinking," Pappa G smiled, and with a sideways nod to David said, "Why don't you take it from here?"

David stepped forward and looked directly at the GAs who stood in a semi-circle around him. His eyes were warm, displaying not the slightest hint of shame or discomfort. "There are many things in my life in Earthtime of which I am proud and for which I was held in high esteem.

Let me be clear: the one we're remembering today was not one of them. In fact, it was probably my lowest, most regrettable moment. The reason we're here is to explain that what human beings fear the most is having their secret sins revealed. As you know, I tried to hide mine by not only abusing Bathsheba, behaving like an animal, but also initiating the murder of her husband. It was only when the prophet Naaman spoke to me very bluntly that I finally acknowledged the depth of my depravity and repented."

The GAs listened intently, simultaneously drawn to his magnetism yet repelled by his sordid actions.

David continued. "The greatest gifts Pappa G has bestowed upon all creation are revelatory truth, absolute forgiveness, and reconciliation. We stand before you as testimonies of those elements at work in our lives. The people you meet in Earthtime will instinctively want to hide, blame, accuse, cover up, and wriggle out of responsibility for what they do, how they think, and what they hold onto. There never has been—and never will be—freedom without truth and forgiveness. For anyone."

Bathsheba led a stranger by the hand and indicated for him to introduce himself. "Hello, my friends. I am Uriah, Bathsheba's first husband."

The GAs gasped.

Uriah smiled and lifted his hands. "There are no heroes in this story. I'd no idea at the time what was playing out behind my back, which is the same for everyone in Earthtime. Sometimes the reality is good; other times it doesn't go so well."

"How do you feel being here with the man who arranged for your death and violated your wife?" Nova asked sheepishly.

Uriah beckoned David and embraced him before continuing. "I bear David no malice. He was wrong and stole my beautiful wife, my future, and my life. If I'd learned that truth in Earthtime, I hate to think what I'd have been capable of. But discovering the truth in the presence of Pappa G removes the sting of everything that went wrong in Earthtime." Uriah paused, released David, whose arm he'd been holding, and continued.

"It's as if in his presence all at once there's a revelation of a larger picture, background history, understanding of motive, even remorse that follows. It doesn't make anything right or justifiable, but it does give powerful perspective, even when reflecting on the unjust and the unfair. He knows all about betrayal, loss, and the rebellion of loved ones. From this reality we see so much more than those living in Earthtime. The miracle in this environment is that we're completely free of anger, pain, unforgiveness, and the desire for revenge."

"And how do you deal with all of this now?" Nova turned to David.

"To be honest, when living in Earthtime, I was a walking contradiction for many years. Courageous and a coward, pure and depraved, self-assured, and terrified, full of faith and haunted by doubt. I was deeply ashamed and troubled by my failures and what I was capable of. I described and confessed these struggles in the songs I wrote, which also contained the key to my survival."

"Which was . . . ?"

"The generosity of grace and forgiveness poured out on me by Pappa G. I still don't understand how I received and knew the reality so deeply, but I did." David nodded to Pappa G.

"We're not going to belabor this," Pappa G said. "Thank you, one and all. The reason we're here is to demonstrate the reality of both the brokenness in Earthtime and the healing and restoration possible. David isn't the only one guilty of wrongdoing. Everyone has their own story, and if we had time Bathsheba could share hers. Uriah has a few tales to tell as well."

"Why is that important?" Asuka asked.

"The snake stirs the pot at every opportunity. When people in Earthtime experience disappointment and failure, he accuses them and convinces them to think that we agree with him. It couldn't be further from the truth." Gale took a deep breath and exhaled slowly. "We are not disillusioned when people stumble. We reach out to help them to keep moving forward, encouraging them to learn and grow with us. Nothing they do can separate them from our love."

"I mean, if they won't ask, we can't force them to receive our love," Pappa G clarified.

"And justice?" said Jenny. "What about justice? Aren't there consequences and responsibility somewhere?"

"The people you'll encounter in Earthtime ask the same question," Pappa G replied soberly. "They want judgment and punishment for everyone else who does wrong. They find it easy to find fault and accuse. However, for themselves they always ask for mercy after long explanations justifying their actions. Jesus took all judgment on the Cross. Justice and love meet there. But consequences and responsibility still have to be worked out every time."

"That's why David's life is important," Gale said. "The point is not how bad you've been in Earthtime, but rather, what have you done about it? David was called 'a man after our own hearts' because he genuinely knew how to keep short accounts and to resolve his mess and mistakes with us—every time."

Pappa G nodded. "It's the opposite learning curve for you GAs because the only perspective you have is from heaven. Just remember, your loss of innocence is going to bless many people when you walk alongside them."

Chapter Twenty-Three

BILL PARKED THE CAR after having dropped Jack at the neon-lit entrance to the Emergency wing of Vancouver Children's Hospital. It was about 7pm when they arrived. "I'll catch up with you later." He'd patted Jack's shoulder as the car stopped. "You're exactly where you need to be right now, Jack. Remember what we talked about on the way here. It's never too late—you can be the man."

Savoring the quiet and the stillness of the parking lot, Bill wondered how his life would have turned out if events had flowed in a different direction. Would he have struggled like Jack? He had no way of knowing. He did know that if he were in Jack's shoes, he would appreciate a few friends alongside to help him bear the load. He sighed, got out of the car, and locked the doors with a click of the fob.

Jack rushed from the Emergency Reception area along the pavement to the Pediatric Intensive Care wing. He'd been informed that Ricky had been moved to the fourth floor. Facilities for family members were available there and that was probably where he'd find Brenda.

He entered a bright reception area with modern architecture, wooden beams splayed from the floor supporting a high ceiling, and inspirational quotations adorning the walls. Jack paid scant attention, his focus on locating the elevator. As the doors slid open on the fourth floor, identified by a large white "4" on an orange wall, Jack could feel his heart pounding a mile a minute.

A long, window-lined hallway stretched to the right of the elevator. On the left were entrances to Intensive Care areas. He noticed a sign for a family room and walked toward the doorway, his body tense with apprehension.

Brenda sat slumped in a chair with her eyes closed. Next to her was a woman Jack didn't recognize. She was holding Brenda's hand.

"Hey, Bren?" Jack whispered from the doorway.

Brenda opened her eyes to find Jack standing at the door like one of her children, looking sheepish, even fearful, wondering whether she was angry with him or not. Exhausted and numb, she had no energy to confront Jack or to fight, or even to cling to the faint hope that things would be different.

"Hi." Brenda waved weakly and turned to Rachel. "Rachel, this is Jack. Jack this is Rachel; she's been with me all the way from Port last night."

"Hello Jack, nice to meet you," said Rachel with a smile.

"Hi Rachel." Jack sat in the chair next to Brenda.

"God, Brenda, I only got your message this morning. I rushed over and Sally told me what happened. I'm really sorry I didn't get here sooner."

Brenda sighed. "Yeah, whatever."

"Have you seen Rick? How is he?" Jack leaned forward.

Brenda was silent. She sat up and faced Jack. She wanted so much to have him hold her close and tell her everything would be all right. She wanted to feel safe and protected. Instead, she felt fragile and vulnerable, not ready to give him an inch of herself.

"JJ, it's really bad." She'd called him JJ ever since they'd started dating; she'd long forgotten why. "Ricky hasn't woken up for over twenty-four hours. We were in to see him a few hours ago. He just lies there with a bunch of tubes stuck in him and no response."

"Can I see him, do you think?" Tears welled up in Jack's eyes—fear, guilt, pain, all mingled together with a deep sense of failure and helplessness.

"Of course, we can see him anytime we want," said Brenda. "I'll show you where his room is."

"I'll wait here," said Rachel. "You two go ahead."

Jack followed Brenda out past the small reception alcove and left into Intensive Care. Brenda swiped a card for access, and Jack followed her down a hallway with rooms on either side, walls of windows, some with curtains pulled. Ricky's was the fourth on the left.

It was large and bright, with natural light flooding in during the day. The walls were painted a soft pale blue with simple darker silhouettes of clouds and trees. The bedclothes were matching blue. Taking in the sight of his normally vibrant, talkative son lying so still and quiet beneath the blue sheet, Jack inhaled sharply. Ricky's tousled brown hair protruded from the bandage wrapped around his head. His bruised eyes were closed. There was no response as Jack took hold of his hand and said, "Hey there bud." There was not the usual broad grin, high five slap of palms, and "Hey Dad" back at him.

Brenda stood on the other side of the bed, gently stroking the top of Ricky's head. The ventilator sounded like a metronome beating a slow waltz accompanied by the beep of the heart monitor.

Brenda recounted the accident.

"His left leg has a fracture and they've set it in a splint. He was hit by a car as he fell off his skateboard so has quite a few scrapes and bruises. Then he slammed his head hard on the road."

"Was he wearing his helmet?"

"No, apparently he was having a last attempt at a trick and had taken it off. I told him so many times to never skate without it."

Jack pulled up a chair and sat with his elbows on the side of the bed holding Ricky's hand in his. "You've gotta wake up, Ricky, there's too much living left to do. Don't give up the fight, we love you man." Then, Jack hung his head and quietly wept.

As Brenda watched Jack, she couldn't help but feel a twinge of sympathy for him. Clearly, he was struggling to find his way back to Ricky and her. She knew him well enough to know he'd be blaming himself, allowing the inner voices to beat him down. And to some degree they would be right. He'd behaved like a selfish jerk, but this was a hell of a wake-up call. She also knew enough about herself to know she couldn't keep up the walls for too long. The sensitive man across from her, speaking words of love to his son, was the man she'd fallen for—the man she still loved, despite everything. She hadn't seen this side of him for years. Even now, amid so much uncertainty and pain, he made her heart race.

"So, what happens now?" Jack looked up at Brenda with frightened, questioning brown eyes.

"We wait and see," she replied, eyes fixed on Ricky. "At least he's not suffering or in pain. But I don't know. We can stay here as long as we want, and there's a pull-out bed over there as well." Brenda waved toward the seating by the window.

"Brenda, look at me," Jack said with an intensity she couldn't ignore. "You have every right to be angry—I've been an idiot. God knows I'm sorry. For not answering your call, for not being here sooner, and for not being around more." He'd decided that he would not mention his failed suicide attempt. "I know this isn't the time or place for a big reconciliation, but I'm here now. I'm not going anywhere."

Brenda remained silent as she continued to caress Ricky's hair. Jack rested his head on the bed.

"The doctor said that Ricky may be able to hear us even though there's no visible response so it's good for us to talk to him. You never know."

The ventilator continued its slow dance with the heart monitor, neither breaking their rhythm. Ricky, normally the life of the party, remained motionless.

"Who's the woman with you, Rachel?" Jack asked.

"She helped me with a flat battery in the school parking lot and then a week later I met her at the hospital in Port. Appeared out of nowhere and offered to keep me company as I had no one else around," Brenda said with no attempt to hide her contempt.

Jack turned away. "I'm sorry."

"It wasn't meant as an accusation, just a fact. Anyway, she's been amazing. Makes me feel safe and somehow not so alone. I don't really know much about her."

"Strange . . . I met a guy called Bill the other day and he's the one who took me to Port and traveled with me here. Also appeared out of nowhere and has been a good man to help me right now. We've had some decent talks."

Brenda sighed heavily. "I don't know, JJ. You've always had a bit of a silver tongue . . . but it never seems to last and I'm tired of hoping things will change. I was exhausted even before all this." She shrugged. "Now, with Ricky here, I've nothing left; I've never felt so empty in my life."

Jack sensed within himself a shift which surprised him. For once he didn't feel defensive, needing to over explain, or justify.

"I'm not assuming anything, Bren. No expectations. Ricky is the focus for now."

They sat in silence for a long while on either side of the bed, Ricky's body a broken bridge between their aching, shattered hearts.

Jack noticed Brenda's head dropping from time to time. Then she'd catch herself and sit up.

"Bren, why don't we go back to the family room and you can get some rest? I'll come back and stay with Ricky."

"Ok." Brenda leaned over and kissed Ricky's forehead. "See you soon, Rick," she whispered.

Returning to the family room, they found Rachel and Bill chatting like long-lost friends. "You guys sound like you know one another," Jack said.

"Well, we do actually; we've met once or twice before," Bill replied. He was a large man with medium length brown hair; Brenda would have described him as "built for comfort not for speed." He wore round, brown-framed glasses. His clothes were Eddie Bauer conservative, she thought. Rising to his feet, he stretched out his hand. "You must be Brenda; nice to meet you. I'm Bill. I'm so deeply sorry for what's happened to your son."

"Thank you." Brenda took his hand briefly. "Jack was just telling me about you."

"Hope it was all good," Bill smiled. "This is a tough time. Anything I can do to help, just say the word."

"Thanks, but if you'll all excuse me, I need to at least *try* to get some sleep. I'm running on empty." Brenda headed for the couch at the far end of the room and lay down.

Chapter Twenty-Four

A TUMBLED PILE OF stones and boulders protruded from the gently curving shore. It formed a crude breakwater where several fishing boats tugged gently against their moorings. A stream gushed white water out of the hillside, bouncing over the rocks into the lake. Behind the GAs, golden, grassy hills sloped gently from the water's edge to form an undulating ridge on the Galilean skyline.

"Follow me," said Jesus, walking onto the pier. They paused beside the second boat where a man in his early twenties was storing nets and filling lamps in preparation for the fishing that night.

"Meet Simon Peter," said Jesus, gesturing toward the solitary figure working in the stern of the broad, flat vessel. Peter had helped build the fishing boat with his father about seven years earlier. It was twenty-three feet long, about seven feet wide, and less than three feet deep. They'd had little access or the means to procure the necessary resources; consequently, they'd scavenged some cedar, which was ideal, but had to make do with pine and willow to complete it. The bottom was smeared with bitumen. This boat was their livelihood—their only means of supplying the family's needs with the profits garnered from what they sold in Magdala's strictly controlled fish market. The Romans monitored every aspect of their lives—and taxed them heavily.

"Damn it!" Peter exclaimed amid a few other choice words as he wrestled with the net, slamming it down then accidentally banging his head against the mast. He was in a foul mood, obviously irritable and upset. Clambering onto the uneven pier, he made his way up the hill shouting for Nathaniel and Thomas to hurry up; the other two boats were already in position.

"Why's he so mad?" asked Gregori. "This place is spectacular."

"You'd probably be angry as well after the week he's endured," Jesus replied. "It's not long after my crucifixion and Peter is laden with guilt because he disowned me. He hates himself for his cowardice. Both he, and the other disciples, are feeling betrayed and let down. This is not a happy fishing trip."

Jesus waved his arm over the lake. "We're on the shore of Galilee; over there to my left is the village of Capernaum where Peter lives. This little harbor is the place of seven springs, where I first called Simon and some of his friends to follow me. We spent many hours along this shoreline. It's one of my favorite places."

Gale looked out across the lake and then up to the cliffs in the direction of Nazareth. Further along the shore was the Roman town of Tiberias. "This lake can change in a heartbeat," she said. "One minute it's calm and the next the wind roars down past those cliffs and turns the water into a heaving monster."

"If you're looking for a lesson in shattered dreams and expectations, Peter's your man." Jesus folded his arms. "He is passionate and sincere, hot-blooded, and never afraid to try something new. We spent three years together in Earthtime; Simon Peter was always the first to volunteer and the last to back down. Most people would never even attempt what he gave up following me. Asking a fisherman to walk on dry land for three years and trust someone else with his livelihood? That was a challenge he embraced with every fiber of his being. Now he's not so sure it was worth it."

"Here they come," said Gale.

Peter led Nathaniel and Thomas down the pathway and along the pier, where they were joined by John. The four men brushed through the GAs and boarded the boat. There was not much talking as they cast off, lit the lamps, and hoisted the sail. Before long they were heading into deeper waters with expectations of returning with a boatload of fish the next morning.

"I'll fend for myself from now on," Peter muttered with one hand on the till, the anger inside him boiling like a pent-up volcano. All he knew was that he had better keep busy, or he'd go insane.

Peter's tired eyes roamed the steep slopes rising from the distant shoreline to a broad plateau; behind him the sky glowed red in the fading light. He remembered the exhilaration he had felt on those hills with Jesus a few years earlier. They had fed nearly ten thousand people with

Mark's meager lunch. So much had changed since those giddy days. A stiff breeze pressed against his back and filled the sail. Despite himself, he began to sink into the familiar routine of night fishing in Galilee.He used to dream of these moments in the dusty, crowded streets of Jerusalem. Maybe something good would come out of all this turmoil—but how?

They were fishing off the place of seven springs where the fresh water flowing into Galilee attracted large shoals of fish. It was a popular spot; two other boats had joined them. As it was warm, they wore only loin cloths, sometimes not even that. Oil lamps affixed to the bow of the boat, they set their seine net, which had cork floats on the top and weights on the bottom. Once the net was in position, the three boats would spread out and move back toward the net, the fishermen banging pots and pounding the sides of the boats to scare fish into the net.

There was none of the normal banter and chatter that night as the fishing boats worked back and forth at varying depths from the shoreline, setting and hauling in nets. Peter's companions were not in a great frame of mind either. The air was charged with their collective disappointment and frustration; each man sensed it. After all, they had grown up together. One wrong word could lead to a fistfight, and a small boat was not the place for grown men to start pounding away at each other. To add to the misery, all night long they hauled in one empty net after the next. The atmosphere could have been cut with a knife when the first hints of light began to tug the darkness from the sky and snuff out the stars.

"This is a waste of time. Let's go in; enough's enough," said Thomas after they had hauled aboard another empty, sagging net. The rest grunted in agreement; they were tired, damp, and the prospect of escaping into a deep sleep on dry ground was enticing.

"We can't even catch fish, not one! God, where are you now?" shouted Peter, slamming his fist into a wet coil of rope. They unfurled the sail and began tacking back to the harbor in the soft morning zephyr. Wise to Peter's moods, the men understood it was best to keep out of the way and let him simmer. Challenging him would merely stoke the fire.

The boat was about fifty yards out from the pier when a lone figure waved and shouted to them across the still waters. "Friends, have you caught any fish?"

"No," they answered in sullen unison. Whoever it was sounded irritatingly pleasant at this hour of the morning.

"Cast your net on the right side of the boat—you may be surprised."

"Jesus!" Gregori interrupted, "You're in two places at the same time. How?"

Jesus placed an arm around his shoulder and pulled him in. "This is nothing, Greg; I can never explain what is possible." He grinned. "Let's focus on Peter for now."

Who is this guy? Peter wondered angrily. *What does he think we've been doing all this time? Better to end this disaster of a night.* The other two boats had already taken off, heading home. He glared at his companions and they shrugged.

"Nothing to lose," said Nathaniel, "Although why we should listen to some stranger shouting at us from the shoreline beats me."

"May as well try once more; the family would love me to come home with fresh fish," said Thomas, unraveling the net. "Here, John, help me throw it out, my arms are killing me. Even if there are fish, I'm not sure I can pull them in."

There was no great sense of anticipation as they repeated the tired motions one more time, releasing the net into the lake as the boat carved a slow circle through the placid water. Normally they would not even have attempted the maneuver at this time of day, as the net was much more visible in the brightening light of dawn. However, they were about to discover that this was no ordinary day upon which the sun rose. Suddenly, the familiar slack indicating another failed attempt metamorphosed into a boiling mass of silver and gray fins and tails thrashing in the water.

Thomas shouted, "This net is about to break with fish!" Eight hands clutched, clawed, strained, and pulled with all their strength to secure the bulging catch at the side of the boat. It wouldn't be a wasted night after all!

They were so preoccupied with hauling the net alongside the boat that they had forgotten the stranger. During the tugging, the shouting, and the laughing, the boat had drifted closer to shore. John glanced up again and exclaimed, "Simon you're not going to believe me: that's the Lord!" Peter looked blankly at John, back to shore, and back to John. Without a word, except for what sounded like a choking cry, he wrapped himself in his clothes, jumped overboard, and swam for all he was worth.

When Peter's feet touched the rocky floor of the lake, he stumbled and crawled across the uneven surface until he stood, dripping and exhausted, before Jesus. There were no sounds on his lips, no words would form; just gasping breath and an expression in his eyes that Jenny knew she would never forget. Desperately confused, frightened, hopeful eyes pleading from an exhausted face beneath wet, bedraggled hair, water cascading from an unkempt beard, hands hanging limp by his side.

Jesus smiled and opened wide his arms. "Peter, my dear, dear friend." They held each other for a long time in a tight embrace.

"Bring some of the fish; let's have breakfast," said Jesus, patting Peter on the shoulder and steering him toward his friends who were securing the boat. "I've prepared a fire, with some fresh bread; you must be starving."

The others walked hesitantly up to the fire, their lingering guilt and awkwardness weighing heavy on tired shoulders. They knew it was Jesus but had absolutely no idea what to do or what to say; they were spent, emotionally and physically.

Jesus broke the bread and distributed it with the fish to the ravenous fishermen. Seated on the rocky pier they devoured the unexpected meal. "Do you remember when we first met here over three years ago?" Jesus smiled as he surveyed the weary men who used to be so at ease in his presence and who were now exhausted and wrung out.

"Will never forget," said Peter. "You asked to borrow our boat on a morning we'd come back with nothing. You taught the crowd, but I was too tired to remember what you said. Then you had us go out and cast for fish. I thought you were an idiot. But anyway, we did what you asked, and our nets were full, just like today. I couldn't believe it."

"And now here we are again." Jesus held the gaze of each of the men: John, Thomas, Nathaniel, and Peter. "I love you guys. Thank you for all that you've given. I know only too well these last days have been hell for you. It will begin to make sense, I promise you. I'm not giving up on you; please don't give up on me. We've come a long way."

The men murmured assurances that they weren't going anywhere. When they had finished eating, Jesus stood up and addressed Peter.

"Simon, son of John, do you truly love me more than these" He gestured at the men and the boats.

"Yes Lord, you know that I love you," Peter responded without looking up.

"Feed my lambs," said Jesus. "Now you understand that I didn't call you because of your strength to obey but because you were willing to try."

"Simon, son of John, do you truly love me?" Jesus asked a second time.

"Yes Lord, you know that I love you," Peter replied, his voice stronger this time.

"Take care of my sheep." Jesus stepped closer and placed a hand on Peter's shoulder. "Don't carry the weight of your denial on these shoulders any longer. I'm not disappointed in you. When you know your weakness, you also discover my strength."

"Simon, son of John, do you love me?"

Peter's lips quivered; he blinked back tears as he looked up at Jesus and replied assuredly, "Lord, you know all things—you know that I love you."

"Feed my sheep. I tell you the truth, when you were younger, you dressed yourself and went where you wanted; but when you are old, you will stretch your hands, and someone else will dress you and lead you where you do not want to go. Follow me!"

Peter paused, looked around at the others, and then pointed to John, saying, "Lord, what about him?"

"If I want him to remain alive until I return, what is that to you? You must follow me. Don't compare yourself to anyone else." Jesus was taller than Peter and lifted his chin with a finger to look him in the eye. "Peter, you are the most faithful and bravest of men. I've never been disappointed with you. But you had to learn that your strength is rooted in my faithfulness to support you, not so much in your abilities alone. You're not the same man I called three years ago. You're more than ready." Jesus pulled him in and embraced him again.

Peter nodded and said nothing—stunned, spent, and mesmerized by what had just transpired. His greatest fear of being rejected and abandoned by Jesus had not materialized. He needed time to rest and gather his thoughts. Like a whisper, he felt the faint stirring of anticipation in his heart, and the relationship he thought he'd lost forever at last restored.

Gale snapped her fingers and it all melted away.

Chapter Twenty-Five

JACK SAT BESIDE RICKY, holding his hand. The nurse had left a few minutes earlier after a routine check-in. Brenda was asleep in the family room, Bill and Rachel talking quietly so as not to disturb her. Everything was still except for the rhythm of the machines providing a relentless reminder that Ricky's life was precariously balanced. The doctor had sent them a message that he'd meet with them in the morning.

Jack couldn't take his eyes off Ricky. He wanted to shake him, to wake him up, to say sorry for not being there enough, to invite him out for another fishing trip.

Their last one had been three years ago on Ricky's eleventh birthday. Jack had promised to take him out for the day. Ricky had been beside himself with excitement the night before. He'd told his friends that he was going fishing with his dad and they'd be leaving early in the morning, when it was still dark.

Ricky wasn't quite so enthusiastic when Jack woke him at 4:30.

"Time to get going, bud."

"I'm so tired, can't we go later?" Ricky pulled the blanket over his head and rolled toward the wall.

"Ok, we won't go then," Jack said casually. "Fish don't bite later so there won't be much point. Sleep well." He left the room and gathered up the breakfast and lunch Brenda had prepared for them. The fourteen-foot aluminum boat was already hooked up to the truck and all the gear was stowed. He started the engine and was doing a final check around the boat trailer when a disheveled, bleary-eyed Ricky appeared, yawning, and dragging his feet. He climbed into the truck without a word and Jack let him be.

They launched at the slipway down at the Harbor Quay only five minutes from their front door. Jack parked the dripping trailer and truck, while Ricky held the boat in the gentle chop of waves on the concrete boat launch. The light was breaking, wisps of clouds feathering a still and brightening sky; it was going to be a beautiful day.

Jack fired up the forty-horsepower Honda outboard. He reversed into deeper water, shoved the outboard hard left and accelerated down the inlet. It stretched like a Norwegian fjord for twenty kilometers through steep mountains and open marshes to the ocean. In the old days, huge tankers navigated through the narrow channel to load logs in Port Alberni bound for the Far East. Only very few came through these days. Ricky sat at the bow, wide awake now, wind blowing in his hair, a large grin across his face.

"Hold tight," Jack shouted. They picked up speed and the boat rose and fell as they hit the waves, which weren't excessively big at this early hour. The wind usually blew stronger in the afternoon, whipping down the inlet from the Pacific Ocean, making conditions more challenging. *Definitely the best time of day to be out here*, Jack thought. They soon passed Polly's Point and within twenty minutes slowed down at China Creek and began preparing the lines.

Jack showed Ricky how to fix the downriggers, one on each side of the boat. Steel wire attached to a weighted lead ball that hung over the side and could be lowered or raised manually with a large flat reel fastened to the side by the seat. They had fished together before, but now Ricky was old enough to share some of the tasks and was keen to learn. He fastened a swivel to his line, then measured three arm stretches long before attaching the lure.

"The sockeye loves bright lures and will follow them a long way before striking the bait," Jack told Ricky. "What do you want to use, fresh herring or a pink hoochie?"

"Hoochie," said Ricky.

"Ok, don't forget to pull off some of the tassels. To catch sockeye, less is more."

"Yeah, I remember that from last time," Ricky replied. The effort of launching the boat and the anticipation of the chase had energized Ricky, erasing the last vestiges of sleep from his eyes. He was ready.

Jack helped Ricky clip his line to the steel wire of the downrigger and they lowered the ball to about thirty feet. "Let's see how that works for you." Jack did the same with his line on the other side of the boat. "I'll set mine for fifteen, Ricky."

They placed their fishing rods in holders and Ricky proudly took the helm as they trolled slowly along the edge of the inlet not too far from the shoreline. The day had brightened as the sun rose behind the mountains, lighting the tops of the hills on the far shore. About fifteen other boats were scattered across the inlet.

"Look Dad," Ricky shouted, pointing ahead. "That guy has a fish on his line!"

"Good sign. Keep your eye on the rod tips; we don't want to miss our chance. Did I ever tell you about my friend Kyle when he was fishing with his dad?"

"No, I don't think so."

"They were on the other side of the island near Nanoose Bay, jigging and fishing for cod that feed on the bottom. Kyle said that he felt this tug and thought it was a smaller fish. He was casually reeling in and chatting with his dad when suddenly his rod was nearly ripped from his hands as something big grabbed the other end. Kyle said it was wild as his line reeled out fast. When he was finally able to wind it back in, he said it was like hauling in an old tyre."

"That sounds weird," said Ricky, all ears,

"When, with great effort, he pulled it to the boat they found a ten-pound salmon on the hook and a massive cod with half the salmon in his mouth. Its jaws were locked firm, so big they couldn't fit it into the net—probably about your size, Ricky."

"Wow," Ricky exclaimed. "Did they catch it?"

"Kyle said they tried but his dad couldn't really reach it with the gaff. Suddenly the big fish shook its head violently and swam away, leaving half a salmon still on the hook. That must have been exciting, eh?"

"That would be cool," Ricky said, standing up. "A fish my size—do they have any like that here?"

"I'm not sure," said Jack. "They used to catch large salmon back in the day up to fifty pounds, but I haven't heard of that happening for a long time."

They trolled in silence, each pondering the big fish story and what it must have been like. The boat puttered along with Ricky at the helm. Jack made sure the net was easily accessible for landing any fish they caught, as well as the wooden club handle to stun it.

"Dad?"

"Yes?" said Jack, turning to Ricky.

"Did you ever go fishing with your dad?"

"Not often that I can remember. He was always busy with work and wasn't that keen. Why are you asking?"

"Just wondered. When I said we were going fishing today, most of my friends were so jealous. They said they hardly ever did anything with their dads—some hardly ever even see their dads." Ricky bit into the peanut butter sandwich he had unwrapped. The comment caught Jack by surprise.

"That's too bad," said Jack. "Too many broken homes and absent fathers these days."

"Lots of my friends don't have dads at home." Ricky scrunched the empty wrapper from his sandwich and tucked it in the bag. "You're not around much, Dad. Mom cries when you're gone. Are you going to leave too?"

The words stung; Jack hadn't anticipated this conversation, certainly not today. "I'm sorry bud . . . Sometimes moms and dads have things they need to work out. We're no different. No, I don't want to leave you or your mom. I promise you that."

"Paul said his dad promised not to leave and then did anyway." Ricky looked around. They had trolled past the China Creek campsite and were heading toward Port Alberni. "Shall I turn now, Dad?"

"Sounds like a plan." Jack smiled. "Don't worry, Ricky, we'll work it all out."

It wasn't long after making the turn that Ricky saw the tip of his rod begin to bend and quiver.

"Dad, look at the rod—there's a fish on mine!" He was so excited he jumped across to take hold of the rod and forgot about the outboard and steering. The boat veered to the left before Jack grabbed hold and steadied their course.

"Whoa, he's a fighter," Jack said, as Ricky clutched his fishing rod tightly. "Go for it, Ricky—tip up, tight lines." Jack switched the engine to neutral and busied himself reeling in his line and then lifting the downriggers.

"Don't want the fish on your line snagged in them. Keep the tip of the rod up, release the reel, and keep your line tight, Rick. You know what to do. Be patient."

The reel ran out through Ricky's fingers, his face taut with concentration and a grin spreading from ear to ear. He began reeling in and then let it run as the fish fought. "It feels like a big one!" he exclaimed.

"Need any help?" Jack asked, knowing Ricky's response.

"No Dad, I can do this."

"You're doing great—keep reeling, watch that tip."

Ten minutes later a beaten and weary sockeye broke the surface alongside the boat. His head was pulled up on Ricky's taut line, no fight left, except for a feeble flick of the tail. Jack leaned over and scooped the dripping silvery mass on board in the net. "Good job." He gave Ricky a high five. "Well done, great catch."

"How big do you think he is, Dad?"

"Looks like a four- or five-pounder to me; they make really tasty eating. Let's get a picture."

Jack pulled out his phone while Ricky lifted his prize catch. His tanned face and arms exuded health. Bright blue eyes alive with pride, blonde hair tufting out beneath his cap. The sky behind him was cloudless, clear, and blue. A perfect day.

"Great photo, Ricky."

Ricky didn't need any persuading to get his line back in the water. Soon he and Jack were trolling again. Every twenty minutes Ricky lifted the lid of the icebox to check out his fish. "Time for another one in the box," he exclaimed, punching the air with his fist, his face all teeth and grin.

Three hours later they headed for home with three more sockeye on ice, making a grand total of four. Three were Ricky's and one was Jack's—much to Ricky's delight. As they turned the corner up the hill toward home, they saw balloons out front and a big sign proclaiming, "Happy Birthday Ricky!" in colorful lettering.

"Looks as if someone I know has a birthday surprise." Jack smiled at his son, who was straining to undo the safety belt and open the door before the truck had stopped in the drive. Ricky was out in a flash, bounding up the stairs. "Hey Mom! Guess how many fish I caught? It was awesome."

Brenda followed Ricky back to the car to view the catch. "Wow Ricky; you're quite the fisherman, eh! Better fry some of this to go with your birthday cake." She laughed and tousled his hair. They unpacked together amid chatter and banter.

Jack was carrying the icebox with fish upstairs when he heard a faint rhythmic beat followed by a higher beep that grew louder. His head was resting on the side of Ricky's bed and a hand was on his shoulder.

"Jack, wake up; I'll take over for a while."

Brenda stood beside him. He lifted his head and rubbed his eyes. "I was dreaming of the day I took Ricky fishing, remember?" He retrieved his phone from his pocket and scrolled through his photos. He found the one with Ricky proudly holding his fish. Big fish, bigger smile, and an entire lifetime ahead to experience and enjoy.

They looked at the photo. So much had happened since then.

"Yep, those were the days." She sighed.

"Do you think we can find them again?" Jack looked up at her, tears in his eyes.

She'd been through this so many times. His tears, his wanting a fresh start, her hopes rising only to be dashed within weeks.

"I honestly have no idea, JJ. It's hard to trust anymore, and now with this situation . . ." her voice trailed into a whisper as she looked out the window at her reflection staring back from the darkness. Why was it that these so-called tough guys were so weak and insecure inside, clueless about relationships and sharing responsibility? She didn't know what she wanted anymore.

"Why don't you get some sleep," Brenda suggested. "We'll talk later. I'll stay here with Ricky and sleep on the roll out."

Jack returned to the family room. Bill was asleep in the corner and Rachel was reading. She looked up and smiled. "Everything ok? Been a long, tough day all around. I'm so sorry, Jack."

"Thanks." Jack smiled wearily, his mind whirling from the stark incongruity of his vivid fishing dream and the reality of Ricky lying in a coma next door. Crowding in was the guilt of not being much of a father or a husband. So much so that a stranger had accompanied Brenda to the hospital because he'd been hungover on his couch.

"I guess you must think I'm a loser." Jack flopped down on the chair opposite Rachel and leaned back with his hands behind his head. He let out a long sigh, feeling awkward and exposed. "Brenda's no doubt told you our story."

"No, I don't see you as a loser, Jack." Rachel set aside her book and looked at him with no hint of judgment or accusation.

She leaned over and quietly whispered, "Let it out Jack. This is a safe place; you don't have to be a hero tonight."

The GAs were seated on benches in a large sports stadium that could hold over 200,000 spectators. It was empty, but a game was scheduled within two hours. They had promised to watch Yesaidu play soccer in the Village League. It was hugely popular, the stadium packed to capacity with cheering fans at every game. Even better was the atmosphere, both on and off the field. While the competition was real, there was no violence, no fouls, no red and yellow card warnings, no injuries. And to top it off, the refreshments were mouth watering and plentiful.

"Of course, we'd love to come!" they had enthusiastically agreed when he'd issued a shy invitation. "Let's do our InSight review before the game."

Yesaidu sported his village soccer jersey with pride—wide white and green horizontal stripes down the front with an emerald green back and collar. The letters "RV" emblazoned on the back—"Romero Village."

"Don't you look sharp?" Jenny exclaimed, punching him playfully in the arm, and then calling the group back to the task at hand. She flipped through her InSight. "Let's start back to front, at one of the most recent episodes we've reviewed. How about that memory Jack recalled of his day fishing with Ricky? Isn't it great that even memories are included in the downloads?"

"It was such a special time for a father and son. I was captivated," Yesaidu said.

"Why's that?" Asuka inquired, ever earnest and thoughtful.

"Ricky was so delighted to hang out with his dad and receive special attention. It was inspiring. And I think Jack enjoyed it too," Gregori said.

"And yet he never made the effort after that to do much with any of his kids. How does that work?" Yesaidu shook his head. "I mean, we all like to receive some attention that makes us feel loved, even here in heaven. Look at you all here, supporting me. I really appreciate it." He smiled broadly. "Although I'm a little nervous, to be honest."

"No worries; we're always here for you, man," Navo said, patting Yesaidu's back playfully.

"Thanks guys." The GAs smiled at Yesaidu and returned to their discussion.

"As Yesaidu commented, isn't it disturbing how easily Jack forgets that day and the impact he had on his son? I wonder why that is?" Jenny said, shifting in her seat.

"You know, I came across the phrase 'You can't give away what you've never received.' I wonder whether that isn't Jack's challenge?" Navo mused. "He hardly had any relationship with his father, so it isn't obvious or easy for him to be there for his own son. It's like he doesn't get it emotionally."

"Yet it sounded as if he was quite close with his mother even though she seemed to allow him to do whatever he wanted," Jenny added. "He said he was very upset when she died shortly before Ricky was born."

"That's interesting," Asuka agreed. "When Jack was describing his family to Bill earlier, they appeared to go on vacation together, yet they weren't close. I can't imagine what that's like—living in such emotional isolation, surrounded by mistrust and estrangement."

"And that disconnect is directed toward God as well." Nova flipped through his screenshots and paused at a picture of Bill and Jack talking together on the ferry. "Jack was pretty alienated from his father, and then didn't really have any idea about God as someone to encounter or to be supported by."

"Yeah, I remember," Gregori said. "Bill was talking to him about being a mechanic, whether it was strange to ask for help when someone had car troubles. I think Jack made the connection, sort of. I'm not sure he really understands though."

"How do you think their friends Bill and Rachel are coping?" Jenny asked. "I mean, I put myself in their situation and I freeze—what to say, what to do? Help!" She smiled.

"Don't get ahead of yourself, Jenny. Remember what Gale promised us? That she will always be with us to help, wherever we are." Navo looked around the group. "Isn't that right?"

"Thanks for the reminder, Navo. It's so easy to forget her promise." Yesaidu patted Navo on the shoulder, as he was sitting next to him. "I think Bill and Rachel are brilliant. Bill is really good at walking alongside Jack and works hard at making him feel comfortable. He uses language and metaphors that are easy for Jack to grasp."

"And Rachel is so patient and gentle with Brenda," Asuka jumped in. "I'm impressed with how she quietly serves her by bringing coffee, and driving, and just being available. Many of her words are spoken through her actions, which strikes me as really important."

"I noticed how Bill and Rachel are each playing a part in helping Jack and Brenda dial down—encouraging them to reflect more deeply about where they've been and where they want to go." Gregori studied his InSight, then looked up. "They were really stuck in a vicious cycle of anger, accusation, blame, and regret. Like freefalling without hope or direction. It was horrible to witness. As Asuka said, I can't imagine how it must be to live like that."

"Was I mistaken, or do you think they're beginning to soften, particularly as they spend time in the hospital with Ricky? I know that Brenda doesn't trust Jack, but I do think Bill and Rachel's presence and support are making a difference, don't you?" Jenny said.

"I agree," said Nova, standing up and stretching. "I remember a wise man talking to me once about how so much of nature quietly grows in the presence of the sun. A flower opens when it feels the warmth, for instance. It's not just the words Bill and Rachel speak. Just by being there, they bring God's presence into the lives of a couple who have never known such warmth and acceptance before. They gradually begin to open up despite themselves. As Guardian Angels I think a significant part of our mission is to intentionally create an unspoken atmosphere around those whom we walk beside. It touches their heart before they're even aware."

"That is so beautiful," Asuka said. "So many layers interlocking, wow!"

Yesaidu jumped to his feet. "Speaking of aware, I'm aware I've got to get going; time to warm up for the game. Thanks for being here with me. I'll meet you outside afterwards. But before that, I have a gift for each of you." He retrieved a bag from under his seat and handed out soccer jerseys to each of them, the same as he was wearing. "Make sure you wear them," he said with a wink. "You've got to show which side you support today."

"How cool! Thanks so much, Yesaidu!" the other GAs exclaimed.

They each embraced their brother, wishing him well. Excitement charged the air, as people began to fill the seats and music boomed from the speakers.

"This is going to be fun. Anyone know anything about soccer?" Gregori asked, having donned his new attire.

"Absolutely!" Jenny exclaimed. "Listen up, I'll give you a quick and simple run down of how it works . . ."

Chapter Twenty-Six

THE GAS SURVEYED THE Tudor-inspired interior of the pub in Jenny's village where she'd invited them to debrief. A log fire flickered in a fireplace framed by a heavy wooden mantel; wooden beams holding the low, sagging roof, with supporting beams straddling the ceiling every couple of feet. The setting was straight out of an English village and similar ones were scattered throughout the area. Jenny had reserved a private room for her fellow GAs, who were joined by Pappa G, Jesus, Gale, and Peter.

They were seated at a long oak table with a variety of drinks before them: beer, wine, coffee, tea, and soft drinks. As neither caffeine nor alcohol existed in heaven, the GAs could savor their drinks without any danger of, or desire for, intoxication.

"Peter, you experienced so much with Jesus before he was crucified—you walked on water with him, and you spent almost three years by his side. Why were you so surprised when he was crucified?" Nova was the first to ask a question.

Peter was a small, ruddy-complexioned, muscular man, oozing energy, and charisma. He found it difficult to sit still. He stood up and began pacing as he talked.

"Many people in Earthtime wish they could have been around at the time of Jesus; they think that it would have been easier to believe. But they have no idea!" He waved his arms. "If they'd been there, like I was, they'd see. Living then was no dream or romantic fantasy; it was hard for us as well, and very confusing. I'm a practical man, brought up to work with my hands and to make things happen. We had to build boats, fabricate nets, catch fish, take our catch to market—all of it. We learned by trial and error. I guess that's how I've always approached life."

"Would you do things differently now?" Asuka asked with a shy smile.

"I don't have much time for wondering 'what if?' I tend to jump first and am not afraid of risk. I experienced some wonderful moments with Jesus. But with all that enthusiasm I often did not really think things through enough. I sometimes assumed I understood, when maybe . . ." Peter shrugged and raised his hands. "Maybe not, I hate to admit."

"You weren't afraid to question or speak your mind, that's for sure," Gregori commented.

Peter smiled. "Jesus used to get frustrated with me and soon learned that subtlety did not work. That's why he was so blunt and didn't mince his words. I refused to believe that Jesus was about to die. After all, we were beginning to build momentum and gain a following. I thought we were just starting and that he'd be around a long time."

"Did you see Jesus as weak?" Gregori leaned back. He sipped at a pint of dark ale from a heavy glass mug, leaving the merest hint of a foam mustache above his upper lip.

"Sometimes I wondered whether he feared conflict, particularly when he wanted to wash my feet and talked about being a servant. He hardly challenged Judas at all—just let him go about his business. When the soldiers showed up in Gethsemane to arrest Jesus, I lunged forward in his defense. No one seemed to be doing anything!"

Peter paused as he paced in front of the fire. He retrieved his glass of ale from the heavy oak mantel, gulped a mouthful, and replaced it. Rubbing his hands together, he continued. "I wasn't going to passively watch as Jesus was led away under Roman guard. I didn't understand that what he was doing was far more courageous than I could ever have imagined. When you are a person who likes to make things happen, it is extremely hard to let go of the instinctive desire to control events. Sitting around 'waiting' is virtually impossible."

"When you were questioned after Jesus' arrest and denied knowing him, what were you thinking?" Nova inquired.

"So much was going on; frankly, everything seemed out of control. I lost my bearings; I panicked. The Roman soldiers are ruthless and brutal. I was scared that I would be dragged off with Jesus, so I said whatever came into my head at the time. I didn't even think I was denying him until I heard the rooster crow. It startled me. As I looked through the crowd and saw Jesus being led away, I froze. I will never forget the look on his face when his gaze caught mine—sad understanding tinged with disappointment. I couldn't handle it; I ran away. I realized that I had betrayed my best friend. in my mind, I was nothing but a weakling with a big mouth."

"I understand that," empathized Jenny. "But then you witnessed Jesus' resurrection appearances! Why were you not more excited when you went back to fishing in Galilee?"

"When you have the benefit of history and perspective, it is always much easier to be sensible, isn't it? Or maybe you don't know what that's like." Peter continued to pace in front of the fireplace. He tugged his bearded chin. "The idea of someone rising from the dead was crazy; I had no idea what would happen next. I fluctuated between hoping that Jesus was alive somehow, to a deep despair and anger that my last three years had been smashed into nothing. Then he appeared and was gone again—what did that mean?"

"Did the other disciples feel the same way?" Asuka asked.

"We certainly all had questions and doubts—not only Thomas, that's for sure. But to finish my earlier comment: I felt enormous guilt because I'd let Jesus down, not to mention myself. I thought I was tougher, more resilient. I was disappointed and disillusioned with myself and wasn't sure how Jesus would respond if we ever met again. I was scared, frightened, angry, tired, irritated, depressed—and not much fun to be around! It was all such a chaotic jumble of thoughts and emotions." Peter shuddered. "It was awful, very lonely, and hard for others to understand. I think I've belabored my point, got the message?" Peter smiled as he looked around the room.

"When did it change? On the beach after you caught the fish?" asked Yesaidu.

"Yes. On our way down to Galilee, John and I talked about Jesus' death on the Cross. John at least had had the guts to remain with him and his mother while the rest of us ran—"

"Sorry to interrupt." A tall, slightly balding man in an apron appeared at the door carrying a large brown teapot. "Anyone like a top up? Just made a fresh pot. I believe our new order came from your neck of the woods," he said, nodding at Asuka.

"Lovely James, thank you." Pappa G raised his bright red mug to be filled.

"Me too, please." Asuka smiled. "Have to support the village, don't we?"

"Anything else I can get anyone while I'm here?" James asked, looking around the table. "No offers? Alrighty then, I'll leave you to it."

"Where was I?" Peter mused.

"Going down to Galilee with John," Jenny reminded him.

"Oh yes, thanks Jenny." Peter nodded his head. "John told us what happened and how Jesus died; then, I recalled some of the other things Jesus had said while we were with him on the road. But I still couldn't put it all together. I was too wrapped up in my own guilt. I felt such a coward, and to be honest, envied John's courage. I never expected him—the youngest of all the disciples—to show such strength. We always used to tease him about that. Everything changed when Jesus said my name and embraced me; that's when my fear and shame dissolved."

Pappa G put his arm around Peter's shoulders. "You know, courage is not something you experience in a vacuum, where fear is absent. Courage is how you behave precisely *when* you are afraid. Courage is what it takes to pick yourself up and dare to persevere and try again. This man illustrates that."

"I need to add one more thing, if that's ok?" Peter asked.

"Go ahead," said Pappa G.

"I'd never have made it after that rooster crowed without my brothers and sisters. They never abandoned me, judged me, or left me to walk alone. When I was despairing and at rock bottom, they were by my side. When I said I was going fishing, they came along despite my foul mood. We made it through together, we finished what we started together, and we continued together."

"So true, well said." Jesus clapped and addressed the GAs. "What's a takeaway for you? What have we learned that could apply for those you will walk alongside? Let's go around and name something that strikes you. Nova, how about we start with you."

"That you can be sincerely wrong? Just because you are passionate and believe strongly doesn't make you right."

"That no matter what mistakes you make, God will never reject you if you're willing to say sorry and change," Jenny answered.

Gregori raised a hand. "Sometimes one can overestimate what they can handle—like Peter thought he was braver than he actually was."

"Adding to that thought," Asuka interjected, "God has no problem with people struggling, questioning, or even expressing anger. We don't have to pretend; God is big enough to handle all our emotions and still love us. That's what I learned from Peter."

"Very good," said Jesus. "Yesaidu, one more from you?"

"Well, you guys took all the easy ones . . . I'm not sure. Maybe that following Jesus doesn't always mean you'll understand reasons, or that life will be easy, without fear, panic, and hardship. In other words, faith can be challenging sometimes. How's that?" Yesaidu smiled and touched his nose.

"All are truths well worth remembering during your assignments," Gale said. "I'll leave you with this final thought to ponder, Jesus was faithful to his disciples no matter how unfaithful they were to him. None of us are disillusioned by human behavior. I think I've mentioned that a few times now. We are for each person—never against them just because they fail or disappoint from time to time. We love grace in word and in action; and that's ultimately what Peter's story is all about."

Chapter Twenty-Seven

BRENDA WOKE THURSDAY MORNING with bright sun streaming through the window. At first, she was disoriented until she heard the familiar rhythmic thrumming of the ventilator. She paled, then took a deep breath and caught her bearings. Across the room lay Ricky. *Could he be awake?* she thought, clinging to a tattered shred of hope. "Good morning Ricky. Wake up, it's a beautiful day."

No response. Throwing aside her blanket, she got up and walked to his bedside. Ricky hadn't moved. Brenda reached out and stroked his cheek; it was cool. "Ricky, I love you so much—please don't leave us. You've got to fight." No response. Same as yesterday. Same as when she knelt by his side at the curb after the accident. Tears rolled down her cheeks. She didn't bother to wipe them away.

There was gentle knock at the door. The morning shift nurse entered.

"Good morning, Mrs. Willard. I'm Christine. How's Ricky today?"

"No sign of change as far as I can see," Brenda whispered, wiping her wet cheeks.

"It takes time," the nurse said gently. "I'm here to check Ricky's vitals and freshen him up. Why don't you take a break and we'll be done here in about an hour?"

"Ok, thank you. You guys are so patient and kind . . . I don't know how you do it day after day."

Passing Brenda a Kleenex, Christine said, "I guess it's because we have families of our own. I have two children around the same age as your Ricky. I can't begin to imagine what you're going through, but I know that if he were my son, I'd want only the best care for him. So, if there's anything I can do to help . . . ?"

"You already are, you already are." Brenda smiled as best she could. "Thank you."

Brenda decided to grab a coffee downstairs. She knew she probably looked a wreck but was beyond caring. Exiting the elevator on the ground floor, she walked wearily along the corridor to the cafeteria. Fortunately, there was no lineup—the last thing she wanted to do was swap sob stories with a stranger. She ordered a medium coffee with cream, no sugar, and a bran muffin, then found a seat by a large window. As she idly picked at the muffin and sipped the coffee, she noticed how tired and dreary the place looked. *Like me—in need of a facelift*, she thought. Outside, there was evidence of building and new expansion plans underway.

Brenda wished her mom could be with her. She thought of her every day. Mary, a down-to-earth, attractive woman with a positive can-do attitude, effusive in showing her love for her two children and her husband, Don. Brenda recalled her mom telling her how she'd met him at an office Christmas party. "I knew that he was the one as soon as I set eyes on him," she said with a wistful look in her eye. Don was fifteen years older than Mary, but age was no barrier to the man she called her soulmate.

Before marrying Don, Mary had worked in an insurance office for eighteen years. Don was employed as a millwright in the local pulp mill. "Don't know why it took us so long to find one another in the same town, but it was worth the wait," she would say with a smile. Mary often told Brenda that being a wife and a mother was "her calling" and that she felt entirely fulfilled in those roles. "Never missed my secretarial work one bit." And Brenda knew it was the truth.

She was one of the most contented people Brenda had ever known, never complaining, and invariably looking at the positive side of life and circumstances. "You can always find something to be thankful for," she'd say. "I prefer to spend five minutes on the problem and the rest on working out a solution. There are some things you can't change, but how we respond is our choice." Brenda had witnessed her living out the truth of these words in the toughest of situations, especially when her brother Paul was ill and when her mother was diagnosed with breast cancer.

Both parents attended the Christian Reformed Church on the other side of town. They never missed a Sunday, and Brenda and Paul were expected to accompany them. She dutifully attended but found little to relate to, particularly as she grew into her teenage years. She'd learned the stories of Jesus but the application to her life was missing, mired in rules and expectations. The thought of a God who loves unconditionally was comforting, as was the message of Easter and Christmas—Brenda loved the Christmas lights, the gifts, the nativity, the carols—but as for the rest, it seemed stuffy and all about being on your best behavior. She just didn't fit in.

Eventually, she managed to persuade her parents to allow her to take a pass on Sundays. But that was only after she'd spent six months trying to be enthusiastic about the youth group. Games and pizza at fifteen with kids mostly younger than her was hardly fun. "I've tried, Mom, but if I'm forced to go it will probably put me off for life." To Brenda's surprise, her father agreed.

"When I was your age my parents made me attend church and I hated it," he said. He was a short man with a kind smile beneath an over-hanging mustache and slicked back silver hair, always long over his collar, despite Mary's frequent appeals that he visit Jimmy the barber. "Attending church didn't seem to do much for them," her dad continued. "My father still drank like a fish and both argued behind the closed doors of our pic-ture-perfect house. I rebelled and refused; it was only after much plead-ing from your mother that I set foot in a church again. Mary, let's give Bren freedom to explore her life and make up her own mind." Brenda's father winked at her as his wife sighed and agreed with some reticence.

"Ok," her mother conceded. "I just worry about the influences out there. Don't want you to fall in with the wrong crowd."

"Don't worry, Mom; I'll be ok. I'm not going to become a drug ad-dict because I don't attend church every week."

However, peer pressure and the desire for acceptance, friends, and a "good time" did cause Brenda to slowly drift. What started as just one drink, or the occasional joint with a few friends, led to a succession of drunken, drug-filled parties, with more than one amorous liaison.

In her last year at school, Brenda enrolled for nursing at North Island College and was looking forward to getting out of town and beginning a new path. Before she left, there was just one more party. Jack would be there; they'd been dating for a few months, but up to then, with Brenda's future hanging in the balance, she had resisted Jack's advances. But on this perfect late summer's evening by the moonlit lake, the combination of one too many drinks, a skinny dip, and overactive hormones would lead Brenda down a different path.

A short while later Brenda discovered she was pregnant. Abortion wasn't a viable choice as far as they were concerned. She and Jack had dis-cussed their options and neither of them wanted to make such a drastic decision. "I couldn't live with myself," Brenda said. Jack had said that it was ultimately up to her what she wanted to do; maybe she didn't want him around. "I want to marry you," he said. What could she do? Nursing was a dream that would have to be put on hold. Her parents were hardly thrilled at the turn of events but supported her, "because you're our daughter and we love you very much."

Consequently, instead of heading to college in September, she was walking down the aisle to marry Jack. Six months later, Ricky was born, a few months after Jack's mother suffered her fatal aneurism. All Brenda's apprehension and regret melted away the moment Ricky burst forth into her world. He was such a gift, and she promised herself that one day she would pursue her dream of nursing. *One day . . .*

Brenda sighed at the memory, glancing around the cafeteria. Nurses changing shift grabbed a coffee or slumped into chairs after a long night. *I was meant to be one of them*, she mused.

Simon was born two years after Brenda. She adored her little brother. He had brown hair, blue eyes, and the cheekiest giggle accentuating his cute dimples. They played together all the time and "Bwenda" relished her role as the responsible older sister, always fussing over him. Then it all abruptly ended. When Simon was five years old, he developed a cough which progressed into pneumonia. Within two weeks he had died. She couldn't process what had happened. For weeks afterwards she would lie on his bed hugging the bear he called Panda and cry.

"Why did Simmie die, Mommy?" she'd ask night after night.

"God only knows, darling. I miss him as much as you do and have lots of questions. I don't know. It's the worst thing in the world for a mother to lose a child . . ."

"And a sister to lose a brother." Brenda squeezed her mother's hand.

"Yes, and a sister." A tear ran down her mother's cheek as she bent over to kiss Brenda and put on a brave face. "We can't bring our little Simmie back, but we can hold him tight in our hearts. We'll always love him and never forget him, right?"

Brenda nodded and hugged Panda tighter. "Can I have a picture of Simmie in my room?"

"Of course, you can."

Nearly thirty years later that picture had never left her bedside table.

"Too many losses," Brenda said under her breath, as she sipped her coffee and ran her fingers through knotted hair.

More tragedy was to follow ten years later, when Brenda came home one day to find her mother and father in the living room, their expression grave. Her heart sank as her mother proceeded to tell her the bad news. "I've just received reports from tests that I have stage three breast cancer."

"What does that mean?" Brenda asked, wanting to run away and bury her head in her pillow.

"It means that I have a large growth in my right breast, which is quite advanced, but they don't think it's spread too far yet. I have to start chemotherapy as soon as possible."

"Are you going to die?" Brenda blurted it out as she knelt at her mother's knees and looked up at the one person who'd been her anchor and rock her entire life.

"No, Brenda, we're going to fight this. Lots of people survive cancer and I'm going to do the same—with God's help." She stroked Brenda's cheek. "It'll be all right, you'll see."

Brenda's father said nothing but the deep sadness in his eyes spoke of his silent sorrow. She got up and hugged him. He held her tight; no words were necessary.

Her mother fought bravely for three years—losing her hair after chemotherapy and joking about the scarves she fashioned into headgear. She tried various naturopathic solutions, quipping one day, "I've been eating so many carrots my complexion is taking on an alluring orange tinge. Suits me, don't you think?" The church prayed and meals were delivered after her treatments. But eventually she weakened and began to waste away to almost nothing. Mary died on a bed in the living room with Brenda and her dad by her side.

Her dad seemed to drift away after her mother's death; he'd lost his best friend and guiding light. He was only in his early sixties when he began to struggle with his memory and became increasingly confused and disoriented.

"You're too young for this, Dad." Brenda's words weren't strong enough to halt the slide. Before much longer he was in a care home. She had visited him there only days before the accident and had to remind him of her name.

"You look far away. Mind if I join you?"

Brenda was jolted from her thoughts back into the hospital cafeteria. Bill smiled down at her as he slid back a chair and placed a mug of coffee on the table.

"Not at all," Brenda smiled weakly. "Afraid I'm rather a mess but I needed space and some caffeine."

Bill nodded and looked at his mug clasped firmly between his hands. "What a hard thing for you to have to go through. I know that words are so limited, but I am sorry." His expression of empathy comforted her. It dawned on her that she couldn't recall the last time she had felt the understanding and strength of a man. For too long she had yearned for it to come from Jack.

"I'm so scared. We have a meeting scheduled with the doctor later this morning. I think I know what I'm going to hear; I can't bear it." Brenda blinked away tears and looked out the window.

"There's no simple and easy response to this one," Bill said quietly. "Just know that you're not alone, Brenda."

"That's hard to believe; certainly feels that way. I was just thinking about the family I've lost—my brother when he was only a little boy, my mom. My own father doesn't recognize me anymore, and my husband has been absent from my life for so long it's hard to believe anyone cares . . ."

"Jack loves you; you do know that don't you?"

"I have no idea anymore. I find myself caring even less. He's disappointed me too many times. I don't trust anything that comes from his lips." Brenda sighed. "You know, I should be wearing scrubs and working here," Brenda continued. "That was the dream—to be a nurse. I gave it all up for him. It would have been worth it if he'd just loved me and been there for me; instead, I've raised his three children almost single-handedly."

"That's not easy for you or the children," said Bill.

"Believe me, it's not been easy . . . but a small part of me knows that it's not fair to throw it all on him. Maybe if he'd been more supportive, I could have found time to study and care for the children. It may have been possible with some help. Honestly, as far as I'm concerned, Jack has behaved like a spoiled brat who must be indulged. I don't trust him for one minute."

"I don't blame you at all." Bill leaned back in the chair. "You'd be crazy to trust him right now. But I must tell you, having spent some time with him over the past few days, he seems to be serious about making changes and fighting for you."

Brenda rose from the table. "It wouldn't be the first time he's said that. I'll believe it when I see it." The expression on her face was one of resignation. "Please excuse me, I'd better go and make myself presentable and get back to Ricky. Thanks for the chat. I do appreciate your concern, truly."

She walked slowly down the long passage into the bright new foyer of the Pediatric Wing and found an elevator ready and waiting. As the doors closed, she looked at the backlit walls with pictures of Bambi and bunnies surrounding her. Her heart constricted her throat as she wondered what she'd find on the fourth floor.

Chapter Twenty-Eight

"WHAT'S GOING ON?" GREGORI asked, brow furrowed in alarm. "This looks serious."

The GAs stood on a rocky mound anxiously watching the scene playing out below them: a boisterous crowd following a group of men storming up the road leading out of the city. The mood was ugly, shouts and jeers charging the air with an edge that grew in violent intensity as the group closed in. The focus of their fury? A man of average build, hands cuffed behind him, being roughly shoved up the hill. With every blow that rained down on him—piercing accusations of "stone him," "traitor," "blasphemer"—the GAs winced, averting their eyes. It was early evening, the sun not yet set, the atmosphere dark.

"Why are they treating him like this?" asked Jenny.

"His name is Stephen," replied Jesus. "A few hours ago he addressed the Sanhedrin and has been accused of blasphemy. They are offended because he challenged them for resisting the work of God and the Holy Spirit. He outlined their common Jewish history but also challenged their unwillingness to be open to God and the promises contained in their Scriptures. The one thing religious leaders will not tolerate is having their traditions questioned, or their spiritual integrity. Stephen is a brave man who is about to die for me."

"But why kill the man for that?" said Yesaidu, shaking his head.

"Human beings are capable of wonderful sensitivity and tenderness, and also a brutality that will shock you to the core—as you've already witnessed," Pappa G answered. "They can very easily become trapped in power struggles. They feel the need to be right and are terrified of losing control. Once people taste power, it becomes like a drug that they cannot do without, whether in the church or in government. The human ego is extremely fickle and unreliable when left unchecked; it's invariably a matter of the heart not the mind that is stung by the forked tongue of the evil one."

The roar from the crowd grew much louder now. A large seething circle had coiled around Stephen standing alone at the center, giving every appearance of being calm amid the hissing chaos. At the fringe of the throng, to the left side, another man watched intensely. Relatively young and of an unassuming stature, he evidently commanded a position of power and respect amongst those gathered before him. Some men placed their outer clothing at his feet and chatted to him before heading back into the fomenting circle.

"Who is that?" asked Asuka.

"He's a rising star, Saul of Tarsus. Very influential. He intends to suppress this new 'Jewish sect' that has arisen since my resurrection," Jesus answered. "Saul is very well educated and is passionate about his religion and the traditions of his fathers. He believes that Stephen and the other followers should be imprisoned or killed before matters get out of hand. He is tough and decisive, convinced that he is being faithful to his God by stamping out this new movement as swiftly and ruthlessly as possible."

"This is a conflict between people who all believe in God?" Yesaidu shook his head. "I thought a shared belief would help?"

"I'm afraid that's often not the case," said Jesus. "Here, they are passionately disagreeing about whether I'm the Messiah. Stephen is declaring that I am the fulfilment of prophecy, while Saul and others oppose the idea. Primarily because my life and teaching doesn't fit into their box about how the Messiah will appear."

"Don't they expect you to do the unexpected sometimes, if you are God?" Nova asked.

"You'll discover that most people in Earthtime prefer me to be distant and abstract—a God in whom they can believe, but who never speaks, never acts, never challenges. They love a religious tradition that is safe and familiar, where they can admire me from a distance like some caged animal. Essentially that's where Saul is trapped, and why they crucified me."

"I find that hard to comprehend." Nova shook his head.

Saul surveyed the crowd, his penetrating eyes lingering on the solitary figure calmly awaiting his fate. He eventually gave the nod to the men gathered around Stephen. At once they raised their hands and their voices in unison and began hurling rocks and stones at him.

"Why won't you do something?" said Gregori, tugging on Jesus' sleeve.

"I could stop them now—just as Pappa G could have saved me from the crucifixion. The problem is that free will is unconditionally given within broad parameters. We cannot change core principles whenever we don't like something, no matter how much we would prefer to do so. Imagine how I felt when John was beheaded? Watch," said Jesus.

The crowd of men laughed and jeered with every rock that was thrown; even some of the children joined in. Stephen, bleeding profusely from head wounds, fell to his knees and mouthed, "Lord Jesus, receive my spirit." No fear was written on his face; in fact, he appeared to those watching to be radiant, more alive than ever. Looking straight at Saul, he continued, "Lord, do not hold this sin against them."

A large stone thudded into the side of Stephen's head. He slumped silently to the earth as the men continued to pommel his body in a mad frenzy long after it lay motionless. They didn't relent until Stephen was half buried beneath a mound of stones and curses.

"Enough!" shouted Saul angrily, his face red with rage. "Now go and find the others and let's put an end to this godless insurrection once and for all!"

The crowd began to disperse and dribbled slowly back toward the city. Stephen's bloody, broken body lay face down, detritus scattered around him, like the ruins of a mighty tower.

"What now?" asked Yesaidu.

"Friends will bury him after dark. They're too scared to come out now. Saul has already authorized that anyone affiliated with his movement should be arrested," Gale explained. "I know this is difficult to stomach, but Stephen accomplished something especially important today, far beyond what he understood or what you have seen. You couldn't see me, but I was right there with him, giving him courage and comfort." Gale's eyes surveyed the distant hills. "I'm always present to do that for anyone who asks me. We have no favorites."

"It looks as if you don't care, and evil always wins," Yesaidu said bluntly.

"Looks can be deceiving, can't they?" Gale smiled. "Our ways are not always apparent to those in Earthtime. Do you want to see what Stephen saw as he died?" Gale swept her arm in front of them, and once again they saw Stephen bleeding, kneeling among the rocks and dust, looking up at Saul. Behind Saul and all around stood a vast army of angels with raised swords. "Stephen, Stephen, take courage, the Lord is with you!" They repeated those words again and again. The GAs gasped in awe. Gale waved her arm again and they disappeared.

"Oh, my goodness!" exclaimed Navo. "Who would have known such a mighty army was so close? Why didn't they save Stephen?"

"As I said, our ways are not the ways of those in Earthtime. We would love to have intervened, and we did to some degree. But our picture and plans are much bigger and broader," Jesus replied.

"Was anything worthwhile accomplished in this barbaric encounter?" Jenny asked, clearly grappling with what had unfolded.

"Stephen's final prayer and the vivid memory of Stephen's death will haunt Saul," Gale said. "He's no longer quite so sure of himself. He will bury this unfamiliar doubt deep within himself and will increase his hostility toward believers in these next days. This ugly event is critical in the life of Saul; the blood of Stephen is on his hands and has seeped into his conscience, fertilizing, and nourishing a new seed of faith."

"Surely you can accomplish that without such cruel violence?" Jenny addressed her question to Pappa G.

"The harshest truth to learn in Earthtime is that actions and choices have consequences. Often innocent people are hurt in the crossfire. Life is never fair on that side of heaven, certainly not where the snake works his curses. People need a revelation about his lies and to realize that even physical death itself is not the final word. That revelation is usually not with mere words. Sometimes it is most powerfully revealed in the way people live and even face their own death. Saul witnessed Stephen dying boldly, with forgiveness on his lips. Such a testimony defies rational logic, which Saul has valued so highly all his life. And that's what unsettles him."

"We'll chat more about this, but right now I think Gale wants us to head out to another venue." Jesus beckoned them to follow him.

Jenny noted how tall he was without his wheelchair.

Chapter Twenty-Nine

"HOW'S RICKY?"

Brenda entered the room to find Jack at his bedside. She'd willed herself to have a shower, and her hair was still damp. She hadn't bothered with makeup. She wore track pants and a loose blue sweat top with a large Nike "swoosh" across the front. *Just do it*, she said to herself as she tugged it over her head. *Do what? Open the door to Jack or close it for the last time?* She shrugged. *I can't think about that now. Ricky is my focus and I'm damned if Jack's going to manipulate me through Bill.*

Jack turned his head as Brenda approached the bed. "No change." His voice was soft. He looked tired. "God it's hard to be here without any response. He just lies there; it feels sooo helpless."

Brenda sat opposite Jack, on the other side of the bed. She took hold of Ricky's hand and stroked his fingers. "Hey Ricky, squeeze my hand if you can hear me." Brenda fixed her eyes on Ricky's fingers limply intertwined in hers. The fleeting hope flooding up from within her dissipated just as fast.

"What happens next?" Jack looked across at Brenda. He wrestled to contain his emotions. The upwelling caught him off guard. He knew what Brenda thought of him. He wanted to tell Brenda he was ashamed and sorry. He wanted to promise that he'd be different from now on, but he was afraid of her reaction. *Typical of you Jack, always avoiding the hard stuff. Anyway, now's not the right time; she's got enough on her plate*, his inner voice goaded him relentlessly.

"Jack!" Brenda leaned across and shook his arm. "I'm talking to you."

"Sorry Bren. Yes, what is it?"

"Do you remember we have a meeting with the doctor soon, nine thirty?"

"Where are we meeting?"

"In the family waiting room. Do you want Bill to be there? I think I'd like Rachel present."

"Sure, maybe good to have him around. He never seems to get flustered."

"Why don't you go and give them the heads up and I'll follow shortly." Brenda stood up to stroke Ricky's hair and bent over to kiss him.

"Sure." Jack nodded and left the room.

The ventilator waltzed, the monitor beeped, and Brenda bit her quivering lip.

Half an hour later, they gathered in the family room with Doctor Pollard.

Smiling weakly, he addressed the group. Brenda tense and taut in her seat as she awaited the update. "I hope you all got some sleep last night," he began. "This is a nightmare for any parent, I'm aware of that. I have a teenage daughter and a younger son. I dread to think how I'd respond faced with what you're enduring." He paused, acknowledging Brenda and Jack in turn with a nod. "I'm afraid the news isn't great."

Brenda gasped and began to cry. Rachel placed her arm around her and pulled her tight. Jack leaned forward, his elbows on his knees, and hung his head. Bill's hand rested on his shoulder. No words, yet again.

Doctor Pollard scratched his tousled head and explained the situation as gently as he knew how. He hated this part of his job—when a life slipped through his fingers and no matter what he tried, it ebbed away.

"We're assessing Ricky continuously to check his vital signs, pressure build up in the brain, and for any indications of improvement."

"What would improvement look like?" Brenda asked with a whisper.

"Some sensitivity to touch, increased eye movement, and a decrease in the intracranial pressure. Until now Ricky has been sedated; we're going to withdraw those medications to see how he responds. This is not an exact science, and we can only do so much."

"If he were your kid . . . ?" Jack interjected.

"I'd be doing exactly what I'm doing for yours," Dr. Pollard assured him. "I would want the doctor to be up front and candid with me and my family."

"So honestly, do you think Ricky has any chance of recovery?" Jack voiced the question that everyone was thinking.

"On a scale of one to ten, where ten is full recovery, I'd have to say it's slipping to perhaps three at this time. Barring a miracle, the prognosis for Ricky isn't looking hopeful."

"Is he in pain?" Brenda asked.

"Fortunately, no. While it's excruciating for us, Ricky has no awareness of what is happening. He's not suffering at all."

"What do we do now?" Brenda asked, her voice a barely audible whisper.

"As I've explained, over the next few days we will be constantly assessing Ricky's condition, particularly as we ease his sedation meds. Other than that, it's a case of giving him more time and waiting to see. I'd encourage you to go for walks and get some fresh air. Try to process what we've been talking about as best you can together. If there's anything you need to ask me, please don't hesitate; you have my contact info."

"Thanks doc. I appreciate you being upfront with us." Jack stood up and shook his hand.

"One day at a time," he said. "We'll do everything we can. Take care."

As Dr. Pollard left the room, Brenda collapsed next to Rachel. "This is a friggin' nightmare. How will we manage? I can't imagine going home without Ricky being there."

"I hope you don't mind . . ." Bill cleared his throat. "This morning I booked a family room at the Ronald McDonald House across the road. It's like an apartment with a couple of rooms, laundry, kitchen, and washroom. Their policy restricts each family to a single unit so I couldn't get separate ones for each of you." Bill looked across at Jack and Brenda. "I'm not trying to make it awkward for you. You can agree to use it at different times."

"Thanks Bill." Jack stood up and stretched. "I guess you'll be heading home?"

"Rachel and I have talked, and we've decided to stay as long as you need us. We booked rooms in a hotel nearby."

"I don't know how to thank you . . ." Brenda began, then her voice became businesslike. "Jack you can use the apartment for now; I'm going to Ricky." She picked up her bag and left the room; Rachel followed.

"How are you doing?" Bill turned to Jack, who was checking his phone, tethered to the wall plug as it recharged.

"I'm trying not to run. Brenda hasn't given me an inch—not sure what I was expecting. And I'm f****d if I know how to deal with Ricky probably never coming home again."

"Brenda needs time," Bill said. "I think I heard her mention 'we' a few times. There's a lot going on. Be patient, Jack."

"There are so many 'if onlys' in my head. Now it's too late. Maybe you shouldn't have fished me out of the lake after all—"

"I pulled you out of the lake because your life is precious, Jack. I pulled you out because you bought into the lie that all was lost. It's never too late to change and make new beginnings. You're no different from anyone else. You can become a great father and a loving husband if you want to. The choice is yours. It takes commitment and work, but the rewards far outweigh the costs. It's really up to you."

"But Brenda . . ."

"Stop waiting for Brenda, accusing Brenda, blaming Brenda," Bill said, leveling his gaze. Jack froze, surprised at Bill's sudden change of tone. "This is on *you*, not her. If I were in her shoes, I certainly wouldn't have much time for you; there've been way too many betrayals and disappointments, empty words, broken promises. You said so yourself."

Jack stood at the window, not really looking at anything, the words stinging, though he knew them to be true. Turning to Bill, hands plunged deep in his jean pockets, he said, "Bill, I'm scared s***less. My oldest son is in a coma on life support, my marriage is hanging by a thread. What if I lose everything?"

"There's a lot of tough stuff in front of you, enough to overwhelm anyone. But you do have some choices, particularly as regards your future with Brenda. No guarantees of course." Bill joined Jack at the window. "From what I can tell," he continued, "Brenda may have closed the door, but I get the feeling that's it's still unlocked. Maybe she's waiting for you to knock, ever so gently. Maybe she'll give you one more chance."

"How do I do that?" Jack removed his hands from his pockets and held them, empty, in front of him.

Bill smiled. "I guess that's for you to figure out."

Chapter Thirty

"WE'RE VISITING ANOTHER ROAD outside a different city," said Gale. "*On the road again . . .*" Gale hummed the tune and laughed. "We're way more fun than most people in Earthtime realize. They seem to believe we're stuck in rules, hidden behind stained-glass windows, always behaving like perfect angels . . ." She winked at the gathered GAs. "And that we only sing worship songs. That would be dull, don't you think? After all, we created music—every note, every instrument, and every style."

Gregori laughed. "I can sing the Russian song 'Katyusha' like Ivan Rebroff." His voice let rip into the lyrical song and surprised them all. He sang of apples and pear trees and mist on the river. Of Katyusha walking along the riverbank singing with longing for her true love.

After holding the last note impressively long, Gregori bowed. "The first two verses anyway."

Jesus applauded. "That was excellent, Gregoritov. We'll have to have a concert sometime."

"Don't think so," said Nova. "I can't sing; I'm tone deaf."

"Oh dear, you're sounding like Moses. Maybe you could if you tried." Gale nudged his shoulder before refocusing the group.

"Let's get 'back on the road again' where you're about to witness a rare event—one of our revelatory interventions, an exception rather than a common practice. Saul has received permission from temple authorities to hunt down more of Stephen's contemporaries—members of 'the Way'—in the synagogues of Damascus."

The GAs found themselves on the turret of a gate in the Damascus city wall through which the meandering dusty road finally deposited its weary travelers and merchants. It was a major thoroughfare, reaching 136 miles back to Jerusalem, which had taken Saul at least six days to walk. The Romans were constantly working to improve it as they strengthened their uncompromising grip on the region. "Roads are the key to power and good governance," they declared everywhere they expanded.

About half a mile from the city gate the GAs watched Saul and his entourage approaching. A colorful, rowdy camel train of traders stretched before them. The rhythmic clink of metal goods strapped to camels mingled with voices, and the smell of spices wafted on a light breeze around their tower. Engrossed in conversation, Saul was lamenting the erosion of the traditions passed down from their fathers.

"We have to act swiftly and firmly against the Way before they cause more trouble. As soon as we arrive in Damascus, we'll arrange meetings in every synagogue, and recruit men to guard prisoners. I will not stand by and allow this sect to come against the ways of God with their heretical teaching about Jesus being the Messiah. If anyone—"

Saul's next words were never uttered. Mid-sentence, a blinding light flashed from the heavens and he was thrown to the ground. Rumblings like thunder shook the sky, as Saul was caught up in a whirlwind of fear and confusion.

"Saul, Saul, why do you persecute me?" a voice asked. The people around him stepped back in alarm, turning in every direction to discover the source of the sound.

"Who are you, Lord?" said Saul, prostrated face down in the dirt, not daring to raise his head.

"I am Jesus, whom you are persecuting. Now, get up and go into the city, and you will be told what you must do."

Silence paralyzed all for a moment before they broke free in frenetic babbling. Saul lay speechless, immobilized in the dust, shrouded in an impenetrable veil of black. Gradually the ringing in his ears subsided, and the voices of his friends and travel companions penetrated the haze of disbelief and shock.

"Saul, are you alright?" "Saul, what happened?" "Saul, get up." "Saul, are you hurt?" Fussing around like turkeys pecking the ground, they reached for him. "What was that? We heard something but saw no one? What's going on?"

Saul grabbed an outstretched arm and slowly rose to his feet. He rubbed his eyes and shook his head. The bravado, arrogance, and belligerence drained from his body, his face pale, caked in dust. "I don't know, I can't see!" he gasped, panicked.

"Here, take my arm. We'd better get you into the city," said one of the men as he led the shaken figure toward the gates of Damascus.

"That was amazing!" Gregori laughed. "Great to see a tyrant fall for a change. What happens now?"

"Saul will be left alone for a while; blind in Damascus for three days. He needs to ponder his actions and try to make sense of what is going on," Pappa G explained slowly. "Of course, he won't find a rational explanation because what we're providing is a revelation. Nevertheless, he needs time to understand that the road along which he has been destructively and cruelly traveling is in direct opposition to the God he professes to believe in and serve."

"We can be tough when we have to," said Gale. "Sometimes people misunderstand that reality. They have no comprehension of what we put up with and how much grace is extended to them."

"I am constantly in awe of your patience," said Asuka.

"It's not so hard to be patient with people you love," Gale responded, embracing her with one arm. "Saul will always argue from his intellect because his ability to reason is his ultimate authority. We had to bring him to his knees, pierce his heart, and confound his logical thought processes. His blindness will keep him in a healthy state of humility and uncertainty for a while. He's hurt enough people in the name of religion."

"And then . . . ?" asked Jenny, sounding like a little girl on her father's lap listening to a bedtime story.

"And then we'll speak to him in a dream, and a humble man named Ananias will come and restore his sight," Pappa G explained. "Saul will discover the love of God that he missed in his years of study with his teacher, Gamaliel. He will come to realize that Jesus knocked but he didn't open the door. He was looking in the wrong direction and the revelation of a messiah was not as he anticipated. His teachers and tradition had God neatly defined and boxed up. And I'm bigger than any box manufactured within the tiny frame of Earthtime." Pappa G smiled. "Sometimes it demands 'don't-argue-with-me' love."

"Why are you going to all this trouble with Saul?" Gregori asked, combing his fingers through his hair.

"That's an interesting observation, Gregori." Gale stood with her hands on her hips looking down the road toward Jerusalem. "There are moments in history where we intervene in a sense and anoint an individual for a special mission. Such was the case with Moses, David, a few others, and now Saul. His transformation and influence will impact history in Earthtime from this day forward."

"But isn't that unfair for everyone else in Earthtime who doesn't get your special attention?" Asuka asked.

"Not really," Jesus replied. "Saul's revelation will help many come to a greater comprehension of who we are and what my life in Earthtime revealed and accomplished. It was a threshold closing one era and opening another. They'll get to share in his revelation and benefit as he did However, with that 'special attention,' as you call it, will also come great suffering. Many desire the revelation, but few welcome or endure the accompanying sacrifice and hardship."

"Let's walk up the road to where Saul had his encounter with us and then we'll head back home." Gale led them down from the tower and they entered the throng of travelers and merchants scurrying in and out of the gate like ants, all oblivious to the extraordinary event that had taken place that afternoon at their doorstep. Some, no doubt, were crying to God for help; when would they realize that he was in their midst, a mere breath away?

Chapter Thirty-One

RICKY HAD NO IDEA what hit him.

It had happened so quickly. He loved the adrenalin rush of skate-boarding, the thrill of mastering a new move. They were practicing the TreFlip, which involved popping the board in the air to rotate 360 degrees before landing. Ricky had completed it successfully only once—after practicing most of the afternoon. He was pumped and didn't give his helmet a second thought when he took to the slope without it.

That afternoon Ben had executed the TreFlip to perfection, twice in a row! Even Tyler had completed it. Ricky's competitive edge couldn't walk away from at least trying to equal the exploits of his friends. "Ok Ben, here I go, one last time—if you can, I can!"

Three days earlier Ricky had been bounced out of a deep sleep by his younger sisters jumping on him singing, "*Happy birthday to youuuu,*" repeatedly, amid laughs, squeals, and prodding. He rolled over and smiled. Today he was fourteen. He sat up quickly and grabbed them both. "Gotcha!"

"Mommy, mommy," they cried in unison, "Ricky won't let us go!" Then they collapsed into giggles again.

The smell of fresh pancakes wafted into the room. "Time for Ricky's birthday breakfast—come and get it!"

Every birthday began the same way. A feast of pancakes drenched with maple syrup, strawberries, cream, and a large glass of fresh orange juice. The kitchen table was set. A "Happy Birthday" balloon floated from a colorful weighted centerpiece. Beside it was an envelope with "Happy Birthday Ricky" scrawled across it in his mother's handwriting.

Kaitlin and Jessica tumbled excitedly into the kitchen followed by a disheveled, smiling Ricky.

"Hey Mom," he said. She turned from the sink and embraced him. "Happy birthday Rick! When did my baby get so old, almost a man?"

Ricky sat at the table and ripped open the envelope. It was brightly decorated with a large "14" on the cover above the words, "It only took 14 years to become this awesome!" Inside, after the printed message "I hope life brings you lots of happiness and laughter," his mother had written:

Have a lovely birthday Rick. So proud of you as my one and only son. Happy skateboarding! All my love, Mom

"Thanks Mom, love you too." Ricky held up the card and waved it at her.

"Open your presents, Ricky!" Kaitlin sat next to him, tugging at his arm.

"Ok, be patient," he said gently. "Which one?"

"This one." Kaitlin stretched across and pointed to a gift wrapped in lilac tissue paper. "That's from me and Jessica."

"Feels soft." Ricky squeezed the wrapped gift and smelled it. "Socks?"

"No, silly." Jessica laughed. "Open it!"

Ricky tore the paper and held up a white tee shirt with "Santa Cruz" emblazoned across the chest.

"Wow, thank you . . . I really like this!" He stood up and pulled off his pajama top and slipped on the shirt. "Fits perfectly. Thanks so much you guys." He embraced both sisters in their chairs as they smiled with delight.

"You're welcome," they said in unison.

"Now the other one." Jessica grabbed a square-box-looking gift wrapped in green with gold stars. "You're going to love this one from Mom."

"Hurry up, pancakes are nearly ready." Brenda turned and smiled while scooping another fresh pancake onto a pile by her side at the stove.

"They smell amazing," said Ricky.

He took the package from Jessica and undid the wrapping very slowly and carefully. Kaitlin jumped up and down. "Come on Ricky, hurry up! You're going slow on purpose." Ricky grinned at her.

"It's *my* birthday Kaitlin." He tore off the rest of the paper to reveal a box. His eyes widened. "No way. Mom, how did you get this?"

Brenda turned. "I have my connections. You've been going on about Tony Hawk for so long."

"Tony Hawk's PlayStation Three!" Ricky held it close to his heart. "Thanks, sooooo much, Mom. I had no idea . . ."

"Well, I hope you enjoy it, Rick. Now let's feed you guys. First Ricky, the birthday boy."

Brenda placed a pile of pancakes in front of Ricky with a candle and sparkler blazing. "*Happy birthday to you, happy birthday to you, Happy birthday dear Ricky, happy birthday to you . . . And many more,*" they all sang at the top of their voices. Ricky laughed and began to pour maple syrup over a pancake.

"Pancakes and Playstation Three, wow!" exclaimed Ricky. "You're the best, Mom."

After serving Kaitlin and Jessica, Brenda joined them at the table with a more modest portion. Their mouths were stuffed with pancake, maple syrup, and cream when the doorbell rang.

"I wonder who that can be?" asked Brenda. She got up and went to the door. "Antoine! How nice to see you!" She gave him a hug.

"I could hear you singing downstairs and realized it was Ricky's big day. I thought I'd better come up and wish him happy birthday."

"You mean you knew there'd be pancakes?" Ricky shouted out and smiled.

"Well, that too." Antoine pulled up a chair after giving Ricky a high five. "Happy birthday buddy boy. You're nearly as old as me eh!"

Antoine lived in the single-room apartment downstairs. He'd struggled for much of his life with schizophrenia and drugs. Originally from back east, he'd moved west with a girl who eventually broke his heart. He'd wasted years in and out of rehab, tried methadone programs, and after many attempts had finally got himself clean.

"I couldn't have done it without support from mental health, my friends at the church, and God," he'd tell anyone who'd listen. He'd moved in about three years ago and often sat at the kitchen table chatting with Brenda. Sometimes he shot hoops with the kids downstairs. "Basketball's my game," he boasted and would invariably dig out clippings highlighting a stellar career in High School that was dashed when he got caught up in the wrong crowd.

Brenda cooked up a few more pancakes and placed them before Antoine. He was chatting with Ricky about Tony Hawk and skateboarding tricks, and when they would watch the next episode of *Band of Brothers*.

Kaitlin and Jessica devoured their pancakes and left the table, talking excitedly about the imaginary game they were going to play—something that involved princesses, pirates, and ice cream.

Ricky turned to his mother and asked hesitantly. "Do you think Dad will be here today?"

"I hope so, Rick, but I can't promise. I haven't heard from him." She stifled a sigh.

Antoine mopped up the last of his pancakes in the maple syrup. He looked at Ricky. "I have children you know, Ricky, and I've missed so many of their birthdays and important events." Tears welled in his eyes. "I was so wasted and out of touch I had no idea. But I love them more than anything in the world. If failure and screw-ups were an Olympic sport I'd be on the podium for Canada. Hey, don't give up on your dad. He's probably going through hell himself, but he loves you. I know that for sure."

Ricky nodded and looked down at his empty plate.

Antoine stood up. "I'd better be going; don't want to overstay my welcome. Thanks for the breakfast, Brenda. It's the best I've had for a long time. Happy birthday Ricky—sorry I didn't get you a card. Come down and hang out anytime, eh?" He and Ricky exchanged more high fives.

"Thanks Antoine, see you around."

After he left, Brenda sat at the table with Ricky. "Had enough, birthday boy?"

"Absolutely Mom, I'm stuffed. Thanks. It was nice of Antoine to stop by. I really like him."

"I do too."

"He's like a big brother. I know he has his problems, but he always makes me feel special—like I felt that time Dad took me fishing on my birthday a few years ago. But then it never happened again . . . Antoine plays with us and he's so *real*."

"How so?" Brenda sipped her coffee from a rustic brown mug.

"He talks about his struggles. You know, his skiz . . . How do you say it?"

"Schizophrenia."

"Yeah, the voices in his head that the medication helps him with. And when we watch *Band of Brothers,* he gets so excited. He must have watched the series a hundred times. He talks about his grandfather in the war and Dunkirk. He's cool. I just wish he had someone so that he wasn't so alone. It must be hard living in a small apartment by yourself."

"Yeah, I know he wishes he could meet somebody, but he doesn't have much confidence in himself; he's traveled a long, hard road. But despite that, he's been there for me when I've been having a rough day." Brenda smiled. "And he always makes me laugh when he starts speaking French with that accent. I have no idea what he's saying—could be telling me I am as lovely as a flower, or the complete opposite! Makes you appreciate what we have, eh Rick, even if it's not perfect. As Antoine said, let's not give up on your dad. I haven't, although it does get harder as time goes by, that's for sure."

Ricky leaned back in his chair with his hands cradled behind his head. "I wonder where I'll be in ten years' time," he said, changing the subject.

"Where would you like to be?"

"I'm not sure. Maybe a skateboarding legend like Tony Hawk or Rodney Mullen, but I doubt that. They were already pro skaters at my age!"

"Well, you have a sharp mind and you're athletic; you could do anything you set your mind to. I know it sounds cliché, but make sure to follow your dream all the way so you don't have regrets later." Brenda smiled and looked out the window.

Ricky was astute. "Do you have regrets Mom?"

"It's a hard question to answer, Rick. I have no regrets about you three children, that's for sure," she said, eyes fixed on Ricky. "But I wish I would have had the chance to pursue a career in nursing as well. I think I'd have found that rewarding."

"Do you ever wish you hadn't married Dad?" he asked pointedly.

"I'm not going to lie to you; you're too smart for that. Sometimes I do when times are hard and he's not here to help. But deep down I still love him and cling to the hope that eventually things will settle down and we can be a proper family again." Brenda sighed. "I wanted so much for you all to grow up in a strong and happy home. I'm sorry it hasn't worked out that way, Rick."

"It's not your fault, Mom." Ricky took her hand and squeezed it. Brenda marveled at how he could be so much more mature than his age. "I wish for that too. Dad can be so much fun."

"What are you going to do for the rest of the day?" Brenda began to collect the sticky, syrup-streaked plates and stack them in a pile by the sink.

"I'll probably get together with Tyler and Ben. We'll definitely be spending time with the PlayStation Three and then probably go skating."

"Well, enjoy it and be careful. Stay safe. As long as you're my son you'll never be too old for me to say that." Brenda smiled and gave Ricky a hug.

"Love you Mom, so much."

Three days later, on a Tuesday in late summer, Ricky lay in a coma.

Chapter Thirty-Two

"CHANGE OF PLAN." GALE smiled and walked over to join the GAs who'd appeared in the doorway of the Rainbow Room. "Could be rather disturbing so be warned."

"Sure," they said hesitantly. Their puzzled faces caused Gale to laugh.

"We thought it wasn't really fair to Saul to only show you his dark side. So, much like with David, we're going to visit him in entirely different circumstances before we chat with him here."

"Great," Nova exclaimed. "Sounds interesting."

"Yeah," Jenny agreed. "We heard about some of these people while we were growing up so it's amazing to be given new insights and perspectives. It's such a different world to what we're used to."

"That's for sure," nodded Yesaidu. "I'm more than grateful that we live here."

The rest murmured agreement as Gale led them through the misty veil wall from light into a dark, damp, stinking hole in the ground.

The smell of urine and feces pervaded the air. A solitary candle flickered. The only other light source filtered through a grate in the door during the day. But it was night and thick with darkness. This was the innermost cell of the Roman prison in Philippi where prisoners were placed awaiting death, the notorious *tullainium*. In the same building were less oppressive cells; the best were well-ventilated cells for minor offenses on the outer courtyard. The rough walls of the jail were built from rocks quarried from the hillside where the jail was located. A cacophony of coughs, muttered complaints, and the occasional shout indicated the building was well populated.

A rat scurried across the filthy floor of the *tullainium*, invisible in the dark but heard by the occupants. Two naked men sat with their backs pressed against the rock wall. Obeying orders for strict security, the jailer, a retired Roman soldier, had locked their feet in heavy wooden stocks. Ankles scraped raw, their agonized moans rent the air, their pain exacerbated by a brutal flogging they'd endured earlier in the day. They'd been subject to mob hysteria, stripped and flogged with a rod before being thrown in jail. Their backs smeared dark stains on the rocks they leaned against from the blood that had coagulated around deep welts and lacerations.

While the two men were in almost total darkness, the GAs viewed the scene as if it were daylight.

"Where on earth are we now?" Jenny held her nose as she spoke.

"In a Philippian prison with Paul and his friend Silas," Jesus replied. "Paul and Silas have been arrested after being accused of destroying the livelihood of merchants by delivering a slave girl of an evil spirit. The merchants were furious, as they could no longer exploit her to tell fortunes, which was making them a fortune."

"Why such a harsh punishment?" Nova asked.

"Philippi is a Roman town with a strong disdain of Jews. Flogging and imprisonment is the Roman solution to mob unrest."

"Remember the Romans weren't the only ones capable of great cruelty," said Pappa G. "Not too long-ago Saul was treating the early disciples of mine with equal brutality—even death."

"Watch this," Gale said.

Paul and Silas conversed in whispers. Both men were in their mid-forties. They'd been followers of "the Way" for many years and were committed to sharing the revelation of Jesus with the Gentiles throughout the region. Life had never been easy, but there was nothing they'd rather be pouring their hearts into, nor did they wish to be anywhere else, despite the grim circumstances in which they now found themselves.

Paul was encouraging Silas, who was encouraging him. The flogging and persecution merely made them more determined, more defiant, and more honored to be suffering for the Lord their God. Which is why, at midnight, their voices were heard throughout the jail, singing songs of praise from their ancient psalms in Hebrew.

> "Though the wicked bind me with ropes,
>   I will not forget your law.
> At midnight I rise to give you thanks
>   for your righteous laws."

As they sang, the rest of the prisoners fell silent. As soon as they finished one song, a voice from a far corner of the jail would call for another, and so they continued, the two men's voices growing in strength even as their torn bodies grew increasingly weak and weary.

Suddenly there was a rumble in the earth and rocks dislodged from the top of the walls; the gates of the cells burst open, some popped off hinges. Prisoners' voices rang out, exclaiming, "We're free! The walls are broken! Praise the God of Paul and Silas, who has spoken!" But no sooner had it started than the shaking ceased, and Paul shouted for everyone to be calm and stay where they were. A minute later the frantic jailer appeared at the entrance, wielding a lamp and a sword. Fully anticipating an empty jail, he was prepared to take his life; he knew the penalty for losing prisoners on his watch.

"We're all here!" Paul shouted above the mayhem, he and Silas still locked in the stocks. The jailer, holding his blazing oil lamp high, shuffled through his jail inspecting the cells. Without a word, he knelt before Paul and Silas, undid the stocks, and beckoned them to follow him. He brought them to his home, where he and his wife washed their wounds and gave them fresh clothes, all the time asking questions about their God and how they could also follow him.

Paul and Silas explained the good news of Jesus, their Messiah, and the implications for both Jew and Gentile. Before returning to the inner cell, the jailer requested that he and his entire household be baptized into the faith.

The GAs watched, mesmerized, as events unfolded.

"How long in Earthtime was it since we met Saul outside Damascus?" Asuka asked.

"About sixteen years," Pappa G replied. "He spent many years in his hometown of Tarsus and the surrounding area before Barnabas located him and he began his missionary journeys in the Mediterranean region."

"What a transformation!" exclaimed Gregori. "You wouldn't know that he was the same person."

"Well, let's meet him and Silas, shall we?" Gale spoke the word and they were back in the Rainbow Room. "Sit down please."

A slightly older Paul was seated in a comfortable chair, with Silas in another by his side. Paul was a short man with a balding head and a beaked nose. His voice was high pitched. When he spoke, he gesticulated with his hands as if to emphasize the point he was intent on making. Silas was the opposite. Of medium height, he was soft spoken, with a gentle face and kind brown eyes. His skin was dark, and when he smiled his teeth shone and he lit up the room.

Well," Jesus said. "We've travelled from Damascus to Philippi and witnessed some harrowing scenes, which is vitally important for your future assignments. As I've said before, many of our followers in Earth-time believe me to be a killjoy, out of step with 'real life.' They tend to be shallow in their beliefs, narrow in their thinking, and end up somewhat hypocritical."

"Why is that?" Yesaidu asked. "Paul and Silas don't appear to be like that at all."

"No, they're not," Jesus agreed. "But down the ages, as Christianity spread and churches became more common, many Christians slipped into a sort of 'comfort religion,' under a polite veneer of faith. When relationship with me is ignored, then the religious pharisee takes over, and that's what's unattractive to many, quite understandably. I called them 'whitewashed sepulchers' in my day in Earthtime."

"Sadly, it's always been that way, but let's address comments and questions to Paul and Silas." Pappa G stretched out his legs and gestured to his two friends. "All yours."

Paul nodded. "Thank you, where would you like to begin?" he asked, surveying the GAs.

After a moment's silence Yesaidu spoke. "I think we're a little shaken by what we've witnessed during this fieldtrip, and nervous as well. I'd be interested to hear how you began by ordering people to be killed and then had such a dramatic conversion?"

Paul nodded. "I received similar reactions during my early years as a Christian. No one trusted me. I spent a great deal of time asking forgiveness for my actions and reassuring people. When I described myself in a letter to the Romans as 'the greatest of sinners,' I wasn't joking. I don't deserve to be here with you; I'm more acutely aware of that fact than anyone."

"I was scared of him at first." Silas smiled. "He was the last person we expected to become a follower of Jesus. Our expectations and our faith weren't that strong. When it happened, it took a while to test whether it was real. I think that's normal and nothing to be apologetic for."

"How do you understand now what happened on the Damascus Road?" Jenny asked.

Paul shifted, lifting his body with his elbows on the arms of the chair. He was a stooped figure of a man, but when he spoke, he was a giant.

"I invested most of my childhood and early adult life being trained and equipped to be a zealous Jewish spiritual leader. I had a strong academic background, was well regarded, on the fast track to become a significant leader. To be honest, I enjoyed the status and the power. This new movement was interfering with my career path and was unsettling me. It clashed with Gamaliel's teaching and contradicted how I believed God accomplished his purposes. Intellectually and spiritually, it was blasphemous."

"And that's why you began hunting down these new believers, imprisoning some, and even murdering others?" Jenny was finding it hard to control her emotions.

"Yes, I'm ashamed to say. And here's the thing. What was most unnerving was how they spoke of Jesus being the Christ and rising after he was dead and buried. They talked of his resurrection, power, and miracles. It seemed the more people we imprisoned and killed; the more followers emerged to take their place. It was disturbingly strange and disquieting."

"Were we imagining it, or did Stephen's death also have an impact on you?" Jenny asked.

"I recall being extremely angry that day, and not comprehending why. Usually I was very controlled, with my intellect processing and directing all my actions. I heard Stephen speak to the assembly in the synagogue and I was impressed with his eloquent summation of our Jewish history. More than that, he spoke with an authority and a conviction that transcended the mere recitation of facts. There was something about him and the look in his eyes that haunted me. I don't know how to put it into words. All I know is that when he looked directly at me and prayed for our forgiveness just before he died, my shame was palpable, like his very words were piercing me. I had never experienced such a degree of conviction or courage."

"But you were convicted enough to murder?" Nova spoke, his voice quivering.

"Yes, you're correct. And I was authorized by the High Priest with letters to prove it. What I did was cowardly. Stephen faced a hostile crowd alone, courageous under the authority of the God he bore witness to. I didn't know God like that."

"You said that these followers of 'the Way' were different. What did you see in them that caused you to question yourself?" Yesaidu asked.

"I couldn't put my finger on it at first. I saw something in Stephen, and in others whose names have been lost to the world. Eventually, I realized that it was their attitude and the incongruity of their lives that was getting under my skin. I was exerting pressure and issuing threats, and they responded with joy and a strength that left me feeling, well, powerless. They were meant to be intimidated and scared of me. Some of course were, but many were not. Death was no threat, but it was the worst thing I could throw at them."

Paul paused and fixed his eyes on the rainbow rug at his feet.

"I had studied God and the Scriptures all my life. I knew far more than they did about history and how he worked in the lives of our forefathers. But they knew God much more personally. Beneath my tough exterior I was the one who was intimidated and insecure. Even if I'd wanted to explore what they were saying, I didn't know how to renege without being humiliated."

"Was the Damascus Road some kind of relief?" Gregori interjected.

"When I lay on the ground hearing Jesus speak and not being able to see, I was totally disoriented. I was not in control and my mind was all over the place. I approached Damascus with my eyes wide open, yet spiritually blind. I entered Damascus without my sight, but my spiritual eyes were beginning to focus, ever so slightly. It was terrifying but wonderful!"

"My dear friend Paul is smart," said Gale, playing with her left earring. "And also, stubborn. When you can process information, think through difficult issues, and translate them into simple language, I'm impressed. But what I truly admire about Paul is the humility beneath his brusque exterior that demands that he be honest with himself and with others. It was not easy for him to realize that his razor-sharp mind had unwittingly severed his connection with God. His intellect alone was not enough for him to know God personally. He would have to lower his defenses and allow his heart to be touched and educated as well. The process began on the Damascus Road—actually, even before the encounter with Stephen—and it continued for many years."

"Sorry Silas, you've hardly been given a chance to talk." Pappa G glanced his way.

"That's all right; I like to leave the public speaking to Paul." He turned sideways and winked. Paul smiled and nodded his head, raising his hands in mock protest.

"However," Silas continued, "Paul's, or Saul's, dilemma is common in Earthtime. You will discover that people form opinions that become deeply embedded and are hard to change. Thinking only goes so far; experience and encounter are more powerful teachers."

"Is that what happened to you?" Asuka asked.

"You could say that. I was in Jerusalem, and a friend had met Peter and was greatly impacted by this simple Galilean fisherman. He claimed to have had his life changed by the crucified Jesus who had appeared after his death. I followed my friend and began to spend time with the group Peter led. It was not only their friendship and love that impressed me. It was the power and authority they exercised in the marketplace, the healing of sick people, and their straightforward teaching. I was thirsty for the reality of God. It was like drinking from a refreshing fountain. Changed my life." Silas fell silent, a distant but contented expression on his face.

Paul raised a hand. "One more thing: I used to think that logical reasoning would persuade anyone about truth and God. That's not the case. You can have the best mind in the world and totally miss the truth that's staring you in the face. If there's no power and encounter with God, then reason seldom carries one to conviction. Many of those you'll walk alongside will be disillusioned and weary of religion, but hungry, like Silas and I were, for the real thing."

"What does the 'real thing' look like?" Jenny asked.

"It's more fun than what I grew up with." Paul stroked his chin thoughtfully and paused. He smiled as he tapped his head. "Everything about God was in here—facts, traditions, knowledge, the conviction that I was right. After the Damascus Road, my heart came alive with God's love and Gale's power present on earth, just as they were present for Jesus." He looked around at the GAs, his eyes alive with wonder. "Can you imagine that? I experienced them renewing my identity, empowering me to speak, and even more amazing, enabling me to lay hands on sick people and see them recover before my eyes." His hand was on his heart as he spoke. It was evident that the revelation still deeply moved him.

"You know most believers in Earthtime have the same disconnect. Too much in the head and too little in the heart. It's not entirely their fault; it's a competitive world, where knowledge reigns supreme, at the expense of everything else. Schools, colleges, workplaces reward those who work hardest, get the best grades; rarely is it about those who have the purest heart, who tap into that voice inside them—Gale's voice—directing them to do the right thing, which sadly isn't always the most popular, or even the most rational option. That makes them angry after a while. They don't realize the reality and power of Gale's presence. She helped me understand that the same spirit that lived and flowed through Jesus could flow through me."

Gale smiled. "Thanks, my brother; what you say is so true and grieves me. We watch people struggle much more than they need to. All the while we stand by longing to help and empower, if only they could let go." She looked at the GAs and nodded. "Everyone needs help to counterbalance blind spots, prejudice, and weakness. Paul had Barnabas, Silas found Peter and other disciples, and people whom you encounter in Earthtime will surely need you."

Chapter Thirty-Three

Thursday
Dere Bren,

not good at this. Sorri for being such a por fathr and husbnd. I know I dont diserve ani more chancss but I beg yu to let me try with yu agen. I do luv yu, and our childrn. I want to make changs that will make yu proud and hapy. Watchg Ricky has ben the wurst thing in the world. I hope we can werk this out togethr.

Yor lovng husband, JJ.
PS. Ive put my stuff in the drawrs next to the single bed. Yu can hav the kween bed. I will not com here when yu are usng the room.

JACK READ HIS NOTE a few times before placing it on the queen size bed. His handwriting was a spidery scrawl. If he overthought what he'd written, his dyslexia would win, and the note would end up in the waste basket. He'd booked in at the Ronald McDonald House while Brenda sat with Ricky. Their room was like a hotel, with two beds, table and chairs, linens, bathroom, and a small fridge. They'd arranged to swop over in six hours.

After trying to sleep without much success, Jack got up and showered. His mind was swirling with thoughts of Ricky, regrets about how little time he'd spent with him over the years, and what a jerk he had been. He half wished he'd drowned, while the other half shouted at him to grow up and be a man. *Think of your struggling wife and your two girls and step up for them!* No matter how hard he tried to focus his thoughts on what he needed to do, the voice of self-deprecation crept in, relentless in its criticism.

Before locking the apartment, Jack checked the bathroom, ensuring it was clean and tidy for Brenda. He walked down the stairs that descended into what was called the Grand Living Room: a large open-plan foyer where chairs and couches were scattered, some around a fireplace. Families were gathered in different areas, some conversing over mugs of coffee or paper cups of fruit juice, others playing games. There was a palpable buzz in the air, punctuated by laughter and the occasional happy shrieks of children on the big yellow slides. Jack marveled at how upbeat everyone seemed, despite the serious circumstances that had brought them all to this place. He nodded and smiled at the woman managing the reception desk. She buzzed open the door and mouthed "thank you" as he opened it. Outside he turned left and made his way around the large hospital complex to meet Bill at the cafeteria.

A few cumulus clouds swelled and floated lazily across a blue sky. The sun shone bright and warm, enticing nurses and doctors in scrubs to gather on the sidewalks and enjoy fresh air with their coffee break. Another warm-to-hot September day for all to enjoy.

The world goes on, yesterday, today, tomorrow. Jack reflected that a few days ago he might have drowned. *This day still would have dawned, and these people would be out here doing what they do. My death would be unnoticed and make no difference to the world. Ricky lies in a coma; my life and marriage are falling apart. No one looking at me walking here would know. But then, maybe it's the same for all of us when we look outward and wonder about those looking in?*

Jack noticed a change in himself that morning. Despite all that was going on around him, he was more present. He had no desire to hide or to run away. For the first time in years, he wanted to be a father and a husband. He hated to acknowledge that much of the time he regarded his children and wife as necessary interruptions. *Keep them happy so I can get on with my life.* Now, they *were* his life, and nothing mattered more to him. Ricky's accident had rocked him. Not only because his son might die, but because he'd taken so long to respond to Brenda's call. The chats with Bill had helped. They'd opened his eyes, perhaps even his heart, to the possibility of hope and change.

But it wasn't going to magically happen. Slowly, Jack had to begin rebuilding some broken bridges. He'd tended to avoid this place of introspection and self-awareness. He found it intimidating, especially when it invariably triggered feelings that were best kept under wraps. With his straight way of talking, Bill had helped unlock the door and shown him that there really was nothing to fear, other than himself. Now, he wanted to be willing. Willing to stop and think. Willing to consider his response and responsibility. He'd always felt too insecure. Bill had helped him understand that he didn't need to be a hero. It wasn't about not being scared or knowing what to do. It was about sharing the journey openly and honestly with those closest to you—then there was some accountability, and change could begin to happen.

Jack hadn't realized how much he had longed to do just that—to confide in someone, to admit his fears and make himself vulnerable. Before Bill, he couldn't have fathomed it. But Bill stood and listened. When he looked him in the eye and accepted him, not just for his failure, but offering friendship and help, that was the game changer. Bill told him that fathers were meant to do that for sons. Jack's father hadn't, but Bill had. For the first time, Jack felt that it was okay to ask for help.

Jack had always seen himself as 'less than.' Not enough. Stupid. Just a son who had mindlessly followed in his father's footsteps and become a dumb mechanic. Bill helped him understand that he wasn't stupid; he was in fact an exceptionally good mechanic. He'd just never had anyone consistently affirm him or encourage him to believe that he brought positive attributes to the table. If Jack didn't believe and respect himself, then he'd merely fulfill what he thought were other people's expectations. He would act the rebel and shun responsibility, giving in yet again to that inner voice, whispering, *let's just have a good time!*

Why had it taken him so long?

He spied Bill at a table in the cafeteria. Bill beckoned him over and pushed a mug with a latte across the table.

"Hi Jack, bought this for you. Before I forget, you have a meeting with Brenda and the surgeon at six o'clock this evening. He wants to talk about where things are and the way ahead."

"Thanks." Jack sat down and grabbed the mug in both hands. "Probably not good news."

"We'll see," said Bill. "From what I can gather, there's not been much change overnight. Brenda asked if you'd come up soon so she can head over to the apartment for a shower."

"Sure," Jack said, looking at his watch. "Guess we'd better get over there."

∽∾

Brenda sat on the bed with Jack's note in her hands. She knew how he labored to write, and his inhibitions about that struggle. A note this long was definitely a big deal.

She'd tried to sleep for a few hours after a restless day with Ricky. Nothing about his condition had changed. No response, just the mechanical repetitious rhythm of the machines. She was beyond exhausted, in every way. They had a meeting scheduled with the surgeon in a few hours. She wasn't expecting good news.

Jack hadn't been so attentive for an awfully long time. She was scared and confused. Scared to even consider opening her heart to him and confused as to why she even entertained the idea of giving their marriage one more chance.

Brenda closed her eyes and sighed. She and Rachel had talked at Ricky's bedside earlier. They sat on opposite sides of the bed in silence for a long time. Brenda watched Rachel and envied her poise and calm; she carried such peace and confidence. Brenda was frightened, as far removed from calm as she could be. Rachel's eyes were closed. Her hand rested softly on Ricky's lower leg and her lips moved ever so slightly.

"What are you doing?" Brenda asked.

Rachel opened her eyes and smiled. "I'm praying."

"To whom?"

"To God. He's been my friend for as long as I can remember."

Brenda shrugged. "Well, he doesn't seem to be my friend. Nothing happens when I throw out a prayer."

Rachel looked over at Brenda with great empathy. "Nothing is simple. It's virtually impossible to link the dots merely by considering your circumstances. All I know is that without God's love I'd have been crushed and destroyed. He brought me back to life."

"My mother used to talk about his love, and I always envied her faith." Brenda rested her eyes on Ricky as she stroked his hand. "But where is God now? My son lies here with no sign of recovery, my marriage is wrecked, my father doesn't even know my name . . ." Her voice tapered into a whisper. Tears flooded in as Brenda shook her head in despair. "I don't get it. I don't get it at all."

After a while Rachel spoke quietly. "Brenda, your heart is so like God's. You're his daughter and you reflect him in more ways than you know."

"How so?"

"What if I were to ask you why you caused Ricky to have an accident and suffer like this?"

Brenda looked up, startled. "What do you mean *why*? What mother would wish this on her son? I'm tired of feeling everything is on my shoulders and that I'm always the one to blame when things go wrong. I'm never enough!"

"Exactly, don't you see? It's not always you. If you wouldn't inflict such a terrible thing on Ricky as his mother, why on earth would God do it to you, or to Ricky?"

Brenda wiped her eyes. "I don't know."

Rachel continued. "If you didn't cause this accident, then why is Ricky lying here?"

"He wanted to skate; he loves doing tricks with his friends."

"And you allowed him to do what he loves even though there was some risk and danger, right?"

"Yes," Brenda nodded. "I was always concerned, but to stop him would have been devastating to him."

"So, your love was expressed by giving him the freedom to pursue his dreams, even if there was risk involved. To make choices and experience consequences. In fact, if you'd only thought about your love and keeping Ricky protected and safe, you'd never have allowed him out of your sight. How do you think that would have worked?"

"He'd have hated me," Brenda replied without hesitation. "He'd have accused me of treating him like a baby. He'd have told me that he'd rather take risks and enjoy adventures with his friends than be locked up safe."

"Well, that's pretty much how it is with God as well," said Rachel. "Freedom is a big deal, but with it comes risk and sometimes heartache. The fact that Ricky lies here in a coma has no bearing on your love for him, does it?"

"Of course not!" Brenda exclaimed. She averted her eyes from Ricky and held Rachel's gaze as if a light were clicking on. "I can see what you're getting at, Rachel. I always thought God was indifferent, and even caused suffering to teach us lessons or to punish us. I found it impossible to trust or believe in a God like that."

"I agree," Rachel replied. "He knows that life is going to be full of ups and downs, fair and unfair. He promises to be with us during any circumstance. Just as you're present here for Ricky now."

"Yes, but if he's all powerful, why doesn't he do something? God knows I'd do anything to make my son better right now . . . What were you praying?"

"For God to heal Ricky and to love you and support you. I was praying for your marriage to be healed, and for you and Jack to have soft hearts in such a difficult time."

"I wish I had your faith, Rachel; I really do. Right now, I just find it hard to believe in anything." Brenda shook her head and bit her lower lip.

Rachel nodded. "That's ok. When faith with God first begins it's like a tiny spark to be fanned into a fire, or a young baby to be gently nurtured. God so respects your free will that all he needs is an invitation to be involved."

"How would I know he cares, let alone what to say?" Brenda asked.

"Well, I'm here telling you about him, aren't I?" Rachel smiled. "How do you know he didn't send me to help you?" she said, a glint in her eye.

"Did he?"

"Perhaps," Rachel replied. "As far as talking to him, all you have to do is talk to him like we're doing now."

"What do I say?"

"Just be truthful and real. Something like, 'God I don't even know if you're real. But if you are, help me to know that. And please help me with Ricky and Jack.'"

"Really?" Brenda whispered. "In church I remember reading lots of prayers that sounded a lot more complicated."

"How did Ricky first talk to you?" Rachel asked. "Wasn't it with gurgles and grunts until eventually 'mama' came out and you were over the moon with joy?"

"Yes, I do remember those days . . . The first time he said a word that resembled 'mom,' my heart melted."

"Maybe that's how God your father feels when you turn to him for the first time. If you can do that for Ricky, Kaitlin, and Jessica, how much more do you think he can do that for you? Just you watch."

Brenda sat silently for a moment, absorbing Rachel's words and continuing to caress Ricky's hand. "It seems so simple when you put it like that. I guess I've nothing to lose in trying."

A nurse came in to check on Ricky, followed shortly thereafter by Jack. Time for a shift change. Brenda could do with a break to digest everything she'd just heard. She smiled weakly at him, then Rachel took hold of Brenda's arm and led her into the corridor.

"Brenda, I detest people pressuring others about God so I'm sorry if that was too much."

"Not at all," Brenda replied. "This is so hard, and it does make me question and wonder what the meaning of everything is. You've been so supportive, so incredibly kind, you've taken the time to be here with me." Brenda shook her head and brushed the hair from her brow. "It blows me away actually. And does make me a little curious about the God you talk about."

"I get passionate because I don't know how I would've made it without the inner strength God has given me. I want everyone to experience his love." Rachel paused as they arrived at the elevator. "Brenda, just think about what we talked about. Think about how you feel when you sit next to Ricky, your love and concern for him. Understand how that is a small glimpse into how God your father feels about you, always. You can be angry, sad, shouting at him or whatever. He never changes. Ok?"

"Yeah, thanks Rachel. Oh, could you please tell Jack that I'm heading to the apartment and will be back for our appointment at six?"

"Will do." Rachel gave Brenda a hug as the elevator doors slid open. A man wheeled a pale young girl out and nodded to them. Rachel smiled, turned, and walked slowly down the corridor to the family room.

Back at the apartment, Brenda sat on the bed and pondered it all, holding the piece of paper with Jack's pleading scrawl. Was this note from Jack God answering her cry? She didn't know what to think.

"God, if you're there, or here, please make Ricky better. Help me to know what to do about Jack. Help me to handle this mess, 'cos I'm falling apart."

After calling Sally to check on the girls Brenda stepped into a hot shower. She stood there for a long time, slowly turning up the heat and enjoying the soothing comfort of the water pulsating down upon her. She wished it could wash away more than her tears.

Chapter Thirty-Four

"Worthy is He
To receive praise
Hallelujah
To our King . . ."

TWO MILLION VOICES ROSE above a crowd from every background and generation, like soccer fans singing, or a standing ovation after a spectacular concert, or passion expressed when receiving great news. Weave them together and there is a glimpse, a mere droplet to sip and savor of worship in heaven. No boredom or drudgery, no half-hearted wishing it were over. No one would have missed it. And this was only the village center where Gregori lived.

The GAs had agreed to meet here after their last InSight review at Yesaidu's soccer game. In the two previous meetings they'd voiced their apprehension and even hints of fear regarding their pending missions into Earthtime, responses unheard of in heaven. Theirs was a special and unique mission which was why the lid of protection was slightly lifted for them. And it came with a cost.

"Why don't we meet in my village for the next Insight review," Gregori suggested, "and instead of talking we take our Insights with us to the worship gathering and lift this entire situation up before the throne?"

"Great idea," said Asuka. "I like that—we can pray for Bill and Rachel, and for breakthrough in awareness for Jack and Brenda, and healing for Ricky."

"Absolutely!" Nova raised his hand. "We are warriors with nothing to fear. We represent the winning side, and we get to help these people find their way home. I'm excited."

"Me too," said Jenny. "I hate seeing people suffer. I keep wondering why we're the ones who get to do this mission, but whatever the reason, I feel privileged."

They were gathered in an enormous open arena surrounding a slightly raised platform where multiple musicians led worship. They blended in exquisite fashion from full orchestra, to piano, violins, guitar, saxophone, hand drums—the list of variations endless. The tempo varied from upbeat and joyful to gentle and intimate, as those gathered engaged and opened wide their hearts and spirits to enter in and respond freely.

Above them diamond clusters of stars shimmered and shifted in glorious patterns across the blue-black heaven as all creation worshipped their Creator. It was breathtaking.

Gregori raised his hands and sang his heart out, tears streaming down his face—tears of wonder and inexpressible gratitude for being part of such an event that never grew old or failed to move him. Swept up in the worship, he called out the names of Jack and Brenda, Ricky, Bill, and Rachel, remembering their need and interceding for healing and a miraculous breakthrough in awareness.

Asuka was on her knees, rocking gently back and forth on her haunches, focusing her thoughts on Brenda as she sang. She saw Brenda weeping beside Ricky, and she prayed for her eyes to open to recognize that she was not alone. She saw Rachel with her arms embracing Brenda. Asuka prayed for the tender touch of the father's love to flow and awaken Brenda's dormant, wounded spirit. She saw Brenda with her eyes wide open and laughter on her face.

Nova moved instinctively to the beat of the music. The hand drums were leading a joyful song, and Nova grinned and shouted as he punched the air. In his heart he was carrying Jack, declaring for hope and a new identity *to infuse my brother Jack as Bill walks with him through his dark journey*. Nova remembered David defeating Goliath and Pappa G in the battledress of a warrior tossing the ugly snake to the ground. "Give my brother Jack such a victory, oh God, let your Kingdom reign all around him. Amen, amen!"

Yesaidu was walking back and forth on the fringe of the gathering. He sang and danced, knelt with hands in the air, then jumped to his feet and continued to pace. The name of Ricky burned on his lips as he pictured Jack and Brenda's young son rising from his bed healed and restored. The music washed in waves over him. He experienced no anxiety or fear, no apprehension or unbelief. Long ago he'd learned that he was never fighting against God or trying to twist his arm; he was always trusting him and adding his heart and voice to the mysterious battle that continued to rage across the universe.

Every worship gathering was unique. Sometimes there was only music. Sometimes the mood was gentle and still, prayers released in whispers that hung in the air like breath vapor on a cold morning. On other occasions, it was a jubilant celebration, where the crowds swayed and danced to the music, singing, and shouting their praise in expressions as diverse as an artist's palette of colors. Then there were the special events, where the whole of heaven gathered, and all the stops were pulled out. Pappa G, Jesus, and Gale would appear in their full majestic glory, surrounded by hosts of angels. Words and music soared from the hearts and spirits of all present in perfect spontaneity. Neither ego nor ritual played a part, but rather a collective sense of awe, praise, and wonder. No words or metaphors in Earthtime could do those occasions justice.

In gatherings such as the one the GAs attended when the music quieted someone would often address the crowd. On this occasion, a mighty roar reverberated through the arena when a diminutive figure appeared on stage—an outpouring of the crowd's genuine affection.

"Hello, dear family, welcome, especially to those of you who are new arrivals. It's wonderful to gather here together with Pappa G, Jesus, and Gale. You know, they often mingle among us; you may not even realize you are next to one of them—which is how they prefer to be at most of our gatherings." The crowd cheered.

"I'm often called a 'mite-y woman of God' because of a seemingly insignificant moment when I lived in Earthtime. My real name is Rebekah. You may recall the story of how one day I went to the temple in Jerusalem and quietly placed a mite, which is the lowest value coin in Jerusalem, in the treasury bowl. It was all I had. I was a widow with few resources, but I loved God with all my heart. I had no idea that Jesus was watching and that my offering was seen, and more importantly, counted for something. That my tiny contribution would be recorded in the Scriptures forever. Imagine that! And now I'm speaking to a massive crowd in heaven. Who would have thought!"

The applause was deafening, accompanied by a crescendo in music and a drumroll. Rebekah raised her hands to the sky and said, "Thanks be to God. Pappa G, Jesus, and Gale . . . We love you so much. We praise you and honor you!"

The cheers swelled higher as the masses voiced their adoration. Re-bekah motioned for silence. "My story in Earthtime demonstrates what is close to God's heart. How he pays attention to the small acts many people perform every day, hidden and seldom even noticed. At our gathering we want to remember those people in Earthtime right now who do acts of service and kindness that no one seems to notice. They are indeed the salt of the earth. As the worship continues let's hold them in our hearts and give thanks. Bless you all."

The music swelled again, the atmosphere buzzing, and the applause morphed into another song. Jenny opened her arms wide and raised her face to the stars. She thought of Jack, Brenda, Ricky, Jessica, and Kaitlin. Tears filled her eyes. She crossed her arms over her chest and bent over as she prayed for them to be reconciled and restored as a family. She cursed the snake and his lies and spoke truth and identity over a fractured family that she was growing to love and hold close to her heart. Around her the music drifted and swirled in a declaration of faith and hope; she grabbed hold of it and folded her words in the praise with confident expectation.

Eventually the music faded, and the GAs headed for home. "That was wonderful," exclaimed Asuka. "So refreshing every time. Hey, why don't we grab something to eat before we part?"

"Sounds like a great idea," Gregori nodded.

"Where do you want to go?" Jenny asked.

"You lead the way," Gregori said. The rest murmured their approval.

"Ok, let's hold hands."

They clasped hands and Jenny blinked. In heaven they could travel anywhere by thinking of the destination, speaking it, and blinking.

Standing in front of Heavenly Ground, she smiled. "I thought we'd revisit the place where we all first met."

Chapter Thirty-Five

"THERE ARE TESTS AND protocols we follow in situations like this." Dr. Pollard sat on the edge of his seat. Jack sat with Bill on his right, and Brenda and Rachel were on his left. Brenda could read the weariness in the doctor's eyes as he faced them wearing scrubs and stethoscope, papers in one hand and spectacles in the other. She guessed he was in his early fifties.

"As you know, we've been keeping a close eye on Ricky since he arrived here on Tuesday evening. That's about forty-eight hours ago, I know it feels so much longer."

"It does indeed," Brenda whispered.

"We've been monitoring Ricky's vital signs, responsiveness, breathing, heart rate, and the like. I won't go into the technicalities. Unfortunately, we're still not seeing much improvement, which is not a good sign."

Jack interjected, "You mean Ricky's not going to make it?"

"It's still too early to be sure." Dr. Pollard exhaled deeply. "I'm afraid I have to prepare you for such a possibility, as much as I'd love to bring you better news. I promised I'd be up front with you."

Brenda, choking with emotion, blurted out, "I've been bracing myself for this . . . So, what now? What's a normal amount of time to be able to tell what's happening?"

"In the first seventy-two hours we're supporting Ricky to allow time for the brain to stabilize. This is one of the hardest scenarios in medicine to predict; it's complex and we still have much to learn." Dr. Pollard placed his tortoiseshell glasses on his nose and scanned his notes before removing them and looking up.

"Tomorrow evening we'll begin to reduce Ricky's sedation and we'll closely monitor him to see whether there are any responses or changes over the next few days. If we do see slight improvement, it would possibly indicate a reduction in brain swelling and some recovery."

"And if nothing changes?" Jack asked.

"If there appears to be no improvement, then I'm afraid the brain damage may be severe. But we'll take it a day at a time."

"Does it help for us to be around?" Jack asked, sitting back with his arms folded. There were tears in his eyes which he tried to blink away.

"Definitely," Dr. Pollard affirmed. "You never know what Ricky can hear, even in this state. It's important for him and I also believe it's important for the family. This is a parent's worst nightmare and is a lot to process and absorb." He glanced at Brenda and Jack in turn. "Is there anything else I can help you with?"

"A miracle perhaps?" Brenda held his gaze. She was surprised at the composure she was feeling amid the helplessness. "If Ricky were to miraculously wake up, could he make a full recovery?"

"In some situations that is a possibility, but with brain injuries the likelihood would be that there is some permanent damage. And that can range from mild to severe. That being said, the body's ability to fight back and recover can be remarkable at times."

"In all honesty, what do you think are the chances with Ricky?" Jack blurted the question then looked away, not really wanting to hear the answer.

"From the test results we have . . ." Dr. Pollard surveyed his notes slowly, glasses slipping to the end of his nose. He looked up over them. "In all honesty it's not looking good, but one can never be sure."

"Ricky's on a ventilator," Brenda leaned forward. "What happens when you take it away?"

"Initially the ventilator supports the patient through the trauma and shock to give time for them to stabilize. Then, as I said earlier, we begin to reduce sedation and monitor that process. After that we consider weaning off and attempting to discontinue the ventilator."

"If the ventilator was removed now, Ricky would die?" Brenda's pleading brown eyes puddled with tears.

"That's entirely possible." Dr. Pollard held her gaze. He was not what they'd expected. Far from being clinical and matter of fact, he was empathic, genuine, and compassionate in his care for them and their questions.

He continued to explain. "This is so hard for families to wrap their heads around. The patient is warm to the touch and breathing because of the ventilator. However, because of severe brain damage, he could be closer to death than life. And while it's excruciating, particularly with young people who have strong bodies, the truth is that recovery at its worst may mean lifelong support and an extremely poor quality of life. The ongoing toll on the family is of course off the charts."

"And if Ricky were your child, what would you do?" Jack asked.

"I see my children every time I treat a child like yours," Dr. Pollard replied. "I've seen so many, too many, over the years. I'd either want them to recover to enjoy a meaningful quality of life or . . ." he looked around the room, "I'd rather they slipped away with no more pain or suffering. I believe that would be the kindest reality for them. For those of us left behind, of course, it's a devastating outcome."

"How do you make the call?" Brenda asked.

"I know it's not a decision any of us want to make. We do what we're doing now. We work hard for recovery and healing while we monitor vital signs and responses. When we eventually remove the ventilator, nature will take its course, one way or another. But before we do that, we will of course run more exhaustive tests to determine if there's life in the brain."

Jack broke the ensuing silence. He surprised Brenda. "Thank you, Dr. Pollard. We know that Ricky's in the best possible care. We appreciate what you and your staff are doing for him, and for us. There's no easy way to absorb this."

"There are many times I feel as helpless as you do; believe me, I wish we could perform miracles." Dr Pollard stood up. "Please don't hesitate to ask me or any of the staff if you have other concerns. Let's see what happens over the next few days. It's good that you have some support, as none of this is easy to bear, and certainly not alone. You all take care now."

Dr. Pollard left the room and they sat, silent, for a while.

"Wow, that was tough." Bill placed his arm around Jack and gave him a hug. "You guys were very brave. Why don't we all take a break and have a change of scenery? Since we've missed lunch, I'll treat you to an early dinner."

Brenda and Jack exchanged awkward glances.

"Are you both ok with that?" Bill asked.

"Yeah, um, I guess so . . ." they replied in stuttering unison.

"But I don't want to leave Ricky for too long," Brenda added. "I just can't do that."

Chapter Thirty-Six

HERE IT WAS, THE historic city on a hill surrounded by valleys. A thick stone wall, wide enough for five people to walk abreast, encircled the inhabitants. Large gates provided access points from every direction. The colossal temple already dominating the landscape was still under construction. Loud conversations and the metallic ring of iron striking stone filled the air as the multitude conducted their daily business. Pilgrims, villagers, and travelers mingled in the area outside the wall where merchant stalls enjoyed steady sales.

The GAs surveyed Jerusalem from the slopes of the Mount of Olives.

"I walked up and down this hill many times with my disciples," said Jesus. "One day I was overwhelmed with sorrow and wept over the city from here." He paused.

"Why was that?" Nova asked, standing beside him.

"I saw so many crying out to God for help but at the same time unwilling or unable to recognize his response in their midst. But more of that another time; we need to make our way to our assignment—which means heading in that direction." Jesus pointed up the hill away from the city.

Bethany was not far beyond the crest of the hill, a mere two miles from the city center. Cypress trees lined the road and bowed deferentially in the breeze. Merchants and visitors with donkeys traveled this road that descended in steep, winding curves through barren hills and valleys to Jericho. It was also a favorite haven for thieves—a good reason to travel in groups during daylight. "You don't want to be caught on the Jericho Road in the dark," was a common warning.

"We're visiting Mary and Martha," Pappa G explained. "They are experiencing a puzzling and difficult time. Their brother Lazarus was sick and died. It appears to them that Jesus is indifferent to their plight."

The group walked in silence down the dusty road into Bethany, soon arriving at the house belonging to Lazarus. Entering his home, they found visitors huddled around two women who looked tired and gaunt, their eyes red with tears. Lazarus had died four days earlier. They were still grieving his unexpected illness, the shock of his death, and the apparent indifference of their friend, Jesus.

"Martha, why don't you sit down? I will look after our guests," an older woman, Hannah, whispered in her ear before leaving the room. For once Martha, ever bustling and busy, relented and allowed another to serve her.

"It's not going to be the same around here without Lazarus," Mary said, her head hung low.

"We'll manage, Mary. Your friends will take care of that," said another woman sitting beside her.

"*Friends?* I thought Jesus was our friend and where is he? He spent many days with us; we opened our home and our hearts to him. Where's he now? Not one word or message. I saw him do miracles for others." Mary clenched her fist, her body tense and quivering. "Why not us?"

Mary always had a special connection with Jesus. She sat at his feet when he visited. He spoke with a depth and sensitivity she'd never encountered in a man. She felt whole and accepted in his presence—appreciated, respected. She was not just a woman with a body to please or to serve his every need. She loved his visits, their shared meals, the laughter, his authenticity, and the many conversations. Which was why his absence when her brother died was such a disappointment.

"I'm surprised too," Martha agreed. "He seems willing to heal other people. Naturally, we expected he would be here right away as soon as he heard that Lazarus was critically ill. Or at least he'd visit when we buried him. He's been like a brother to this family. I don't understand his absence either."

"Jesus, why didn't you go to them?" Jenny tugged on his sleeve.

Yesaidu overheard the question and added, "You must have known how your friends would be feeling?"

Jesus nodded his head. "When I received the news that Lazarus was sick, possibly dying, I was not far away. I could have been by his side within a few hours. But I only did what my Father authorized. He instructed me to wait. I argued with him in my heart because I wanted to comfort my friends. I knew they'd misunderstand and be upset."

Pappa G stepped forward and faced the group with Gale beside him. "There are a variety of perspectives that I have to hold in creative tension. I did not cause or desire Lazarus to be ill and die."

"We never want that," Gale interjected. "If I had my way, I'd use our power to heal every sick person and to prevent all suffering. We hate standing on the sidelines watching what we've created with such love and care be hurt and even destroyed. I feel so passionately about the injustices in Earthtime." Gale had tears in her eyes as she blurted out the words. Any doubt that she was indifferent was dispelled.

Pappa G continued. "When Lazarus became ill, I could have encouraged Jesus to go and heal his friend immediately. On the other hand, another vital aspect of Jesus' life and teaching was to model the power and authority of our Kingdom in a fallen and hostile world. The worst that satan can throw at human beings is to threaten with death."

"You mean that you allowed this dreadful trauma to happen to this family to teach others a lesson?" said Asuka, looking upset. "I'm confused."

"No, of course we didn't cause Lazarus to die. We never cause sickness, suffering, or death. It's not in our nature and we would never abuse our power or any human being like that," Pappa G answered reassuringly. "We merely used the occasion for a larger purpose that was not immediately apparent."

Gale continued, "We needed to demonstrate that not even the darkness of death can extinguish the light of the Kingdom of God. We were confident that the bonds of friendship between Mary, Martha, and Jesus were strong enough to survive this time of understandable disillusionment and pain. Jesus had to stay away in order that there would be no doubt that Lazarus had indeed died. Please, keep watching and see how this plays out."

Pappa G added, "We redeem and take what is often intended for evil and use it for good. And such was the case with Lazarus and his family. It merely took a little longer."

The women huddled in the room around Mary and Martha, muttering among themselves in agreement. They too couldn't understand Jesus' absence.

"Martha, Mary," a figure appeared at the door, "Jesus is coming!"

"Speak of . . . I'll go out and meet him," said Martha, springing to her feet and rushing out the door. As she rounded the corner, she spotted the familiar figure of Jesus with his ever-present group of followers, striding in her direction. Extending open arms he embraced her as she spluttered breathlessly, "Lord, if you had been here, my brother would not have died."

"Martha, I am so sorry for what you've endured. But take heart, your brother will rise again," Jesus assured her.

"I know he will eventually rise." Martha's voice was muffled in his shoulder as she spoke.

"I think you're misunderstanding me . . . I am the resurrection and the life. He who believes in me will live forever. Even though he physically dies, he will live. Do you believe this?"

Martha drew back and looked at Jesus, still holding her at arm's length. "Yes Lord, I believe that you are who you say you are. But my brother Lazarus is dead, and I'm confused."

"Where is Mary?" Jesus asked.

"She's in the house with the guests; I'll call her." Martha hurried back down the road. Bursting into the house, she called Mary. "The Teacher is here and is asking for you."

Mary's face lit up. "Really?"

Both women raced outside to where a crowd was already gathering around Jesus. Pushing through the mass of people, Mary fell, weeping, at his feet, "Lord, if you had been here, my brother would not have died."

Jesus was moved and his brow furrowed in concern. Tears filled his eyes and blurred his vision as he gently reached out to Mary. She returned his embrace.

"Mary, did you really think I do not care? Tell me, where have you buried your brother?" he asked.

"Come and see, Lord," Mary and Martha replied as they led the way further up the street. Jesus followed and wept. People around noticed his distress.

"Why couldn't he have done something earlier?" a voice in the crowd muttered. "They say he has healed a blind person before . . ."

"Jesus, did you know that you would be raising Lazarus from the dead?" Yesaidu asked.

"Not at all. I was walking by faith, trusting Pappa G for the outcome—the same as everyone else in Earthtime."

"What is the key to faith in Earthtime?" Jenny asked. "Or maybe that's a silly question?"

Jesus replied, "There's no formula, magic word, ritual, or discipline really. It's rooted in the intimacy and relaxed trust of relationship between each individual and us. Which means that in one instance we may answer one way, and in another something different. Outcomes may vary, but loving kindness together with grace is always our heartbeat and our only motive."

"This is one of the toughest dilemmas of faith in Earthtime," Gale said as they walked. "People pray in faith and one person is healed and another doesn't appear to be. If the healing comes, then God is good, and if not, then he doesn't care. It's so not like that!"

"Does the snake have power that can heal?" Nova asked.

"Yes, he does," said Jesus. "He loves to attack and bare his fangs to those who are closest to me. Come over here a minute." He gestured for them to gather at the side of the path and pointed to the distant horizon. "Remember where we were a while ago in the wilderness? That's the desert region where the snake tried to tempt me. He promised me power, status, and influence. He promised me bread because I was starving, authority and influence in Earthtime, and protection if I jumped from a high cliff to demonstrate my power. He can make sick people well and perform all kinds of miracles."

"Why do you allow him to do that?" Yesaidu asked.

"As we told you before, we never withdraw gifts we have given. It's freedom of choice, even for him." Jesus gazed into the distance. "But he has been overcome."

"It's so confusing for people in Earthtime," Gale said. "They want to see immediate results and the snake gives them what they crave—instant gratification. The only problem is that when he works, he also hooks people into his selfish schemes to enslave rather than set free."

"How so?" said Jenny.

"He infiltrates people who speak in our name and seduces them with the same temptations he brought to Jesus: fame, influence, power, miracles," Gale explained. "There are many who have succumbed, often unwittingly. The result has been destruction, confusion, and even enmity between those who profess to believe and follow us. Which is exactly what the snake intended. One of your main tasks is to counter those lies by revealing the truth of our love, and restore confidence in our faithfulness, in life and even through death."

"It's no simple or easy task, believe me," said Jesus. "Let's return to Mary and Martha."

Following a path off to the side of the road, they approached a hillside where a cave was carved into the rock under an overhang. A large stone was rolled across the entrance.

"This is where we buried Lazarus, four days ago." Martha pointed toward the entrance.

They waited in silence, all eyes fixed on Jesus. He stood, arms by his side, gazing at the large stone rolled over the entrance to the grave of his friend.

"Roll away the stone." Jesus sighed, evidently moved and distressed.

"Lord," Martha protested, "we can't open the grave now, after four days! Can you imagine the smell?"

"Martha, did I not tell you that if you believed, you would see God do miraculous things?" Jesus responded.

Martha was silent for a long time, unsure of what she believed or understood. She stared at Jesus and slowly shook her head. She turned toward her sister; there was no need for words. Eventually they both nodded. "Move the stone," Martha said.

Four men rolled the stone to the side, exposing the hollow entrance where the dead entered and never emerged. Mary and Martha linked arms, leaning on one another, tears flowing, at a loss to know what to think or expect.

Jesus looked up to the heavens and opened his arms, "Father, I thank you that you have heard me. I know that you always hear me, but I speak these words for the benefit of the people standing here, that they may believe that you sent me." Stepping toward the gaping mouth of the cave, he called in a loud voice, "Lazarus, Lazarus, come out!"

A minute passed and nothing happened. They waited—mute, staring, transfixed. Mary thought she heard a sound, but it could have been her imagination.

"Look, he's coming out of the tomb!" someone gasped.

Slowly, out of the darkness a figure shuffled into the light. He was laboring within the restrictive grave clothes covering his entire body. His outstretched hand against the crudely hewn rock supported him. A cloth was draped over his face.

"Remove the grave clothes, and let him go," said Jesus. Mary and Martha shrieked with delight, laughing, and crying as they joyfully embraced their brother. They tore off the facecloth and kept touching

Lazarus, who had a rather confused look on his face, like one waking from a deep sleep. All frustration with Jesus was forgotten as the sisters praised God for the miracle.

Gale twirled around. "Yes!" she exclaimed. "That's what we do, how we overcome. Sometimes the healing happens on earth, and many more times it is realized in heaven. Either way, there's joy and celebration." She smiled and pointed her finger at each GA in turn. "Do you want to know what your real mission is? To be the hands and feet of Jesus today in Earthtime, just as he was present in the flesh for Mary and Martha over two thousand years ago. And I'll be there to help you as much as I was present to help him. I can't wait, I'm getting all fired up. I love, I love, I *love* rescuing people from the snake's self-serving snares." Gale did a little jig, dancing in circles and grinning.

"A few more sessions and we're done," Pappa G laughed and took hold of her hand. "You want to dance?"

"Sure thing, Mr. God, why not? Music maestro!" To everyone's surprise "On the Road Again" began to blast out across the hills. Before long they'd all joined in, even Mary, Martha, and Lazarus, in front of the empty grave.

Chapter Thirty-Seven

"GOODNESS, I DON'T KNOW where to start." Brenda looked through the menu, bewildered by the vast array of choices.

"Don't be shy; order something you've always wanted but never have," Bill said. He had driven them to a restaurant he'd found recommended online not far from the hospital. They were seated in a booth with a stunning view across Vancouver. Rachel and Brenda sat on one side, Jack and Bill on the other. The style was West Coast Rustic with log posts, thick fir beams overhead, river rock fireplace, and wall-to-ceiling windows.

"This is great; what a view," exclaimed Rachel. "Thanks Bill."

"You're welcome. And just so you know, I'm very aware that it feels strange being here while Ricky is alone in hospital. But unless you take care of yourselves you won't be much use to him. Have you decided, Brenda?"

"Well, since you suggested I try something new . . . I'll have the lobster and salad. Never had lobster before."

"I'm a man of simple taste," said Jack. "The burger with all the trimmings and fries will do me fine, thanks."

Rachel chose a Greek salad and Bill settled for the filet mignon with peppercorn sauce. Bill suggested water all round and Jack opted for a diet coke. They chatted about some of the landmarks of Vancouver they could see through the window before the conversation turned back to Jack and Brenda.

Brenda shot a glance across at Jack and smiled. "It's probably been nearly two years since we had a meal out together."

"Yep, way too long." Jack scratched the back of his neck awkwardly. His cheeks flushed. He looked down and fiddled with his knife and fork.

Brenda leaned on the table with folded elbows and glanced sideways at Rachel and then across at Bill. "And if it wasn't for the two of you, we'd never be here at all."

"You can say that again," Jack agreed. "I mean, where do you guys come from and why are you being so kind to us? You seem to have all the time in the world, and you can afford to treat us to dinner in a place like this?"

Rachel smiled, twirling dark strands of her hair around her middle finger. "Yes, Bill and I have known each other a long time. Hmm . . ." she turned to Bill, "how would you describe what we do?"

"Let's just say it's a little different from the norm," Bill responded, leaning back. "We serve a worldwide organization with many branches distributed in almost every country on earth. It has been established for many, many years. Our benefactor is very wealthy and has a deep concern and compassion for all people, particularly those who are struggling in life. Our task . . . oh, here comes the food." Bill smiled at the waitress as she placed their meals before them. "Thank you."

"Looks good, I'm starving." Jack grabbed his burger with both hands and took a bite.

"Go on, Bill, you were saying . . ." said Brenda after they'd received their food and tasted a few mouthfuls.

"I can't divulge too much detail, I'm afraid. We're commissioned to walk alongside people such as yourselves and offer support, encouragement, and a helping hand—no strings attached."

"Why *us*?" Jack wiped his mouth with a paper serviette. "We're, I mean *I'm* nothing special. In fact, it's embarrassing to admit how screwed up my life is and what a mess I've made of my family. I'm a bloody nightmare. Just ask Brenda."

"Why not you?" Rachel looked up at Jack and tilted her head sideways. "Who deserves anything? Everyone alive has value and significance."

"I don't get it . . . it's been hard for me to believe in myself, let alone complete strangers. To be honest, while I'm grateful for the support you've given us, you also scare me a little."

"*Scare you?* Why on earth would we scare you?" Bill spoke with a mouth full of steak. Wiping his lips, he smiled. "You've no reason to fear us, we have no agenda."

"Everyone has an agenda . . ."

"Jack!" Brenda interjected. "Please don't mess this up by being rude, for God's sake!"

"It's ok Brenda." Rachel touched her arm reassuringly. "Jack's free to express himself." Holding Jack's gaze, she said, "I'm glad you're open. I'd rather that than keeping your thoughts private. We need more honest conversation, don't you think? What's the fear, Jack?"

"Well . . . that you'll give up on us because I'll probably screw up, like I always do. That's why Brenda jumped on me. And your talk about God. That makes me nervous, 'cos we're not religious and I don't plan on going to church."

"Guess I'd be scared too," said Bill. "I don't blame you for being wary and maybe fearful; there's a lot going on right now for the two of you. How are you feeling after our chat with Dr. Pollard?"

"Makes me sick to my stomach," Brenda said quietly. "I'm on the brink of tears all the time, and my heart aches. I look across at that family over there." She nodded in the direction of a family of five seated around a table with a birthday balloon floating in the center. "One of those boys is close to Ricky's age. That should be us. It was my dream, all I ever really wanted. And now . . ."

"I feel angry, mostly at myself, for how stupid and selfish I've been." A tear rolled down Jack's stubbled cheek, but he was beyond caring. "I always wanted to not be like my dad—distant, often drunk, someone who never seemed to care about us kids. He'd spend hours fixing a friend's motor but not even five minutes to find out what makes us tick. Next thing I discover I've become him."

"From what I observe," said Rachel, "both of you are understandably overwhelmed. You're fearful of what will happen with Ricky, and you're very uncertain of one another. Trust is almost nonexistent. On top of that you're locked up inside emotionally, and desperately alone. Would that be a fair summary?"

"Yes," said Brenda without hesitation.

Jack nodded.

"Jack, we're not here to add to your sense of failure and shame." Bill placed his hand on Jack's shoulder and squeezed. "We're here because we believe that both of you are worth fighting for. As you look back on your lives so far, what is your biggest regret or sorrow?"

"I don't want to blame, but as I've already said about my dad, I wish he'd cared more. We never had anything like the conversations I've had with you, Bill, over the past few days. I've just floundered around and hurt Brenda and the kids in the process. It was like my dad just shoved me off from the shore and said, 'You'd better learn to sail kid, good luck, and don't call me when you screw up.'"

"My family was much more supportive," said Brenda, idly picking at her salad. "I knew that I was loved and cared for. Don't get me wrong, I absolutely adore my children, but I do regret not having taken the opportunity to go to nursing college before marriage. Jack and I needed people like you around us before we were married. Instead, we tried to keep fixing our mistakes with more wrong decisions, one after the other. We don't have a clue how to talk to one another, or listen, for that matter."

"Thank you both for your transparency; it's not easy." Rachel looked from Jack to Brenda, then back again. "But what if it's not too late to change? If you could write the script for the rest of your life and dare to dream, what might that look like?" Rachel smiled.

Jack took off his baseball cap and scratched his head before replacing it. It was blue with the Molson logo on the front.

"Shoot, that's a question! If anything was possible? Easy, I'd like to be married to Brenda, have a steady job, and be a way better husband and father than I've managed so far. And that's the honest truth."

"And you, Brenda?" Rachel turned to Brenda beside her who was quietly finishing the last of the lobster, breaking a leg and retrieving the white meat. Licking her fingers and wiping them on her napkin, she leaned back and looked at the ceiling. When she spoke, her voice was measured.

"To be scary honest, I want to trust Jack and risk saving our marriage, but I'm really terrified of him hurting me again. I couldn't take that. Personally, I'd love to go to college and qualify for nursing at any level, so that I could work in the hospital." She kept her head low, avoiding eye contact with Jack.

"That's brave, Brenda, thank you for trusting us." Rachel looked across at Jack, "Do you want to respond to what Brenda's just said?"

"Bren, I really do get that you are scared of me. So am I. I respect you so much and want more than anything in the world to make it up to you and the kids. And I don't want to hurt you ever again." Jack's lip quivered and he took another bite of his burger.

Brenda stared back and nodded. "Thanks, JJ."

They were silent around the table for a while, aware of the family birthday celebration not far away. Bill broke the silence.

"Returning to your reaction to God." He gave Jack a friendly nudge with his shoulder. "Why so negative and fearful?"

Jack shrugged. "I've never been one for church. Seems depressing, full of rules about what you're not allowed to do. Don't drink, don't dance, don't have sex before marriage, don't party. I mean, how attractive is that? They're prejudiced against gays, hate abortion, and seem uptight about everything. Not for me."

"Clarify one thing for me, Jack," Bill said, eyeing him skeptically. "What's that got to do with God?" Bill thanked the waitress who'd appeared to clear the dishes. They all agreed on ice cream and chocolate sauce for dessert washed down with three coffees and a glass of water for Jack.

"Aren't the ones who attend church his favorites? They hang around with him?" Jack leaned against the corner, agitated about the turn the conversation had taken.

Brenda caught his vibe. "Chill out JJ, we're only talking."

Jack sighed. "Sorry, the subject makes me uncomfortable, and I can't handle any more pressure."

"No pressure from us." Bill threw up his hands, palms out, before resting them on the table. "If we're being honest, it seems you've placed quite a lot of pressure on yourself. You know what you don't want, and you've said where you'd like to go. The only real challenge is how to bring those two elements together—and to be blunt, your track record isn't great. I'd bet you often feel misunderstood and blamed when you don't think life's been fair?"

"Yes, I do, on occasion," Jack agreed, wondering where this was heading.

"Would it surprise you if God feels the same way much of the time? Misrepresented by those who claim to know him. Often obscured in the fog of dubious facts that question his character, his motives, and even his very existence?"

Rachel cleared her throat before speaking. "You know, Jack, we're only here because God wanted us to show you how real and caring he is. He's not at all like many churches portray him. He's certainly not 'religious,' uptight, and full of rules. His bottom line is love and grace, understanding and acceptance. Relationship is the door to his heart, not rules. Does that make sense?"

"I'd have to think about it," Jack replied. "It's hard to let go of my knee-jerk beliefs."

"It makes sense to me," Brenda said quietly. "I always envied my mother's faith, but as a kid there was not much I could relate to. I've felt quite alone these past years, and now with Ricky so critically ill I'd love to have someone I can trust. This is when I most miss my mom being here, and even my dad."

"I've always felt alone." Jack swirled the diet coke in his glass and took another sip. "I can't even imagine that relationship you describe with your parents, Bren, let alone with God."

Suddenly, as if from nowhere, Brenda felt emboldened to speak openly to Jack. Locking eyes with his, she said, "Well, answer me this, JJ. From what we've been through, why should I trust you? Why should I risk my heart again when you've broken it so many times with empty promises, no support, and leaving me to raise the kids alone?"

Silence filled the fragile bubble that seemed to surround them. If it popped now, there may never be another opportunity.

"I've just told you Bren, I get it. I have no idea what to say other than I want to be with you and the kids and make our family work. More than anything. And yes, we're going to need help. Maybe Bill and Rachel can help us, I don't know. But I hear you Bren, I really do."

"Ok, but it's going to take time and we're not just going to pick up where we left off and hope things magically change. I'm done with that." Brenda spoke with quiet firmness as she held Jack's gaze.

"This is a tough place for you guys. I applaud you for setting a boundary Brenda, and Jack for listening and not getting defensive. Perhaps Bill and I can be supportive in some way, we'll see." Rachel spoke with gentle affirmation, adding, "And I know God is definitely rooting for you and will help, if you want."

"Thanks Rachel, appreciate that, but right now my focus is on Ricky before anything else." Brenda sipped her water and Jack nodded.

Bill broke in gently. "Following up on what Rachel said and about God helping, I think I understand it's not very appealing to you, Jack." He smiled and nudged Jack again with his shoulder.

"Let me use this restaurant as a metaphor. We were presented with menus. We examined the offerings and made our orders. Imagine your response if the waitress returned with a photograph of the meal and a description alongside. How would you respond?"

"I'd be pissed off," said Jack. "Without a doubt."

"I'd feel a bit of a fool, like I'd been tricked," Brenda added. "It certainly wouldn't take away my hunger."

"And so you should be. Unfortunately, many churches are like that. It would be wrong to not affirm the positives in the church, and we can look at those later. For now, these are probably on your negative list. People attending church tend to talk about God's love and they invite you to join them. When you attend you read and hear what the menu (in this case the Bible) says about God. Before long you struggle with the great disconnect between what you read and your experience. And when you draw attention to the discrepancy, you're made to believe that you're the problem."

"That sounds about right." Jack and Brenda nodded.

"For instance," Bill continued, "you read about forgiveness but find judgment; grace but find accusation and blame; kindness but often only extended to a select few. I can go on: generosity, but only as much as is comfortable; loving one another but maybe only those who are like-minded; and so on."

"I don't know how to say this without sounding rude, but church is boring. I'd rather go fishing or be riding quads with my buddies." Jack shrugged his shoulders. "Sorry, that's how I feel."

"You're not alone," Bill responded.

"I agree," said Brenda. "I've always felt that I'm not good enough, or spiritual enough, or acceptable to God. More like a great disappointment."

"It's sad for God too," said Rachel. "He longs for everyone to really know his love and compassion. But often, those who profess to follow him diminish who he is by judging others, focusing on rules, and making it so hard for people to even want to know more."

"Oh, here comes the ice cream; it's not a photo, it's real!" Bill exclaimed. "With chocolate!" The waitress placed white plates before them filled with scoops of vanilla ice cream drizzled generously with dark chocolate.

"Oh my goodness, this looks wonderful," Brenda said, picking up her spoon and scooping a mouthful. "Mmmmm, so good."

"You know your feelings about God are really not so weird, and . . ." Bill said. "You're right—that does taste good." He licked his spoon and smiled at Brenda.

"And?" Jack added.

"You must have both had teachers at school to help you learn to read and write? Jack, did you just magically know how to be a mechanic? I know I asked you that on the ferry."

"Of course not. I had teachers and my dad taught me mechanics as well as courses I took," Jack replied.

"Yet when it comes to living life and finding out who we are, it seems we accept it as normal to muddle along without any guidance or input." Bill scraped his ice cream out of the bowl and licked his spoon with relish. "So, how's it worked for you, Jack? I mean, without anyone schooling you in life. How have drugs and alcohol benefitted your life? How has being married young with a child worked out? I'm not being cruel, but let's be brutally honest here. Has doing it your way been so great?"

Jack took off his cap and scratched his head again. He held the cap in his hands and ran his finger over the Molson logo. "Nope. It's been a disaster. One stuff up after another."

"And Jack, for that I'm sorry," Bill said with tenderness. "The truth is, it's not all your fault. Yes, you have choices and responsibility, but you've also been let down by others and left to your own resources. God certainly never desired that for you. No one is meant to live as an orphan. Your parents failed (as did theirs before them), the church failed in the message they portrayed, and individuals have failed you as you have failed them. Everyone's failed and had to endure consequences not of their making. That's life."

"But it's not fair!" Brenda put down her spoon and leaned forward. "If God is so good and real, why doesn't he do anything to help? Why does a kid like Ricky have to go through this hell? Why do we? I feel so angry, and guilty, sitting here when he's lying there—alone."

Rachel placed her arm around Brenda's hunched shoulders. "Brenda, I know it hurts and you're angry. I'd be too. But what if it's no more God's fault than it is yours that Ricky is lying in hospital? Forgive me for repeating myself. What if your love and concern as a mother is remarkably like God's love and concern for his children, for you, and Jack, and everyone else?"

"But I'm not God, damn it!" Brenda protested. "Why doesn't he do something—isn't he meant to be the great almighty?"

"Perhaps the choice is not his alone. Maybe some of the reasons rest upon our choices as individuals and as communities. What if freedom to choose has consequences that even God will not violate? Why does he get ignored for much of the time and then blamed when things go wrong?"

Bill interjected. "You know, God never said life would be easy, or even fair. But he has promised to never leave his children and to come and support them whenever they ask. What if he's here right now assuring you of his love through Rachel and me? Would that mean anything, or make a difference?"

"Sort of, I guess, but it's a lot to wrap my head around." Brenda glanced at her watch. "Sorry to be rude, but we've got to get back to the hospital." She pressed back into the red vinyl seat, crumpled her serviette, and placed it next to her plate. Chocolate smears fractured the white china and her spoon bore the delicate lines of her lips after her last mouthful. "Thank you so much, you two. The meal was lovely. I'm sorry that I'm a bit on edge. I do appreciate your care, truly." She reached out and squeezed Rachel's hand.

"Yes, thanks a lot," Jack agreed. "Bren, do you want to spend time with Ricky first and I'll come later?" he asked.

"Yes. Maybe we can change over at midnight."

"Glad we could do this together." Bill slid out of his seat and stretched. "I'll settle up at the counter. Either Rachel or I will be in the family room when we get back, not far away."

Chapter Thirty-Eight

"WE'RE NOT GOING ON a fieldtrip this time," Pappa G informed the group as they reconvened in the Rainbow Room. "This session is definitely the most difficult, but it is essential. We're going to focus on you for a change."

"Me?" said Yesaidu.

"No, all of you. You are Guardian Angels being trained to support and protect people in Earthtime as they face the challenges of life in their fractured realm. We've been on various assignments to educate you as to how people there think, act, and feel. It's almost the exact opposite to the environment in which you live. Where you have trust and security, they experience insecurity and mistrust. Where you know love unconditionally, their experience of love is usually conditional, often fleeting. The list of contrasts between a perfect heaven and a broken earth is, sadly, endless.

"This is what we call an Earthtime simulation exercise, which will be explained as we continue. It will also answer some of your questions that have, as yet been unanswered."

The GAs glanced nervously at one another. Their hearts missed a beat wondering what was coming.

"How long do you think you have lived in heaven?" asked Pappa G, eyes scanning the room.

"I don't know," replied Jenny. "It seems like always; isn't it?"

"I'm not conscious of living anywhere else," Yesaidu said. "We've grown up here. That's what I've always believed."

"It has been *almost* always, but not quite." Pappa G held each of their gazes for a second with an expression they hadn't seen before. Turning to Gale, he nodded for her to take over the session.

"I'd like each of you to face a different wall. Because there are five GAs, we'll split this wall here. Gregori, this half is yours; Jenny, you can have the other section. Yesaidu, you have this wall, Asuka the opposite end, and Nova the last wall is yours."

The five GAs repositioned their chairs accordingly without saying a word. Jesus, Pappa G, and Gale stood behind them in the middle of the room on the rainbow carpet.

"Is everyone ready?" Gale asked. "I want you to merely observe what appears on your wall and we'll talk later."

The walls melted and different people appeared in each of the allocated sections in what appeared to be five different video clips. There was no sound accompanying the vibrantly colored pictures.

Nova saw a girl of about fifteen walking along a red, dusty road with a boy who was probably around seventeen. They were holding hands and the girl was giggling as the boy spoke with animated passion. The verdant vegetation was various shades of green as far as the eye could see. They approached a clearing, which was evidently the shore of a large lake. The boy picked up a pebble and skimmed it across the water. The girl tried but couldn't get hers to bounce even once. They both laughed and then embraced.

Gregori saw a couple driving a car through a university campus. Students riding bikes filled the street, and the sidewalks spilled over with young people clutching books, backpacks, and laptops. The couple were smiling, her head leaning on his shoulder as he drove slowly through the traffic. They appeared to be in their mid-twenties; the man had flame-red hair that caused Gregori to gasp.

In Jenny's section of the wall, she saw a disheveled woman in her mid-twenties sitting on a park bench. She looked distressed and was rocking backwards and forwards with arms folded and her body hunched. A man was shouting at her from a distance; Jenny noticed the woman was crying. Neither of them looked healthy or well clothed. They may have been living on the street or in the park of a large city.

Yesaidu saw a man and woman dressed in business suits riding an escalator in an affluent business complex. They appeared to be successful and preoccupied; neither held eye contact with the other and both carried monogrammed briefcases of genuine leather. The woman was perhaps in her late thirties, a brunette with blue eyes. The man was closer to fifty, light gray streaks in a thick head of black hair that he wore long.

They exchanged a few words before walking together down a brightly lit hallway beneath a sign that said "Alderbrook Business Associates."

Asuka saw two women in their mid-thirties chatting in a downtown coffee shop. One woman wore an elegant flowing print dress over a pale-yellow blouse. Her long brown hair was tied in a ponytail. Her blue eyes were alive and dancing as she sipped from a white mug. Across from her sat another woman speaking very excitedly, gesticulating with her hands as she talked. Her hair was short on one side and long on the other with dark and blonde streaks. She wore jeans and a large, pink, baggy tee shirt untucked, "Make my day!" emblazoned in black across the front. The sun streamed through the open shop door, and in the street, trees sprouting green leaves announced that spring was in the air.

Asuka watched as a tall Asian man joined them. He pulled back a third chair from the table, legs scratching across the granite slate floor. They greeted him warmly. He dipped his teabag a few times in the steaming water, squeezed it with his spoon, and placed it beside his cup. The woman in the dress stood up and smiled, then pressed her hands against her belly, which was beginning to show her pregnancy, while the other two applauded enthusiastically.

The GAs gazed on these scenes before them for a long time, until Gale broke the silence.

"During this module we have been reviewing moments in the lives of characters throughout history as they faced unexpected challenges. We have talked to them, listened to their stories, and hopefully gained some useful insights from their experiences. You've journeyed via your InSights with Bill and Rachel, as they support Jack and Brenda in Earthtime. But we all know that the real learning penetrates most deeply when the lessons are woven into the fabric of our own lives. Now it's your turn to listen, to learn, and to support each other."

"Who are these people?" said Gregori, peering around the room at the other figures visible on the walls.

"The people directly in front of each of you are your parents," Gale said quietly.

"No way!" said Yesaidu.

"Despite what people in Earthtime debate, every single life germinating in the womb of a woman produces a human life ignited from a spiritual center. In our entire universe humans are the only species specifically created in our image—people capable of love, reflection, complex thought, a conscience, and other unique attributes."

Pappa G interjected. "Because humanity carries our DNA, every person intuitively desires love, cares about justice, looks for purpose, and requires healthy relationships to flourish. It doesn't matter whether they believe in us or not; those traits will be evident in every tribe, race, and creed. They yearn for meaning and will always worship something."

Gale continued. "When the spirit germinates, it sets in motion the growth of a human baby." She paused, allowing the perplexed-looking GAs time to process the magnitude of her words. "What I'm saying is: Guardian Angels are the children who were conceived in Earthtime but who died before or soon after their birth."

"*What?* I thought we were always here?" said Jenny.

"Me too," added Nova. "We weren't born in Earthtime, why?"

Gale sat on the arm of Jenny's chair. "We'll go around the room and I'll tell you something about each of the people you see before you. Let's give one another time to absorb what we're hearing and learning. I'm sensitive that this news is a shock for you. But it's important that you know the truth and have time to process some disillusionment of your own."

The Rainbow Room was quiet. They had never seen anything like this before in heaven. Filled with a mixture of apprehension, shock, and even fear, the GAs stared, transfixed, at the images in front of them, their minds racing, hearts pounding, emotions in turmoil.

Gale turned to Jenny first, addressing her gently but matter-of-factly. "Jenny, I'm afraid your parents were neither happy nor well adjusted. That's Gabby, your mother, sitting on the bench. She's a drug addict. The man shouting at her is Ben, your father. He's an alcoholic who is homeless in a large city in the North of England. Both come from tough, working-class backgrounds with no family stability. Unfortunately, in their mid-teens they discovered that alcohol and drugs effectively numbed their pain. They were never married."

Gale rubbed her hand across Jenny's shoulders like any mother would do to comfort her daughter.

"Jenny, your father raped your mother one night in a drunken frenzy. Despite the trauma when your mother found out she was pregnant she was secretly delighted. But she was confused and scared as to how she would deal with a child in her situation. Your father wanted to have nothing to do with her when she told him she was carrying his child. His addictions meant that he was very seldom rational.

"One of the side effects of your mother's addiction was paranoia. I'm afraid that the result of increased drug use was a miscarriage when you were three months' gestational age. You were discarded in a garbage bag. Your mother died five years later but never forgot you. She'd said that if her baby was a girl, she wanted to name her Jenny after her mother, your grandmother. Your father died of sclerosis of the liver eight years after the miscarriage."

The ache in Jenny's stomach caused her to double over as waves of grief enveloped her. Gale continued to rub her back. After a period of silence, she said, "You're experiencing a combination of your pain, your mother's angst, and your father's hurt. It's not going to last long." As Gale spoke, Jenny felt the pain lift and peace return.

"When we bring you to heaven, any memory of abandonment or rejection is gone." Jesus smiled at Jenny. "Your identity is not rooted in the past and the pain of your parents; it is fulfilled in who we created you to be. In heaven what was taken from you is restored. You have had the opportunity to grow up in an environment of love and security in a manner you'd never have experienced in Earthtime."

Jenny nodded quietly. "Oh my goodness, this is going to take a while to absorb. I wasn't expecting that. How could anyone live with such sorrow and pain inside them?"

"Many do," Pappa G replied. "Far too many do. It breaks our hearts."

"We won't rush," said Gale. "After I've shared each story, we'll have a short pause to silently reflect before we move on, ok?"

The group nodded, already taken aback by Jenny's story.

"Gregori," Gale began, turning to him. He paled in anticipation of what he was about to hear. "This young couple are students attending a university in central Europe. Your mother, Olivia, is studying art and your father, Ivan, is halfway through his architectural degree. They grew up in different cities and countries in Europe, met at university in Heidelberg, and had been living together for two years in a student apartment. When Olivia discovered that she was pregnant, both agreed they were not ready for children. You were aborted in a hospital clinic six weeks after conception.

"Both your parents graduated and now live in Frankfurt with three children—two boys and a girl, all in their teens. They never speak of you, neither did they name you. They believe a fetus is not a baby until birth." Gale paused before delivering the final blow. "As far as they're concerned, you never existed."

Gregori was quiet, his entire body numb. He had a lump in his throat as he experienced abandonment for the first time. Tears tumbled down his cheeks. The words *you never existed* rang in his ears. He looked so much like his father. From what he could tell, he seemed like a man he'd love to have known. It was as if he'd been punched in the stomach, as he absorbed the pain of not being acknowledged or taken seriously. He wanted to scream out and grab their attention. He wanted to hear the words "Mom, Dad," roll off his tongue. He sobbed. Not a moment too soon, peace and calm filled him, burying the cruel flotsam of his abandonment forever.

Jesus was beside him with his hand on his arm. "I've always been proud of you Greg. I mean that. Everything about you is rich and has depth. You look like your dad and you have your mother's sharp sensitivity. They had no idea what they were doing, and we certainly won't allow anyone to be discarded. Now as a GA you have an opportunity to perhaps help others grow in awareness."

"Thanks," Gregori sniffed. "That helps, but it's still a shock, whew!" He sighed heavily and took a deep breath, then placed his hand over Jesus' scarred wrist.

There was a lengthy pause before Gale moved alongside Nova and placed her hand on his shoulder. "Nova, the boy and girl walking along the road are teenage sweethearts in Africa. They attended the same school in Kampala and had known each other for about six months. The girl, Anne, is your mother, and she became pregnant at fifteen. Her father is a pastor of a large church in the city. Her boyfriend Philo is seventeen, and he is your father. They were both upset and frightened when they found out Anne was expecting a child and decided to tell no one. Anne secretly aborted you in a backyard 'clinic' eight weeks after conception. Philo helped to pay for the procedure from odd jobs he was doing.

"Anne and Philo's relationship ended a few months later. Anne feared another pregnancy and Philo put her under pressure to continue to be sexually active. Anne kept her abortion secret and Philo wasn't too concerned either way. Anne is now a secretary in Kampala, married with two girls. Philo was killed in a car crash two years after he and Anne broke up. Every year Anne remembers the day she lost you and still talks to Pappa G about you."

Nova shook his head. He leaned forward and cupped his chin between his hands. "No, no," he cried. "It can't be. Why?" He had his mother's eyes and could tell from even the short clip that much of his father lived on in him. He wanted to walk along that road holding his mother's hand and hear her calling him by name. He wanted to meet his sisters and experience sitting around the table for a meal together as a family. He wanted to face his father and ask him why he hadn't cared. Anger and sorrow simmered and boiled inside of Nova to the point where he thought he'd burst. Then, in God's great healing mercy, a calm fell upon him and soothed the deep ache he would never feel again but he'd also never forget.

Pappa G stood behind him and rested his hands on Nova's shoulders. "Peace, my son, peace. I've always loved you and am so glad you're here. Like many others, your parents were naïve and didn't think anything would happen to them. Anne's father was a strict Christian pastor with little understanding of grace in these matters. She was terrified of him, and the shame she would face in the church community. She was entirely alone and frightened. It took a long time for her to forgive herself. Philo didn't do anything to support her other than help pay for the procedure. In his defense, his own father abandoned the family when he was born. He'd virtually grown up fending for himself on the streets of Kampala until he found the church."

Gale gestured for their attention and spoke in a soft voice. "This is unquestionably the toughest session in any GA training. It's a lot to absorb and process. Every one of the millions of children you've seen growing up in your villages here in heaven have similar stories. Let's take a break and give you time to collect your thoughts, and then we'll continue. If you'd like to talk to any of us, you're welcome; we're always here for you."

Chapter Thirty-Nine

FIVE MORE DAYS PASSED.

The machines in Ricky's room never missed a beat. The sedatives were withdrawn but no change was evident. Ricky showed no response to various stimuli, he wasn't fighting the ventilator, and his pupils offered no reaction to light.

Jack and Brenda traded places, passing like ships in the night. But there was a gradual thawing that both could feel; yet each was nervous to test it or reach out.

It was late Wednesday evening when Brenda walked the quiet corridor to Ricky's room to give Jack a chance to rest. He'd been more attentive than she'd ever known before. Perhaps change was possible? Was it evidence of God hearing their cries for help? She had no idea. If it were up to her, she'd have chosen for Ricky to live and her marriage to die. It would have been much easier to process and accept. Losing Ricky and having Jack back was almost too much to bear.

At least that's what she'd have said a few days ago. Ever since their dinner out she'd felt her heart soften toward Jack. He'd left flowers in a vase by her bed the following day and made sure the room was tidy whenever she returned. He'd not made any attempt to encroach on her space, nor was there any of the normal pressure or guilt-tripping that had been his past modus operandi.

She and Rachel had talked. "Trust the process," Rachel had told her. "There's so much you both have to deal with right now. Be gentle, create space. When a ship is wrecked and sinks, after a while it becomes a reef teeming with life. That happens when it hits the bottom: the ocean fills its empty spaces and they become one. When we open our hearts to God's love and allow him in, all kinds of things can happen, from the inside out—even things you never asked for or expected. This time at Ricky's bedside will change you forever, and it will change Jack. That change can be for good or for something not so positive. It all depends on how you process and respond to it."

"You know I can feel that." Brenda placed her hand over her heart. "Something that was empty and lost inside is being filled. I don't really understand why it's different, but it is. That gives me hope. I'm not so much a victim of circumstances as I thought I was, and I'm determined to make it through. I mean, if this really is the end for Ricky—I can hardly bear to say that—and his life has been cut short." She choked at the thought and could barely utter the words. "Then, surely, I need to make the best use of the life I still have, for me and my children?"

One minute Brenda felt strong; the next she was weak-kneed, and her heart was in her throat with the ache of losing Ricky. Then, she prayed for a miracle and hoped. Maybe Rachel *was* a messenger from God, and all would be ok? But most of the time she was off balance, disoriented. She would sit and scroll through photos on her phone. Ricky's broad smile was everywhere. Jack was notably absent.

She'd known Jack from such a young age. Her first love. She was familiar with his dreams, his fears, his funny ways, how to make him laugh, and how to tug and console his orphaned heart. He was a Peter Pan like many of his peers, never wanting to grow up, be held accountable, or take responsibility. But this week had been different. She felt she was witnessing a gradual transformation, where the boy was becoming a man. Better late than never. But why does it take such tragedy for the penny to drop?

She quietly entered Ricky's room. Jack was sitting by the bed holding Ricky's hand and singing softly.

> "Ally, bally, ally bally bee,
> Sittin' on yer mammy's knee
> Greeting for a wee baw-bee
> To buy some Coulter's Candy."

Brenda paused in the doorway and listened. Tears welled up yet again and rolled down her cheeks at the simple sight of a father singing to his only son, dim light casting shadows around the room, the machines waltzing and beeping in mechanical harmony. Brenda approached Jack slowly from behind. She couldn't help herself. Gently, she rested her hands on his shoulders and sang with him. He reached up to his right shoulder without looking and placed his hand on hers.

"Poor wee Jennie's lookin' awful thin
A rickle of bones covered over with skin
Now she's gettin' a wee double chin
From sucking Coulter's Candy"

Ricky lay still, neither of them knowing whether he heard his parents' aching lament poured out like ointment: Mary anointing the feet of Jesus with tears and drying them with her hair. It was like that in this room two thousand years later. A man and a woman in another age with the same wrenching sorrow, struggling to express a grief for which they lacked vocabulary. As the song ended, silence filled the room with a gentle, tender stillness. They agonized, together, watching over their son for what seemed an eternity.

Eventually Brenda squeezed Jack's shoulders and sat down opposite him, and as always, gently took Ricky's hand in hers. She looked at Jack staring at her, their mutual pain screaming in the quiet intimacy of the night. She could see the lines down Jack's cheeks where tears had flowed freely.

"Get some sleep, JJ. I'll be ok here."

Jack nodded wearily, got up slowly, walked around the bed and kissed her on the cheek, and left the room. He poked his head around the door of the family room and found Rachel and Bill in conversation.

"I'm off to get some sleep. Bren's with Ricky."

Bill turned and rose to his feet. "Hi Jack, I'll walk over with you."

"Goodnight." Rachel came to the door and embraced Jack warmly. "You take care, Jack. You're a wonderful man. I'm so proud of you."

"Thanks Rachel," Jack mumbled. Moved by her words, he fought the tears that once again welled inside him. Quickly he turned for the elevator, Bill following behind.

They stood side by side in the elevator. Bill placed his arm around Jack like a brother, or like a father would a much-loved son.

"You know, something's changing in you, Jack. Can you sense it? You've come a long way from the man I fished out of the lake eight days ago."

They stepped out on the ground floor and made their way through the brightly lit foyer into the fresh night air. Jack tugged on the rim of his cap and tucked his hands deep into his jean pockets.

"I think so. To be honest I'm not used to all this emotion being so close to the surface. Usually, I stuff it down and have a drink. But now I honestly have no desire to do that—or to run. I'm very broken inside about Ricky. I just want to be present and strong for Bren."

They crossed the street and ambled through the yellow spheres of light cast by the lamps overhead. Insects filled the air. Jack swatted one away.

"You're beginning to discover what it's like to find life and strength from the inside out. It's how God works."

"But I hardly know how to spell God," Jack protested. "Most of the time I've used Jesus in the same breath as f**k you, excuse my language. I'm not proud of it. I have no clue really what you're talking about, but I can't deny that something's changing."

"You realize by now, I think, that it's impossible to know God by focusing on yourself and how bad you've been. Has Ricky had to earn your love?"

"Never," said Jack. "From the moment he was born, and I held him in my arms for the first time, I've loved him. As best as I could, and I've often done that badly, which is why I feel such guilt now. But no—there's nothing he could do to make me stop loving him."

"You sound like God speaking about you." Bill stopped in the street and looked at Jack with a smile. "Do you understand that?"

"Yeah! Maybe I'm beginning to." Jack stared down and kicked the pavement.

"You are like most people when it comes to God, so don't be discouraged, Jack." Bill was leaning against a lamppost, his arms folded. "How can someone believe in a God they can't see? That's why Jesus walked this earth, to do what I'm doing with you. To walk alongside and help you make sense of what seems unbelievable."

Jack shuffled his feet, took off his cap, and ruffled his hair. Bill noticed that he often did that when he was confused or unsure. "It's so different. Up to now I've just lived for the moment and that's it."

"Remember when you went fishing with Ricky?" Bill asked.

"Of course, his eleventh birthday, one of my best memories."

"Imagine trying to convince a fish that there was more to the world than merely his wet environment. That beyond the water there's dry ground where people live in a totally different dimension. How would you explain, describe, or convince? It would seem unbelievable."

Jack smiled and nodded.

"Imagine, if you can, trying to persuade a fish that someone was out to get them by placing a hook in their favorite food. If they ate it, they would die. Try to tell them that something called evil is real. Get the picture?"

"Put like that," Jack replied, rubbing his chin thoughtfully, "Some of it makes more sense, even though it seems weird. I keep thinking I'll wake up and this will be a dream."

"Jesus, entering earth as a man, a human being, was like God becoming a fish, to help you see how much more there is to life, and even death. To introduce you to a dimension of the world of which you'd been totally unaware."

"Isn't that a cruel joke?" Jack asked with a quizzical look.

"Not at all. Because he not only revealed that there's more to life than meets the eye; he also invited you to enlarge your perspective and to follow him into it. He gave hope that life has more depth and purpose and meaning than you can dream of. With the ultimate unbelievable revelation—that death itself isn't the end of life."

"What do you mean?"

"When a fish is caught it flops around, dies, and often is eaten. That's it. When a human being dies and leaves our 'wet' world, Jesus shows us there is another life beyond this one to look forward to—a massive adventure on dry land! I could go into his crucifixion and resurrection, but we'll leave that for another time. Another analogy would be that of the caterpillar becoming a butterfly. How would you explain that to a caterpillar crawling around on a branch?"

"You know I've never heard this stuff explained in my language before. Even I can understand about fish and butterflies." Jack punched Bill's shoulder playfully. "But I still struggle with believing that I'm included or invited to the party, after all I've done."

They began to walk again. Bill could see that Jack was exhausted and needed to rest.

"Let me tell you a story as we head home—you need to get some sleep. Jesus told a story about a man who had two sons. One son worked around the farm and dutifully did what his father asked of him, but inside he was angry and resentful. The reason was that his younger brother had decided to take off and explore the world in far off places. He'd even managed to persuade his father to give him his portion of his inheritance to fund his rebellion—which was pretty much telling his dad that he wished he were dead so he could get his money.

"Anyway, his father relented and gave the younger son what he asked for and he departed. At first, he couldn't believe his freedom and the resources he had to indulge himself. He traveled, he partied, he enjoyed the proverbial wine, women, and much more. Life was great—until the money ran out, the women were no longer interested, and he could only drink water. He did a bunch of menial jobs because he wasn't qualified for much. He even resorted to looking after pigs.

"Only then did he begin to reflect on his downward spiral. He thought to himself that his life had been so good with his father and yet he'd squandered everything. Now he was living in poverty and squalor. He wondered whether if he returned home and apologized, his father would allow him to look after the pigs there. At least it would be on his father's farm, though he knew he had a huge debt he could never repay.

"He began a long journey home filled with shame and trepidation as to how he'd be received. Finally, the day dawned when he walked through the gate and up the long driveway to his father's house. He remembered how cocky and self-assured he'd been when he left. Now he dragged his feet, his clothes were in rags, his hair and beard unkempt, and he was as thin as a rake. He kept rehearsing what he'd say: *Please forgive me, father, I'm not worthy, I'm so ashamed. Can I just work as a servant?*

"His thoughts were interrupted by the sound of shouts—shouts of joy. He looked up and saw a sight he never, in his wildest dreams, would have expected, nor would he ever forget—his father, running down the road, waving his arms, shouting, smiling. Servants and dogs trailed behind him. He didn't stop until he was right in front of his son. Sweating and gasping for air, he grabbed his boy in a bear hug.

"'My son, welcome home! I've looked out for you every day since you left, welcome home.'

"'But father, I have . . . '

"'Forget that, my son. I thought you were dead and now you're alive!'

"'I'm so ashamed, can I just serve—'

"'Of course not; you're my beloved son.' Turning to his servants, he gestured. 'Place a cloak on his shoulders, a ring on his finger, and sandals on his feet. My son has come home—he's alive—let's have a great feast and a celebration in his honor!'"

"That's cool, make a great movie," Jack said as they arrived at the front door of the Ronald McDonald House.

"Jack, that story describes the love of God, a father, for all his children, including you. In these past few days, he's run down the road to embrace you and welcome you home. Stop protesting and beating your-self up. Receive and accept. That is the greatest gift a prodigal can give a father. Now go and get some sleep and dream of a banquet honoring you. You're seated at the right hand of a father who is delighted that you've looked his way and nodded without fully understanding."

Bill embraced Jack without giving him a chance to reply. "See you in the morning. Goodnight, prodigal Jack."

Chapter Forty

Nova was in an animated conversation with Pappa G. Jenny walked around the room talking to Jesus as he kept pace in his wheelchair beside her. Gregori sat alone, looking at the floor, lost in thought. Yesaidu and Asuka, the only ones who hadn't heard their background stories, chatted together with Gale.

"How did heaven become what it is now?" they asked.

"It has always been our home," said Gale. "When Adam and Eve joined us, it was the beginning of creating a home after life in Earthtime."

"Did you create it all at once?" Yesaidu asked.

"Oh no, not at all. As people arrived, we invited them to create with us whatever they wanted. Gradually villages formed that reflected the diverse homes and cultures in Earthtime. There's no competition or greed so no one builds to be better than another. Rather, it's a lovely expression of wide-ranging creativity that everyone gets to enjoy and appreciate. It's a project that never ceases to expand and grow."

Eventually Gale stood up to signal the resumption of the session. The misty walls returned to the family history graphics.

"Yesaidu, your turn. The business couple before you are your parents, Juan and Lucia. They both have high-powered careers in business development and management consulting in Caracas, Venezuela. Initially, when they married, they agreed not to have children as they wanted to pursue their career goals. Then Lucia accidently became pregnant, and they changed their minds and eagerly anticipated your birth. They were excited, and then heartbroken when Lucia miscarried you in the second trimester of her pregnancy.

"Your mother thinks of you often, particularly around the month she lost you, in April. She knew you as her son, and she and your father never had any other children. There is a void you left in her heart that's never been filled. Your father was married previously and has two children from his first marriage. Your parents often mention you and wonder how different their life might have been had you been born."

Yesaidu's lower lip quivered. He wanted to reach out and embrace his mother and tell her that she still had a son, who bore an uncanny resemblance to her. He jumped to his feet and placed his hands behind his head and walked to and fro across the rainbow carpet, fighting back tears.

"They look so cool; we could have had such fun together. We never had a chance to enjoy the life and relationship God intended for us. It's not fair, Gale."

"You're quite right, Yesaidu—it's not fair. However, it is the sad reality for many who live in Earthtime. They experience suffering and loss that often come out of nowhere and is through no fault of theirs. You were a casualty of a situation far beyond your responsibility or control. Your life was a precious gift that we brought to heaven to allow to grow into who you are now. I know that if your mother and father could see you now, they'd be so proud."

Gale looked at him with deep affection and drew him close in a warm embrace. Yesaidu placed his arm around her shoulders and rested his head on top of hers.

"Thank you, Gale. Thank you for redeeming my life and not giving up on me, or my parents. This is a lot to take in, such a change so suddenly." He sighed as a lump formed in his throat.

"I know it is, Yesaidu. When you have an assignment, this memory will help you empathize with those you'll meet in Earthtime. Because you won't be there to judge or accuse; you'll be there to reveal our love and mercy, always."

After a pause Gale finally turned to Asuka and smiled. "Asuka, you've had to wait a long time. Thank you for your patience."

Asuka looked up and nodded nervously.

"Asuka, the couple in the coffee shop are Julie and Samantha—or Sam, as she prefers to be called. They've been in a relationship for two years and were keen to have a baby and share the parenting. The man who joined them at their table was your father, Raymond. He agreed to be a donor for his close friend Julie. Five months into her pregnancy Julie was hit by a drunken driver while walking home from work. She suffered

multiple injuries and lost you. It took her a long time to physically heal
and even longer to recover from her terminated pregnancy. As you observed, no doubt, you get your looks from your father Raymond. He was
a musician living and working in Los Angeles at the time. He was born
in Hong Kong.

"Julie and Sam planned to raise you without reference to your bio-
logical father. They believed in same-sex marriage, were committed to
one another, and desperately wanted you. They are still in a relationship.
Your father, Raymond, moved to New York, where he is married with a
young son of two years old. Despite his promises to Julie, he still thinks
about you and wonders who you might have grown up to become."

Asuka had assumed her parents would have been a variation of the
others she had listened to; she hadn't anticipated a revelation quite like
this. She loved the thought of Julie being her mother, and the fact that
she resembled her father so much gave her comfort. But that she would
have grown up never engaging with him upset her. She was conflicted
and confused.

"What do you do in a situation like this?" Asuka couldn't help her
tears as Gale gently rocked her in her arms.

"The world is quick to judge. Sometimes arguing merely entrenches
people who feel strongly from opposite sides of an issue. They define
themselves by their point of view and never the two shall meet. We prefer
to start with their identities as sons and daughters and work from there."

Pappa G stood with his arms folded. "You'll discover that this is a
hot issue in Earthtime. It's complicated and deeply emotional for all parties. We'll talk more later—is that all right?"

Asuka nodded. She didn't know what to feel; her head and her heart
pounded. But as Gale continued to hold her, peace enveloped her. She
could wait for her many questions to be answered later.

The images faded into the blank walls. But for each GA those "snap-
shots" were indelibly imprinted in their minds; "back to normal" had to
be discovered somewhere other than where they had lived before. They
felt a stillness they had not experienced together before, each silently gazing at their empty space of wall, lost in their own thoughts. The silence,
gentle and safe, without threat or awkwardness, lingered. All tension dissipated as they allowed themselves to be fully immersed in the moment.

Eventually Pappa G invited them to face the center again.

"It's hard, isn't it?" he said gently. "Suddenly being exposed to a truth
or a reality that you never anticipated, or even imagined would appear on

your horizon. Never saw it coming and then 'bam' it hits you. Just when you thought you were safe, and maybe well adjusted, you discover you are as frail and as easily unglued as the next person. How are you feeling now?"

"All kinds of things," said Nova. "I am stunned, confused, rejected, sad . . ."

"I am feeling an 'aloneness' that I don't understand," said Jenny. "Maybe 'orphaned' is a good word?"

"I feel angry and sad," said Yesaidu. "And if I'm honest, Pappa G, I want to get mad at you for allowing this to happen."

"I feel a sense of longing," said Gregori. "When I saw my parents, I wanted to talk to them and show them who I've become. I so much wanted to make them aware that their only son is alive."

Asuka spoke in a mere whisper. "I am confused. I don't know what more to say right now."

"It's very humbling," said Yesaidu. "When we were reviewing the others in our previous assignments—their difficult situations, their tragedies and heartbreak—I felt we were superior, privileged, not remotely like those in Earthtime with all their struggles and unanswered questions. Now, in one moment, when the veil is pulled aside, I'm faced with the reality that I'm no different at all."

Pappa G spoke tenderly, his voice brimming with emotion. "I'm sorry for the shock, but there was no way we could prepare you for this revelation concerning your origins. If the truth were hidden you may have escaped the pain, but would you ever have journeyed alongside anyone in Earthtime with authentic humility and compassion?" He let the question hang in the air.

"Why? Why? Why?" said Jenny, tears streaming down her face. "Why? I don't understand. My mother was destitute, my father a drunk; I never had a chance and neither did they. How can you just stand there as if we are a little object lesson for a normal class? This is *my life*, and now I have no clue what to do with what I know!"

Gale walked across to Jenny, knelt, and embraced her. Jenny sobbed quietly into her shoulder. "I'm sorry," she sniffed. "I'm so confused and surprised by my own emotions; I didn't see this coming at all."

"I know," said Gale, squeezing her tight. "There's no shame in your response."

"I'm so upset to see my parents as such screwed-up people. They looked so impoverished," sniffed Jenny.

"It is shocking and tragic to learn how life becomes desperately mixed up," said Jesus, "with surprises and consequences that are undeserved and seldom fair. Your life has always been very precious, Jenny. We created you, and each person here. The intention was for you to be fully alive in Earthtime and then reunited with us in heaven for eternity."

Gale knelt at Jenny's feet and looked up into her red-rimmed brown eyes and smiled. She touched her cheek. "You know that couple you meet quite often in your village, Jane and Dave? And you chat over coffee?"

"Yes, they're so kind to me. I love my time with them."

"That's them."

"Who?" Jenny's brow furrowed.

"Your parents." Gale smiled.

"Really, how . . . what . . . ?"

"They were ravaged by the snake to the point of death and they cried out to us in their pain. Our grace is always more than ready to respond. We gave them new names and asked them not to say anything. Does that help?"

Jenny nodded, half a smile playing on her lips, tears in her eyes; it would take time. "What about the other parents?" she whispered. "What's happened to them?"

"We'll have those conversations shortly," Gale assured them.

"So why does it all get so messed up?" said Nova, "My parents looked like nice people, hard-working, maybe too ambitious, but . . ."

"I share your frustration and your grief," said Pappa G. "Every human being is created to enjoy my creation as in Eden. I intended them to live in love and relationship with me that would be a delight for them in surroundings of joy and safety. Instead, many see me as a disciplinarian. They're unaware of the prince of lies whispering in their ear and instinctively blame me for every mishap, negative experience, or situation they endure. Never for one moment did I desire or wish any of you to be prematurely killed, aborted, rejected, or discarded. Neither did I create the circumstances that your parents found themselves in, good or bad."

"But surely you are responsible for allowing all of this? Or are we merely pawns in a game you're playing, and we get to suffer so that you have someone to save?" Nova shook with emotion.

Pappa G seated himself in his favorite chair. Rather than respond sharply to Nova's outburst, he nodded and replied slowly with deliberate words. "Life in Earthtime is about living within the parameters laid down at the beginning of creation. I cannot violate them or abrogate the gift of free will. Jesus, Gale, and I work within that reality to reach out to a creation we are committed to. And take responsibility for."

Asuka stood up and spoke with a strength no one had witnessed before. "Were you taken by surprise when the snake rebelled, and the earth became his domain? If you created everything, why didn't you *not* create him, and then none of this would have happened?" She paced the floor with her arms folded.

"No, we weren't surprised," Pappa G replied. "We were thrilled with the beauty of our creation and wanted to share it with others. The real possibility of rebellion had to be an intricate part of the psyche of our creation to give it life, love, and free choice. Otherwise, you're left with pre-programmed robots."

"The elephant in the room," said Jesus wheeling himself behind their chairs, "Is that, yes, we are ultimately responsible for the existence of evil, because we allowed for it. At the same time, we also planned how to overcome evil within the parameters of the world we created. That is why when I became a man in Earthtime, I paid the penalty for rebellion on behalf of our creation.

"In other words, what Adam and Eve lost, I restored through taking their punishment upon myself, namely death. We have never abandoned anyone, nor have we left them to make the best of a bad experiment. We desire all to be restored and redeemed. That invitation is given in love, with respect to their choices, not by force or intimidation."

"But didn't you violate that principle by intimidating Moses and virtually forcing Saul?" Yesaidu challenged.

"At first glance it does appear that way, doesn't it?" Pappa G agreed and pressed his fingers together, with his elbows resting on the arms of his chair. "However, consider most of the men and women whom I call up for leadership to accomplish a great task. What is their initial response? Invariably, they see themselves as unworthy, not smart enough, not articulate enough, and a host of other excuses. That's not how I perceive them to be. But living in the broken culture of Earthtime, they're profoundly conditioned toward the negative. My love must be tough and firm to propel them to recognize their full potential. Some of them need strong words and even a good shake to awaken them from their stupor."

Gale picked up as Pappa G paused. "We never call anyone into something for which I don't empower and equip them. They come to that realization in all manner of ways. In Saul's case, his heart was totally devoted to us, but he was sincerely misguided. Our only recourse was to shake him up with revelation that transcended his closed mind. We're not merely love manifest in hugs." All three smiled. "We can rise up if we have to," Gale declared and raised her arm.

"Does that help make sense of what you witnessed, Yesaidu?" Jesus rocked his chair back as he checked in.

"I think so." Yesaidu looked at the carpet thoughtfully. "It's increasingly clear that how one interprets your actions depends upon the relationship. Firmness in the context of love is part of the equation. Firmness without love can easily be received as abuse or control. Because none of you are swayed by emotional manipulation, I can understand why some would interpret you through the abuse lens when they haven't experienced the love."

Gregori waved his hand. "The part I don't understand is the rationale for terminating a pregnancy. How can anyone do that?"

Pappa G answered. "Some reasons are selfish and irresponsible; others are complex and not so easy to explain. The biggest lie is that life only begins at birth and not conception. We won't go into a long debate here, but I will say this: people can be distressingly short sighted, thinking only of their current circumstances, rather than the bigger picture, or how things might be different in the future. If only they had the ability to see what we can see, then things might have turned out differently for some of you."

"I, as your heavenly Father, know you and see you from the moment of conception. I know who you are, what you are capable of, your personality, and the purpose for which you were given the gift of life. If people can dehumanize you and consider you as a non-person then they don't have to face the fact that they are ending the life of a personality. But . . ." Pappa G paused.

"Life is my gift and my creation. Although people can choose to destroy life in Earthtime, I do not permit that action to be the final decision over anyone's eternal life. Your life is precious and matters to me, which is why you are here, and I'm so delighted that you are."

"But if you know what will happen, why don't you prevent those people from having children?" Nova interjected with some passion.

"I know we sound like a broken record, Nova; it is because of free will and choices," Pappa G said. "When satan rebelled as an angel with many powers we did not withhold those powers. He now exercises them against our creation and us, although we could crush him at any time. My point is that either free will is a fundamental gift and foundation for all of creation, or it is highly selective and conditional—in which case we get to manipulate, control, and dispense like a master puppeteer. The fact that we may be aware of what will happen does not mean that we desire the outcome. Nor that we can override the principles we have prescribed, even if we'd like to."

"Thanks, Pappa G," Gale said. "I hope that you do see evidence through what has transpired of our love and commitment to you. Guardian Angels are particularly important in accomplishing our purposes and helping people in Earthtime grow in wisdom to make better choices. You are in the unique position of having been conceived in Earthtime and lived your life in heaven, which means you can return there in a manner other angels cannot."

Jesus wheeled into the middle of the carpet.

"Everyone take a deep breath. Well done, this hasn't been easy for any of us, but knowing the truth is important. This rainbow carpet is a sign for all eternity of our commitment to creation. We never break our promises. Next time we'll have an encouraging session to wrap this series up. In the meantime, any issues, or questions, you know where to find us. Well done again. You make us proud, and never forget, you are deeply loved."

Chapter Forty-One

Jack and Brenda waited anxiously in the family room for Dr. Pollard. In their hearts they had clung to some wild hope that Ricky would awaken. A miracle perhaps. They'd both prayed in their own way: "God if you're real please make Ricky better, bring him back to us." But as the days slipped by their hope unraveled like a fishing line, hooked to the bottom of the ocean to something they couldn't see. Tugging in vain, nothing changed or budged. Exhausted, they dreaded the moment their line would snap. Ricky seemed much the same to their eyes as he had since his arrival at the hospital last Tuesday.

"This is the moment we've all been dreading," Dr. Pollard said with sad eyes and a grim expression. "Unfortunately, Ricky has shown no signs of improvement since we withdrew the sedation and throughout our routine tests and monitoring."

Dr. Pollard explained the variety of procedures, assuring them of the broad and deep experience and expertise of his team. Their overwhelming conclusion was that the brain damage was irreversible, that Ricky's brain had ceased to function because of the pressure and trauma resulting from the accident.

"We can keep Ricky 'looking alive' mechanically, probably for a long time, but the chances of recovery are virtually nil I'm afraid."

Brenda could hardly bear it. Her insides ached and exploded from the depths of her being in a convulsion of sorrow and despair; she doubled over in her chair clutching her heart, wracked by heaving sobs. Jack sat next to her, expressionless, with stoic numbness. He placed an arm across Brenda's bent back and gently caressed her shoulders.

Dr. Pollard sat with them in the messy wreckage of their agony. This was no time for empty words. He knew that nothing he said could possibly help. He could have shared with them stories of others in their situation and how events had played out for them. About Peter, who was ten years old and had suffered a severe injury in a diving accident. How he'd been kept alive for over a year before they finally accepted that he was not coming back. Or Janet, who'd slipped and fallen on an icy sidewalk and never regained consciousness. How her husband struggled to come to terms with letting her go; an exhausting journey that nearly destroyed him as well.

Dr. Pollard wanted to admit that their medical skills and advances were an enormous blessing and yet, on occasion, a real curse. The ventilator could mask natural death so effectively it often left those beside their loved ones hanging onto false hope and confusion. It forced them to make a decision that had already been made. But they just couldn't see it because the body was still warm and breathing. Their loved one looked as if they would wake up and be reunited with them at any minute. And of course, they clung to that optimism and faint expectation. It was as useless as trying to carve an anchor from rotting driftwood.

And Dr. Pollard could have shared the story closest to his heart— the pain of walking alongside his younger sister, Caroline, as she battled breast cancer. It was detected late, and they fought hard, but to no avail. He journeyed every step with her, Barry her husband, and their two young children. All the medicine in the world couldn't save her. He always remembered Caroline in times like this and felt the loss and the longing all over again, like a sutured cut that had been ripped open.

But Dr. Pollard said nothing. He'd learned the painful lesson of how to be at peace with approaching death and helplessness. Years ago, a Swedish psychiatrist, Elizabeth Kubler Ross, had initiated groundbreaking research on death and dying and the five stages of grief. Conducting her research, she discovered that many doctors were reluctant to face the reality of death among their patients. Death was failure and their job was solely to make people healthy. Mercifully, times had changed.

Dr. Pollard represented the best of medicine, technical expertise, teamwork, and humble empathic caring. And it cost him. He did not hold Ricky at arm's length. He permitted himself to feel Jack and Brenda's pain. And at this agonizing window his presence without a solution was the most precious medicine he could offer them.

"How long will Ricky live with the ventilator removed?" Jack asked quietly.

"It's hard to say. Usually no more than a few days. But there is no pressure for you to decide right now. Frankly, it's never the right time."

"What would you do if you were us?" Brenda lifted her tear-stained eyes and blew her nose on a Kleenex she tore from the box on the coffee table.

"I've seen too much and know too much, Brenda. But with all of that, if Ricky were my son, as hard as it is, I'd let him go and allow nature to take its course. We've done the best we possibly can, and so have you."

Silence.

"Thank you, doctor. I know you've done everything you can. Maybe we can have a little time to process right now and get back to you?"

"By all means, take all the time you need." Dr. Pollard stood up to leave. "You know where to find me if you need anything at all. Please don't hesitate."

Shortly after he left, Bill and Rachel appeared. They'd been waiting outside. Brenda embraced Rachel and sobbed on her shoulder. Jack sat motionless while Bill placed a hand on his back and stood by his side.

"Dr. Pollard told us that there's nothing more they can do for Ricky," Jack said seething. "He's suggesting that we consider removing the ventilator."

Jack was a time bomb ready to explode. He'd never been good at controlling himself and the most natural response for him was blame and anger. He stood up and began pacing the room, clenching and unclenching his fists.

"Where the f**k is God now!" he spat, with no attempt to hide the vitriol he felt. "It's all words but nothing changes. Ricky still suffers, we suffer, his sisters suffer. 'We're praying for you, trust God'; how can you believe that bulls***t?"

Rachel quietly moved to the kitchen area and began making coffee for everyone. Brenda looked up and said, "JJ, please, not now." *Here we go again*, she thought. *The bubble's burst, and when the pressure is on Jack goes ballistic, blames, shouts, runs.*

Bill left the room while Jack continued to pace. His baseball cap turned backward on his head merely increased the resemblance of a kid having a tantrum. Thirty seconds later Bill returned and beckoned Jack. Jack followed him down the hallway into an empty room. Bill shut the door quietly and turned to Jack.

"Jack, I know this is tough, probably the hardest thing you'll ever have to face—the loss of your firstborn son. But you have a choice right now that will impact the rest of your life. How are you going to conduct yourself? Are you going to rant and rave and blame with obscenities, or are you going to be a man of strength and integrity, supporting, and caring for your wife and children? What's it going to be?"

Jack was breathing heavily, pacing the room, and staring at the carpet. "I'm not in the mood Bill, leave me alone."

Bill stood watching him for a while. "I'm not going away, Jack."

"For God's sake, Bill, what do you want from me?" Jack looked up and glared.

"I don't want anything. I'm fighting for you to be the husband Brenda so desperately needs, right now! I'm fighting for you and your children. I'm fighting for you to be the father that Ricky would be proud of."

"Don't drag him into this. He's going to die, and your talk of God doesn't seem to make much difference, does it?"

"Ok Jack let's face some truth here. What if I came to you and expressed anger toward you for Ricky's situation and asked you where you've been as a father over these years? Why do you play around and conceive a boy when you have no intention of being a responsible father? It takes no brain or effort to make someone pregnant but it's a totally different thing to be a father to a son. So why shouldn't I blame *you* for Ricky's situation?

"You think God is about weak people needing a crutch and dressing up for church while living hypocritical lives. What have you done with your life that's so wonderful? Get off your high horse and find some truth to stand on. And by the way, talking of crutches, you've leaned on a few crutches: sex, drugs, alcohol, blame and anger, for a start. I'm sorry, sometimes truth hurts, but it's now or never."

Jack stopped pacing. "I'm scared, Bill. I'm hurting so much for Ricky and my guilt for failing him. I don't know how to deal with this, so I panic and lash out."

Bill placed his hands upon Jack's shoulders. He towered above him. "Look at me, Jack."

Jack looked up, his face red with anger and his lip trembling.

"There was a guy in the Bible called Job. He was rich and lost everything and had many questions as to 'why?' Eventually God spoke to him as sternly as I'm speaking to you now. And he said to Job, 'Brace yourself like a man. Who are you to question me? What do you know?' and he outlined examples that Job couldn't answer.'"

"I'm not following you."

"The point is, Jack, that there's much about God and his ways that we'll never understand. But blaming him for Ricky's situation is as stupid as blaming you. Ricky's accident has nothing to do with you. There is no blame or accusation that you must carry. Failures and regrets about being a father and a husband? Yes, there are plenty. But I'm here to tell you that God loves you more than you love Ricky. He wants to help, not judge, condemn, or accuse. Can you understand that truth?"

"I think I'm beginning to. Funny thing is, I'm so used to the struggle I'm unsure of what to do with acceptance and love." Jack mumbled as he looked down.

Bill's hands remained resting on Jack's shoulders. "Look at me, Jack." Jack looked up awkwardly.

"You are not an accident. When God made you, he was intentional and knew exactly who he was creating. Your invitation is to find out who that man is out of the tangle of the person you've become in your own strength. You're not used to anyone believing in you. I'm doing that right now. I look at you and see a son who God loves and in whom he delights and is well pleased. He promises to be with you and help you become the man he created you to be. The thing is, you can't be much of a father, or a husband for that matter, until you've learned how to be a beloved son. It's about identity. So that's what I'm declaring over you and calling up in you right now." Bill smiled, squeezed Jack's shoulders, and let him go.

Jack's expression softened. "When you say those words, something changes inside; I feel the tension leaving. Not being condemned or judged is like lifting a weight off my shoulders. It's weird."

"Which man do you want to be?" This time Bill paced the room while Jack stood, following him with his eyes.

"Do you want to be angry and lashing out, or do you want to be a son who handles responsibility well because he knows he's accepted, and that God is with him? It's not about having all the strength and all the answers. It's about being in relationship with One who does, that's all—and everything."

"It sounds good, but I haven't a clue how to do that."

"You've already begun. Everyone needs help and support. A child doesn't learn to walk in a day, but with gentle encouragement from parents it doesn't take long. I'm happy to help if you'll allow me. But I won't put up with your tantrums either." Bill raised his eyebrows.

Jack smiled sheepishly. "Thank you, Bill. I'm sorry for losing it. I'm tired of falling flat on my face. I know I can be a challenge at times. But thank you for believing in me despite everything you've seen."

"That's why I'm here. Now let's get back to the girls and Ricky."

When they returned Brenda was lying with her head on Rachel's lap and Rachel was running her hand through Brenda's hair. Brenda's eyes were closed. Rachel looked up and smiled.

Jack knelt beside Brenda and kissed her cheek. "I'm sorry, Bren, for my behavior. Sorry, Rachel, I acted like a jerk."

Brenda whispered, "Ok." Rachel nodded and smiled gently.

Brenda sat up and rubbed her eyes. "We have to tell Dr. Pollard what we've decided. I don't think we've much choice, do you?"

"I don't know how to say 'yes' and cause Ricky to die." Jack blurted out the words as tears flooded out. He knelt on one knee and sobbed, all the tension and anxiety of the past days breaking the surface.

Bill spoke into the silence that followed. "Be assured that you are not causing Ricky's death. When the doctor says that they can find no brain activity he's really saying that Ricky's already dying, and they can't bring him back. Without the support of machines that would have already probably happened. He's told us that maintaining the ventilator will merely prolong the inevitable, as well as be increasingly traumatic for you. I agree with him. Rachel, what do you think?"

"Tough though it is, I agree with what you've said, Bill. We can make this decision together, so Jack and Brenda aren't carrying it alone. Just know that if I believed there was any hope for Ricky, I'd be the first to say so. This is so hard to say yes to, but I believe it's the kindest decision for everyone, including Ricky."

"I hate to agree, but I do." Brenda stood up and went over to Jack and hugged him. "I'm so sorry, JJ. Ricky's our son." She cried into his shoulder, her body shaking. He wrapped her in his arms and wept with her.

Brenda turned in Jack's arms to Bill. "Bill, could you tell Dr. Pollard please? I don't think I can do that."

"I'll do that, for sure." Bill hugged them both and left the room.

Three hours later Brenda cradled Ricky in her arms. Jack sat alongside in a chair by the bed. The room was unusually still except for her quiet sobs. The rhythmic pulsating of the ventilator had ceased when it was unplugged an hour earlier. Ricky's breathing was shallow, his face gaunt and pale. If she could have traded places with her son she would have, in a bleeping heartbeat.

Brenda spoke softly beside Ricky's inert form. She told him how proud she was to be his mother, what fun they'd enjoyed, and things that no one else could hear. Jack sat beside the bed; his head buried in the blankets. Brenda reached out and offered him her hand. When Jack looked up and noticed, he took hold of it in both of his and squeezed.

Chapter Forty-Two

"THANKS TO THOSE OF you who came to talk after the last session." Pappa G paced the carpet with his hands in his pockets. "How are you?"

Asuka responded immediately. "I feel much better after a chat with Gale. It helped me make sense of a difficult situation. Thank you."

The others nodded in agreement. "The five of us met and also debriefed afterwards," said Jenny. "It's a lot to process. I've already noticed how it's impacted the way I regard Earthtime, and Jack and Brenda. There's a deeper bond, I think."

"Yeah, I've been aware of the same shift in me. It's subtle but real," Nova agreed.

Yesaidu added, "I most appreciate the freedom—or permission—you've given us to ask hard questions, to challenge, and even let our feelings out. It's helped to find a place of peaceful acceptance even if we may never like or agree with actions taken."

"And that's what we desire to accomplish with all our children in Earthtime," Gale said. "Their lives often don't make sense within circumstances beyond their control. If they can learn to live from the inside out, it makes all the difference in the world. That means, quite simply, that their identity is rooted in our love from which flows their sense of purpose. And the assurance that we are for them, not against them; no matter what they experience in Earthtime."

"How have you found your shared journey with Jack and Brenda? You know, the ones we invited you to follow through your InSights?" Jesus asked from the doorway, which was closed behind him.

"I'm not sure whether their situation raises more questions than it answers for me," Nova said. "It's been quite a journey with them."

"Interesting, distressing, and tragic are words that come to mind." Jenny shook her head sadly. "I found it heartbreaking."

"That it is," said Gale. "There are no easy answers to the dilemmas people face in Earthtime. Maybe I should rephrase that. It's deceptively easy to have solutions for people but working toward a positive outcome is the real challenge—so that, in the end, they're not forced into something but rather they desire it for themselves."

"The reason you've been observing Jack and Brenda in particular," Gale continued, is because we wanted you to learn from the experts, Bill and Rachel . . ."

A collective gasp rose from the GAs. "You mean that Bill and Rachel—" Gregori began

"Are Guardian Angels!" Yesaidu exclaimed.

Jenny nodded knowingly. "I had an inkling . . ."

"You're right, of course," Gale said, smiling. "I thought you would figure it out but didn't want you to feel intimidated by telling you straight-away. They have been doing this job for some years so have a lot of experience, in all types of situations. Why don't we ask them about it?" Gale turned to the wall behind her . . . "Come on in you two."

Bill and Rachel entered the room, greeting everyone with a smile as Gale gestured to some empty chairs. "Welcome, Bill and Rachel. Here's the group who have been watching you and are in awe of how you accomplished your assignment."

"I remember being where you are now," said Rachel, making herself comfortable in a seat next to Yesaidu. "I couldn't imagine how I'd cope. If left to my own devices I'd have chosen to remain safe and sound in heaven."

"Me too," said Bill. "But I can assure you that when Pappa G, Jesus, and Gale promise to never leave you, that's true."

"How does the assignment work?" Jenny asked.

"We went through training like you are. Then we are placed on a roster of about," he looked at Rachel, "how many?"

"Oh, I'm not sure," said Rachel. "More than ten million?"

"There are many more Guardian Angels, of course. That's about ten million every week, and we have two assignments for each year in Earthtime," Bill explained.

Rachel continued. "We usually work in teams of two chosen from a larger team of ten. We're paired together depending on the nature of the assignment to ensure that we have complementary strengths and personalities."

"When you prepare for an assignment, like the one you've just been on with Jack and Brenda, how much do you know when you head out?" Nova asked.

"Gale usually does the briefing and gives us some background and insight into underlying issues. After that we follow the threads and see how things play out," said Bill.

"Does it always have a happy ending?" Jenny asked.

"No, not always," Rachel replied, shaking her head. "Sometimes, no matter how hard we try, people choose to go their own way and never seem to learn from their mistakes."

"It can be tough," said Bill. "We grow very attached to the people we're walking alongside, but we can't wave magic wands or force anything."

"How was it with Jack and Brenda . . . did you know that their marriage would work, and that Ricky was going to die?"

"I think in this instance," said Bill, "they were ready for change and really wanted it but didn't know how. The tragedy with Ricky could have been the end for them, as it often is, but I believe our presence made a difference. To answer the other question—no, we don't know what the outcome will be on any assignment. We are authentically in their situation alongside them, trusting God and walking by faith."

Rachel continued. "You know most people in Earthtime are hungry for love, hope, and significance. Even churches are often unsafe communities. Religion can be oppressive. Many people have never experienced the kindness of Pappa G or known the forgiveness Jesus brings. They have no idea how much Gale can empower them in their weakness. Our task is to model some of that as best we can—within the confines of human relationships, and their significant limitations to understand of course."

"Could you have prayed for Ricky to be healed?" Yesaidu asked.

"We did," said Bill. "There's mystery here and we trust Pappa G with the answer completely. We never try to force an issue."

"Do your prayers ever heal?" Asuka asked.

"Absolutely," said Rachel. "On my last assignment a mother of three was diagnosed with leukemia. She was a single parent and beside herself with fear and concern. I walked alongside her, and we prayed and over two months she was completely healed. It was wonderful!"

"We've both worked with many men and women through the centuries of Earthtime who have endured childhood abuse. They have been locked up inside, afraid, and ashamed. As they have grown to trust and share in relationship with us, they've often received healing. Sometimes it's physical, sometimes emotional, sometimes both, and sometime none," Bill shared. "They don't have to wait for heaven to taste freedom!"

"How safe do you feel on assignment?" Gregori asked.

"We're completely safe. We can't be injured and in fact are always accompanied by angels who are never visible. While we appear very human and limited on the ground, we can withdraw at any time, but I've never had to." Bill smiled. "It's actually an amazing privilege and joy."

"I agree," said Rachel. "While initially I was nervous, I absolutely love that we make a difference. The fact that we know something of our history helps us connect. For instance, as I sat next to Ricky in hospital and Brenda was by my side, I felt a tinge of pain about not having children. God protects us while allowing some of those emotions to be a reality, which also enables us to be authentic."

"Is there any advice you'd give us?" Nova asked.

"Be yourself and trust the process. You'll be amazed how much you've learned that will come to mind when you're in the moment. Of course, you have a far deeper and greater awareness of the reality of both heaven and earth than do those you're encouraging. Sometimes you need patience as well as wisdom. Listen well and let them lead you. Be willing to travel at their pace. The most powerful gift you'll ever give them is your time, attention, unconditional love, and authentic presence." Bill turned to Rachel. "What would you say, Rachel?"

"I'd merely add that in Earthtime you are the human face of God. Be willing to serve and don't carry the weight of outcomes because that is their responsibility. When we return from assignment we always debrief and ask questions. I've never been disappointed or discouraged with the answers I've received. Now, I don't think about it. I trust completely."

"I nearly forgot." Bill leaned forward. "In Earthtime so many people try to find God through their intellect, strength, good behavior, or whatever. It's all the wrong way around. They need to encounter his love, and from there everything else flows and makes much more sense. We help that happen, and that's what changed Jack and Brenda, even with the traumatic death of Ricky."

"We've come a long way in a short time." Pappa G rose from his chair. "In this context we can appear to be meek and mild, but I assure you there are other occasions when our might and power are more than you could handle. I say that to merely underscore what Bill's just said. It's our grace and love that you Guardian Angels will be sharing in Earthtime. You are working with people who have been captured, abused, blinded, deceived, and robbed of their inheritance. This battle is about rescuing and freeing as many as we can. The outcome is not in doubt. It's for the sake of the lost that we stay our hand rather than allow our fist to come crashing down now."

Gregori raised his hand slowly. "Before we go, I have a question I've been pondering for a long time. What happens to those who don't respond to you positively? Did you really create hell to punish them?"

"That's a big question Gregori, and a fair one. Maybe we'll each try to give you a portion of the answer." Pappa G remained standing. He continued, "We didn't create hell, but we did create space for it."

"Meaning?" Gregori leaned forward, scratching his chin.

"Meaning that we've spoken a great deal about free will and consequences. The snake, satan, has no intention of ever reuniting with us. Therefore, to respect his decision he has been given space to do what he wants without our interference. All those who choose to go their own way will join him there. Hell is a place where we are not present. When people make their choices, they've never experienced what that place is actually like."

"I'm not sure I'm following you," Jenny said.

Gale interjected, "I'll take this. Life in Earthtime unfolds on the threshold between light and dark, good and evil, heaven and hell. The best things that ever happen in Earthtime are a small taste of heaven with us. The worst atrocities ever experienced in Earthtime are a small taste of hell with him, the snake."

"But there are many people in Earthtime who never hear of Jesus, you know, people who follow other religions. Do they go to hell?" Nova asked the question as he leaned with his back against the door.

"That's a topic that many of our followers in Earthtime love to debate," said Jesus. "And when they do, they are often very quick to send much of the population into what they call 'the burning fires of hell.' They forget that every human being on earth is a beloved son or daughter of ours. We detest the fact that any are lost. What do we do when through no fault of theirs they do not learn about Jesus? Or, as is sometimes the case, they hear in such a distorted manner that they turn away?"

Pappa G continued with a quiet earnestness. "We hold love and justice firmly in our hands and in our hearts. We created every man, woman, boy, and girl with love and intention. We see everything about them, know every secret, and understand every challenge. We remember every word, every thought, and every deed whether selfish or generous. We know what they inherited, what inhibited, what hurt, and what brought joy. We are aware of every opportunity taken, and every opportunity missed. We hear every prayer, every cry, every curse, and every act of worship. All those factors, and more, are considered within the context of our love for them."

Jesus added, "We live and love from a position of how someone can be welcomed home, rather than what they have done wrong to deserve exclusion. No one enters heaven on merit or because they have been 'good enough.' Everyone has fallen short of what we call 'the glory of God.' Entry into our Kingdom is solely through grace and my work on the Cross. Consequently we 'judge' every person according to the revelation they have received. In other words, we are very, times a hundred, fair."

Gale smiled and gave Jesus a high five, exclaiming, "Yes, we are!"

"We'll talk again. We have lots of time. There's always more, and more, layer upon layer. Never cease asking questions. Encourage those in Earthtime to do the same. We created you with the capacity to explore, ask, think, and to understand—at least to some degree. But never forget there are limitations." Pappa G smiled. "A few things you'll have to leave with us and trust without understanding, even for eternity."

"Let's go and enjoy a little slice of heaven." Gale laughed and walked to the door. "Thank you, Bill and Rachel; your assignment was profoundly significant. There's a great little coffee shop around the corner, anyone want to join me?"

"Oh, by the way," Pappa G spoke up, "before you go. No one asked what happens now." He smiled.

"What happens now?" Gregori said, with a mischievous expression.

"You'll be heading into Earthtime with Bill and Rachel for about a week—to get oriented. They can chat with you about the details. Full of surprises around here. Off you go." Pappa G laughed as he turned toward the door.

"Oh my goodness; that news has my heart racing," Asuka said.

"Mine too," said Yesaidu.

"Bill and Rachel, we're all ears," Jenny said as they headed out chattering excitedly.

Chapter Forty-Three

"RICKY, RICKY, WAKE UP." It was a voice of calm, kindness, and strength.

Ricky opened his eyes and blinked. His mother was lying next to him, her arms enfolding him. She was crying and speaking, but he could neither hear, nor feel her. He was enveloped in a deep warmth and peace as his eyes met those of a bearded figure sitting beside him. Ricky recognized him immediately and couldn't explain the sense of excitement rising in him. He wasn't afraid, but he was confused.

"What's happened?"

He remembered skateboarding down the hill and going for a TreFlip, missing his landing, and tumbling into an oncoming car. He remembered it was red.

"You had an accident and hit your head hard, causing severe brain damage. You've been in the hospital for the past eight days with the doctors fighting for your life. Unfortunately, the damage is too severe."

"Can't you make me better?" Ricky had heard about Jesus when he went to Sunday School with his grandmother, Nana Mary. He didn't even know how he knew, or why it felt as if he was talking to an old and trusted friend.

"I'm afraid that's not possible for many reasons, but not one of them is because I wouldn't love for you to have lived a long life on earth. Do you remember when you first talked to me?"

"No."

"You attended Sunday School with your Nana and were asking her about me on the way home. You were about five years old at the time. Your Nana told you how she prayed for you and your family every day.

She asked you if you'd like to meet me, and with the innocent trust of a child you asked me to come into your heart. I did, and I never left."

"I forgot all about that; we hardly ever went to church, especially after Nana died," Ricky replied, smiling without feeling awkward.

"I know," Jesus said. "You missed so much of what I had to give you in those years. But I kept my promise and have never left you."

"If you were with me, why did I have such a bad accident?"

"My presence doesn't mean controlling you like a puppet. You rode your skateboard down a hill and tried a difficult trick without a helmet."

"Yeah, that was dumb."

"The good news is that your dumb decision leading to a premature death is not the end. I've overcome death. You watch and see—there's more ahead, Ricky. I'm giving you a new life with me and my friends. Stretch out your hand."

Without a second thought Ricky stretched out his hand. He gasped. He lifted out of his body lying on the bed yet retained his shape and form. He realized he was looking down on the room where his mother lay beside him and his father sat next to his bed.

He was sitting on Jesus' lap and Jesus was seated in a wheelchair.

"Why are you . . . ?" Ricky began.

Jesus smiled and put his arms around him and whispered, "I'll tell you later. It's time to say goodbye."

Ricky felt no sorrow and yet at the same time he knew he was in the presence of great grief, that of his parents. "What will happen to them?"

"I love them very much Ricky. I've sent some dear friends to comfort them and to help them heal and move forward. We allow for what we do not always desire. And we did not desire for you to lose your life on earth so young."

"What happens now?" Ricky lifted his eyes from the room and up into the face of Jesus. He felt safe and loved; more secure and protected than he'd ever known. There was no sense of loss, no broken body, no damaged brain.

"You're on the threshold of heaven," Jesus smiled. "No more pain, no more tears, no more sorrow, no more sickness, no more fear, or loneliness, or anything bad."

"Can I skateboard?" Ricky's eyes lit up at the prospect.

"You can do many things," Jesus laughed. "Let's go, I'll show you."

In the blink of an eye, they were beside a large park filled with a stunning array of trees scattered across wide expanses of the greenest grass Ricky had ever seen. People were everywhere: talking, playing games, sitting reading, or strolling along pathways lined with flower beds splattered with every color of the rainbow.

Then he saw the skatepark. It was huge, complete with every ramp, bowl, and angle he could imagine. Kids and adults were rolling, jumping, flipping, and spinning with various degrees of expertise. There were a few elderly men who on earth would require walkers performing tricks that Ricky could only dream of.

Ricky looked at Jesus with the broadest of smiles. "This is so cool!"

"I remember when a young man of your age first came here and asked about skateboarding," Jesus said. "We didn't have a skateboard park, so I suggested he meet with a few people and they design one. Now they're everywhere."

"It's amazing," Ricky exclaimed.

"That's how everything has grown in heaven," Jesus said, rocking back on his wheelchair. "From the very beginning. It never ends."

"What's this surface made of?" Ricky bent down and rubbed his hand on a deep yellow pavement. "It's gold," Jesus replied. All our roads and skateparks are made with gold. And the beauty is that when you fall or stumble you can't get hurt. It's as if you're falling onto a soft mattress. No helmet required." He smiled.

"Wow! I can't wait to try." Ricky didn't have to plead.

Jesus gestured him to go. "That's why we're here. Go on over and one of the boys will give you a skateboard. Welcome home, Ricky. Have fun."

Ricky walked across the grass that pressed thick and lush beneath his feet. He noticed that it yielded to the pressure of his foot and then immediately sprang back without any hint of damage or an imprint. As he approached the skatepark he realized that he knew the names of those around him. He could hear what they were saying in his heart as well as when they used their voice. It was a strange knowing.

Peter approached him with a welcoming hug and showed him where the skateboards were stored. They were all shapes and sizes. "Pick whichever you want to try; they're all great rides."

Ricky had no idea how long he spent flipping, spinning, grinding, and flying. He truly was in heaven. He didn't know what caused him to look around, but he did. And there on the fringe of the park was Nana Mary.

"Nana!" he exclaimed. He picked up the board and ran over to her and they embraced.

"Oh Ricky, how lovely to see you!"

Nana Mary glowed with life and health. "I've come to show you where you'll be living. You have the most beautiful room close to me. Do you want to come now or later?"

Ricky linked arms with her and said, "Let's go now, Nana. It's weird—I could skate forever. I don't feel tired and falling doesn't hurt. It's amazing. I don't even need to wear a helmet!"

"That's what's so beautiful about heaven." Nana smiled. "There is no weariness or danger. It's the world as it was always meant to be. We have lots of catching up to do." She squeezed his hand and together they strolled down the golden sidewalk to discover Ricky's new home.

Chapter Forty-Four

RICKY DIED SOON AFTER the ventilator was removed. Dr. Pollard said it was exceptionally quick. Brenda and Jack couldn't explain the presence they felt in the room when Ricky left them. Bill and Rachel said it was God's love embracing them and comforting them.

Jack and Brenda wept beside Ricky. Brenda tidied his hair with her fingers, tenderly brushing a stray lock from his forehead. There was the hint of a smile on his lips. It was impossible to grasp the fact that Ricky was not merely asleep, that he wouldn't suddenly wake up and they could embrace, get him dressed, and go somewhere for pancakes and maple syrup.

Jack clutched Ricky's skateboard close to his chest. It was battered and bruised, well used, and much loved. They would cherish this bittersweet memento forever. Bill and Rachel quietly came alongside and held them in their arms. Neither Jack nor Brenda had any fight left, no more questions to ask, no more of anything at all.

Bill placed his hand on Ricky's shoulder and spoke soft words committing him into the hands of God. He thanked him for Ricky's short life and for the joy he'd shared with all. Rachel prayed for strength and comfort for Jack and Brenda, Kaitlin, and Jessica.

This time, neither Jack nor Brenda ran away to avoid their harsh reality. They faced it together, vulnerable in their grief, sensitive with their words. "Take all the time you need," they were told. And they did.

Later, on the ferry back to Vancouver Island, Jack and Brenda sat by the large upper deck window, holding hands, staring into the distance.

"Who would guess," Brenda thought, looking around, "that I've just lost my precious son?" She dabbed away the tears, leaned her head on Jack's shoulder, and closed her eyes. "How quickly life changes."

Back at home they shared with Kaitlin and Jessica that their brother wasn't coming back. "Ricky was too badly hurt. He's gone to heaven, maybe he's with Nana now."

"But we want him here with us," Kaitlin sobbed.

"So do we, honey," Jack replied as he held a distraught Jessica close. "But sometimes terrible things happen, and we have to be strong together, and help one another."

"It's ok to cry," said Brenda. She blew her nose. "It's going to hurt all of us for a while. I think Ricky would want us to be brave and remember the good times, don't you?" The girls nodded.

"Daddy, will you be coming home?" Jessica looked up at her father expectantly, her face streaked with tears.

Jack glanced across at Brenda. She nodded and buried her face in Kaitlin's hair. "Your mother and I are talking. We need a little time; this has been a terrible shock for all of us. I've made some big mistakes that I'm really sorry for."

"That's alright Daddy. Please come home."

"Your mother and I will work it out," he reassured her. "I think Ricky would also be happy if we were a family again." He kissed Jessica on the forehead. "Ok?"

She nodded. "Can I sleep in Ricky's room tonight?"

A little more than a week later, the following Saturday, they held an emotional "Celebration of Life" service at the Chapel of Memories. Ricky's teachers and schoolmates were present. They reminisced with tears and laughter. Slides of Ricky's short life were shared with anecdotal stories. His skateboard held pride of place on a table at the front alongside a large photograph of him. Brenda spoke of her love for Ricky and how proud she was. He'd never be forgotten, always missed. Jack stood beside her but couldn't speak.

Over the next month Bill and Rachel remained close. Rachel cooked meals which she delivered every few days, usually lingering for coffee and a chat with Brenda. Bill hung out with Jack. Together they tidied up the mobile home after Jack gave a month's notice.

Bill organized a boat and the four of them went down the inlet to China Creek early one Sunday morning. The fishing season was over. The water was calm. The early morning sun peaked through, gilding grey clouds with silver linings.

Brenda placed a beautiful floral wreath on the water that she and Rachel had made the day before. A photo in a plastic Ziploc bag, Ricky smiling, proudly holding his fish, was pinned to it. Tucked in beside the photo Kaitlin and Jessica had drawn pictures of Ricky and his skateboard. Kaitlin wrote, "Bye bye big brother, I miss you so much. Love you always." Jessica's picture said, "Luv you Ricky. I'm sleeping in your bed to be close. Say hi to Nana."

Jack slowly poured Ricky's ashes into the ebbing ocean and reluctantly released the container to sink with them. Silently they watched the ashes melt below the surface and the wreath bob and float away. Bill said a short prayer. Rachel squeezed Brenda's hand.

Jack wistfully recalled his fishing trip with Ricky. He glanced down at his watch and noted the date, 10th October. *Almost a month ago I wanted to end it all. Now it's Ricky sinking beneath the surface. It feels like five lifetimes.*

At the end of the month Jack moved back home with Brenda. As they had mutually agreed, they attended counselling for over a year with the pastor of a local church. It was helpful to have a third person to vent to when pressure inevitably began to build. Sometimes they both wondered whether they could do this. Pastor Ben facilitated and coached them in healthier communication skills: how to accept each other's flaws with grace, take ownership, and say sorry. How to take responsibility and be self-aware, initiate conversation, no shifting blame. How to say what you think and feel, earlier rather than later—no "you make me . . ." accusations. How to actively listen before responding and embrace patience. How to have some fun together, be thankful, believe the best.

They began to attend his church. They dressed casually, the girls loved it, and they were surprised by the contemporary music and teaching they could relate to.

They discovered there were others on the same journey; they weren't the only ones who struggled. They joined a weekly group called Alpha to ask questions and learn more about this God whom they'd encountered at such a critical time in their lives. Jack made friends with men who took him under their wing. He grew to love them as brothers, particularly because they could be real with one another. Jack realized that most were as confused and as complex as he was. Talking helped, accepting each other's imperfections released hope, and mutual accountability and support kept them growing. It was good to not have to pretend anymore.

He'd been invited back to his old job with a friend who owned a heavy-duty mechanic shop, and he hadn't missed a shift in nearly two years.

Brenda enrolled in the local college part-time to gain credentials for nursing and felt fulfilled in a way she could not have imagined. She'd never dreamed that she and Jack could be so close. He was a different man, no longer running away, but instead motivating her to be hungry for more. "Let's not waste the years we have left," he said. "Let's honor Ricky's memory by being the best husband and wife we can be; we've so much catching up to do."

A photo of Ricky riding his skateboard hung proudly in the living room of the new house they'd moved into after Jack had been working solid for fifteen months. Antoine joined them for supper every Thursday and cried in Jack's arms when they talked about Ricky.

Almost two years after Ricky's death, the family spent the afternoon swimming from the beach at Cameron Lake. The sun was beginning to sink as they packed up picnic paraphernalia and towels to head back to Port. Many who had shared the beach with them had already trickled home. Kaitlin and Jessica were growing up fast and were the best of friends. They'd gone ahead to the car and were playing games on their phones.

Jack and Brenda stood looking across the lake. The water reflected the evening sky, shivering black lines and multiple shades of burnt orange. Brenda held her distended belly in her hands and smiled. The setting sun shone on her face and cast a golden glow in her hair. She looked almost angelic.

"You look lovely Bren. I love you more than ever. Thank you for giving me, and us, another chance. What will we call him?" Jack looked at her with a funny expression and stretched out his arm to draw her closer.

"Wait and see." Brenda snuggled into his embrace.

"To think that two years ago I was floating on this lake wanting to die." They both pondered the prospect and tears welled up.

Brenda looked at Jack. "I never in a thousand years imagined we could find this place together again or recover from the loss of Ricky."

"Me neither, although I know we'll never get over the hurt." Jack paused, then his lips curved into the slightest of smiles. "He'd be sixteen now—probably have a girlfriend and causing us all kinds of worry." He laughed. "No matter what, he's always with us in our hearts. At least we know he's happy and in a better place. And we have God as a friend. Who'd have imagined me ever saying that?" Jack kissed Brenda on the forehead.

A speedboat roared around the corner, wake fanning out behind. It swerved and headed toward them. Pulling up on the beach, two figures jumped out.

"Bill and Rachel! What a surprise! How are you?" Brenda laughed and she and Jack embraced them.

"It's been a while," said Bill. "Just thought we'd check in. Looks like you're both doing well."

"We are, thanks to you." Jack smiled and shifted his baseball cap; it was dark green with a golden logo of a cross beside a rising sun.

"We haven't seen you for nearly a year, but you've never been far from our hearts." Rachel smiled and rubbed Brenda's stomach. "And who do we have here?"

"This little fella will be born in two months, God willing."

"Do you have a name?"

"Not yet," Jack said.

"Actually, we might," Brenda interjected with a twinkle in her eyes. There was many a day when she never thought she'd ever stop crying or feeling the ache for Ricky. Rachel had promised that time and God's love would heal her pain. She was right.

"Oh, we have?" Jack took a step back and grinned. "Do tell."

"We can't name him Ricky, much as I'd like to, but Richard is close. And Bill, I thought your name would be an honor to include. After all, you and Rachel gave us our life and our marriage back." Brenda smiled and blinked away tears. "Every time I see you two, I cry."

"Richard Bill Willard—I couldn't think of a better name for our son," Jack beamed from ear to ear. "Rachel, I'm sorry we can't add yours but, you know, kinda sounds strange."

Rachel laughed. "I'm glad about that. Call him 'RB' then we're covered."

"Come on up and meet the girls; they'll be thrilled to see you," Brenda said with her arm around Rachel.

"It's so good to see you guys. Bren and I often think of you. You've been like guardian angels to us—if such creatures even exist." Jack laughed. "No, I mean it, we're so grateful."

Bill winked at Rachel and they walked slowly up the beach to the car.

Epilogue

GREGORI RUFFLED HIS HAIR as he approached the skate park. He'd enjoyed the course with Pappa G and the others. The revelation about his parents and his "beginning" had initially upset him. But after talking to Pappa G he felt more rooted than ever. Joy bubbled up as he stood on the golden pavement in the warm sunshine and watched kids of all ages tumble and turn on their skateboards. He wondered about all the stories behind each person here, how much grace. An elderly man who looked about eighty in Earthtime years was yelling with delight as he completed a 360 without taking a tumble.

Gregori smiled. A teenager approached on his skateboard. Gregori had been admiring his style and fluid moves on his board.

"Hey Ricky, can you teach me a few tricks? I'm just learning."

"Sure Gregori." Ricky pulled up with a grin.

"Great."

"Do you know how to Pop an Ollie?" said Ricky.

Gregori shook his head. "No clue."

"Why don't we start there? But first, do you skate regular or goofy?"

Gregori scratched his mop of hair again. "You tell me."

For now we see only a reflection as in a mirror; then we shall see face to face. Now I know in part; then I shall know fully, even as I am fully known.

1 CORINTHIANS 13:12 NIV

Acknowledgements

WRITING IS BOTH SOLITARY and collaborative. I began this story many years ago. Then it gathered dust for years before waking up and breathing again.

Thank you, Brian, for sharing your family story with me. Thank you, Kyle, for countless coffees, chats, feedback, initial edits, and much encouragement. Your friendship with an old man is a gift. Thank you to Alex and Juliette for advice regarding medical matters; any inaccuracies are solely mine. And to Adam for teaching me about the wonderful world of skateboarding.

Huge appreciation to my editors Jonathan Pountney and Julie Frederick who enhanced my offering with their experience, insights, and encouragement. Your input made such a difference.

To my publisher, Wipf & Stock, and Matt Wimer my Project Manager. Thank you for believing, for providing opportunities for writers, and for your wisdom and guidance.

Finally, to my wife Vi, there are no words to express appreciation for your generosity, kindness, and encouragement that gave me the space and time to complete this project. It is dedicated to you, with love.

Comments and feedback are welcome through my blog or email: johncoxauthor.ca | johncox@shaw.ca

www.ingramcontent.com/pod-product-compliance
Lightning Source LLC
Chambersburg PA
CBHW070222030726
47505CB00006B/1772